THE

RELUCTANT TIME TRAVELLER

BY

JOHN DAWSON

To our great friends
Antony and Virginia (née Ponsonby) Phipps
Thank you for your comments &
suggested corrections, particularly
those connected to history including
riding and shooting.

'May your horses always win'

SECRETS
'The Reticent Volcano Keeps'.
Emily Dickinson

30th July 2021

WISDOM

"The gift of intelligence leads to curiosity
and then to ambition and then success
But success is an empty prophecy,
Only from mistakes and failures do you progress
and when old age overtakes you,
and you stop blaming others,
Then, and only then, can you claim wisdom,
- more or less."

John Dawson

Success is not final; failure is not fatal it is the courage to continue that counts.

Winston Churchill

TABLE OF CONTENTS

1 - THE BEGINNING

I looked at my watch, and it was just after 7 p.m. I was sitting behind my desk, with paper piled high all around me. It was mainly represented by manuscripts that had to be keyed into a computer for the typesetter to set the pages to be able to produce negatives for printing. I stretched back in my chair and rubbed my eyes. It seemed to alleviate the tiredness I felt momentarily. I realised I was exhausted and highly stressed. I could feel the tension building up in the back of my neck and shoulders. Recently this had been spreading down to my chest, a danger sign I thought.

For some reason, as I sat there, I allowed my mind to wander back to the beginning. After a meteoric career in the city, all had gone wrong just over ten years ago. Afterwards, I had started a small, computerised data capture business, concentrating on scientific journals from all over the world. I built up a good solid customer base, but in recent years, the market had begun to change. The bigger houses having merged, thoroughly exploiting most other forms of publishing, now recognised that the world of scientific journals was a lucrative one. In the last two years, the competition had become almost unbearable. Whereas I could give a personal service to my clients, the large houses could cut their costs by sending manuscripts offshore to China, the West Indies, and other areas in the third world where labour was cheap. The market was changing. To combat the intense competition, I relied on inventiveness and ingenuity.

Eighteen months ago, I approached Barons, the large

merchant bank in the city with an idea for producing electronic text cheaply. The publishing industry was all about costs nowadays. Typed manuscripts had to be read by proof-readers for accuracy, sometimes up to three times after corrections. The method was expensive, slow, and not always accurate. My invention comprised of software written in Borland's C+, utilising a technique where everything was typed twice into a word processor by two different people. My software then merged the computer text from the two files into a third file. The result my program created was, wherever there was a difference between one typist and another, the computer highlighted the text in colour, one colour for the first typist and another colour for the second.

This system meant that manuscripts could be corrected more efficiently, more accurately, and the speed of the correction was three times faster. The bank liked the idea, but I had to give them my patent rights as security as well as the security on my home.

It was now clear to me that I hadn't asked for enough money, and by the end of this month, unless I could borrow more, I would have no more cash to continue the business.

Oh, our customers owed us plenty, but credit in the industry continued to be slow, and cash is king. I should have known that a new idea would be suspect, particularly in such a conservative business. I tentatively asked the bank if they would put up more, but they had been adamant in their refusal. No doubt the thought of selling my invention on to one of the large publishers partly motivated their decision. They wouldn't lose.

I rose from my chair wearily and walked across to the window that overlooked a small courtyard. My car was the only one parked there. The office where I worked was part of a complex. An old paint works had been modernised and turned into a small number of comfortable suites. The reception area on the ground floor was communal to us all, as was the impressive lobby.

My office consisted of two small rooms, both facing the courtyard, which was at the back of the complex. The other room was where Debbie sat. Debbie was my secretary, editor, tea maker, gopher and much more. She controlled the small number of home typists who did our work. I lifted the Venetian blinds and was surprised to see that the sun was still shining outside. I looked at the calendar on my desk. It showed Friday, June 4th, realising that I hadn't changed the date that morning, I walked back across to my desk and changed it for the 5th, and then muttering to myself how stupid I was, I changed it again to 8th, ready for Tuesday, the next morning. I wondered if Debbie would have put the correct dates on the letter I sent out, but of course she would, I told myself, at least she was efficient in what she did.

To get to the outside door, I had to walk through Debbie's office. She'd long gone of course, but I wondered what would become of her at the month-end if I could not pay her. I knew she was struggling to bring up two young children, her husband having been killed in an oil rig accident some years before. It was with a sinking feeling in my stomach that I closed the outside door and turned the key. For some reason, the 6th of June came back into my mind. Was there something special about it? My brow furrowed as I went down the stairs to the ground floor.

'Oh my god,' I stood rooted to the spot. A security man coming up the other way stopped suddenly.

'Are you all right sor?' He sounded Irish.

I smiled weakly, 'my wedding anniversary, it was yesterday, and I forgot it.'

'Oh, dear sor, you'd better make it up to the missus tonight, eh.'

I nodded and hurried on down, trying to think of a flower shop that might be still open. I could not think of one. I reached the car and electronically opened the door with the infra-red button on my key and climbed in, throwing my case on the rear seat.

I looked at the car clock it showed 7.25 p.m. I had told Victoria I would be home by 6 p.m. at the latest, 'Damn.'

I started the engine of my second-hand BMW, reversed, and unnecessarily screeched forward stopping briefly at the main road before turning left.

I took a detour past the florists, but as I thought, it was closed. Driving through the narrow streets of Stony Stratford, I headed for the A5. The roads were quite busy, due to summer traffic, and I had time to think about what I would say on my return home.

Victoria, who I called Tory, had been my wife for twenty-five years, we were both twenty when we married. She was a pretty brunette, and I was a serious and ambitious young man still in the army based at Larkhill near Andover. I had met her at one of the dances organised by the officer's mess. Her father was invited as he was the leader of the local Conservative Council at the time. Tory's mother had died the year before, so she had taken the place of her mother's hostessing duties.

It was love at first sight, and despite the Army discouraging the match because of our age, we were married in a little church near Ringwood in Dorset. Tory's personality was almost directly opposite to mine. She was effervescent, whereas I was quiet. She enjoyed dancing and entertaining and made friends easily, I did not. An astrologer would have said that we were typical of our star signs, Tory was a Leo, I was a Scorpio. Paradoxically she'd a serious side to her in that her cultural pursuits were reading good books and listening to serious classical music. Mine was reading spy novels and watching sport on television, particularly cricket. Her voice, when she sang, was like a nightingale in song. I've no doubt that had she wished to take up singing professionally, she could have done so with ease. I was virtually tone-deaf.

Like a lot of good-looking women, she was quite tall,

over 5 feet eight inches.

Her skin was smooth and peach-like, and she had the sort of hair that just seemed to fall into place. Strangely what I first noticed about her were her teeth, which were exceptionally even and white. When she smiled, her whole face lit up. I hadn't seen that smile for many a month now. The last of our two children having left home over a year ago should have meant that we could have enjoyed each other's company to the full and done all the things that we could not do due to our parental responsibilities. The problems with our business put such a strain on our relationship that three weeks ago Tory had moved into a separate bedroom, and since then we had barely spoken to one another. I knew it was my fault. I could not leave my problems at work, but I had thought to try and break the ice on our wedding anniversary.

I drove onto the A5 and gunned the engine. I felt the pleasure of a fast car beneath my feet. I could not control my life, but I was a natural driver and felt entirely in control as I weaved through the traffic. I was overtaking on the outside lane when I came up behind a small Morris Minor going at a steady seventy. I flashed my lights. The woman driver didn't move into the empty left lane. I was about to press the horn but changed down to third, pressing the accelerator hard, and moving into the inside lane, within seconds the Morris had been left behind. I felt a smug feeling of satisfaction. I was startled to hear a siren coming up close behind me and looking in the mirror, I groaned. There was a police car on my tail. I slowed down as it shot past me, the driver waving his arm, indicating I should pull in. I did so and patiently waited for the policeman to get out of the car. I noticed the Morris Minor cruise past, the woman with a smile on her face. I grimaced.

After about a minute, the police driver got out and walked up to my door. I pressed the electric window button.

The man in uniform bent down and looked at me. He could not have been much more than twenty-five.

'Do you know the speed limit on this road, sir?' I told him that I thought it was seventy. His lips compressed into a thin line. 'And do you know what speed you were doing?'

'Er... seventy-five,' I answered uncertainly.

'Ninety-six to be precise sir,' he added unnecessarily, 'and you passed one car on the wrong side, which contravened road traffic act...' I stopped listening.

The day had not been a good one, I had forgotten my wedding anniversary of twenty-five years, and now I wouldn't be home much before eight-o-clock. I mechanically handed the officer my driving licence and insurance certificate, which I always kept in the glove compartment. I noticed the other policeman from the police car walking around my vehicle looking at the tyres, and I felt a tinge of unease when he stared at the windscreen on the near side.

He then walked around the front of the BMW and said something to his colleague. The first policeman bent down again and leaned towards me 'Excuse me, sir, your road fund tax is one month out of date, which is an offence under...' I groaned again. I meant to renew it and had forgotten. The officer handed me a ticket, and when he had walked back to their car, I gently pulled away, driving the remaining six miles or so to my home at a gentle cruising speed of not more than forty miles an hour.

I lived in a modest house, it was a converted barn, in what had been part of the land belonging to Hammond Farm close to Leighton Buzzard. As I pulled off the main road into the private drive, I noticed the garden looked clean and tidy. It was a small garden, with a lawn enclosed on the north and west side by the L shaped house. There was a brick wall on the east side, which divided us from our neighbours and in front, on the south side was another converted farm building, which served as the garage. It was therefore almost a walled garden, enclosed on all sides, except for the entrance, which led to the short drive I had just driven down.

I stopped the car on the gravel with a crunch. I got my case from the back and climbed out, walking through the garden to the back door. The front door of the house was at the top end of the L, which faced the drive opening, but we rarely used this, preferring to use the door in the middle of the house next to the rectangular garden. We called it our back door, although it faced the same direction as the front. The hanging baskets, on which Tory had spent so much time, were overflowing with flowers and colour, there were Fuchsias, Begonias, Geraniums, and some small blue flowers whose name I could not remember. I saw someone had recently watered them.

There was a time when Tory would have met me with a welcoming kiss, but she didn't appear. I opened the door and stepped inside. It was quite chilly in the house, a change from the sultry evening outside. I turned right in the small

HAMMOND FARM

hallway that led to the sitting room. Tory was sitting knitting, probably for the newest grandchild on the way, and watching television. She looked up as I entered, still beautiful even though there were small tell-tale lines around her mouth. Tory looked pensive, as though awaiting the usual row, which inevitably exploded nowadays when I arrived home.

I went across and kissed her, and she looked surprised. 'I'm sorry I forgot our wedding anniversary, I...'

Tory cut me short. 'I'm used to it by now,' she said grimly. She turned back to watch the screen. 'Your supper is in the oven because you are so late,' she inclined her head towards the kitchen.

'I thought we could go out...' I didn't finish. Tory looked at me as though I was out of my mind. 'You know darned well we can't afford to go out, I can feed both of us for a week for the same price as a restaurant meal.'

'Well, a twenty-fifth wedding anniversary is rather special,' I answered lamely.

Tory looked at me contemptuously and shook her head. 'I would just have been satisfied with you remembering,' her lower lip was starting to tremble, her eyes glistened.

'Well, I said I was sorry,' I said roughly, starting to show my anger at being rebuffed, 'but I've had a hell of a week, a hell of a day, and I just felt like relaxing.'

Tory stood up. 'Do you think it's any different for me, just because I stay at home? I went to the butchers today, and he asked me when I was going to pay our bill. We have a demand from the local council for overdue council tax, our electricity is about to be cut off, and my dentist won't see me because we owe him for our last visit. I'm fed up with being short of money and making excuses, and you suggesting we spend what little we have left on a meal out is more than I can stand tonight.'

She threw her knitting on the couch. 'I'm going to bed.' She was in tears now, and she swept out of the room. A few minutes later, I heard the bedroom door slam.

I wanted desperately to go up and comfort her, but pride prevented it. I had always been the breadwinner, the decision-maker, but I had to admit that I wasn't the most practical of people. I did spend too much money, and the worse my financial situation, the more I spent. It was a sort of escapism.

Tory had relied on me, and I had let her down, I thought self pityingly. For the first time, the thought of suicide entered my mind. I just as quickly relegated the idea as hunger became the stronger emotion. I went through to the kitchen and opened the oven door. There was a piece of dried-up chicken in tarragon with soggy vegetables. I knew what a good cook Tory was, and that the meal would have been delicious at 6-o-clock, the time I had told her I would be home. Even dried up, it tasted good, and I opened a bottle of wine, drinking the whole bottle. I have always liked wine, but the occasional glass with the odd meal had increased imperceptibly to a glass every meal and rising to two drinks and then to half a bottle. Now I regularly consumed a bottle each evening, and tonight it became two. I was drunk when I staggered up the stairs to go to bed. I thought of going into the bedroom where Tory was but wisely thought better of it. I didn't get undressed but simply threw myself on the bed and was almost immediately enveloped in a deep sleep.

I awoke with a blinding headache. Looking at my watch, I could see it was just after 5 a.m. I rose and went down to the kitchen for some aspirin. As I opened the first aid box, I saw there was a bottle with over a hundred tablets. I stared at them for what seemed like an age. Suicide again crossed my mind.

How simple it would be to take an overdose. I pulled myself up short. I realised that Tory would probably find me before I could claim oblivion; she was always an early riser. The sum of my action would be me ignominiously raced off to the hospital for a stomach pump. 'Failed again,' I could hear her imaginary voice say. I took three tablets and crawled back upstairs, but I could not sleep. At 5-45, I climbed off my bed, undressed, and had a shower, after shaving, I felt a little better.

It had always been our practice to go for an early morning walk before breakfast. Nowadays, we went separately, but the walk had become a habit, and I wanted to get out early this morning. A walk cleared my mind and enabled me to think without pressure and the unending telephone ringing. I put on my dark blue tracksuit, Nike tennis shoes and just before leaving I looked in the mirror to comb my thinning grey hair. My face looked worn and tired, the bags under my eyes were evidence of this, and the previous night's alcohol could not have helped. Despite my appearance that morning, I was still very fit, and certainly not overweight at 145 pounds for my five-foot-ten height. At least I can do something right, I thought to myself. I went quietly downstairs and let myself out of the back door. The car was streaked with dew because I had forgotten to put it in the garage the night before. The day was going to be a warm one, but now there was a light cool breeze with some ground mist. The air smelled fresh. I filled my lungs as I got into the car and put the key into the ignition. It started on the first try.

There was a large park near us with a circular walk. I hated any walk where one had to retrace one's steps. The Park was about a mile away, so we always took the car and parked it at the beginning of the walk. The circular route was just over three miles, which we accomplished within forty-five minutes. I had considered leaving the car for Tory, but I didn't relish walking on main roads, which I would have had to do to get there. I reasoned that I would be back in time for her to take the car for her walk.

I reversed out of the drive and drove along the main Leighton Buzzard road turning right after half a mile towards Milton Keynes. There was almost no traffic and within five minutes I had steered the car off the main road and across a narrow bridge that spanned the Grand Union Canal. There was a small space for parking cars on the other side, which was ideal, because no one could see it from the main road. I locked the car door and started on the walk that took me away from the canal towards a small river. The local council had laid the path, and it twisted between trees and bushes, while running alongside the riverbank. I noticed that the water was extremely high from recent rains and the heron that usually fished the section I passed was standing on the bank instead of in the rushing water. As always, when it saw me, it took off with a squawk in the direction of a cornfield the other side of the river. Within ten minutes, I reached the weir, where the banks had overflowed, and I had to make a detour to get around it. The water was rushing through the overflow, and the force of the current was carrying all before it. I saw tree stumps, dead birds, uprooted bushes and even a child's dolls pram floating by. As I stood and watched the fast-flowing water, I again thought about the prospect of ending my life.

Just jump in, a siren voice whispered to me, drowning is supposed to be quite a pleasant way to die. I resisted the urge, mainly because I was an excellent swimmer, and I doubted if I would allow myself to drown without fighting to save myself. All I would get for my pains would be a ducking.

I skirted the flooded water and walked on. The path started to move away from the river towards the canal. It ran parallel about a quarter of a mile away. I crossed a small wooden bridge and came to a lane with a farmhouse on my left.

Walking up the lane, I then moved right, back into the upper section of the park. The breeze had dropped, the air was muggy, and it felt as though there was an electrical storm somewhere. I noticed thick clouds had covered the sky. I hoped it wouldn't break before I got back to the car. I quickened my pace as the path led me back to the riverside. The birds were enjoying their early morning feast of worms and snails. I crossed over several snail tracks as I walked on, I remember thinking that it must be just as dangerous for a snail to cross the open path as it was for me to cross a busy road. I wondered if they knew how dangerous it was or whether they were sublimely ignorant that they could become a bird's breakfast. The path wound around, heading away from the river, and now I was walking towards the canal again. I saw a barge chimney floating by, proud over the hedgerow, which hid the canal water from view.

Within a few minutes, I reached the tow-path and turned left-back in the direction I had come. I was now just over halfway on my walk. I saw the stern of the barge I had noticed earlier. It was moving more quickly than me, but not a great deal faster. I guessed it was one of the holiday boats hired out in the season. I was startled by a pigeon that suddenly decided I was too close to its perch, and it shot out in front of me.

The water in the canal was murky, and there were signs of trash. What a shame, I thought. I also noticed that the parks authority had repaired some of the new saplings they had planted, every so often these young trees would be vandalised, either broken, pulled up or their ties ripped off so that they had no support in their continuing growth. I could never understand the mentality of people who caused such damage. It was these thoughts that brought me back to the real world, and I could feel my stomach tighten as I reviewed what I had to do today. I would have to tell Debbie the bad news, and it was a job I didn't relish. She was not a fool though she probably guessed that her career with me was coming to an end. I wondered if I could obtain more credit, and if so, where from, another bank but what would I give as security? I had been walking along the tow-path for some time, with all my yesterday's thoughts churning in my bowels when I was conscious that it was getting cold. I saw an elderly couple coming towards me and a Golden Retriever with its nose burrowing into the hedgerow, suddenly I found myself in a ground mist. I was surprised because it had come from nowhere. The figures in front were now only shadows in the mist. The dog shot past me on some important errand, almost knocking me over as it did so. As I tried to recover my balance, I felt myself getting dizzy, almost floating. I knew I was falling, but I remembered no more.

2 - THE JOURNEY

I awoke, aware that there was some soil in my mouth. I had hit the tow-path quite hard, and I tested each part of my body as I moved to sit up. My mouth was painful, I instinctively put my hand to it, and it came away with blood and earth. It wasn't severe, but I could feel a small amount of torn skin inside my mouth that I gently probed with my tongue. I got to my feet, and although feeling a bit light-headed, I was otherwise in good shape. I remembered the two older people and the dog, but I looked around me, and could not see any sign of them. I felt I was lucky not to have landed in the canal, and I thought of the irony of the situation, only half an hour before I had considered ending my life, now I was feeling lucky that I was still alive.

I started walking along the tow-path, the sun was shining brightly, there were hardly any clouds to be seen, and I began to wonder how long I had been unconscious.

I instinctively looked at my left wrist, and then remembered that I never wore my watch on my morning walk. Sweat and leather watch straps aren't compatible, I decided. I looked up at the sun, and it was in much the same position as it had been, so I reckoned that I was unconscious for a short time only. There was no sign whatsoever of mist though, and I found this puzzling. I had walked another few hundred metres when I realised something was wrong. I reached the little bridge, which I had crossed in the car earlier, and as I climbed the bank to get back to where it was parked, I was astonished to see that there was no car. My first reaction was that someone had stolen it, but then I realised that there was no area where you could park a car. In front of me was a plain cornfield. I looked at the little bridge with a feeling of panic. It seemed to be the same bridge, and yet when I ran across it expecting to see the main road on the other side, there was only a narrow country lane with a mud track, no tarmac. I told myself to get a grip on my mind, I wasn't in the same place, somehow, I must have walked further down the tow-path, but I wasn't conscious of doing so. It would explain why the older people and their dog had disappeared, I told myself. But if that was the case, which way had I walked, east or west?

Of course, I thought to myself that's easy to resolve. I knew by the sun that I had not lost more than half an hour or so, if that, and if I had walked west, I would now be in the town of Bletchley. I certainly wasn't near any village, so I must have walked to the east. If I followed the canal back, I must come across the bridge where I parked my car. Feeling better, I turned around and started striding at quite a fast pace. As I was walking, I tried to analyse what had happened to me. Not a heart attack, as I hadn't experienced any chest pain. Was it a stroke? I shrugged, I had perfect movement of all my limbs. Nevertheless, I told myself, the best thing I could do when I got home was to telephone the doctor to arrange to have a thorough check-up. If I had become unconscious while driving my car, the results could have been disastrous both for other road users and me.

After walking for over half an hour, there was still no sign of any buildings. I stopped suddenly, I was puzzled, and for the first time, I realised I was lost. If in doubt, find a telephone I muttered to myself. I decided I would make a reverse charge call for a taxi to take me back to the car. Otherwise, I reasoned, I could be wandering around the countryside all day.

I walked on for another ten minutes until I saw a farmhouse about a quarter of a mile away. I left the canal tow-path and struck out for the small stone building. By accident, I stumbled across a narrow lane, which led straight to the house, and I shortly found myself in a wildly disorganised and smelly farmyard through which I had to navigate to get to the front door.

The door was open, and as I approached it, a chicken ran out with a large red-faced woman chasing it with what looked like a broomstick. She saw me and stopped dead in her tracks; her mouth fell open as she looked me up and down as though I were something from outer space. I suppose I did look a little odd, with my tracksuit and tennis shoes and what was a bit of a bloody face. I could feel the stinging of the cut inside my mouth. I smiled as best I could.

'I'm sorry to bother you, but I am a bit disoriented... well, lost,' I admitted, 'I wonder if I could borrow your telephone to call for a taxi?'

As soon as she heard my voice, her demeanour seemed to change, and she became almost servile. 'Oh, you'd be from the big 'ouse I 'spect? My 'usband be back soon, e can take you there.' She gestured for me to go inside the house. 'If you'd come sur, you can wait for 'im in the cool.' She looked closely at my face.

'I fell and hit my face on the ground,' I explained.

She nodded knowingly, 'Arh you've been riding one of Lord Crowley's horses I 'spect, my 'usband says they're not broken proper...' She stopped with a hiss of breath, as though she'd said too much. 'Course, gentlemen like you are taught to ride proper like,' she grinned showing a row of bad blackened teeth.

I didn't enlighten her as to my horse-riding skills, which were zero, and by now I gathered that the woman was a bit simple, so the less said, the better. I followed her into the house, which was just one room with a kitchen area behind. I gathered from what I could see up the steep stairs that there was only one bedroom.

'If I could just borrow your telephone...' I stopped as she gestured for me to sit on a worn Victorian couch.

'Telephon?' she repeated, her brows furrowed. She shook her head. I looked around, there was no sign of a telephone anywhere, and I guessed that they didn't have one. It was just my luck I thought to have picked the only house in Buckinghamshire not to have a telephone line. I was starting to sit down when I felt a very definite call to nature. 'Well, if you've no telephone, could I please use your bathroom?' I inquired.

I received another puzzled look, 'bathroom?' She repeated looking perplexed. I was starting to get irritated, 'yes, bathroom, lavatory, toilet, I would like to have a pee,' I almost shouted in frustration.

'Ah,' she grinned hugely, 'this way sur,' she led the way through the kitchen area that would have been more at home in a Dickens novel. We stopped at a little shed near the bottom of the garden, she pointed and left. I wasn't at all surprised that the shed was at the bottom of the piece of land, the smell was putrid, and inside was a rudimentary tin barrel with a makeshift seat. The lavatory inside the shed had flies that rose in a mass like a mushroom cloud when I entered. I relieved myself as quickly as I could, holding my breath as I did so. I was halfway up the garden path before I took in a gasp of clean air. Jesus, I thought, I never realised that people still lived like that.

I looked up to see a wizened man walking down the path to meet me.

'Good mornin sur,' he half bowed, as his eyes bulged at the sight of me. I got the impression he found me a little strange. 'My missus 'as asked me to take you up to the big 'ouse sur and I got the wagon hitched up ready,'

'The wagon?' I said incredulously, I frowned, then realised he meant a station wagon, probably a Land Rover.

'That's truly kind of you,' I said, 'I left my car somewhere, but when I became lost, I couldn't find it.'

'Car?' The man looked at me strangely again. 'Arh, you be talkin about them new automobiles the 'orseless carriages,' he grinned; 'no sur, don't ave one of them, Lord Crowley as one though,' he said with what sounded like pride in his voice.

I didn't realise that there were still rural backwaters around the Milton Keynes area, I was surprised as I walked through the small house and was about to walk out through the front door when the woman came behind me and tapped me on the back.

"Done a small cloth for ye sur, to rub your face with.' I took it gratefully and wiped my face. It had a pleasant smell, it seemed she had soaked it in some herbal liniment. I thanked her as I handed the earth and bloodstained cloth back.

When I went outside, the man whose name I learned was George was already waiting on the wagon. It wasn't a Land Rover but a horse-drawn contraption; it had a bench seat at the front with a large flat area behind with sides about a foot high. The Shire horse attached to it looked as though it had seen better days. I climbed up beside George, he cracked the reins, and we began to move. Each time we encountered a small obstruction, the wooden spoke wheels groaned and squealed. There was no padding on the seat, and it wasn't long before I began to feel a little sore. I held on tight as we hit a rock in the lane, as the wagon clattered over it. I was now getting worried, it must be getting quite late, and Tory would be wondering where I was.

'Do you have the time, George?' I asked.

He pulled out a large timepiece from his waistcoat pocket and showed it to me. It was nearly nine-o-clock. I had somehow or other lost two hours.

'How far is it to the big house George?' I asked. 'Jus over the ridge sur,' George pointed ahead.

I didn't ask if they had a telephone, as I knew they must have one. I smiled to myself, the wagon was so slow, I could have easily walked faster, but I realised George had put himself out to take me, so I stayed put. I noticed for the first time that he was well dressed, in that he had on a suit with full waistcoat. The tie was missing, but a soft peaked hat was on his head, and his boots were brightly polished. It appeared that he had been working on the farm, but he must have changed to escort me. He had not bathed, however, as I caught a distinct smell of body odour and I moved further away to the left-hand edge of the seat but decided I should engage him in a little conversation to pass the time away.

'Been farming long George?'

'Arh, all my life sur, and my father and granddad before me,' he negotiated the wagon around a rock, for which I was grateful.

'Is this your farm?'

He looked at me in surprise. 'No sur, the likes of me don't own land sur, it belongs to Lord Crowley, all the land around ere belongs to 'is Lordship.' We had just topped the rise, and I could see that the narrow lane joined a wider mud road, with trees leading up to a large country house perched on a small hill. The setting, from where I viewed the house, was exceptional, there was a wood that stretched behind the house, and in front were well laid out gardens, both sides of which were full of rhododendron bushes in full bloom.

CROWLEY HALL

It was clear that the original owners of the house had travelled. In addition to the rhododendrons, there were all sorts of tropical and semi-tropical flora I recognised from my travels in Africa and the West Indies. The incongruity of the situation suddenly struck me. Here I was sitting on a horse-driven wagon, with a driver that looked as though he was straight out of Gulliver's Travels, staring down on a beautiful country mansion. The scene could have been England a hundred years ago. I smiled to myself as I remembered the garden lavatory. Even down to the sanitary arrangements, I thought.

Crowley Hall, as I later found it was called, was impressive. As we approached the front entrance from the tree-lined driveway, I took stock of the architecture. It was a Georgian mansion, beautifully proportioned. It was quite square with no wings. The front entrance had steps on three sides that were protected from the rain by a portico balanced on colleens. There was no sign of outhouses, and I guessed these were at the rear, well hidden from the frontal approach. On the right-hand side, as I was looking at it, there was what appeared to be a closed garden behind beech hedges, and I could see the top of what I guessed correctly was a summer house.

A beech hedge also screened the left-hand side, and one could not see what was behind. At the rear of the house was quite a large wood, but as the front faced south, the trees would have no effect on the light in the house itself except for some of the rear rooms that I suspected in days gone by had been used for junior guests or children, and perhaps a staff area. The wagon was now coming level with the front door, and I felt the crunch of gravel under us as we drew to a halt.

'If you wouldn't mind waiting ere sur I will go around the back and ask the butler to receive you.'

George ponderously climbed down and walked away around the right-hand side of the house. I watched as he went. Although wizened and hunched, he was quite a lean man and appeared quite fit. I decided to climb down and stretch my legs and felt better doing so. The view back, from where we had come. was utterly unspoilt.

There was an air of tranquillity in the area I had not felt on the drive up to it, but there was also a tinge of sadness. I've always been sensitive to an atmosphere, and I wondered why I felt this way. I walked to the edge of the gravel and looked over the rhododendron bushes to the fields beyond. There was a gentle slope down from the house, and then open fields and woods on the near horizon. The road we had just come up was yellowish and twisted away to some large entrance gates a mile or so away.

I smiled to myself as I thought of the Yellow Brick Road in the Wizard Oz. The sun was hot; it was a beautiful June day with scarcely a cloud in the sky. The thing that caught my attention most was the lack of sound, no traffic, or aircraft, just the birds and the slight rustle of grass in the light breeze.

George reached the kitchen at the back of the house. He was let in by one of the kitchen maids. As he walked in through the door, the butler, a man called Porter came into the kitchen from inside the house and asked George what it was he wanted, as it was most unusual to see him anywhere near the house. George relayed the fact that a stranger had turned up at his home about an hour ago, saying he'd had a fall and although he was wearing funny clothes, it was apparent he was a gentleman. "e speaks like a toff an 'e as a motor car,' George said with reverence 'although 'e doesn't know where 'e left it. Said 'e wanted to use a telephon, well I knew is Lordship as one, but as 'e's a gentleman, I thought maybe 'e was staying ere with....' George stopped as he saw the butler shake his head. 'No, we've no guests this week,' he frowned. Gentlemen didn't turn up in funny clothes at country houses unless they were properly invited; there was something strange here he thought.

On the other hand, Lord Crowley did have some very strange friends. It could be someone he'd invited without his knowledge. 'I had better see the gentleman George, where is he?'

"Es waitin outside the front door, I told I'm to wait,' he added unnecessarily.

'How did you get him here, George?'

'I brought 'im up on the wagon Mr Porter, it's outside at the front.'

'Well, get it moved and quickly, you know his Lordship doesn't like trade vehicles at the front of the house, quickly now,' he added, 'I will deal with the gentleman.'

Porter turned, picked up his jacket that he'd draped over a kitchen chair and went back through the house.

I had turned to look back at the house from the edge of the gravel where I was standing, and saw the double doors opening, a tall man in some sort of uniform emerged, he moved quickly down the steps, and walked across to me, the gravel crunching under his shining shoes. As he approached, I could see a brief look of horror on his face as he eyed me from head to foot, and then one of intense curiosity, which I didn't quite understand. I went forward to meet him. I somehow felt that this wasn't a man to be friendly with; I didn't offer my hand and looked him straight in the eyes.

3 - CROWLEY HALL

'Good morning,' I said.

'Good morning, sir, can I be of help to you?' He'd a trace of a west-country accent. 'I'm Lord Crowley's butler, sir, and I'm at your service. My name is Porter.'

'Thank you, Porter,' I said. 'Yes. where was I..., ah... yes, I came across George's house hoping there would be a telephone there so that I could call for a car, but he doesn't seem to have one, he kindly brought me here in the wagon, which I must admit I found rather quaint.' I added, 'if I could just borrow your phone, I won't trouble you further.' I smiled at him.

Porter smiled back, 'of course, sir, that can be arranged, if you'd like to follow me, I will take you to his Lordship's study, and you can use the instrument there.' As we were walking towards the house, Porter asked, 'in case his Lordship asks sir, can I give a name?'

'My name is Alexander, James Alexander,' I replied.

'Are you a relative of his Lordship by any chance?'

'Good Lord no,' I answered, surprised at the question.

Porter peered at me closely. 'If you don't mind me saying so, sir, it's just that you are remarkably similar in looks to Lord Crowley, in fact, sir, you could easily pass as brothers.'

I resisted saying what was going through my mind, *must be a good-looking chap then* but I somehow felt that Porter was a man not inclined to a sense of humour.

We reached the still open front doors, and Porter stepped aside for me to enter first. The hallway of Crowley

Hall was quite magnificent, with two large tapestries on each side and a gorgeous painted ceiling. The floor was polished wood, with the odd Turkish carpet laid down, the room was sparsely furnished, but with pieces, I guessed Christies would give their eye teeth for. How the rich live, I thought to myself I was starting to feel under-dressed in the surroundings.

Porter had overtaken me and went to open the door to a room off the hall, at the far end. I passed a beautifully carved semi-circular staircase on my right, and I could see an attractive minstrel gallery at the top of the stairs. As I entered the room, I noticed that books filled the wall by the door, the remainder of the study was panelled in mahogany, always a favourite wood of mine. The desk in the centre was also mahogany, and behind was a large window and glass doors that opened on to what seemed to be a croquet lawn outside. The room was sparsely furnished; there was a small nest of tables on the left of me as I walked in, sumptuous rugs laid about the polished floor, and a wonderful brass fireplace to the right, with a white marble fire surround and mantelpiece. The contrast from the dark mahogany wood was startling. In front of the fireplace were two comfortable two-person sofas.

There was a tall thin window in the far-right hand corner, which overlooked the rear garden, but net curtains prevented me from seeing what was there. There were two armchairs in front of the desk, and a similar one behind it. On my left, there was a chaise longue. An unmistakable Canaletto was hanging above the fireplace. It looked as though it was an original. The room suggested someone of balanced tastes, who was ordered in his life but had a flair for the unexpected. It was a warm room, and I immediately felt at home within it.

Porter passed in front of me and handed me the telephone. It appeared to be one of the converted antiques, and I looked for the buttons to press, but could not find any. Porter saw I was in difficulty and smiled. 'Most people can't deal with these new ones, allow me, sir.' He took it out of my hands, laying the base on the desk and picked up the listening section. He held it to his ear, 'do you have a number, sir?' He enquired. I had decided to call my home, as it would be easier to get Tory to accept the reverse charge call. I reeled off my number, which was six digit's, Porter frowned, 'I don't think there are more than three numbers, sir...'

'May I?' I said a trifle impatiently holding out my hand for the receiving end.

Porter gave it to me and told me to speak clearly into the mouthpiece on the desk. I moved closer to do so.

The line wasn't clear and crackled a lot.

'Lord Crowley?' asked a voice from the other end. I was surprised the operator knew where the call was coming from. 'No, this is not Lord Crowley, although I'm calling from his house. As I can't dial on this phone, do you think you could get me Milton Keynes 123491?'

I waited for the familiar ring.

'Could you repeat that number please, sir?' I did.

'I'm very sorry sir, but all our numbers are only up to three digits, and there's no exchange called Milton Keynes.' I laughed, 'but of course, there is, the number I've just given you is my number,' I had that slight feeling of panic again.

' I'm sorry sir, but I've no number like that, who are you wanting to contact.'

'My name is James Alexander, A-L-E-X-A-N-D-E-R, Alexander,' I repeated down the mouthpiece.

There was a silence for about two minutes, and the woman came back on the line. 'I'm sorry sir, I've looked at all our international numbers, and there's nothing like that here,' she said firmly.

'International,' I said, becoming exasperated, 'Milton Keynes is within the county of Buckinghamshire...'

'I'm sorry sir,' she repeated.

I rudely hung up on the operator and turned to Porter, who had been listening intently. 'Do you by any chance have a yellow pages?' rather than call home, I thought I would ring directly for a taxi.

'I beg your pardon sir, yellow pages?' Porter repeated, looking puzzled.

'Yes, you know a telephone book.' Porter looked a bit taken aback. 'I don't think his Lordship has such a thing, but I can ask Lady Crowley for you, sir.'

'I would be most grateful,' I said now becoming more worried about the time.

Porter coughed, 'in that case sir, would you like to follow me into the drawing-room, and I will find Lady Crowley for you, his Lordship won't be back until later this afternoon.'

I nodded. Porter opened the study door and held it while I passed through. He closed it quietly and headed towards the front door, opening the last door on the right, I walked into a charming room, a complete contrast to the study. The room was large, with French windows either side of the pale green marble fireplace set into the left-hand wall. The French windows overlooked the front garden. On the far wall were more windows with glass doors that opened onto the same croquet lawn as the study. There was a thick piled Persian carpet on the floor, and I felt my feet sinking into it as I walked. The ceiling was high with a pretty glass chandelier in the centre. It was the furnishings that most caught my eye, everywhere I looked there was Chippendale mixed with French Regency furniture, the sofas were large and comfortable, covered with a rich print on a white background. I could swear that there were two Monet's on the wall by the fireplace, and other paintings carefully placed around the room. Someone had taken a lot of trouble with the design, I thought.

'If you'd care to sit here sir,' Porter pointed to the large couch. 'Would sir like some tea while you are waiting?' he inquired.

'That's most kind of you Porter, yes please,' I realised I was quite thirsty.

'Oh, there is a newspaper over there, sir.' Porter pointed to the small Chippendale table in the centre of the room.'

As he quietly exited, I got up to get the paper. It was the Times, but obviously, a commemorative issue, as it was printed in the old style and dated 5th June 1910. Some of the articles were quite interesting. I was reading intently when a maid came in with the tray of tea. She poured it into a Dresden China teacup and left me with some delicious home-made scones. Porter came in a few minutes later. 'I've told madam that you are here, and she will be with you presently.' He bowed slightly to take his leave.

'Oh Porter, this isn't today's paper,' I smiled, 'you don't by any chance have a copy of today's, do you?' Porter came across and looked at it. 'Ah, I'm sorry sir the maid should have changed it. We have yesterday's paper, but today's will be brought in by his Lordship this afternoon.' 'Yesterdays will be fine,' I said.

Porter looked over the top of me, to a round table near the window. Ah, there it is, he walked over, picked it up and brought it back to me picking up the old one. 'Is there anything else, sir?' I told him there wasn't, and he left, closing the door behind him.

I got hold of the paper and was irritated to find that it appeared to be a copy of the one Porter had just removed. I then looked closer; the date was two days later, 7th June 1910. The headline was about Scott's expedition to the Antarctic. I suddenly had a most uneasy feeling. I stood and walked over to the glass doors and looked out onto the croquet lawn and the trees beyond. For the first time in the last two hours, I started to take stock of what had happened. In my mind, I retraced my steps back to the place where I had fallen and realised, I had not seen any houses, apart from the farmhouse and Crowley Hall. That was strange, but I had not come across a tarmac road, a farm tractor, electricity pylons or even telephone lines. I frowned. My thoughts went back to the farmhouse, I hadn't realised it at the time, but something was missing in the main room. What was it? I concentrated hard. I heard the door open behind me, and as I started to turn, I realised what it was. There had been an old paraffin lamp hanging from the low ceiling, but no sign of electricity. As I turned around, I felt my heart beating faster, and as the person entering the room came through the door, my jaw dropped. 'Tory,' I blurted out, I could not believe my eyes. The woman had stopped too, a look of complete astonishment on her face. 'How... How on earth did you know my name?' She looked at me, incredulously.

'I...I don't know,' I said, 'you remind of someone I know,' I stammered. Lady Crowley: for I was sure that's who she was, was still standing by the door she had just closed behind her. She was wearing a long beige coloured skirt with a startlingly white blouse. The blouse had a high neck to it with a small gold filigree chain hanging from her neck. There was a gold locket at the end of the chain, which rested between her breasts. The sleeves of the blouse were tight at the wrist and forearm ballooning from the elbow to the shoulder. She looked stunning but in an innocent school girlish way. I judged her age to be late twenties. I had mistaken her for Tory, simply because that's how Tory looked about fifteen years ago, but I could now see slight differences. Her hair was lighter in colour, and although pretty, it was straighter, and she wore it up and tied at the back. Her teeth were not as white and straight either, but she had the same dark blue eyes and the slightly downward pointing mouth.

She recovered herself first, 'I'm so sorry Mr Alexander, please do sit down,' as she advanced towards one of the couches. I noticed she walked well, with her head held high on her shoulders. As she sat down, she was speaking again. 'I... I didn't mean to be rude, but you see Tory is the name only my husband uses,' *or used to use in happier days*, she thought to herself. 'My real name is Victoria, and most people call me that,' she smiled, and as she did so, her whole personality seemed to light up. After the initial shock, I walked over from the window and sat down in a chair opposite. My mind was still racing with a jumble of thoughts.

I was conscious of her looking at my clothes, without it appearing too obvious.

I shook my head. 'No, Lady Crowley, it's me who should apologise, I'm afraid I've not been myself this morning.'

She nodded, 'Porter told me that you had a fall and that you were lost.' I affirmed that was the case and recounted my story to her from the time I left home in the morning.

'And you say you left your, er... automobile near a bridge?' I nodded. 'The thing I've found confusing, is that your telephone exchange doesn't seem to have a record my telephone number, or even the exchange,' I thought for a few seconds, 'but there's one thing you can do for me, Lady Crowley.'

She tipped her head up on one side and looked at me with raised eyebrows.

'Can you confirm today's date?' She looked a little taken aback. Shrugging her shoulders, she picked up the Times that I had left on the small table between us. 'Well, this is yesterday's paper, so the date today is Tuesday, 8th, June,' she smiled, but with a slight frown.

'The year, Lady Crowley, what is the year?'

She looked at me as though I was slightly out of my mind. '1910 of course.'

'1910?' now I was the one to look at her as though she were crazy.

Lady Crowley looked slightly taken aback. 'Yes, nineteen hundred and ten,' she repeated.

My head started to swim. 'The monarch, who is on the throne...?' I didn't finish.

'Why, George V of course, King Edward VII died a month ago yesterday, and the Prime Minister in power is

Herbert Asquith. My husband says he's trying to ruin the country by preventing the Lords from continuing with their veto. They won't succeed of course,' she added.

She must have seen my face go pale. 'Are you all right, Mr Alexander? You've gone quite ashen,' she now looked genuinely concerned.

I put my head in my hands. 'I'm not sure, you see... when I set out this morning, the date was 8th June 2010,' I now began to wonder about my sanity, and I looked up at her. 'I can't explain it, but somehow, I seemed to have moved back in time... I know how stupid that must seem to you...'

She shook her head, sympathetically. 'Well, I do assure you that you are not in 2000... What did you say, 2010, we still have, er... one hundred years to live before then, and I certainly won't be around to see it,' she laughed. 'You probably hit your head when you fell, and... Well, I've read about these things. I suspect you have a temporary loss of memory.' I stood up and started to pace the room, a habit I had when I needed to think.

'No, no, I remember everything so clearly. I thrust my hand into my trouser pocket and felt something there. My car keys, of course, my car keys. I was elated. Suddenly I had a connection with my movements earlier this morning. I pulled them out of my pocket in triumph and held them up. 'There, you see, these are my car keys...' Lady Crowley got up and took them from me and stared at them. 'These are keys?' She looked doubtful. 'Yes, car keys,' I repeated, relief still in my voice, 'this larger one fit's the ignition, and the smaller one is for the alarm system, and the little red light when I press the top of the large key opens the doors....' My voice trailed off as I saw Lady Crowley was looking at me intently. 'You don't believe me, do you?' I said deflated.

'I believe you are sincere in your belief,' she answered, 'but automobiles don't have keys, even I know that, why would you want an alarm on an automobile and I certainly don't understand how a little thing like that could open a heavy door.'

I was now getting desperate. I realised that the only connection I had with this morning was unexplainable, how would someone living in 1910 understand an infra-red key. I knew it was useless. 'But what am I to do?' I felt utterly helpless.

Lady Crowley looked at me for what seemed to be an interminable time. It appeared that she was trying to make up her mind about how to deal with me. Then it seemed her mind was made up.

'I know what we will do; first, you should bathe and get out of those clothes. My husband used to be of a similar build to you, he's rather portlier now,' she added, 'but some of his older clothes will fit you. They may be a little out of fashion, but that doesn't matter for now. After that, I suggest you take lunch with me, and then I will get Porter to prepare a room for you where you can rest this afternoon.'

'Lord Crowley will be home just after four, and then we can decide what we should do with you. But don't worry, you can stay with us for tonight if we don't get you home.' She smiled.

Underneath, Victoria's heart was beating. To have offered succour to a stranger, let alone a room for the night would, in normal circumstances have been foolish and particularly so for one who had lost his mind. And yet there was something strange about this man James Alexander, she thought. She liked him instinctively, was it because he reminded her of John Crowley, her husband when she first met him eight years ago? The man she'd once loved with all her heart and now despised, hardly, she thought, James Alexander was about her husband's age. She frowned.

There was a likeness though, perhaps he's some lost member of John Crowley's family. Whatever the case, she trusted the stranger, and in some intuitive way, she felt their futures were to be intertwined. The thought sent a pleasant thrill through her body.

LADY VICTORIA CROWLEY

4 - THE QUESTIONING

I thanked Lady Crowley for her kindness, and she called Porter, telling him to take me up to her husband's dressing room and find a suitable day suit. 'In case we can't get Mr Alexander home, or find his automobile before this evening, you had better add to that some evening clothes that will fit Mr Alexander, it looks as though he may be staying for dinner.'

Lord Crowley's bedroom was at the front of the house on the right-hand corner. His dressing room was attached and overlooked the croquet garden. The two rooms together must have been directly over the drawing-room. Crowley's bedroom was completely masculine, with no sign of femininity whatsoever. I noticed a picture of two Golden Retrievers by his bedside. There were none of Lady Crowley. There was a communicating door between the dressing room and what I assumed to be a bedroom towards the rear of the house. A chest of drawers in front of it blocked this, suggesting it was not used. There were wardrobes full of clothes. I had never seen so many. Porter went to the area furthest away from the window and picked a brown sports jacket, which I noticed had high lapels, a pair of trousers with narrow bottoms and no turn-ups. Soon he was laden with various garments, including white shirts, cravats, an evening suit with tails, and polished ankle-high boots. Asking me if I approved, I told him I was most grateful. Porter then led the way out of Lord Crowley's room to the next room down, the one with the communicating door. This room was a little smaller than Lord Crowley's and must have sat over a room that I hadn't yet seen between the drawing-room and the study. Glass doors were leading out to a tiny balcony, and Porter opened them to allow air in to refresh the stuffy atmosphere. The net curtains blew inwards with the light breeze.

Porter hung the clothes in an adjoining dressing room, and he told me he'd asked one of the maids to draw my bath for me. 'The bathroom is next to Lady Crowley's room,' he explained, 'you turn left out of this room, go to the end of the corridor, turn right, and it's the second door on your left. I will leave a bathrobe in there for you sir. Oh, and madam said you'd be resting this afternoon, would you like someone to call you?' I nodded, 'thank you, Porter, I am tired, and it would be safer to ensure I am woken by 4 p.m.'

Porter bowed as he was going out, and then remembering something, he came back into the room. 'Oh, by the way, sir, the maid's bell is over the bed.' He walked across to a long tassel dangling at the centre of the wall by the four-poster bed. 'You just pull this, and someone will attend your needs.' He looked at his timepiece that he took out of his waistcoat. It's now twelve-fifteen, 'lunch is at 1.30 p.m. Madam is expecting you to join her. The dining room is between the drawing-room and the study.' Porter withdrew without smiling. I had the feeling he disapproved of Lady Crowley's decision for me to stay in the house.

I walked down to the bathroom some five minutes later, to find a steaming hot bath awaiting me. I was also delighted to find a flush lavatory. While in the bath I noticed the Victorian fittings now so popular with the trendy set in 2010.

I must have dozed because there was a knock at the bathroom door and a woman's voice asked if I was all right. I said I was, but hurriedly got out and dried myself putting on the bathrobe to walk back to the bedroom. I quickly dressed in the clothes I had been given, and before leaving the room, I looked in the mirror. Apart from the high lapels of the jacket, and the cravat, I could have been dressed to go anywhere. The clothes fitted me perfectly, although I found the boots to be a little small, and I was conscious of my feet being pinched. I noticed that the boots had not been worn, so the tightness may well have been due to that. I was 5 minutes late for lunch, and as Porter opened the dining-room door, I saw Lady Crowley was already at the table. She was reading what looked to be a small book. I saw the name of the author; it was Jules Verne. I apologised for my lateness and went to sit down. 'No. no, wait, let me look at you,' Lady Crowley sat back in her chair and looked me up and down carefully. 'What a change of clothes makes to a man.' she smiled, 'they look as though they were made for you.'

Porter drew out my chair, and I sat down. Lady Crowley was at the head of the table, and I sat next to her facing the window. The room was bigger than I had thought, as the dining area was the size of three large rooms put together and I realised that there must be several bedrooms next to the one I was in upstairs. The table could have held at least thirty guests, but I could see from the centre that it could be extended even further. There were several large sideboards down the wall that backed on to the hall, and a large painting at the far end, which covered the whole wall area. It was a picture of Lady Crowley on a horse. Lady Crowley saw me looking at it. 'It was painted just after my marriage to Lord Crowley, my father commissioned it for my twenty-first birthday.' There was a trace of sadness in her voice when she spoke about the picture, but I didn't comment.

I found Lady Crowley delightful to talk to, but I was surprised when she told me that she'd never travelled abroad. I told her about my travels in Africa, the West Indies, America, and the Far East. She seemed enthralled, although I was careful to exclude any suggestion of modern travel, such as the aeroplane. Many of the areas she had not heard about, such as Nigeria and Ghana, but she had heard of the Gold Coast. Africa was apparently in the news as the

British government had recently declared South Africa a dominion. The conversation went so well, and I can't remember what we ate. I know the end of lunch came all too quickly, and when I had taken my leave of her, I was in high spirits.

I got back to my bedroom at quarter to three and knowing I didn't have time for sleep, I took off my jacket, and lay on the bed. My mind started to take in the day's events as I tried to think logically about what had happened. My mind told me that it was impossible to have travelled back through time. Even to think it was ridiculous. But Lady Crowley wasn't acting, and why should she lie? So, what had happened? I pinched myself to see if I was dreaming, and then I remembered the car keys. I wasn't dreaming. *What were the possibilities, think it through logically,* I told myself angrily? First, let's consider the impossible. If I had somehow tripped into 1910, infeasible though the thought was, the problem I had to face was that I had no background and no history in this strange environment. So far, I had been lucky, but what if Lord Crowley threw me out, or worse, had me certified. How should I tackle the situation, if I insisted on the truth, would they have to consider me mad?

I began to think about how I could prove where I had come from. The car keys would mean nothing.

The tracksuit... I bounded off the bed, and grabbed the trousers, looking at the label inside the waistband. It read:

CHEROKEE
65% POLYESTER
35% COTTON
MADE IN CHINA
SEE OVER FOR CARE
And over the other side:
MACHINE WASH WARM
SEPARATELY OR WITH

LIKE COLOURS
ONLY NON-CHLORINE
BLEACH WHEN NEEDED
TUMBLE DRY LOW

I groaned, if the tracksuit had been manufactured in the USA or Europe, it would have been much easier to demonstrate that there was no such manufacturing plant, but made in China... Nevertheless, I knew that polyester was not invented in 1910, but did that mean anyone would know the difference between man-made and natural fibres, I wondered. I started to think about what I knew of the period and was horrified to realise just how little I did know. I knew World War 1 was due to the assassination of Archduke Franz Ferdinand, and it was declared on August 4th, 1914. Still, I was generally ignorant except for specific significant facts, political and financial, which I had studied due to my interest in history. Had I for instance known in detail what had transpired in 1910 directly after June 8th, I might have been able to convince people of my sincerity, but to forecast the First World War, would mean waiting four years for verification. And what, if now I appeared to be in the past, the future changed? *I was getting nowhere. Let me try a different tack*, I thought to myself, *why am I here, what is the reason I've been catapulted back in time if that is what has happened*? Then I thought, *what is the reason for living anyway, who am I, what am I. Is all life just a dream?* I sighed. That branch of questioning wasn't getting me too much further either. One thing that was odd though, Victoria Crowley was almost the double, albeit a younger version of my Tory, she even had the same name.

I frowned. It appeared that John Crowley looked like me; indeed, his clothes fit perfectly. Why, why? Was someone trying to tell me something? I had already got the feeling that there was a sadness attached to the house, was that because John Crowley and Victoria Crowley didn't have a good marriage? I had no evidence of that only a feeling. I thought back to the separate bedrooms, but I also knew that this was normal in certain upper-class circles, particularly in the early part of the century. Again, my mind came back to the question of whether I was in 1910. Could I have stumbled on some strange sect who lived as though they were in the past? It seemed unlikely, mainly as I had seen no evidence of 2010 since my fall, and I felt I would have come across something even if it were only a telegraph pole. But did they have telegraph poles in 1910?

I looked up at the ceiling; there was an electric light bulb under a shade. I reasoned that didn't tell me anything either. Electricity would have been available to the better off in 1910. It came down to this. How could I get conclusive proof of the time I was living in, and if I had travelled back through time, how could I convince everyone around me that I was from the future? And if I could not do so, would it be wise to press the point? I knew enough about astronomy to know that the stars would be in a different position in 1910 from 2010, but I didn't know enough to be able to tell the difference. God, it was frustrating. Perhaps my best plan with Lord Crowley was to pretend amnesia, in that way he'd not assume I was mad, and I may then have a better chance of finding a way to make a living. I reasoned he must be well connected, and I did have knowledge that could be of immense value. Or did I? Yes, I can use a computer with some skill, but when there are no computers to use, it's a bit pointless. I realised just how useless most of my knowledge was, what I knew I could not put to commercial use. I could not manufacture computer parts, or a television or an aeroplane or... The list was endless as to what I could not do. There must be a way...

I had not thought of one when I fell asleep.

The chauffeur stopped the Rolls Royce 40/50 Silver Ghost on the gravel at the front of the house, and he stepped out to open the rear door for Lord Crowley who was resplendent in a dark blue suit, wing collar, silk tie and top hat. He got out and climbed the steps to the front of the house. The chauffeur carried his small case that he handed to Porter, who met them at the door. Lord Crowley nodded perfunctorily at Porter and was about to pass him to go inside, when Porter said, 'Excuse me your Lordship, but Lady Crowley has asked if you can spare her a few minutes?' Crowley's eyes narrowed, but he nodded in assent.

He wondered what his wife wanted; it was rare that they spoke to each other. Nowadays, she carried on her pursuit's, and Lord Crowley his interests. Of course, in company, they acted as a loving man and wife, but that was for public consumption. Money was never a problem, he was rich, but she was wealthier in her own right, her father had been one of the first steel magnates. The marriage had seemed perfect, Crowley from an old aristocratic family and Victoria from the new merchant elite.

Although she'd experienced the best education money could buy, she was relatively naive when she met the handsome Crowley. Age wasn't a problem he was thirty-five, she twenty, a perfect match some said. Crowley destined to be made the chairman of the family bank,

Crowley & Company. His future seemed to be assured, titled with lands and a beautiful family home, the major shareholder of a well-respected bank, albeit a little conservative in its policies, and a lovely wife.

What more could a man want? Crowley cringed inwardly. He knew that he'd made a massive blunder in continuing liaisons with doubtful women in London. He loved his wife dearly, but the excitement of being with a new woman on each of his frequent stopovers in the city provided him with an adrenaline surge. The last woman he bedded was introduced to him by Jules Byron, the son of the present chairman of Byron's Bank, one of the fastest-growing banks in the city. Soon afterwards, signs had appeared, and upon consulting his doctor, he found he'd contracted syphilis.

Fortunately, Victoria had been staying with her aunt during this period. It was on her return that John Crowley had confessed to her what had happened. Victoria was understandably shattered. She had only been married for two years at the time. Victoria knew then that any physical side to her married life was over; she also knew that due to a genetic problem, having children was denied to her. Since then, the two of them had grown apart, and the deep hurt felt by Victoria made worse by the fact that she bottled up her frustration. To an onlooker, the marriage seemed as good as any other. Of course, some knew the truth, but they were few and kept silent.

Strangely Victoria hadn't left John Crowley; he didn't know quite why. He had heard of a new treatment called Halverson, invented by a Dr Paul Ehrlich and because of his wealth, he'd managed to persuade him to treat him as a guinea pig. Ehrlich had noted some improvement, but John Crowley knew it would be many years before he could get back to normal, if ever... There was always the chance that the treatment had come too late and was just allowing him more time. All these thoughts rushed through his brain as *he headed for his study.*

He sat down at his desk and opened the Times that he'd brought with him from the city. He'd been reading for about five minutes when he heard the door open.

He looked up.

Victoria Crowley came through the door, and barely glancing at her husband, she sat down in one of the comfortable chairs opposite him. Her face was severe, and he thought he could detect contempt in her eyes. Oh my God, she's beautiful, he thought, and he could feel himself gritting his teeth as she started to speak. Outwardly, his face hadn't changed from his usual aloof composure. She told him about the arrival of James Alexander, his strange clothes, his extraordinary likeness to John Crowley himself, and his easy manner. When she finished, Lord Crowley frowned. 'You asked him to stay here?' he said incredulously.

'Yes, and I've loaned him some of your clothes, the ones you can no longer get into,' she said unkindly. 'The point is, there's a family likeness, and the man is highly educated and well-travelled and...,' she emphasized the point, 'he's knowledgeable... and quite different from anyone else I've ever met.' John Crowley felt a pang of jealousy. 'I could not turn someone like that away, particularly as he's had a fall and suffered what I assume to be a memory loss. He appears to be about 40 years of age, obviously wealthy he owns an automobile, although he doesn't know where he left it. I think you should talk to him before making any decision. I've offered for him to stay tonight as our guest.' Victoria Crowley looked at her husband, defiantly.

John Crowley was about to make a sarcastic remark but thought better of it.

Victoria was no fool, he knew that, and what she'd told him about the man was just enough to interest him. Could it be that this man was a distant relative? 'Oh, and one more thing,' Victoria smiled, 'he has the impression that he lived in the future...'

'WHAT...?'

She nodded. 'Probably due to the blow on his head, but the stories of his trips to other parts of the world don't tie up with my reading of the places he's been, and yet... well... there's something strange about him, that's all I can say.'

'He sounds to me as though he should be in an asylum,' said John Crowley. He was now intrigued. He read Jules Verne avidly, although he'd never have admitted that to Victoria.

Victoria got up. 'You may be right John, but this man isn't mad. It may be he hasn't come from the future. That's highly unlikely and could only be believed by those people who read such childish ideas as those propounded by Jules Verne,' she said maliciously, 'but he may have had some sort of vision, certainly the detail is too great to be tossed away lightly. He could author an excellent book about the future if nothing else.' She smiled in a business-like way as she got up. 'I will ask Porter to send him into you.' She didn't wait for an answer, and within a couple of seconds, she had left the room, leaving behind her perfume, which made John Crowley's teeth clamp yet again.

A few moments later, Porter came through the door. There was no knock, servants didn't announce themselves when entering the downstairs rooms.

'Madam said you'd like to see Mr Alexander, sir; shall I show him in?' Porter was aware of the animosity between husband and wife without knowing the reason for it, so he was his usual careful self.

'What do you think of our new-found friend, Charles?' Porter thought for a minute. 'He appears to be a gentleman, sir, he speaks well, carries himself well, I should think Mr Alexander has served under the Kings colours at some time, and he's very self-assured.' Porter leaned over, 'There's a family likeness, sir, but there's

something strange about him.'

'Oh?'

'Yes, sir, although a gentleman, the maid told me he emptied his bathwater, not something a gentleman would normally do,' Porter frowned, 'and another thing sir, he turned up in the most extraordinary clothes, he called them a tracksuit...'

'Is that all?'

'No, sir, he says please and thank you to servants, I think you'll agree with me, sir, that's not normal behaviour from a gentleman either. Err, should I show him in now, sir?'

John Crowley nodded, 'yes, Charles that'll be in order.' Porter went out, and a few minutes later the door opened, and he came in with the stranger, 'Mr James Alexander, sir,' John Crowley got up, and walked around his desk, holding his hand out. I grasped it firmly.

'Is there anything I can get you, sir?' asked Porter,

John Crowley steered me towards the comfortable chairs in front of the fireplace and gestured for me to sit down.

'Some tea Mr Alexander or would you like something stronger?' he asked.

'Thank you, if you are having tea, I would be delighted to join you.'

Crowley turned around to Porter. 'Tea for two and bring some of the cook's scones as well. Oh, and Porter, tell Sidney to put the Rolls Royce away, I shall not need it again today.' Porter bowed and went out, closing the door softly behind him.

While he was giving Porter his instructions, Crowley was weighing up the man sitting opposite him. He was clean-shaven and lean, very lean for his age. Lord Crowley noticed that Alexander was suntanned, and as Porter had said, he was well-spoken and held himself ramrod straight when standing. In comparison, he sported a King George V beard and was 20 pounds or so overweight, but there was a similarity between the two men. Both about the same height, both with similar hair, although James Alexander was greyer, he had more of it. He guessed his age at forty, some five years younger than himself. He was astounded when he found out later that John Alexander and he were the same age. The eye colour was the same, deep brown, but it was the shape of the head and the forehead that was most similar. Alexander's head was square, with a good chin and a large nose. The forehead broad with dark brown eyebrows that almost met in the middle, he felt he could be looking at a younger brother, and as Crowley knew he had no brothers or sisters, he wondered if the stranger was a product of his father's philandering. Perhaps he thought Alexander had wheedled his way in, to try and claim some of the fortune left by his father. Some hope, he thought, an estate that cost him £250 a year to run and a bank that was now losing even more than that.

Crowley's debts were mounting.

'My wife has told me something of your arrival here, and I confess I'm intrigued, perhaps you'd not mind me asking you to tell me your story direct?'

I nodded, and for some reason, changed my original plan and decided to tell the story as it was. I knew I was taking a risk, but I somehow felt I would sound more convincing with the truth. I told Lord Crowley of my early life, my time in the army and of my travels and work abroad. I also told him how I became a millionaire businessman flying a helicopter to work each day, how I lost all my money and set up the small publishing business I now ran. I included something of my family, including the coincidence of my wife having the same name as Lady Crowley. Lord Crowley frequently interrupted when there was something he didn't understand. Helli-copter, he pronounced it in two separate syllables. What is a helli-copter? At that point, a maid brought in the tea and poured out two cups, and I took one of the delicious scones. 'Is there anything else, sir?'

'No Mary, you can go,' Lord Crowley said in dismissive

terms. As she closed the door behind her, I told him in some detail what a helicopter was, and the principles of how it flew, that I had, of course, learned when I was learning to fly the machine.

He seemed particularly interested in modern technology, but as I started to explain more details, I could see he was no longer concentrating on what I was saying. By then, we had been talking for over two hours, and I reasoned that the information I gave him must have been difficult to assimilate. For a couple of minutes, Lord Crowley had seemed to go into some sort of trance state. When I stopped talking, he snapped out of it. I wasn't sure how much he'd taken in. 'I do apologise, Mr Alexander,' he said, straightening himself in the chair, 'I have an, er... an unfortunate illness that interferes with my concentration from time to time. What you've told me is most interesting, most entertaining even, but we both know that you could not have come from the future, so what is it you are wanting?' He said it bluntly and I thought uncharacteristically. His lack of concentration irritated him, and he wanted to end the interview.

'Want?' I was surprised, 'I don't want anything Lord Crowley, except to get back to my house and my wife.' My answer was slightly belligerent, and Lord Crowley recognised it as such. He looked at me for a long time, and I returned his stare. Lord Crowley got up and went to his desk, took a cigarette out of a silver case, and lit it with a Swan Vestas match. He started pacing the floor. 'Let's assume for the minute that your fall somehow created a fictional picture in your mind, blanking out all knowledge of your past, causing amnesia.' He stopped pacing and looked down at me and then blew smoke in the air. 'While you've told me of flying craft that carry hundreds of people, boxes that transmit images, and machines that do the work of our current servants, none of what you've told me is outside the imagination of some of our current writers. I could even fantasise about men going to the Moon or Mars. Of course, we know that such things will never happen.' I stayed silent.

'I thought you might be a charlatan, but I don't think so now...' He stopped pacing again and looked for my reaction. There was none.

'So, let us consider the medical possibilities. You could be mad...' He thought of his illness and shuddered. 'But you don't appear to be deranged, so it leaves the possibility of some sort of complete memory loss due to a bang on the head. Perhaps the story you've retained is from some book or other you'd just completed reading.' He turned to look at me, triumphant.

'And the car keys and tracksuit?' I inquired.

Lord Crowley shrugged. 'I admit the key you've given me is different from anything I've seen before, as is the suit you refer to, but I'm simply not qualified to comment on either, I'm afraid I know little about what goes on in China. I can, of course, give the garments to a textile manufacturer I know, and get his opinion...'

I agreed that such an opinion would at least clear up one of the puzzles in this saga, and I could see Lord Crowley's point of view. I wondered how I would have dealt with someone landing on my doorstep and telling me he was from one hundred years in the future, probably not as kindly as Lord Crowley had done.

'I think you should see my doctor, you are quite welcome to stay here at least until we've heard his report, and in the meantime, I will speak to the local constabulary, to see if they've any reports of missing people... I might also have a word with the war office too. There is just a chance that you could have been on some army training course that might account for your odd clothes.' Lord Crowley turned to me and held out his hand. 'We will see you at dinner then, 8.30?'

I smiled and got up realising that the interview was at an end, but with the knowledge that at least I had a roof over my head for a few more days. I thanked him, and as I left the room, I saw him pick up the telephone mouthpiece.

When I returned to my bedroom, I realised I was tired. I pulled the tassel behind the bed, and soon there was a knock on the door. I opened it, and an older woman was standing there, 'I am Mrs Carter sir, I'm the housekeeper, can I help you?'

'Yes, Mrs Carter, I wonder if you'd mind telling Lord Crowley that I'm grateful for his dinner invitation, but I am exhausted and would prefer to go straight to bed.' Mrs Carter looked sympathetic. 'I will relay your comments to Mr Porter, the butler, sir, but is there anything I can get you?' I thanked her and said no, firmly closing the door after she had gone.

I undressed without covering the windows and got into bed naked.

Although it was still light outside, I must have fallen asleep very quickly.

The next thing I knew was a sharp knock on the door. I woke up with a start.

'It's Mary, sir, madam has had your breakfast sent up.' I sat up in bed and shouted for her to come in and that the door was not locked. The door opened, and Mary entered carrying a large tray, which she went to put on the table in front of the window. As she was putting it down, she turned to say something to me, and suddenly let out a little screech. She dropped the tray with a crash; fortunately, it only had a few inches to travel, so there was more noise than damage. 'Oh, I do beg your pardon sir,' she giggled and then her face went a puce red. 'It's... well sir, I've never seen a gentleman undressed before...' She was giggling as she almost ran out of the room, closing the door quickly. Undressed, I thought, how odd. I was sitting up in bed, but everything that should be covered was well under the sheets. I shook my head, and climbed out of bed, hoping to find some evidence of modern breakfast cereals, there was none. There was a pot of tea, toast and marmalade and scones along with some fresh apples. I felt hungry and did the food justice. As I was

49

pouring out my tea, which was made a little too strong for my liking, I noticed a sealed envelope tucked under the plate of scones. It was addressed to me. I tore it open.

Crowley Hall
Buckinghamshire

Dear Mr Alexander,

I'm sorry you could not join us for dinner last evening, but I do understand how tired you must have been after your accident. Lord Crowley has arranged for Doctor Simpson, he is our family doctor and well qualified, to attend you at the house at 10.00 this morning. Porter will make all the arrangements, but I have suggested he attends to you in your bedroom, which will ensure you the privacy you need for any examination.

I so enjoyed our lunch talk yesterday; I do hope you will join me again today at 1.30 p.m.

Sincerely

Victoria Crowley.

The writing was small and neat, as I would have expected. I took it across to the desk in my room and using the quill pen provided, drew a sheet of headed notepaper from the desk drawer. I scribbled a message saying I would be delighted to join her in the dining room at 1.30 I put the note into a new envelope, printing LADY CROWLEY in bold letters on the front and put it back on the tray.

I didn't know what time it was, and as my bedroom was on the west side of the house, I could not easily assess the time from the sun. After visiting the bathroom, I dressed, using a clean shirt and undergarments loaned to me. I then folded the two pieces of the tracksuit and put them along with my tennis shoes in one of the drawers I found in the dressing room.

I thought it better to await Dr Simpson in my room, so I gave up the idea of an early morning walk and sat on the bed. I was thinking about what I would do for my future when there was a knock on the door. I assumed it was the maid to take the tray away, so I went and opened it. Porter was standing there with a medium-sized man of about sixty years. Porter seemed genuinely surprised that I had opened the door, and it took him a few seconds to compose himself. He coughed. 'Excuse me, sir, this is Dr Simpson.' Simpson came forward with a bulbous bag in his left hand and his right hand outstretched. I took it and shook it warmly.

'Please come in doctor,' I smiled at him. Porter followed us through and was displeased to see the tray still in my room. He let out a tut and collected it before exiting, closing the door behind him.

Dr Simpson put his heavy bag on the unmade bed. 'Now, Mr Alexander, tell me what the trouble is?' He spoke with a heavy Scottish accent.

I smiled again, offering him a seat on one of the two-bedroom chairs near the window. He took it, and I sat in the other. 'Well, tell me what you know so far, and Ill fill in the rest.'

'Ay,' he looked at me a little suspiciously, 'well, Lord Crowley has given me a run-down on yer accident yesterday and thinks ye may have lost your memory. Is that the case, Mr Alexander?' He was observing me. I guessed that John Crowley had said more than he admitted.

'I certainly have no memory of 1910, or before, I do appear to have a memory of 2010, a period 100 years into the future. I remember falling while out walking, I became disoriented and lost, eventually finding Crowley Hall, where Lord and Lady Crowley have been most kind in offering me accommodation.'

'Ay, ay, they're nice people right enough. Well, I had better examine you first,' he got up and came over to me, putting his expert hands around my neck and feeling for glands. 'Bit of swelling there,' he frowned.

I confirmed that I had always had large tonsils.

His hands were now feeling my scalp. 'Do you feel any

pain?'

I shook my head. 'No, I seem to have fallen on my face and cut the inside of my mouth. Apart from that...' I put my hand up to my cheek where it was still sore.

Dr Simpson went over to the wash-bowl and poured some water in it from a jug that was on a marble washstand nearby. He thoroughly washed his hands, drying them on the small towel hung underneath. He approached me again.

'Ay, let me look, open your mouth wide and turn yer head towards the window,' I did so. I could feel his fingers probing the inside of my cheek. 'Ay it's healing okay,' he withdrew his hand and peered into my gaping mouth. There was a sudden gasp of amazement. I closed my mouth hurriedly, 'something wrong doctor?' I asked, feeling uneasy. He looked at me strangely and was puzzled. 'Noo, noo, there's nothing wrong exactly, but it's... it's your teeth. They are filled with some substance.' He frowned.

Teeth, of course, I thought with a surge of excitement, dental treatment must have made huge strides since 1910, and this was a way to prove my story.

I laughed. 'Oh, is that all,' I said, 'I've crowns too,' I opened my mouth and showed my front teeth, 'this one on the left is a crown, a false tooth made from porcelain and stuck on to my natural tooth that was reduced to a peg to give it support. The original was bad, of course.' Dr Simpson was excited. 'May I have another look at your mouth?'

'Of course,' I said.

He got a small metal instrument from his case and probed around my teeth for a few minutes. 'And this one near the back is this not a natural tooth either?'

'No, that's a crown too,' I answered, glad to be able to close my mouth at last.

Dr Simpson went back to sit down, completely forgetting that I was supposed to have a loss of memory. 'But where did you receive such superb treatment?'

'A lot of the treatment was carried out when I was in the United States,' I admitted truthfully, 'but some was done recently in Leighton Buzzard.'

'In Leighton Buzzard, but I know of no doctor who…?'

'It wasn't a doctor, it was a dentist,' I was enjoying myself now.

'A dentist? I don't know of any dentists outside of the city of London,' he said.

Doctor Simpson shook his head, 'I must make enquiries, this treatment you've had is revolutionary, it's, it's fantastic.' He thought for a minute. 'I assume this dentist used ether to make you unconscious. Otherwise, the pain would have been unbearable?' I shook my head. 'He used a local anaesthetic, injected into the nerve connected to the tooth, and this numbs the whole area for a period, long enough to carry out the restructuring.'

'How interesting, what is the dentist's name? I really must contact him as I usually deal with teeth in this area.'

I told him.

He frowned, 'I've never heard of the man… well I never, I thought I had seen everything in my thirty-five years of medicine, but it seems I have a lot to learn.' He seemed to ponder, deep in thought for a time. He got up again.

'Now, would you mind taking your shirt off and I will give you a full examination.' I did so, and as I faced him half-naked, I saw his eyes go straight to my appendix scar.

'What is that?' he pointed towards the scar.

'Oh, I had an appendectomy when I was ten years old.' I saw a blank look. 'I had my appendix out,' I explained.

He scrutinized the scar. 'Beautiful surgery such a small cut, who…?'

I told him I had no idea, as it was thirty-five years ago. He looked at me strangely.

He continued the examination, tapping my chest, taking my blood pressure just as a doctor would have done in 2010. He could not resist another look inside my mouth, shaking his head with wonder as he did so.

'Well?' I said as he finished.

'What age did you say you were Mr Alexander?'

'Forty-five,' he looked surprised as he put his various instruments back in his case, he stood back and looked at me. 'I put your biological age at thirty-five, there's nothing wrong with you, and you are supremely fit. However, I'm not a doctor of the mind;' he lowered his head and looked at me over his metal-rimmed glasses. 'I'm going to suggest to his Lordship that Sir Ernest Cottingham see you, he's the best man in the world for the workings of the brain.'

'Do I appear to be mentally deranged?' I half-smiled.

He turned away from me to pick up his bag. 'Just the opposite, Mr Alexander, but your obvious amnesia needs some understanding and treatment, and I'm not qualified to give you any help in that area.' He shook my hand and took his leave, still deep in thought. Altogether his examination had taken just under two hours. I decided to take another bath, and pulling on my bathrobe, walked along to the bathroom. I was surprised to find there was no lock on the door. I took my robe off and went to turn the taps on in the bath, but there were none. I realised that the bath must be filled from hot water carried up from the kitchens. I had not noticed this yesterday. *Oh, for a modern shower,* I thought.

Putting my bathrobe back on, I went back to my bedroom and pulled the tassel above my bed. Shortly afterwards there was a knock at the door, and I was surprised that it was Porter who stood there. I suddenly realised that my half nakedness, when Mary came into my room earlier in the morning, might have somehow embarrassed her, I supposed that men in 1910 didn't sleep naked. I was to have my thoughts not so subtly confirmed by Lady Crowley over lunch.

'Yes, sir, can I get you anything?'

'Is it possible for someone to run... er fill the bath for me?'

'You wish to take another bath, sir?'

Porter seemed surprised.

I nodded. 'Where I come from, people have a bath every day.' Porter looked astonished

'Oh, really, sir, well if you give me instructions, I will ensure your bath is prepared for you daily. Give me a few moments, sir, I will get the staff to prepare it for you.' He disappeared through the door, looking put out.

As I waited, I went over to the bedroom window and looked out. It was another glorious day, with hardly a hint of a cloud in the sky. I usually suffered from acute hay fever at this time of year, but I realised I had no problems now. Could it be that my allergy was caused by pollution in 2010 I wondered? I started to think about how servants filled the bath, and I realised just how dependent people must have been on them. Not to have servants in 1910, would be akin to not having electricity in 2010 I mused. It seemed that electricity in 1910 was used purely for lighting, though I assumed industry used it too, or perhaps they still used steam.

As I looked down from the window, I saw Lady Crowley walking across the croquet lawn, and heading for some rose bushes at the far edge where she picked a large red rose and held it to her nose. I was entranced by her and was caught off guard when she turned and looked directly up to my window. I smiled and waved. She looked embarrassed, but returned the smile and waved back, hastily but proudly moving back towards the house with the single rose clutched in her hand.

It was then I felt a strange urge to jump out of the window. I can't explain the feeling adequately, but it was strong, and I was a little frightened by it. It was to take me six years to understand the reason for the feeling. It was interrupted by a knock at the door. Porter came in with something laid out on a towel. It was a cut-throat razor. I had completely forgotten I had not shaved.

'Your bath is ready, sir, and I assumed you'd want to shave?' He put the dangerous-looking instrument on the marble stand. 'While you are bathing, I will arrange for Mary to change your water, is there anything else...?'

I shook my head.

Shortly afterwards, I made my way down to the bathroom, and after closing the door, I had a good look at the lavatory system. It was apparent that the cistern was refilled by gravity from a tank in the roof. I assumed rightly that the tank was topped up by rainwater. As I sank into the warm water in the bath, I wondered idly if pumps had been invented for household use. If they had, Lord Crowley hadn't put them to use in Crowley Hall.

When I got back to my room, I saw my clothes for the day had been laid out on the freshly made bed. I smiled at the thought that the servants even decided what I was to wear. I saw a garment folded over the chair next to the bed. It was a nightshirt.

I did much more damage to my face with the cut-throat razor than I did during the fall, and when I turned up for lunch, the clumsy ministrations were obvious.

Lady Crowley was in her usual seat, and as I sat down, she expressed some concern at the sight of my face.

'You really must let my husband's valet shave you in the morning, Mr. Alexander.'

Valet? I had not seen another male in the house apart from Lord Crowley and Porter.

'His name is Donald. He's a nice lad and well trained, he came to us by recommendation from Sir Pierce Dominion, who went to live in the West Indies. He laid out your clothes this morning, and I hope left you a nightshirt.' She giggled. 'You quite shocked poor Mary this morning, she thought you had nothing on when she delivered your breakfast.' I didn't enlighten her.

Soon our conversation, like that of yesterdays, turned to other things. We talked about the West Indies, and I told her that I had sailed to all the islands in the Leeward and Windward chain. I had been interested in studying something of the varying cultures left first by the Arawak Indians, then the Caribs from whom the name Caribbean was taken. Since then, the Europeans, starting with the Spanish, Swedish, Dutch, French, English and later the Americans, had left their mark. 'Of course, most of the natives are Negros from West Africa,' I explained.

'But why did you take so much interest in islands that are so small and far away?' She asked.

'The islands are beautiful, and each one is quite different, even the cultures between certain islands. Of course, the larger ones were important as producers of sugar'.

'Are,' she corrected me with a smile. I didn't argue.

'To give you an idea of how important the islands were, Lord Cornwallis the head of the British army fighting against Washington, was ordered by the British government of 1795 to ship half of his army to defend St Lucia. Can you believe that we considered the small island of St Lucia more important than the colonies in North America?' She shook her head, unbelievingly.

'And after the war of independence was won by the Americans the first state to recognise the new power, was tiny Eustatius, a small Dutch island in the Leeward Islands'.

She showed tremendous interest in everything I told her. Since our conversation yesterday, she had been reading up on West Africa, particularly the story of Mary Slessor, the missionary who tried to prevent the West African tribes from killing twins at birth.

'Have you heard of her?' she asked, and then, 'did you meet her?' She leaned over towards me; her eyebrows raised.

I laughed. 'She was rather before my time, but in a way, I did meet her.' Lady Crowley's eyes grew larger.

'I visited Calabar, which is a small town in Eastern Nigeria, and came across her grave in the little church there, she died quite young you know.' I then told her of the old European club in Calabar where the bar stools had brass plates engraved with the name of the owner, but not only that, the seats were scooped out to fit the incumbent, and the largest of them all belonged to the female nurse on the station. 'It was this big,' I said, exaggerating with my hands held out wide.

She laughed, trying to visualize the scene. She had an infectious laugh.

The conversation ranged on until finally we somehow got on to Freud and his ideas that were still revolutionary for 1910. 'No doubt Mr Freud would make something of your dream of the future,' she said.

'I can't see what sort of sexual connotation he'd attach to it though,' I answered as I laughed at the thought.

I was aware of Lady Crowley looking at me intently. I looked back at her. I'm not sure how long we looked into each other's eyes, but it was she who first tore her gaze away, looking slightly flustered. I felt I had known her forever; we just seemed natural together; it was an uncanny feeling. I thought of my wife Tory, and the resemblance between the two. I knew then I was falling in love with Lady Crowley, but somehow, I didn't have a feeling of guilt. I broke the silence.

'By the way Lady Crowley, I would prefer you to call me James instead of Mr Alexander.'

For some reason, her eyes swelled up with tears, and she looked away for a minute, her thoughts far away. When she turned back, she was entirely composed. 'I would like that' she smiled, 'and I'm Victoria.' *She wanted to say, Tory, please call me Tory, a name she had known from happier days. But she could not, of course, only John Crowley had called her that name, but she connected it with love and happiness.*

She knew that this man, James Alexander, had appeared precisely at a time when she was most vulnerable. She knew she would become his lover, and it had a sort of inevitability about it. But perhaps by becoming intimate, everything would be spoiled, and she resolved to fight her emotions if she could bear to do so.

She was aware that James Alexander was talking again. 'I thought I might go out for a walk this afternoon, to try and retrace my steps of yesterday, would you like to join me?' Victoria shook her head sadly. 'I'm afraid it wouldn't be proper for me to walk with you as you suggest, but we could ride,' she suggested brightly.

My last encounter with a horse wasn't a happy one, and I rubbed my nose where I had broken it many years before, as the memory flooded back into my mind. 'I did have the use of a pony when I was young, but my experience with a horse has not left me with good memories, so, I regret that I can't ride,' I stated blandly.

Victoria tipped her head up. 'Then I shall teach you,' she smiled. There appeared to be no further argument on the matter. It was with some trepidation that I heard her giving instructions to Porter to relay to the groom that she and Mr Alexander were going riding at 3.30 p.m. and would he arrange for two horses to be saddled ready. 'Oh, and Porter, would you please arrange for some suitable riding breeches and a jacket from my husband's wardrobe.'

I met Victoria at the stables behind the house, Johnson, the groom, led out the horse I was about to ride. I gulped when I first saw her. She was a magnificent gleaming chestnut filly with a lovely head. But she was exceptionally large. I was about to climb on to her back when Victoria came to my side. 'No, no, James, you must talk to her first, so that she has confidence in you. You should never just ride a horse as though it were a piece of furniture, treat her as if she were a beautiful woman and the intelligent animal she is.'

I remembered a friend of mine who bred and trained horses who told me that a horse's brain was the size of a walnut, but I didn't impart that knowledge to Victoria.

I felt self-conscious in talking to the animal as Victoria Crowley suggested, but I found when I had done so, the horse whose name was Bright Star, was more comfortable with her nervous passenger.

As we rode off, Victoria leaned over to me and told me

how to sit in the saddle so that I would not become so sore afterwards, but at the same time have better control. 'We won't go any faster than a trot today,' she said, 'you should just get used to being in the saddle and for Bright Star to get used to you.' I looked across at her, she was wholly at home riding side-saddle, and I noticed she had removed the pin holding in her hair so that it was now flowing out behind her.

'Don't you wear a hat?' I asked conscious that I was without one too.

'No, I love to feel the wind in my hair,' she smiled, 'it gives me a sense of freedom.'

I led her to the canal tow-path, and with some surprise quickly found the area where I had fallen. We then headed east away from the spot, and sure enough, we soon came across a large farmhouse with several barns separate from the main building. I recognised the farmhouse immediately and the barn that I knew was my home in 2010. It was quite definitely a barn and not a house. If I needed conclusive proof that I was in another time, I now had it.

'This is where I live... lived,' I corrected myself as I turned to Victoria.

'The farm?' She looked surprised. 'No, the Barn was converted into quite a large house, it looks quite different now though.'

We both sat side by side on our respective mounts, as the horses munched from the fresh grass where we were standing. I looked at the various buildings, and I felt a tinge of sadness as I thought of my Tory. Would I ever see her again?

Victoria somehow felt my mood and moved her horse closer to mine. I could smell her perfume, and I wanted her more than anything else in the world. The sudden switch in affection, or was it lust, was confusing, and I felt tears well up inside me. I needed to getaway. I wheeled my horse sharply, and Bright Star was surprised at my harsh treatment and whinnied in protest.

As we rode back towards Crowley Hall, Victoria told me that Charles Porter's father had tenanted the farm, and as tenant farms went, it was one of the larger farms on the Crowley estate.

'It had a sad ending though,' Victoria held in the rein of her horse as it tried to forge ahead, 'Porter's mother died of consumption, caught from the cow's milk, and his father just let everything go. Eventually, John's father had to evict him, even though Porter, the son, was by then in service to the Crowley family. The poor man died in a debtor's prison.'

I listened to the story but said nothing. My feelings were in turmoil, and I could not trust myself to speak. Victoria realised this, and we returned to Crowley Hall in silence, but without any feeling of embarrassment because of it.

When we joined the main entrance road to the house, I saw Lord Crowley's 40/50 Silver Ghost Rolls Royce just disappearing around the side of the house, and I assumed he'd returned from the city. I thanked Victoria for her company and tuition, and she suggested that we continue with the lessons if I felt up to it.

I felt pleased and answered that I would like nothing better.

'Tomorrow then,' I nodded in agreement.

'And I hope you'll join us for dinner tonight, James.'

I assured her that I would.

I went back to my room, not meeting anyone on the way, and although it was only around five-o-clock, I took off my riding clothes and lay on the bed, my thoughts still confused I fell asleep.

Victoria had spent some time with the horses, before turning them over to Johnson the groom and returning to the house. As she entered the hall, John Crowley was just coming out of his study. 'Ah, there you are Victoria; Johnson told me that you and Alexander had gone for a ride.' Victoria walked up to him. 'Yes, he... he wanted to retrace his steps of yesterday, and I felt it would be better if I went with him, in case he, he became lost again...' She had the feeling that she had over-explained herself, and she stopped herself going further.

'Of course, you did the right thing, I'm sure. Do you have a moment to spare?' Victoria frowned; her husband was unusually polite.

'Of course,' Crowley opened the door to his study and ushered Victoria inside. She sat down in front of his desk. Crowley sat in his usual seat. It was strange, she thought, they both felt safer nowadays when they did talk to each other, they did so across a desk.

Crowley opened the conversation.

'I've been thinking about taking a permanent room in my London club,' he saw a look of alarm cross Victoria's face. 'I'm finding the daily trips most tiring, and there are problems at the bank that I need to spend more time on, what I'm suggesting is that I leave on Monday morning and stay away until Friday night,' Victoria's heart was racing. If John Crowley had suggested this two days ago, she would have whooped for joy, but now she knew that James Alexander could not stay at Crowley Hall with only herself as a resident. She was desperately thinking of a solution when John Crowley spoke again.

'Now, let us talk about Mr Alexander.' He moved on hastily and lifted a sheet of paper on which he'd written some notes. 'I've spoken to Dr Simpson, and he thinks that Alexander is suffering from amnesia. There is no doubt that either he or his family, wherever they might be, are extremely wealthy. He told me that the work done on his teeth alone was extraordinary and must have cost a small fortune.' Crowley ran his tongue over his false teeth with a grim reminder that he had all his own out over ten years ago. 'Simpson says that such treatment is not available in Britain, and he assumes that only in America could he have had such technologically advanced work done, even though Alexander said some of the work was done locally. He mentioned the name of a doctor that doesn't appear to

exist. He is very fit, and Simpson says he has the blood pressure of someone ten years younger than Alexander admits to being. Incredibly Alexander says he's forty-five years old, which is most unlikely. He has undergone surgery that again shows an advance in medicine that's not apparent here. The feeling, therefore, is that Alexander, although English from his speech, must have lived for some time in America. Perhaps he was educated over here, although none of the schools he mentioned to me are known institutions. The local constabulary has no record of a person of Alexander's description missing, nor have the War Office, although both are going to make further enquiries. I've written to my cousin in America to see if Alexander is in any way related to us. I hope this will throw some light on the mystery. It's clear that there's a family likeness, and that can't be a coincidence. I think he may have come from America to visit us, and experienced an accident on the way, but part of his brain retained where he was headed, which is why he landed here. I assume his memory is so confused that he's mixing up places and things so that anything he says about his past cannot be relied upon.'

John Crowley sat back in his chair and dropped the piece of paper back on his desk.

Victoria thought of the ride that afternoon, the farmhouse, and what James Alexander had said. She decided to remain silent.

John Crowley went on as though to convince himself of his argument.

'We must assume that there's a strong possibility that he's related to my family, and as such, we should at least care for him until we can obtain more information on his background. After all, he may well have a wife and children who are extremely worried about him. Apart from his memory loss, he appears quite normal except for this fantasy that he lived in the future. Simpson has recommended that we get Sir Ernest Cottingham, the famous brain specialist to see him, and I've sent a message to his club asking him to contact me.'

Victoria nodded in approval.

John Crowley sighed. 'The only problem we now have, until this matter is sorted out is that with me away, it would be quite improper for a lady to be living in the same house alone with Alexander,' Victoria drew in her breath. 'What I suggest is that you ask your cousin Priscilla to come and stay with you for the summer, her mother would like her out of the house I'm sure, and she would be a most suitable chaperon, don't you think?'

Victoria did think so. Priscilla was the daughter of her mother's sister, who hadn't married as well as her mother. Although on the surface they retained a wealthy front, Victoria knew that the family was extremely hard up, only being able to afford a small number of servants. Priscilla was nearly twenty-seven, and because of the lack of family funds and an austere countenance, she had not married, and it was now doubtful she would. A strange girl thought Victoria, but she liked her company, the situation demanded a solution, and she could not think of a better one. She looked at John Crowley in a slightly new light and was grateful to him for his suggestion, although she could not say so.

'I think that's an excellent idea, and agree with you about James, he's so like you, there just must be a family connection somewhere.' Victoria thought for a moment, 'I will send Johnson to Oxford tomorrow with the invitation to Priscilla..., tomorrow being Thursday, and suggest we send the Rolls for her on Saturday, if that fits in with your plans?'

'Good, that's settled then,' said John Crowley, relieved that his wife didn't complain about his idea of staying in London during the weekdays.

Victoria stood up. 'What happens if we can't trace James Alexander's past?' she said, almost to herself.

John Crowley reached for his cigarette case, 'I think

we should deal with that problem when it is reached, but I have no doubt that we could ensure an income for him from somewhere,' he leaned over, 'what you could do is to get to know him better, get to know what he's good at, and what he could do well if our enquiries fail.' He tapped the end of his cigarette on the desk before lighting it.

'Don't forget my dear, we have the Lloyd Georges and the Churchill's staying with us for the weekend.'

Victoria groaned, 'oh my lord, I had quite forgotten with everything else going on. I do dislike that arrogant man Winston Churchill. He's so full of himself.' She remembered last time when they were invited to the Churchill's; the conversation was politics, politics, politics, and mainly how important Winston was, in his mind, to the future of Britain.

Lord Crowley sighed. 'Yes, he's a bit of a bore, I must admit, but his wife makes up for his crassness,' he paused to inhale the cigarette smoke, 'and the bank has just recently lost the main Marlborough account,' he blew the smoke out at the ceiling. 'Winston has some influence with the family, and I don't want us to lose all their business to Byron's.'

He reflected that the main banking competitor and the threat to the Crowley Bank was by far Byron's Bank. Twenty years ago, they had been an insignificant counting-house. Still, the grandfather who started it had the foresight to invest heavily in South African mining, and the current dominion status of that country had cemented their future, making huge returns for their shareholders and investors. The Crowley Bank had been much more conservative, investing in European projects that had not gone so well. John Crowley had high hopes of their latest investment in Russia however and felt that the next few years would prove Crowley's conservatism to be the correct approach.

While he'd been talking, Victoria had been in deep thought. She knew what her husband had said, and she now had every excuse to get closer to James Alexander, and the idea excited her, but John Crowley was not a fool, was he deliberately steering her in that direction, and if so why. Was it to compensate her for the lost love, or something much crueller and more devious?

5 - THE DINNER

The week passed quickly. On Thursday and Friday, I had lunch with Victoria Crowley, and then in the afternoons, she accompanied me for rides into the beautiful countryside. In that short time, I started to enjoy the freedom of being with her and riding Bright Star. It was on the Friday afternoon when we had stopped under a large oak tree near to the house that she told me of her conversation with John Crowley and the arrangement with Priscilla Fortescue, who had accepted the invitation. I knew then that Victoria wanted our new relationship to continue, but my feelings were mixed, I thought about my Tory and sadness overcame me; I thought about John Crowley and the fact that I was clearly thinking of abusing his kindness, and yet the power of my attachment to Victoria Crowley was too strong to ignore. She saw that I was deep in thought. 'A penny for them,' she smiled.

I smiled back, 'well at least there are some sayings that are similar,' I laughed, 'although I think a penny would be worth considerably more today than in my time.' Victoria cocked her head on to one side and raised her eyebrows.

'I was thinking of how strange everything is,' I said, 'and how comfortable I am in your company, and yet I've only known you for a few days...'

Victoria blushed; *my God she thought, I want this man more than anything else I have ever wished for, but I must not fall, not yet it is too early.*

'It must be the sunshine,' she said laughingly as she wheeled her horse away and trotted back towards Crowley Hall. I caught up with her, and we slowed to a walk, travelling in silence back to the stables.

After dinner that night John Crowley told me that he had arranged for me to see the brain specialist Sir Ernest

Cottingham at his Harley Street address on Monday next. I was about to ask how I would be able to travel there, when John suggested I rode with him in the Rolls. He said he would be dropped off at the bank and the chauffeur, Sidney Blenkinsop, would deliver me to Cottingham's establishment in time for the appointment that was at 10 a.m.

'As soon as Cottingham has finished with you, Sidney will bring you back to the bank then we will have lunch at my club, and afterwards, I will arrange for you to have a tour of the bank so that you can see the various departments.' I thanked him, saying I would be most interested to see around the bank and how it operated.

'Now, on another completely different subject,' said John Crowley, 'we have the Churchill's and the Lloyd George's coming for the weekend and we would obviously like you to join us for dinner. Priscilla Fortescue will be staying with us by then, you can accompany her so that she doesn't feel that she's without a partner.'

'Of course, I would be delighted,' I said, wondering whether Priscilla Fortescue was a good conversationalist.

'That's settled then,' said John as he rose from the table, 'and perhaps you'd like to join us for a shoot on Saturday, you can borrow one of my Purdie's,' he added, 'and then we can have a late lunch outside on the lawn, as the weather is looking to remain good for the next few days.'

I thanked him for the invitation, and although not very keen on the killing of birds for the sake of it, I didn't feel I could refuse without offending.

'If you don't mind, my dear,' John turned to Victoria as they walked through to the drawing-room, 'I've had a rather heavy day, and am rather tired, so if you'll both forgive me, I intend to retire.'

I wished him goodnight and accepted a glass of excellent port before sitting down and facing Victoria who had taken a sherry. We talked about a whole range of things, and she was so easy to talk to that I was amazed when Porter came in stating that it was past midnight, asking if we would want anything else before he retired.

'Absolutely not,' I said, I hadn't realised the time, Victoria said that she hadn't either and told Porter he could go. As Porter closed the door quietly behind him, I got up and turned to Victoria, 'I'm extremely sorry,' I said, 'I'm afraid I talk too much...'

She smiled, 'well, it was me that did most of the talking, but we will have plenty of time to continue our discussion, although I have to say that I'm not looking forward to tomorrow evening.'

'Oh?'

'Well, it's Mr Churchill, you'll see what I mean,' she grimaced as I held the drawing-room door open for her.

As we stepped into the hallway, the soft light played on her hair, she looked quite beautiful, and as she tilted her head up to say goodnight her lips parted slightly, and it took all my inner strength not to hold her and kiss her. Instead, I thanked her for a most pleasant evening and turned quickly away to head for the sweeping staircase.

As I turned, I didn't notice that Victoria was trembling with a longing for my touch, and she closed her eyes to compose herself, waiting until I had disappeared and then went straight to her room. She undressed and slipped in between the sheets, but it was some time before she slept.

When I reached my bedroom, I read for a while. Victoria had picked a book from the study as I had mentioned I had nothing to read. The book was called Clouds in the East, by V. Baker, first printed in 1876. She had chosen well, as I had discussed the Middle East situation with her and the problem, we were experiencing with it, particularly Russia and Iran. The book was slightly damaged, but the original maps and watercolour paintings inside were superb. The book was about the gradual and subtle expansion of the Russian Empire. Interestingly, Valentine Baker was responsible for the creation of corridors in railway carriages due to him being accused and imprisoned for allegedly interfering with a lone lady in his compartment. I must have read for over an hour until I felt my eyelids drooping and I crawled into bed without my nightshirt, something I found I could not get used to. The memories from the day before flooded back and my longing for Victoria Crowley came back to me. I had fallen in love with her and wondered whether she thought of me in the same way. With that thought, I fell into a blissful sleep.

The next morning was a busy one getting ready for the guests who were due to arrive in the late afternoon. I kept myself well out the way and took my book into the garden. Just before lunch, John Crowley approached me, carrying what was a beautiful 12 bore gun.

'I had a pair of Purdie's made for me some years ago,' he said, 'but as you are roughly my size, you should be comfortable with this one, and I will use the other,' he handed me the gun with a box of cartridges. 'Oh, by the way, it's tails for dinner, but Donald will have yours laid out for you, another of my old suit's I can no longer get into I'm afraid,' he looked slightly embarrassed, whether because I was wearing his hand me downs or whether it was because he'd grown too large for them, I wasn't sure. I thanked him and took the gun up to my room staying there until I was informed lunch was about to be served.

The conversation over lunch was basically for my benefit.

'I thought it might be helpful to let you know a bit about our guests,' said John. 'The Right Honourable Winston Churchill has just been promoted to Home Secretary from being President of the Board of Trade. He's serving in the Liberal government headed by Herbert Asquith. Winston is from the Marlborough family. You may know from your history books that his ancestor was created a duke by Queen Anne in 1702 mainly due to his service to the crown in defeating the French at Blenheim.

'In fact, the name Churchill disappeared for a time as

the dukedom passed to the Spencer family and it wasn't until the 5ᵗʰ duke that the name Churchill was added to that of Spencer, so officially they're known as the Spencer-Churchills.

'Winston's family have always been reformist conservatives, but Winston crossed the floor from them to the Liberal party in 1904, something the conservatives will never forgive him for. He's not nearly as clever as his father Randolph Churchill who died early of a particularly horrible disease.' His words faltered when he mentioned Randolph Churchill's disease, and I noticed a furtive look at Victoria, who responded with a sniff and looked away. 'Churchill is an over-ambitious renegade who will almost certainly come to a sticky end. His wife, who he married two years ago is Clementine Ogilvy Hozier, a lovely girl with good connections, although it isn't known who her biological father was, it was reputed to be a man called Captain

CHURCHILL AND LLOYD GEORGE

William George Bay Middleton who was a noted horseman.'

'Did you say Middleton?' I asked. I was thinking about the romance between Prince William and Kate Middleton and wondering if there was a family connection, but I decided not to mention it.

'Yes, that was reputed to be the claim of Clementine's mother.' He raised his eyebrows.

I shook my head, 'it's just that I feel I know of someone called Middleton and wondered if there was a connection, but probably not, it's a common name.'

John nodded and continued. 'The Lloyd George's have a vastly different background altogether, he's the son of an ordinary schoolmaster and was brought up at some institution or other in Wales. His wife Margaret is also from the lower classes, but how long the marriage will last is anyone's guess as David is already reputed to be eyeing one of his female assistants. He's currently Chancellor of the Exchequer and has big ambitions.'

'Horrible little man,' said Victoria, 'he gives women the feeling that...'

'Yes, yes,' interjected John, 'but both hold considerable power now, and we must live with that until we can rid ourselves of them, we were hoping to do that as the Lords have voted down Lloyd George's last year's budget, so he may not last too much longer thank goodness.'

One of the facts I did know was that Lloyd George would win against the Lords by creating the 1911 Act preventing the Lords from stopping legislation enacted by the commons after a third reading. I didn't comment on what John had told me but was amused at his attitude to what he considered to be the lower classes. I asked him why he invited them when he didn't like either of them.

'I've no choice but to keep in with these people,' he said, 'Winston because of the Marlborough account, which I would like to get back for the bank. Lloyd George is hugely influential now, and I would like to buttonhole him after dinner so that I can try to elicit what his government's future is.'

Victoria sniffed again, 'you won't get anything out of him, he's far too slippery... and clever,' she said, slightly suggesting that John Crowley was not.

Crowley ignored her remark, 'normally we would have invited more guests, but they're so universally disliked by our social set, that I would be embarrassed to ask anyone else.'

'That's most interesting,' I replied, 'but as it's not going to be a nice evening, are you sure you want me to come?'

'Oh, YES,' almost shouted Victoria, 'I could not bear dealing with them without someone else to help.'

'But you'll have Priscilla,' I started.

'Indeed, that is another reason you should be present,' said John Crowley.

I nodded, 'I was just worried that I might say the wrong thing, or...' I stopped, 'By the way how are you going to introduce me?' I asked.

'We will simply say that you are a distant cousin from part of the family who moved to America and that you've come over to see how our banking system works.' He threw his hands out in front of him as if to say, simple...

We broke up from the lunch table, and I decided to go out for a short walk around the estate, which was larger than I had thought. Although I kept Crowley Hall within sight, I hadn't covered the estate within in the time I allotted to myself, so I turned around and headed back promising myself that I would walk the whole estate on another day. I went straight to my room and then had a leisurely bath before dressing. Victoria had invited me down to the drawing-room for an early drink at 7 p.m. and so at 6.45 p.m. I went back to my room to find my dinner clothes had been laid out for me. I went through them one by one. The largest garment was the swallow tailcoat with slight shoulder padding and peaked lapels. Alongside was a white single-breasted waistcoat in silk, then black trousers

73

matching the coat, which were tapered with straight outside seams, a neatly folded white shirt and cuffs, a wing collar, and a white cravat in linen, and white gloves. The shoes were black patent leather and suspenders accompanied the black socks. I wondered if I would be able to move when I had dressed, but I found the clothes not only fitted me perfectly but that they were remarkably comfortable.

I felt self-conscious when I arrived in the drawing-room but felt better when I saw only John there.

'Am I a little too early?' I asked.

'Not at all,' he said, eyeing me up and down. 'My goodness my clothes do fit you well,' he exclaimed as a young thing entered with full sherry glasses. I took one and took a sip just as Victoria came into the room. She took my breath away, looking gorgeous. She wore a simple light-coloured green dress with a narrow bodice, slim skirt and a slightly raised waistline. The front of the dress showed an ample bosom with the expensive-looking filigree chain with a gold locket around her neck. But it was the fitting of the dress that was stunning; the fabric flowed as she walked, it reminded me of a soft green evening dress I had bought for my Tory, that had been made by Yuki, a Japanese designer. I was later to learn that Victoria's dress was designed by Poiret, a French designer who based his creations on the Japanese kimono.

Out of the corner of my eye, I saw John Crowley gasp and then turn away, as though the sight of her was too much for him to behold. I was more than a little surprised at this, not understanding why they seemed to be barely noticing each other, let alone conversing. Victoria came across and kissed me lightly on the cheek, it was soft kiss, and I had felt her hands placed lightly on my waist as she did so. There was a smell of exquisite perfume.

'You look magnificent Victoria,' I stammered. She blushed slightly and drew away from me, smiling. John Crowley approached her with a glass of sherry and kissed her in a perfunctory manner, not commenting on her attire.

I was about to speak when Porter opened the door and announced The Right Honourable David Lloyd George and Mrs Lloyd George, and almost immediately afterwards the Right Honourable Winston Spencer-Churchill and Mrs Spencer-Churchill. I was introduced to them, and as the polite small talk was engaged, Priscilla Fortescue entered. She was dressed adequately for the evening, but not in a designer dress, and I felt rather sorry for her, as, against Victoria, she looked dowdy. She was a plain girl, and having her hair tied up didn't improve her looks. After all the introductions were made, I took it as my duty to look after Priscilla, and she responded well to my attention.

The meal was exceptionally good with eight courses and different wines to go with each course, but the food was too rich for me, and I drank more than I should have. I spent most of my time talking to Priscilla and Clementine Churchill, to whom I took an instant liking.

After dinner, the gentlemen retired to the smoking room, a room I had not seen before, and the ladies went to back to the drawing-room. I was offered a large cigar by John, which much to his surprise I refused saying that I didn't smoke. Then the port came out in large glasses, and I noticed John Crowley and Lloyd George talking earnestly in one part of the room, and although Churchill was with them initially, he broke away and came to sit opposite me. He had a habit of staring at one, which was a little disconcerting.

'They're talking money,' he growled, jerking his thumb in the direction of Lloyd George and John. 'One thing I know nothing about is money!' he exclaimed. I smiled *thinking that after the First World War, he would become Chancellor of the Exchequer, an excellent job for someone who didn't know anything about money I thought.*

Churchill sat down heavily in one of the armchairs, cigar in one hand and his drink in the other. I noted that he was quite good looking and still reasonably slim. Of course, I was comparing him with the Churchill I knew from Second World War photographs. The most surprising thing I noticed about him was his height, and I reckoned he could not have been more than 5 foot eight inches, (1.727 metres) much smaller than I had imagined.

'Now, I understand you've just come from America,' he said. 'My mother is American you know.'

'Yes, I know,' I answered, 'and she's exceptionally beautiful, I've recently seen pictures of her,' I recalled a picture I had seen in the latest copy of the Times that Lord Crowley had brought from London.

Churchill frowned, 'hmm, well tell me what you are doing here, I take it from your accent that you are English?' He was a man who got straight to the point.

'Yes, I was born here, but have spent quite a lot of time in Africa the West Indies and the United States as well.'

'Ah, you know I spent some time in Africa.'

'Yes, but you were in the south, whereas I was on the Gold Coast.'

'What on earth were you doing there?' He frowned again.

I realised I had to be careful as I felt this wasn't a man who would be put off by vague answers. I also realised that his questioning might soon reach a point where I could not give satisfactory answers, so I said, I was helping set up a trading company out there, nothing interesting. I smiled, and then changing the subject completely I said, 'but enough about me, I should congratulate you on your new appointment as Home Secretary.' The tack worked, Churchill's interest was moved from me to himself, and for the next half hour, I was in receipt of what he'd done and what he'd achieved. It was when he came to what he was going to do that I slipped up, probably because I had drunk too much port.

We started talking about politics and the recent vote by the Lords. 'I'm confident that we will win against the Lords at the end of the day,' Churchill blew a large plume of smoke he'd inhaled from his cigar, 'we can't allow them to dictate to the people,' he said.

I said to myself, silently that it was nothing to do with the people, more to do with the grasp for power over people. But of course, I kept those thoughts to myself. I nodded, 'I'm sure you'll win,' I said, 'but you'll almost certainly have some major problems coming your way.'

'Problems. What problems?'

'Mainly with Germany,' I said.

I realised that I had made a mistake and now had to follow through with my argument.

Churchill moved forward in his chair, 'puff, what can Germany do against the British Empire? They are trying to match us with capital ships, but they'll never catch up, and if they don't stop their nonsense, well starve em out.' He glared at me as I noticed he was handed a large brandy by one of the servants as we spoke.

'Yes, I understand that's Admiral Fisher's view, but it may not be so easy, particularly as they've allies such as Austria Hungary and perhaps Turkey.'

Churchill frowned, 'why should they be involved in any conflict?'

'Because they have a treaty with Germany, so if one goes to war, they all do, thanks to Chancellor Bismarck's work. I suspect everything would have been fine had he still been in power, but now that the Kaiser handles politics, I think things may not go in a direction that suit's our interests.'

Churchill looked a little taken aback, 'you are remarkably well informed, have you heard this from John Crowley...?'

'I understood it to be common knowledge,' I said looking surprised.

'Well, it isn't, and you can take it from me that Great Britain will never go to war with Germany.' I was angered at his arrogance, so compounded my original error. 'I'm afraid you are wrong,' I said, 'Germany will be at war with Britain, France, and Russia within the next four years. The war will be the bloodiest in our history and last until the end of 1918.

Austria Hungary will start it by going for Serbia, that'll bring in Russia, and Germany will follow as will Turkey.'

Churchill was astounded. 'Oh, you can see the future, can you?' he said sarcastically. 'You are raving mad; how can you envisage these things?'

I shrugged, 'perhaps it's the excellent port,' I smiled, trying to play down what I had just said. To try and move the subject back to him, I continued, 'but I could tell you much more, just to prove my point, let me tell you about your next post in Government.'

Churchill looked at me, contemptuously. 'Please do...'

'In one year's, time, in 1911 you'll be appointed as First Lord of the Admiralty. But your greatest contribution to the war will be the development of the tank.'

'The TANK? The water tank is already invented. What other forms of the tank could there be, and how would that help in war?' But Churchill knew that secret developments were being undertaken at that precise moment and he also knew that John Crowley wouldn't have that knowledge. His eyes narrowed, but fortunately, I was let off the hook, as it was at that point that John came over and said his conversation with Lloyd George had ended, unfortunately in disagreement. He suggested that we all join the ladies. He turned to Churchill and said that Lloyd George would fill him in later.

Before leaving, Churchill steered John to another part of the room. 'I don't know who this man Alexander is, but he has some confidential information that he shouldn't have,' he glared, looking for a reaction, which he didn't get, 'and he's making wild predictions of the future, his talk could be dangerous,' he growled.

John looked over at me and shook his head slightly. I took the hint, when we went back into the drawing-room, I said that I was tired and excused myself. I had a run-in with Winston Churchill, which probably did me no good, but I wondered how he'd feel when my predictions came true. I promised myself that I would not drink to excess in the future.

I found out later that Churchill had put in a request to the intelligence service of the day to have me checked out. I never did find the result of their enquiries.

6 - THE BANK

I awoke late on Sunday morning and didn't feel at all well. It wasn't just the port; the rich food had upset me too, and I decided that I wouldn't rise until later in the day. In 2010, I would have taken medication, but I wasn't at all sure that there would be anything available to settle my stomach. When I heard a knock at the door, I rushed out of bed, put on the nightshirt, and quickly climbed back into the bed and called the person outside to come in.

It was Mary; the maid had overcome her previous shock; she told me that Lady Crowley had sent up my breakfast. I told her to put it on the table at the end of my bed, and to apologise and inform Lord Crowley that I wouldn't be joining the shoot as I was feeling rather unwell and would be spending the morning in bed.

'Is there anything else I can get you, sir?' She asked.

'Thank you, no Mary, I probably won't be down for lunch either if you could let Lady Crowley know.'

'Yes, of course, sir,' with that she went out closing the door behind her.

It was about thirty minutes later when there was another knock on the door. I did my quick change again and called, 'Come in,' I was hoping that it was Victoria, so was a bit disappointed when Mary appeared again. She was carrying some steaming liquid in a glass. 'This is for you, sir.' She came in and put it by my bedside table and went to collect the breakfast tray, the contents of which I had not touched. 'Oh, you haven't had time to have your breakfast, sir?' She said diplomatically. 'It's all right Mary you can take the tray, I'm afraid my stomach isn't up to food just now.'

'Yes, of course, sir,' she said moving toward the tray, she turned, 'oh, I almost forgot, Lady Crowley sent this up for you, sir,' she pointed at the glass of liquid she had put on my bedside table. 'She asks you to drink it as it'll ease your stomach,' she smiled.

'What is it, Mary?' I asked.

'I believe it's chamomile, sir, it's particularly good for you.'

I asked her to thank Lady Crowley, and when she had gone, I drank the medicine, and I admit it did have a good effect on me, so much so, I was able to get up in the afternoon and sit on the balcony. It was while I was there that I heard the guests leaving at the front of the house. I decided then to dress, as I felt like walking, I went downstairs hoping I would get outside without being seen. Unfortunately, Victoria was just coming in with some picked wild-flowers, and she saw me.

'Oh James, are you, alright?' she showed real concern.

'Thanks to your potion,' I smiled.

She laughed, 'oh, it has been handed down in my family for years, my mother used to prepare it for my father when he was a little under the weather, after a heavy night,' she cocked her head and raised her eyebrows.

'Well, it worked for me,' I said. 'I'm just going to go for a short walk around the garden. Would you like to accompany me?' Victoria thought quickly, 'providing we stay in sight of the house. I think that would be delightful, I so missed our talk over lunch, although it would have been a little difficult with the guests...'

'That's another reason I didn't come down before they left,' I said, as we walked through the front door, 'you see Winston was probing, and I was foolish enough to say some things I shouldn't have done.'

'Yes, John told me that he was quite inquisitive about you, so you were right to stay away, but we missed you.' She looked up at me as we were walking and smiled. It was a smile that said so much, and I felt a warm glow inside. We walked around the gardens for about half an hour, and we were joined by Priscilla, which rather stilted our conversation. I told Victoria I wasn't going to join them for dinner, as my stomach, although recovered hadn't done so completely.

She understood and told me that I should get to bed early as it was to be an early start in the morning, 'I'm told,' she said, 'that John will be leaving about 7.30 a.m. so I will have your breakfast sent up about an hour before and I've asked the valet to call at your room to shave you.'

'You are spoiling me Victoria,' I laughed, 'I'm not used to all this attention.'

'I'm feeding you up for the strenuous work John has set for you,' I looked a little startled. 'Don't worry,' she said smiling, 'I've no doubt he'll tell you about it tomorrow.'

The next morning, I dressed hurriedly after being shaved and was downstairs early, I told the maid not to take my breakfast to the room. I had a light breakfast alone in the breakfast room and was finished in good time to meet John, who was waiting for me at the front door. We climbed into the back of the Rolls, the sun hadn't yet risen high into the sky, and it was a bit chilly. A heavy rug was pulled over our knees by Sidney, the chauffeur. With that, he climbed into the driving seat, and the car effortlessly moved down the drive towards the gates to the estate.

John spoke for the first time. 'I'm sorry you were unwell yesterday, we had a good shoot, bagging some 60 braces of pheasant and even a few grouse. Of course, it was totally incorrect to have a shoot on a Sunday, but Churchill seemed oblivious to that, and Lloyd George would not have known anyway.'

'Yes, I too am sorry,' I said untruthfully, 'but I did feel a little nauseous so I wouldn't have been good company. I must also apologise for the night before,' I said, 'you see I'm not used to eating such rich food, nor the quantity that was given. The wine and port had an unfortunate effect on me, which is why I was a little careless when talking to Churchill.'

John roared with laughter. 'Don't think anything of it,' he smiled, 'he could not make you out, which made him a bit peevish. I think he thought you were either a German spy or an illegitimate brother, but he was concerned that you knew of certain matters concerning military developments. He asked me about it, and I had to tell him that I knew nothing.'

'Did he believe you?' I asked.

'Oh, yes, I'm afraid that the Lords aren't acquainted with top secrets, unless of course they're in government, and since we voted against Lloyd George's budget, we've been kept very much in the cold.' John became serious, 'of course, you could be a spy, but then if you were, you wouldn't have been so foolish as to discuss such matters with Winston, so I'm satisfied that you are not.'

'What about an illegitimate brother?' I queried smiling.

He gave me a piercing stare. 'I have to say that it isn't beyond possibility, my father liked women, and he had several mistresses in his life, one who I remember was remarkably like my mother, but much younger. I'm not aware that she had a child, but of course, I wouldn't have been told if she had. Nevertheless, the family likeness can't be a coincidence, and we must consider that fact. This is another reason it's important that we try and see if we can get your memory back, so we will see what Cottingham has to say. In the meantime, we will stick with the line that you are a distant cousin from America.'

I nodded. 'I too am not sure why there's a likeness between us, but my memory is fine except it's 100 years into the future.'

'Yes, that's another matter that Cottingham will explore with you.'

With that, John apologised and said he had a board meeting later in the morning and had to read up some notes that had been prepared for him. He took out a heavy-looking ledger opening it and started to read.

I noticed that the road was narrow and winding and I reckoned that our top speed was less than 30 M.P.H. which was just as well as anything faster would have made running on bad roads rather uncomfortable. The road was more like a country lane, and apart from the odd horse and rider and one or two carts, the road was empty until we reached the city, and even then, I could not help but compare the road system in 1910 to 2010. In 2010 by the time, we would have reached the outskirts of London, we would be in gridlock. Of course, in this case, the outskirts of London were only a few miles from the city. As we moved nearer to our destination I was shocked at the apparent poverty as we motored through the streets, and I was appalled to see some children without shoes. I remembered the only place I had been to where white children had no shoes, was the Azores, where our ship docked on the journey from Jamaica to the United Kingdom.

The Rolls pulled up in front of a very Imposing building with four Palladian pillars adorning the front. I could see two large, polished doors opening and a liveried man running down the steps to open the door for John

Crowley.

As he got out, he waved me goodbye, and Sidney moved the Rolls smoothly away from the side of the road heading for Harley Street, which took only a few minutes. I told him that he didn't need to wait to collect me as I would walk back to the bank when I had finished. He got out and opened the door, doffing his cap as he did so. I watched him drive off before I entered the imposing house in front of me. It was Georgian, built as a terrace where the façade was the same on all the houses but each one quite different behind.

I walked up the steps and rang the bell noticing the brass plate stating it was the residence of Sir Ernest Cottingham. It didn't, unsurprisingly, indicate his speciality.

The door was opened by a middle-aged woman wearing what I assumed was a nurse's uniform in 1910. She led me to a large room on the right-hand side of the building, and I walked over to the window that overlooked the street.

'Sir Ernest will be with you presently Mr Alexander.'

I thanked her, noting that she had called me by my name. Not too many appointments this morning, I thought to myself. I was about to sit down on one of the comfortable sofas in the well-proportioned room when the door opened. 'Sir Ernest will see you now, sir,' she smiled in a business-like way.

I followed her down a short hallway to what I assumed was the back of the house, and she opened a door on the left. As I walked in a sprightly man with thinning grey hair sprang up from a swivel chair and held his hand out. 'Ernest Cottingham at your service, sir, please enter, why don't you sit over here?' He pointed to a small armchair next to his desk. I heard the door close behind me.

Cottingham started the conversation by making a comment on the lovely weather but soon turned to the reason for my visit. 'Lord Crowley asked me to see you because he believes you may have suffered a memory loss after a fall is that correct?'

'It appears to be the case,' I answered, 'I certainly can't

remember anything before June 8th, 1910, but I have a memory of 2010, 100 years into the future,' I added.

Cottingham put on his pince-nez glasses and peered at me, leaning forward as he did so.

'Hmm, how interesting, I have of course a report from Lord Crowley's doctor, but while I've come across loss of memory cases before, I must admit that I've never dealt with someone from the future,' he laughed.

'Well, I suppose there's a first time for everything,' I smiled.

'Indeed, indeed, well let me have a good look at you, would you mind stripping to the waist?' I did so, and after sounding my chest and heartbeat, he asked me to sit down and roll my trousers up, he then tested my reflexes. After that, he told me to dress and then carried out a thorough investigation of my head and eyes and then my mouth where he exclaimed in surprise at my teeth much the same as Lord Crowley's doctor had done. He was taking copious notes and asked if I had any dubious liaisons with women of the night, I confirmed I hadn't.

The full examination, including word tests, took over one and a half hours, and during that time, I had to explain in some detail my movements since my fall. When he had finished, he sat back in his chair and removed his glasses. 'To be honest, there's nothing wrong with you as far as I can tell, and I can't in all conscience recommend any treatment. You appear very fit indeed for your age, indeed extremely fit, and your cognitive processes are better than any patient I've seen in a long time. You are a puzzle, Mr Alexander,' he said, sucking his teeth. 'All I can recommend at this time is that you go about your business, I hope with time your memory will return. I must assume that your memory of the future has come from some book you've read, and that will gradually fade. I suggest however that you call back and see me in say three months, and we will have another look at you. If in the meantime, your memory re-appears, I would be most grateful if you'd call me.' I thanked him, got up and was walking out when he sprang a question at me, 'tell me, Mr Alexander, what is the date today?' I thought for a second, 'I believe it's 20th June'. Cottingham smiled, 'and what day is it, my dear fellow?'

I frowned, 'why it's Monday.'

'Quite, quite,' he said, 'now what would be the day and date today in 2010?'

'Oh, that's easy,' I said, 'it's the same, Monday 20th June,' I answered.

'The same?' asked Cottingham surprised.

'Yes, I'm sure,' I smiled.

He stood and held out his hand, which I shook. 'Thank you again for so much for your time,' I said, 'and oh, how much do I owe...' I stopped, realising I had no money.

Cottingham waved his hand, 'it's all taken care of my good fellow, good morning.'

As I was closing his door, I saw him sitting down at his desk with a pencil and piece of paper scribbling some notes.

I was soon on the street outside Ernest Cottingham's house retracing the route the car had taken and arriving back at the bank after about fifteen minutes. I walked up the broad steps into the interior, the doors now being open. There was a man sitting at the desk near the door who raised his eyebrows, 'may I help you, sir?'

'Yes, my name is Alexander, I've come to see...'

'Oh, yes, sir, we were expecting you, I will call someone to take you up to Lord Crowley's office.' His demeanour changed to one of how an important client would be treated. It brought back memories of the offhand way my bank treated me in 2010.

A tall man in a smart suit and polished shoes came down the stairs and ushered me up to the top floor of the building, where the carpets became thicker and the furnishing much more luxurious. We walked to the end of the corridor, and the man knocked on the door at the end.

'Come.'

The man opened the door, 'Mr James Alexander, sir.'

'Ah, James, do come in,' John Crowley got up from his desk and walked towards me.

'Is there anything else, sir?'

'No, thank you, we will be lunching at my club if there's anything urgent.' The man closed the door.

'Well now how did you get on?' John said enquiringly

I looked at him, 'I have a feeling you know exactly how I got on, don't tell me that Cottingham didn't call you as soon as I left his office.'

John laughed, 'yes of course he did, but I was interested in your view. I had a good laugh, though, because he asked you a trick question before you left.'

'Yes, that was a surprise, he asked me the day and date in 2010?'

'And you answered that it was the same as today, and he asked me if I could get my staff to find out if that was correct, I did, and it was, so I phoned him back, and he was quite shaken. Anyway, we can discuss that over lunch, and there's something else I want to talk to you about. Hold on a minute, and I will bring the folder I was reading this morning with me, because the information in it is pertinent.'

While John was getting the folder from his desk, I looked around the room. It was a long office heavily carpeted with an enormous mahogany desk at the end in front of a large window looking out on to the city. There were several couches and comfortable chairs and a large mahogany table with 12 chairs. I guessed this was the office where he held his board meetings. There was a sizeable communicating door near the other end of the room, which I assumed led into another office. There were some paintings on the far wall including La Gare Saint-Lazare, by Monet and a beautiful Renoir that I knew as the Path through the high grass, on the other side was a painting by Mitchell of a sailing ship on the high seas called Round Cape

Horn.

John noticed me studying the paintings and asked if I liked them. I told him that I did and owned exact copies of all three.

'Copies,' John looked puzzled.

I laughed, 'yes copies, in my day these paintings would be worth millions of pounds.'

'I had better hang on to them then,' he said as he opened the door of his office.

'Yes,'I answered, 'I think you should.'

We walked down the stairs and through the front doors, I noticed staff walking in the corridors and the man at the front desk all stood to attention as we passed by.

'My club is only five minutes' walk from here,' he said. 'Incidentally, James, I think you must be careful who you talk to about the future, I know you believe that's where you've come from, but you are not an unintelligent man, and you must see what people will think of you if you persevere in doing so. Indeed, it'll make it difficult for me to take you into the bank unless you plant yourself firmly in 1910.'

I was surprised, 'take me into the bank?'

'Yes, I have the feeling that you could be useful to me, I'm not sure why, perhaps an instinct,' he looked for my reaction as we walked.

'But you've only known me for less than two weeks,' I said puzzled. I was walking quickly, and I noticed that John Crowley was getting out of breath trying to keep up with me, so I slowed down. 'Well, I asked Victoria for her view, and she's had several conversations with you, the first point is that you look like a family member, and I think that there is a connection somewhere, there must be,' he added. 'Then there's your experience you've discussed with Victoria regarding the West Indies, Africa and the United States, all areas where investment is desperately needed.' We reached the doors of John's club, and he was greeted by the doorman who passed us on to the head waiter who showed us to his table. I noticed the number of people who knew John

Crowley and who acknowledged him.

'She told me that you had financial experience too, now that's of great interest to me, and I will tell you why, in the meantime lets order some lunch.'

Over lunch, John told me that his bank was losing money. He appreciated they had lost business to Byron's, but he still could not reconcile the losses with the business they still retained. He'd discussed the matter with his chief clerk, a man called Anderson, but Anderson put it purely down to the loss of business.

'I assume that there are accounting companies that could carry out some sort of investigation for you.'

John Crowley smiled, 'yes there are, but the city is a very small community, if it were seen that I was putting in outside investigators the word would spread that perhaps the bank wasn't safe, Byron's would take full advantage of such a story.'

'So, you want me to...'

'What I need is someone with my authority to work within the bank and look at our financial systems and how things work, members of our staff who can be trusted and who can't. I know there's a leakage of information going from the bank to Byron's, but I've no concrete evidence of it, just too many coincidences.'

I nodded; 'you do realise that I know virtually nothing about banking?'

John Crowley laughed,' well, that makes two of us.'

I must have looked surprised. 'Let me explain,' said John. 'My father died quite young, and I had no siblings, at least I wasn't aware of any,' he smiled. 'So, while I was essentially running the Crowley estate, I was suddenly thrown into a completely new business environment, and because my father's death was very sudden, I didn't even have a handover. I found that I didn't get the support I needed from the senior people, and I probably made things worse when I turned down an offer from Byron's.'

'Oh, why was that?' I asked.

'They pounced as soon as my father died and started buying Crowley Bank shares, what they didn't know was that Victoria had previously invested heavily. She already held a substantial amount of bank shares, which, coupled with my father's shares, that became mine when he died, gave the family absolute control. Victoria's shares were in a closed trust, so at the time, they could not know the ownership of them, but once it became clear, they could not obtain control they sold off all the shares they had bought at a considerable loss. It was Victoria's trust that bought them, which means it's she who now controls the bank.'

I pondered John's explanation and wondered to myself why it was that their marriage wasn't working, as they were tied to each other financially.

'Of course, Victoria is hugely wealthy in her own right,' continued John, 'she inherited the Oldham Steel Company from her father, and that was sold by the trustees of the will for millions, so the bank is only a small part of her investment. Apart from Priscilla, and her side of the family, Victoria has no other surviving relatives.'

'And you've no children?' I enquired.

John looked sorrowful. 'No, I knew when I married Victoria that she could not have children, and we were resigned to the fact. Perhaps in the future, they'll be able to deal with her problem, but I suspect not within her lifetime. In any case, my illness would now prohibit us from having children.' I felt he was close to telling me what his illness was, but he didn't think that the time was appropriate to do so.

'Now, to get back to our discussion, Cottingham has told me that as far as he's concerned, you are very fit, and there's nothing wrong with your cognitive abilities, just the reverse. My plan, as you know, is to introduce you as my cousin who has worked in the United States, the fact that you've worked there's helpful. What do you think?'

John had just finished his roast beef lunch, and wiping

his mouth with a napkin, he sat back on his chair.

'Oh, and there's one other thing that's important,' he said.

'And that is?'

'I trust you implicitly, I don't know why, but I do instinctively.'

I felt a little uncomfortable when I remembered my feelings for Victoria, but I knew he was referring to financial matters, at least I hoped so.

I was a bit concerned, while I had run a large public company, I had not been involved with the banking sector. On the other hand, I told myself I was experienced enough to understand the financial side of any business. As far as investment was concerned, I had an unfair advantage instead, knowing as I did, the main events that were to occur in the future. If I refused to do what John asked of me, it would be ungrateful, to say the least, and anyway I could not expect to continue to live on their kindness for much longer. Then there was Victoria... I made my decision.

'You asked me what I thought,' I said. 'Both you and Victoria have been most kind to me since my unexpected arrival, and I would certainly like to repay that kindness, the earlier, the better.

'If you are agreeable, I suggest that I start with the bank on Monday next, that'll give me time to think about how I might tackle the problem' *and give me some time to spend with Victoria* I thought to myself, 'and then I will need three things at the bank to start with.'

John Crowley raised his eyebrows.

'An office preferably next to yours, and a bright young man not connected with the hierarchy, who will be my assistant, and of course, I will need some salary.'

'Done and agreed,' said John Crowley. 'There just happens to be an office next to mine that has a communicating door, it used to be the office of my father's secretary, but I now use a senior girl from the typing pool. The young man let me see...' He thought for a minute, 'ah yes, I know who would fit that position perfectly, and that's Gerald Phipps. He's obtained a first from Cambridge, and as he joined only last week, he's not familiar with the system or in any way loyal to anyone but me. I know his father well, and their family is very well connected. Finally, you must earn a salary commensurate with your position, and I suggest £400 per annum as a starting figure.'

I smiled at that, wondering what £400 a year would buy in 2010.

I shrugged, 'I'm sure I will not starve on such a generous stipend.'

'Good, if that's settled, well go back to the bank, I will get Miss Parkinson to accompany you around the various departments and introduce you to the managers, when that is done, I will instruct Sidney to take you back to Crowley Hall.' John had suddenly become bustling and efficient.

I could see that my acceptance had eased his usual apprehensive countenance.

As we were walking back to the bank, I wondered if it was feasible for me to stay at Crowley Hall once I started work, and I decided to take notice of the trip back and how long it took.

7 - THE LOVE TRYST

The trip back to Crowley Hall took just under 2 hours, and I decided I would spend one week in London, and one week at Crowley Hall, my thinking was to assimilate the information I had gained during my city week and assess what I would plan for the week ahead.

When I arrived back at Crowley Hall, I was disappointed to find that Victoria had left with Priscilla to visit Priscilla's family near Newmarket in Cambridgeshire and would not return until Thursday.

Victoria left Porter with instructions, and I was well looked after during her absence, I missed her company and particularly the daily rides on Bright Star. In a way, though it was quite useful to be alone and able to think about the job ahead, I did most of this by walking in the garden and then jotting my thoughts down on paper when I got back. I made a list of areas I would start on.

1.   What sort of financial system did the bank run and what type of controls were in place?
2.   What investments did they hold and what was the validity of them?
3.   Who did they loan money to, and what was the state of the repayments of such loans? What security was held, and was it enough to cover the loan in a break-up situation?
4.   What sort of stocks did they hold, particularly gold and cash?
5.   What sort of business did they do with other

banks worldwide, but particularly Byron's bank?

6.   Who was responsible for dealing with all the above and who reported to whom?

7.   What did the balance sheet show the bank was worth and how was it constructed?

I thought that would be enough to get on with, but the more I thought of it, the more I realised I would soon need a small team of people to go through all the paperwork. Still, I thought the seven-point plan was a start. Then I considered the indicated leak, which, to be meaningful to Byron's Bank must come from senior management, so I needed to look at the people involved very carefully, their employment record, how they lived, and their relationships.

I realised that I had taken on quite a job, but I was quietly confident I could achieve something worthwhile for John Crowley. The last thought I had on the subject was the inevitable animosity I was bound to get from the senior managers, who had been working blissfully on while the bank lost money. The point was puzzling, as a bust bank would not be in their interests, or would it? Perhaps John had more enemies than he perceived, or maybe, as he was an inexperienced newcomer, relatively speaking, some were feathering their own nest.

Once I had my plan worked out, I decided to rest while finishing the book Victoria had loaned me.

I did little during the next few days, and Thursday came around surprisingly quickly, Victoria and Priscilla returning late on Thursday afternoon. I was in my room when I heard a knock at the door, and Porter told me that Lady Crowley had returned and would very much like my company for dinner.

I went down to the drawing-room early and sat in one of the comfortable armchairs, with sherry, and had just started to read the paper I had brought with me from London, now several days old, when Victoria entered the room. She looked quite beautiful as usual; despite the plain dress she wore. I rose from my chair and kissed her on the cheek. I noticed she held me for a second longer than I expected.

'I'm so sorry, I wasn't here when you came back from London, but Priscilla's widowed mother was ill, and she needed to go and arrange for her to be cared for in her absence.'

'And is everything okay?' I asked.

'Oh yes,' Victoria smiled, 'she had just picked up a bad cold, and was feeling a little lonely, but by the time we left, she was in good spirits. I did invite her to come to Crowley Hall, but she declined,' Victoria shrugged.

'And Priscilla?' I asked.

Just then, the door opened, and Priscilla walked in, I went forward and gave her a perfunctory kiss. I felt her tense as I did so and realised that Priscilla could very quickly get the wrong idea about my attentiveness if I were not careful. Unusually, she was particularly talkative and showed that she had a comprehensive knowledge of wild-flowers, and I was able to tell her about the various flora I had come across in Africa and the West Indies, some of which are here at Crowley Hall.

She told me that a family who had sugar estates in Jamaica had initially built the house. I found this fascinating, as I had visited Worthy Park Estate while in Jamaica, and I told her that I was able to study the book containing the names of all the slaves who had worked there.

We had pheasant for dinner, beautifully cooked, and as the game was relatively high, I assumed it was from an earlier shoot, Victoria later confirmed this. Afterwards, we went back to the drawing-room, and Priscilla thanked me for letting her know about plants that she had not come across, she then excused herself, saying she was tired after the journey. I had the feeling though that she was deliberately leaving us alone

After she had left the room, Victoria and I took off from our previous conversation, and I told her about my visit to London and Cottingham, then my lunch with John and the offer he'd made. I told her of my basic plan for the investigation and that I would be spending every other week in London.

'Oh, I'm delighted that John has talked to you and that he's made you an offer, but watch out for Cecil Anderson, who is the managing director, I don't trust that man.' She thought for a minute then she asked me if I had taken Bright Star out while she was away. I told her no; I did not feel like riding without her company. She smiled, 'in that case, why don't we ride tomorrow, and take a light lunch with us, I know of a beautiful place by the river where we could stop.'

I agreed that it would be perfect, as Porter had told me that the forecast for the following day was good.

'Will Priscilla be joining us?' I asked.

Victoria laughed, 'absolutely not, Priscilla doesn't ride, she hates horses so that it will be just the two of us,' she had a mischievous smile on her face, 'quite improper of course, but who is to know. The spot I mentioned is quite isolated,' she added.

We talked some more and agreed to set off the next morning about 11-o-clock. I kissed her lightly on the cheek as I said goodnight, and noticed the electricity between us was palpable, I reluctantly let go of her as I turned for the door.

'Tomorrow then?' She said, with raised eyebrows.

'Tomorrow,' I answered smiling, as I paused by the open door. There seemed to be a lot of meaning in that word, I thought as I climbed the stairs.

I slept soundly and as I was up early, I decided to go for a walk before breakfast. I was so deep in thought that I wandered further than I intended, and when I saw the sun rising, I realised I had been away for over an hour. I tried to retrace my steps but found the ground to be unfamiliar. I was fortunate to come across my original saviour, the farmer George out for an early morning shoot, and he gave me correct directions back to Crowley Hall.

When I returned, I entered through the kitchen door at the back, much to the consternation of the staff. 'Oh, sir, Lady Crowley was most worried about you,' said a cook who I knew as Mrs. Bamford, 'Lady Crowley has sent Mr. Blenkinsop out to find you,' she explained.

I smiled and told her that I had got lost, but that George had directed me back. With that, I made my way to the breakfast room where Victoria and Priscilla were finishing breakfast.

'James, oh thank goodness, did Sidney find you?' Victoria had stood up from the table, looking concerned. 'I...I thought we had lost you,' she said, and I noticed that her eyes were moist.

'I'm sorry,' I said, 'I just went out for an early walk and got a little lost. Fortunately, I came across George, who directed me back, but I'm afraid I didn't see Sidney.' I sat down at the table next to Victoria, having said good morning to Priscilla. I learnt from Victoria that there were marshes to the east of the estate, and there were some dangerous spots, which is why she was concerned, but I somehow didn't wholly believe that was the reason for her anxiety.

We discussed the day ahead as I ate a hearty breakfast. Victoria told Priscilla that we had planned to go riding and take a light lunch with us. Out of courtesy, she invited Priscilla to join us, for a few seconds Priscilla considered the invitation, 'it's kind of you Victoria, but you know that I don't ride, and besides I've some writing to do this morning, so if you don't mind, I will stay behind.'

Victoria did not press the point, she nodded and turned to me, '11-o-clock James, I will arrange the lunch and send someone out to find Sidney before he gets lost too,' she smiled, 'I will see you at the stables?'

It turned out to be a glorious day, and I found that I was relatively warm in my riding gear but assumed that a gallop might cool me down as there was a slight breeze. I was pleased that I had become used to riding Bright Star and although I had little experience of riding a horse before I arrived at Crowley Hall, I found it somehow natural and yet I had always been afraid of horses, and I wondered why.

We rode due west through some beautiful countryside and after about 30 minutes we came across a wooded area where we slowed to a trot, Victoria knew where we were going as she weaved her horse through the trees. I realised that we had left the estate behind and there was no sign of any habitation, but I had seen a signpost to a village called Newton Blossomville, which sounded quaint, and I wondered if there was such a place in 2010. Suddenly we came into a clearing, and I noticed a patch of green grass leading down to a small river. It reminded me of a picture I owned called the Secret Place by John H. Kauffmann, and I had always wondered what had drawn me to the oil painting. The sun streamed through the trees and fell in a pool of light on the clearing. Victoria dismounted, took a thick blanket, that she had rolled up on the rear of the saddle, and spread it on the ground. She then unpacked the food and champagne from the saddlebags. I was still mounted taking in the scene around me when I noticed Victoria standing, legs astride, and hands on her hips looking up at me. She was wearing a dark blue velvet jacket with a split skirt that I found later had been introduced by Mrs. Adolph Landenberg, to allow ladies to ride astride the saddle properly instead of side saddle as was the custom of the day. Victoria wore polished boots the tops of which disappeared under the folds of her skirt, they appeared to be from some brushed leather. The decoration around her neck was a white silk cravat with the filigree chain and locket that she often wore, even with day dresses. I was captivated by her, the surrounding scenery, and the warmth of the sun. As I dismounted from Bright Star and tethered her to a nearby tree, I felt completely and utterly relaxed, a feeling I hadn't experienced for many years.

'Well, are you going to stand there all day?' Victoria tilted her head on one side and raised her eyebrows, a position she adopted when she expected a reaction. I walked towards her, and she held out her hand, I clasped it, and we walked down to the river hand in hand.

We reached the river's edge, it was not too wide, about three yards, but it flowed effortlessly from right to left, disappearing into the foliage about 100 yards or so away from where we stood. We both stared at the running water without speaking, and I was aware of Victoria's head tilting upwards towards me with slightly parted lips, just as she had that night back in Crowley Hall. This time I did not ignore her. I gently took her chin in my hand and kissed her full on the lips. I felt her body close with mine, and her hands tightened around my waist as we lost ourselves in each other's embrace.

I am not sure how long we were there by the river, but when we parted, she led me by the hand back to the area where she had laid out the picnic. We both sat down on the ground and kissed again, this time more passionately.

I felt incredibly tender towards her, but she reacted with enormous passion, I felt engulfed by her lovemaking removing clothes that were not made to be undone quickly. Buttons were ripped off, and clasps broken, clothes were torn in desperation to get to the final act, so much so that we became one both working desperately for a climax that came with a cry of pleasure from Victoria. We lay there for what seemed an endless amount of time quite breathless in each other arms unaware of time, space or of our beautiful surroundings.

I knew I had completely fallen in love again as had she. It was the same strange feeling that I had experienced when I first made love to my Tory all those years ago, or should I say, all those years in the future. Strangely I did not feel guilty; it was purely natural, as though we had been together for eternity.

We slept together afterwards; the passion expunged. When we awoke, we realised that we had been lying in each other's arms, for almost two hours.

'How about a swim?' I said as I sat up.

Victoria looked startled, 'but I didn't bring any swimwear,' she protested.

'Nor me,' I said, 'so let's just go in naked.'

Victoria laughed, 'why not,' and with that, she took off what few clothes she had on, and we walked down to the river together, wading into the cool water as it stirred around us. We spent some time in the water, and it was there that Victoria told me that John Crowley's illness was syphilis and that he had caught it from a prostitute who had been introduced to him by the young Jules Byron of Byron's Bank. She told me that she had been away during that time and so, fortunately, she did not contract the disease, but that she had to undergo the indignity of having a thorough medical check to make sure. 'I've never been able to forgive him,' she said, 'and we've spoken hardly a word to each other until you appeared and then something seemed to change in him, and at the same time, for some reason, I became more sympathetic towards him. Of course, our marriage is over, but I know he is dying, and I don't wish him to suffer any more than he must.' There were tears in her eyes as she spoke, and we left the river lying again on our picnic spot. I pulled her close to me, and we made love again, this time it was tender and even more loving. Afterwards, we lay together entirely naked for some time, suddenly Victoria sat up. 'Oh, my goodness, look at the sun, it must be well past 4-o-clock,' she said, as she started dressing, looking at me sheepishly. 'This has always been my secret place,' she said, 'I found peace here, now I've found love again, thanks to you, and so this is now our secret place, and we'll come here to be alone.' She looked at me and smiled. As she was dressing, she dropped the filigree chain and locket, and it fell on the ground. I picked it up, and for some reason, I opened the locket. Inside was a hand-painted picture of Victoria. I guessed it was an image of her about two years ago. It was exquisite.

'I had it made just after the doctors told me the truth

about John, I've kept it with me ever since.'

'It's quite beautiful,' I said, 'both you and the locket'.

'Do you like it?' she asked.

'Of course, I do...' I didn't finish.

'Then you must keep it,'

I protested that I could not possibly do so.

'I want you to have it, James, so that if we are ever parted, you'll have part of me with you, and if we are destined to be together, then you can give it back to me, but only when that time comes, as it must.'

I was going to protest again, but something in her eyes stopped me. 'I will keep it only until then,' I promised, 'and you'll have it back when were together permanently.'

She smiled, 'well we've some pheasant sandwiches and a bottle of champagne, so why don't we drink it?'

I uncorked the bottle and filled the two glasses.

'To the future,' I said, as the glasses clinked.

'To the future together, whatever it may bring,' she said.

It took us over an hour to ride back as we were talking most of the way, and when Crowley Hall came into view, I turned to her, 'why were you so worried when I was late this morning?'

She did not answer.

I looked at her again.

'I...I am afraid of losing you James, you came into my life from seemingly nowhere, I'm afraid you might suddenly disappear, I know it's stupid to think this way,' she looked across at me, her cheeks wet with tears, 'but I could not bear for you to go.'

I leaned over and kissed her, 'I'm not going anywhere silly, so just take that thought out of your head.' I kicked Bright Star into a gallop for the remaining few hundred metres.

When we were walking back to the house, Victoria turned to me. 'James, your idea of spending one week in London and one week here won't work, much as I want you by my side. You should plan to spend the weekdays at the bank and return here on a Friday evening, as you are going to be busy, and you'll need to keep your eyes on business matters daily. You should plan to stay at John's club, I'm sure he can arrange it, but you must return each Friday evening so that we can have our Saturdays together and ride out to our special place. That's the only claim I can have on you now, Saturdays are mine,' she said firmly.

'What about John?' I asked, 'because he'll be home on Saturday, won't that be a problem for you? It's perhaps embarrassing too, as he's been extremely kind to me in offering me a position at the bank.'

Victoria smiled; 'John has burned his own boat, I can't change what he's done, neither can he. He's so exhausted when he returns home at the weekend that he spends most Saturdays in bed. In any case, I feel that he wants us to become close, he indicated as much when we spoke last week, so guilt shouldn't be part of your thinking. From my point of view, I want to be with you, and now I know the feeling I have for you is shared, let's enjoy each other while we have each other to enjoy.' The tilted head and the raised eyebrows were evident again, and she smiled. I realised that Victoria was much stronger mentally than I had given her credit for. I also realised that she was right about me staying in London, and I was happy with the Saturday arrangement.

When I got back to my room, I took the filigree chain and the locket and looked for somewhere to place it that would be safe. It then dawned on me that my tracksuit was still folded in a drawer in the wardrobe. I took it out, carefully putting the locket and chain in one of the pockets and folded it back precisely as it had been placed after it had been washed.

8 - THE INVESTIGATION

The rest of the weekend went by quickly as I prepared for starting at the bank on Monday. John Crowley arranged for me to have a room at his club, but I felt that it should be a temporary affair, not wishing to impinge on his generosity longer than necessary. On the other hand, I realised that in the beginning, it would be useful to be able to discuss matters with him on a day-to-day basis over dinner in the evening. Victoria had warned me that his illness created gaps in his memory, so I needed to ensure that everything agreed with him was in writing. I, therefore, wrote out the agreement we had made at the club and gave him a copy of my seven-point plan. Because of Victoria being the major shareholder, I also decided to copy her with everything I wrote.

I spent some time trying to compare my salary in 2010. I found to my surprise that by multiplying the figure by 300, £400 a year was equivalent to £120,000 in 2010 terms, and I felt that I was well paid for the job, particularly so, as I was living free.

On Monday, when we arrived at the bank, John called Gerald Phipps to his office and introduced him to me. He was quite tall, strikingly good looking and exceptionally well dressed coming from a wealthy background. He had a pleasant charm, not at all overbearing and as I was quick to find out a keen intelligence.

I spent the morning organizing my new office. It was not as large as John Crowley's but large enough for two desks and a small boardroom table with eight chairs. There was ample cupboard room and three telephones, one internal.

John had arranged for all his eight senior managers to

assemble in his office at 2 p.m. that afternoon and that included Cecil Anderson.

At five minutes to two, the managers filed into John's office led by Anderson, who had the air of superiority born from being in control. He did not like being summoned to the meeting, saying that he was busy and could only spare 15 minutes. The rest of the managers, including two directors, were subservient to Anderson.

When everyone was seated, John took the floor. 'You are all aware that the bank has been losing custom over the last two years and is inexplicably, losing money too. As you are all busy in your respective jobs.' He looked pointedly at Cecil Anderson, 'my wife and I have decided to bring in my cousin from America to look at the way we do things here and what, if anything, we can do to improve the situation. You all met James Alexander when he visited the bank last week, and I would now like to introduce him to you formally. Mr. Alexander has been engaged as my assistant and has full authority from the major shareholders to carry out a thorough investigation of the business. Mr. Alexander has chosen Gerald Phipps to help him, and so you'll be seeing quite a lot of both during the next few months.'

Cecil Anderson spoke. 'I'm sure we will give Mr. Alexander all the cooperation he needs,' he smiled, 'but I think that we all have enough to do without any outside interference. We are all experienced bankers here,' he intoned, suggesting by implication that John Crowley was not. 'I doubt if we have anything to learn from America whose banking sector doesn't have the experience that the City of London enjoys,' he looked around the table and received nods from various members present.

John Crowley looked at me with raised eyebrows as I stood up. 'Good morning gentlemen,' they all responded. 'I am of course, aware of the tremendous respect the financial centre of the City of London has overseas, and certainly in the United States.' I paused, 'it's not my intention to try to teach anyone here how to run a bank,' I smiled, 'you are all well experienced in your jobs. As a result, you'll all be aware that banks shouldn't lose money, and as my cousins are substantial shareholders (*I lied*), they are naturally concerned to ensure their investment is safe. Each one of you has a busy schedule, and you haven't had the time to take a close look at the problem, although some of you may have an idea.' I looked pointedly at Cecil Anderson. 'My past skills concentrated in looking at organisations to find out what has gone wrong,' I said truthfully, 'and by doing so, I hope that all your jobs will remain safe,' I emphasized the last word. 'In the first instance, I would like to make an appointment with each of you to meet in your own offices to establish what ideas you may have. Having done that I will correlate all the information and then take a close look at the systems you use, who is responsible for what, and see if together we can come up with a plan that I can then discuss with Lord Crowley to help make the bank stronger. There's one thing I also claim to be particularly good at, and that's regarding solid investment opportunities not just in England, but also elsewhere in the world. That may well be of help to people you give investment advice to. I understand that Claude Auchinleck oversees investment opportunities, and Michael Smith, who is head of finance who I would like to start with.' I smiled at them all as I sat down and asked Auchinleck and Smith to remain behind so that I could set up appointments. As Cecil Anderson stood up, he asked John Crowley if he could talk to him privately and John agreed they could meet the next day.

John then closed the meeting, everyone leaving apart from the two I mentioned who stayed behind, and I set up appointments with them for the following day. When they had left the office, John congratulated me on my approach. 'That was well done. It would have been difficult for any of them to take offence, but I expect some problems from Anderson tomorrow when I meet him.'

I nodded, 'I must leave it with you to be firm John, as he could well be a disruptive influence on the rest of the management, you may even have to consider moving him on,' I said, looking for a reaction from him.

'Yes, you are right, I know Victoria doesn't trust him, but the problem I have is there's no one to replace him. Certainly, I don't have the skills necessary.'

'Let's not get ahead of ourselves we must see what turns up,' I turned to Gerald Phipps who had been sitting quietly in the back of the room. 'Gerald, I picked financial matters and investment first because that's where we need to start. What I suggest is that you pick up all the ledgers for 1909 and bring them up to my...' I smiled, 'our office. I want to see what sort of system we're running. By the way,' I asked, 'what sort of financial experience do you have?'

Gerald smiled, 'hmm, not a great deal I'm afraid, I covered basic economics at Cambridge, but I'm keen to be taught, and you'll find me a fast learner, which is why I'm grateful to you for picking me for this job.'

'Okay,' I said, 'once you've all the ledgers, we will initially go through them together, and I will show you what to look for, the priority is to find out why the bank is losing money. It can only be down to four principal areas. 1. The staff expenses are too high for the income, but I have not noticed a high staff count, bearing in mind the turnover. 2. The business we are bringing in is unprofitable, but again that's difficult for a bank if it's run properly 3. Loans not repaid as per the schedules and bad loans hidden. If the latter is the case, well soon find them, and 4. There's a leakage of cash due to either mismanagement or theft. These are the main areas we will attack first, so off you go and get hold of the ledgers from the finance department.'

As Gerald left the office, I turned to John. 'It would probably be a good idea if you phoned Smith and told him to release the files to Gerald.' John nodded in assent and picked up the internal phone as I went back into my office.

Gerald returned about an hour later with a security man carrying ten heavy ledgers between them, and he

	DEBIT	CREDIT
ASSET	INCREASE	DECREASE
LIABILITY	DECREASE	INCREASE
INCOME	DECREASE	INCREASE
EXPENSE	INCREASE	DECREASE
CAPITAL	DECREASE	INCREASE

placed them on the floor. I picked one up and flipped through the pages; I then did this with several others. I looked up at Gerald, 'I'm amazed, it appears the bank is still using single-entry bookkeeping.' Gerald looked puzzled, 'what does that mean?' he asked. 'It means that there's no balancing figure, so it's much easier for someone dishonest to fiddle the books. For a business of this size, we should be on double-entry bookkeeping.'

'How does double-entry bookkeeping work?' asked Gerald. I took a piece of paper and drew a table.

'In the double-entry accounting system, two accounting entries are required to record each financial transaction. The aggregate balance of all accounts having positive balances will be equal to the aggregate balance of all accounts having negative balances.

'Accounting entries for related accounts typically include the same date and identifying code in both accounts, so that in case of error, each can be traced back to a journal and transaction source document, thus preserving an audit trail.

'The rules for formulating accounting entries known as Golden Rules of Accounting. The accounting entries are recorded in the Books of Accounts. The fundamental accounting equation A = L + OE will hold, i.e., assets equal liabilities plus owners' equity

'Yes, I see sense in that system,' said [Grab your reader's attention with a great quote from the document or use

Gerald, 'but surely this means that every entry is done twice, that would increase cost, rather than the opposite?'

'Yes, it would,' I said, 'but the accounts must balance, and the single-entry system of record-keeping doesn't include equal debits and credits to the balance sheet and income statement accounts, so this means the following:

'1. A single-entry accounting system isn't self-balancing, so mathematical errors in the account totals are suspect.

'2. Lack of systematic and precise bookkeeping will almost certainly lead to inefficient administration and reduced control over the affairs of the business and finally,

'3. Theft and other losses are easier to conceal.

'It would be possible to use a single-entry system for a small business, perhaps run by the owner with one or two employees, but to use this system for a large bank is quite extraordinary. Frankly, I'm not sure how they could have got away with it, even with a private bank.' I continued. 'What this means is that data may not be available to management for effectively planning and controlling the business.'

I sat back in my chair and looked at Gerald. 'Well,' I exclaimed, 'this is something I certainly didn't expect, and it means a complete overhaul of the financial system.'

'Where do we go from here?' asked Gerald.

'Well, I'm seeing Smith tomorrow at 10 a.m., and I will be asking him some pertinent questions. From there I will have to take the matter up with Lord Crowley I am dining with him tonight, so if it's appropriate, I will raise the question during dinner.

'In the meantime, I think we now need to follow the cash paid out. With each payment, there should be an authorization. A signature from a senior manager and a document, say an invoice for each payment. In the case of wages, there should be contracts. Now to save time, I would only look at larger amounts, say £250,' I thought *that would be the equivalent of £15,000 in 2010.* 'But also look for continuous payments to the same person and amounts with no paperwork or authorization. Do that for the first three months of last year and let's look at the result.'

Gerald immediately got a pad of paper and opened the payment ledger. When I eventually left the office in the evening, he was still working away.

When I reached John's club, I was directed by the doorman to the manager, a relatively thin-faced man with an exaggerated accent. 'Ah, Mr. Alexander, how pleased I am to meet you,' he did not hold his hand out. 'Lord Crowley has booked a small suite for you in the west wing, I will just get the key,' he disappeared behind a large reception area, and returned with a large key attached to a metal anchor. I realised the Club was called the Anchor, which I suppose was entirely appropriate. 'Please follow me, sir. Oh, by the way, my name is Smithers,' he said, as we climbed two sets of stairs. We came to a door with the name painted in gold leaf CARLTON suite. He opened the door, and I entered. I must admit I expected just a bedroom, but this was a proper suite, with sitting room, bathroom, and large bedroom. Smithers showed me around and pointed out the Club rules pasted behind the doors. I noted the main ones: keys should always be left with the reception, no ladies allowed in the club, laundry to be left outside the door in the bag provided in the bathroom, and shoes for cleaning the night before. My case was already there, dropped in by Sidney, and I noted it had been unpacked and clothes put away.

'I understand that you prefer to be shaved each morning, so I've arranged for a valet to attend you at 7.30 a.m. Will there be anything else, sir?'

'Yes, Smithers, what time do you serve dinner?'

'Ah, Lord Crowley left a message that he would be dining at 8.30 p.m. and would be delighted for you to join him.'

I thanked him as he closed the door. I looked in at the bathroom and was pleased to see taps on the bath, so I thought I would indulge myself before going down to eat. Used to a shower in 2010, I reflected how relaxing a bath was, and how it helped the thinking process, I had plenty of thinking to do.

John was already at his table when I arrived in the dining room.

'Good evening, John,' he stood up and held out his hand, 'good evening, James, how was your first day?'

I unfolded my napkin, 'I'm afraid you are probably not going to be happy with what I have to say.'

'Oh dear, as bad as that,' John leaned across the table and put his hand on mine. 'To be honest James, I didn't expect good news, only when the problems are identified and dealt with, will I be able to relax.'

I nodded, 'well the first bullet is the most damaging, the bank is going to have to change its financial system I'm afraid, you can't run a business of this size on a single-entry bookkeeping system.'

'Ah, I see,' said John, he paused, 'it's interesting because I was advised to change to the double-entry system over two years ago and Anderson was vehemently against it, to the extent that he said he would resign if I insisted on it. He claims it would be too expensive.'

'He is certainly right there, John, but you've no choice, with a single-entry system you've no proper administrative or financial control, and I strongly suspect that cash is lost because of it. I guess your choice may be to keep Anderson and lose the bank or get rid of Anderson if he insists on resigning. The point I do not understand is that he must know that by having a proper accounting system, the bank would be easier to control and that in the end would save money or at least highlight where it is lost. Why should he be against that?'

'So, where do we go from here?' asked John.

The waiter came to take our order, and John ordered grouse while I asked for a light salad.

'I've got Gerald looking into payments at this time,

and I will keep on that for the moment. You are seeing Anderson tomorrow morning, and you must deal with him as you think fit, but he must agree to the system changes. Now, that is going to be a big job, it will take at least six months, and we need to bring in good people to initiate it, which means bringing in an accounting company. The public story should be that Crowley's Bank is streamlining its systems to meet the modern age. I can instruct them accordingly and leave them to do their job. Gerald will continue delving into payments, and I will concentrate with Auchinleck on new investment customers.'

John appeared impressed, 'I could not have imagined that in one afternoon you could have come up with such a sweeping change for the bank,' but he also looked worried.

'I must confess,' I said, 'that I had no idea that there would be a single-entry accounting system for such an important bank. The problem is simple John. It is so inefficient that the immediate answer is also simple. Once the accounts are right, we can delve further.'

As our aperitif arrived, a gentleman with grey hair and wearing a frockcoat tapped John on the shoulder. John turned around in his chair and smiled, 'Joseph, how nice to see you here, I thought you were in Portugal.'

'I've just got back, with this,' he held up a rolled-up document, 'your man Auchinleck recommended that I invest in this project with the government of Portugal, so I have the document here to sign.' John was suddenly aware that he'd not introduced me, and he turned to me, 'Joseph, this is my cousin from America, who has recently joined the bank, James Alexander this is Joseph Ward, one of our best customers.' I stood up and shook his hand. John suggested Joseph join us for dinner, and he agreed to do so, allowing the waiter to take his frockcoat to hang up at reception. The waiter brought the menu, and Joseph ordered.

When our meal arrived, we moved from the weather to talking about other things, and eventually, we came around to investment opportunities. 'As you are aware

Joseph, we've been quite conservative over our views about recommendations to our clients, and we've kept our portfolio mainly in Europe,' said John.

I interjected, 'it depends where in Europe the bank has been looking,' I said, 'but I will discuss that tomorrow, with Auchinleck,' I turned to Joseph Ward, 'I'm afraid that I must warn you against any investment in Portugal.'

Joseph Ward looked most perturbed, and I could see that John was concerned with my comment.

'I'm sure Auchinleck acted in good faith,' I said as I took a sip of wine, 'but I've information that within three months, the government of Portugal will fall, and any contract with them will be worthless. Unfortunately, I have not yet had time to discuss these matters with Auchinleck, but I intend to do so tomorrow.' *I happened to know about the collapse of the Portugal financial system in late 1910. It was caused mainly due to the revolution overturning the monarchy and the new Republican government printing money which caused hyperinflation. I had studied their financial history when considering the buying of a large motor business there with the public company I ran before setting up my own company. The purchase did not go ahead because of Portugal's weak economy.* Joseph Ward looked surprised, 'if that's the case, then I'm truly fortunate to have met you, Mr. Alexander, but tell me how you come to know about this information.'

'Now Mr. Ward,' I smiled, 'you wouldn't expect a banker to explain his sources', I raised my eyebrows. Ward nodded slowly, 'so you don't think I should sign this document.'

'No, you shouldn't, if you want a good investment that's going to accumulate over the next ten years, go for the Noble Explosives Company, it's Swedish, you'll not be disappointed.'

Joseph Ward looked at John Crowley for confirmation.

John was still concerned but realised that one of his

best clients may have been saved from a disastrous investment, and thus he concurred.

After the meal, Joseph Ward left saying he had to get back home, as he was not staying at the Club that night but thanked both John and me for the advice.

When he left, John turned to me, 'I do have confidence in you, James, but that was a bit unnerving, particularly as he's one of our best clients.'

'And I suspect he will remain so,' I said. 'The areas we must avoid at all costs are Germany, Austria Hungary, Russia and Turkey, and I must add Portugal I'm afraid.' John dropped his knife on his plate in shock, 'but Germany is one of the faster-growing economies in the world,' he said, 'we must concentrate on those economies that are doing best surely?'

'I'm afraid you are going to have to trust me, John,' I said, 'we are going to be at war with Germany by 1914 and by 1918 it'll be a broken economy. Austria Hungary will destroy itself; Russia will be taken over by a communist state and Turkey will lose virtually all its possessions. I will draw up a list of ten countries we should encourage our customers to invest in, and I promise you, that within five years Byron's Bank will be far behind us.' I smiled.

John had stopped eating altogether, 'Churchill mentioned to me that you'd indicated a war with Germany, but he told me you were mad and that our relations had never been better, rivals, yes, but war never.'

I looked at John Crowley, 'Churchill is wrong John, as you'll find out, there are going to be huge changes in power in the world, and it's the United States that'll become the principal world power after 1918, not the British Empire nor France.'

John picked up his knife and fork again. 'I'm afraid it'll take me some time to assimilate all this James.'

'I fully understand, but I do know the future, how I do I don't know, but I'm quite certain in my deliberations.' I was desperately trying to remember certain things that happened in 1910, and I suddenly remembered going to an evening quiz in a pub near our home. I had forgotten most of the questions and answers, but I remembered one because I studied history, and it stuck in my mind.

'While I'm taking your sensible advice on whom I talk to about the future, here's one thing that's about to happen: by the end of this month, Russia will annex Finland,' I stated.

'My God James, for goodness's sake, don't go around with predictions like this. Otherwise, they'll have you certified.' John Crowley was shocked.

I smiled, 'well, let us wait for the end of this month, shall we?'

I Immediately changed the subject, and we discussed philosophy and art, and by the time we had finished the meal, John was back to his usual self. Still, I could see he was concerned that I might be leading him up the wrong path, so I resolved not to push too hard until he had more confidence in me.

I was extremely busy over the next few days, and John had told Anderson that a team of accountants were to come in to change the system and that they would be working under my control. Anderson had threatened resignation, but when he realised that it would be accepted if he continued to interfere with the decision, he backed down but put everything he possibly could in the way of the change-over of the accounting system being made. John had rushed into my office on 4th of July with a newspaper story that told of the Russian annexation of Finland on 30th June as I had forecast. He was delighted and much comforted by this news, as indeed was I because although I had gone back 100 years, I did not know whether this reality was the same as the one I had come from, but I remember breathing a sigh of relief at the receipt of the news.

Gerald continued digging and came up with some interesting facts. The first was that there was a large amount of money being paid out to a Mr. H. Truscott, the amount being £100.00 per month a figure equal to £30,000 on 2010 figures. There appeared to be no authorization for this figure to be paid. However, it had been regularly sent to an account in Luxembourg under the same name. Paradoxically Gerald also found that the Crowley Bank had a depositor called Herr Dieter Schneider, who was paying in precisely that amount from the same bank on similar dates. Both payments started around the time of John Crowley's father's death some two years ago. The sums were now considerable, amounting to £2,400 or £0.72 million based on 2010 values. I had not questioned Smith or Anderson over these amounts as I decided that I first wanted to try and trace the two people concerned.

In the first instance, I hired a very highly respected law firm to create dossiers on the senior managers of the bank and gave them one month to report.

The bank in Luxembourg was a highly respected private bank that had strong connections with Germany at the time. Once the lawyers report had been received, I decided to travel personally to Luxembourg to meet the Chairman and major shareholder of the Banque les Germain, as I did not wish to put anything in writing at this stage.

During this time, I also created the list of 10 countries that the bank should encourage people to invest in and ten companies or organisations that should be supported. I placed the plan in my safe for future use.

COUNTRIES:
United States of America (Until 1920)
Canada
Australia
Rhodesia
India
Malaya
New Zealand

Barbados
Egypt
South Africa

COMPANIES:

De Beers – Mining
Noble Explosives – Dynamite
CTR (the forerunner of ICI)
NCR (the forerunner of IBM)
British Petroleum
Shell Oil
Rolls Royce Limited
Ford Motor Company
Sainsbury
Blackburn Aeroplane and Motor Company.

Some of these companies were not yet on the public stock market, and I would be suggesting that they be considered for loans when they were raising capital, as they surely would be.

After meeting all the managers, I found that they were essentially supervisors, having almost no authority. The exceptions being Smith and Auchinleck, but even then, Anderson kept practically total control. He ruled the bank with a rod of iron. Even relatively small decisions could not be taken without him, which meant that the bank was utterly moribund in its decision making. I also discovered, from reading past board minutes that Anderson's decisions were not faithfully reported, or if they were, they were well hidden in the text.

Gerald subsequently found several loan accounts that were not serviced, but there was no report on why.

At the end of three months, I was almost ready to write a full report to the board with my recommendations. The changeover to the new accounting system was more straightforward than I had at first thought, and this was because Crowley's, being a private bank did not have small deposits, so most of the figures were quite large. There were fewer figures to work with, on the interim report from the accounting company, there appeared to be a giant hole of some £6,300 equivalent to just over £1.89 million on a 2010 valuation, amounting to just over 32% of the net worth of Crowley's bank. After mandatory government reserves of 46% in 1910, it left only 22% of capital to loan out or invest. The net worth figures included a revaluation of loans with some large doubtful debts written off, a valuation of gold stocks written down to the current price that had been valued at USD 37.94 per troy ounce instead of its correct price of precisely half that amount. The exchange rate against the pound was 4.98 USD, and a valuation was written in at 7.47 one and a half times its value. The value of the building and land on which the bank sat was in the accounts at an inflated value of £65,000 against the Bank of England property worth £100,000. There had been some very dubious dealings with other banks, notably Byron's Bank, which needed substantial explanation. By the end of September, I had almost everything I needed, when I received the report from the lawyers on their investigation into the private lives of the bank's managers. It transpired that most were living normal lives and well within their incomes. One was a homosexual, and I decided the best way to deal with him was to let him know that I was aware of the situation and although against the law of the day, I did not consider it a dismissible offence. At least it would obviate anyone blackmailing him to the detriment of the bank. In any case, his position was not a sensitive one, in that he did not control a department that had access to either cash or contracts. The three I was most interested in were Anderson, Auchinleck and Smith. Anderson had bought a grand house in Belgravia, and a large estate near Haywards Heath in Sussex and was living far beyond his salary from the bank. The report stated that his wife had a small private income believed to be less than £20 per annum, and so far as could be ascertained, Anderson had come up from a relatively poor Scottish family, his father was a shepherd. I learned that he had a German mistress who he visited periodically.

Auchinleck had a German father and an English mother. The parents no longer lived together, and he'd recently bought his mother, who had been left destitute, a modest property near Romsey in Hampshire. He and his wife lived quietly near Wrotham in Kent, his income appeared to be adequate for his lifestyle, and he was very friendly with Smith, in that their families regularly socialised.

Smith had an expensive country house near Oxford and another two properties; one that he leased out and one that he lived in during the week, both were just across from Hyde Park. His wife lived the whole of her time in Oxford, and it appeared that she was not from a wealthy family, her father being a station master. The purchase of the two properties in London was priced far beyond his capability to buy without a loan, but there were no external liens on any of his properties. He appeared to be keen on gambling at his local club and was known to have lost quite large sums, although not beyond his capacity to pay from his adequate salary.

9 - LUXEMBOURG

When I returned to Crowley Hall at the weekend. I discussed these matters with John and Victoria and said that all I needed to do now was to visit with the Chairman of the Banque Les Germain in Luxembourg and I asked John if he knew the man.

John nodded, 'yes as a matter of a fact I do, last time we met was at the Lord Mayors banquet about three years ago, he had come over with a delegation with Kaiser Wilhelm II. We got on quite well, and I seem to remember Victoria and his wife did too.'

Victoria agreed. 'Oh yes, I do remember, she was a genuinely nice lady, originally from a well-known Yorkshire family, and she had three darling children of 6, 8 and 10 who were very well behaved. Her husband, who I believe is a German Count, was most civil and they invited us to go and stay with them in Luxembourg, but I haven't been able to take up her offer,' she smiled, 'perhaps this is the time to contact her?'

John nodded, 'I think that's an excellent idea Victoria, and as you are the largest shareholder of the bank anyway, it would be appropriate. However, I don't think that I'm well enough to make the trip, so why don't you take James and Priscilla. I will write an introductory letter to Count Heidelberg. I think that was his name, letting him know that James is my trusted confidant and that he may discuss any private business with both of you. By the way, James, you should know that the Banque Les Germain deals with the Kaiser's private accounts, so you may find it difficult to obtain information from him.'

'Thank you for that John,' I said, 'I think the

arrangements are splendid,' I glanced across at Victoria, who smiled, 'and I think the best way to get there is by train and ferry, don't you agree?' *I thought of the trip in 2010 taking about 2 hours and wondered how long it would take in 1910.*

'Yes, that would be sensible, you'll probably have to stay overnight in Dover and then again in Paris, but I will ask Maggie, our social secretary, to make all the arrangements.' John was writing down notes.

'I don't think you should do that,' said Victoria, 'let me make the arrangements through Porter, and therefore the bank staff are not involved. There is no point in forewarning anyone there, and you never know with Anderson.'

We had been sitting in John's study, and as I got up to leave, I noticed a framed photograph on one of the bookshelves. I walked across to it and saw several senior employees of Crowley's Bank in it. It was like a school photograph where one sits in line with the most senior person on the first line at the bottom in the middle. 'Is that your father, John?' I asked, pointing to the central figure.

John got up from his desk and walked across, 'yes, the photograph was taken on the 50th anniversary of the formation of the ban, my grandfather originally started in 1857.'

I turned to John; 'do you mind if I borrow it?' I asked.

He looked surprised, and raised his eyebrows, 'of course not, but why...?'

I smiled, 'just an instinctive feeling, I could be wrong, but I will return it.' John shrugged and handed it to me.

After the meeting, John excused himself, saying he was tired and wished to turn in, bidding us good night.

We walked back to the drawing-room where Victoria poured me a sherry. 'I think we're going to have to change our place of assignation,' she laughed, 'our secret place has worked well for us over the summer, but it's starting to get a bit chilly and damp, so I suggest you arrange to stay at John's Club over the weekends now.' My face must have looked crestfallen, as I so enjoyed our somewhat furtive journeys each Saturday where I could indulge in her company, and I suddenly wondered whether she was tired of me.

She laughed at my face, 'oh, James, 'I can read you like a book. You don't think for a moment that I would give up my Saturdays with you, I could never do that.'

'What do you suggest then?' I frowned, somewhat mollified.

'I intend to take a suite at Langham's Hotel for the winter season, this will allow Priscilla to go back to look after her mother and instead of just Saturday, we can spend the whole weekend together, it will be bliss. For the moment it will also be useful as I intend to become more involved with the bank to support John and you until this business is over and then I will come back and spend each weekday at Crowley Hall.'

'What about John at weekends, he would be on his own?'

'Yes, I have thought of that, and there is no doubt that his health is still gradually deteriorating, I'm going to engage a very experienced nurse so that he will be looked after at the weekends. I have discussed this with him, and he agrees that it would make sense, but of course, I am sure he knows we're lovers, and in some strange way, he's pleased that I'm happy and this has changed my view of him who only weeks ago I utterly despised.'

I was not sure she was correct that John Crowley was aware of the situation as far as Victoria and I were concerned and I still had guilty pangs over him and my Tory whom I had left behind, but I could not change what was. My love for Victoria was far too strong for that.

Of course, Pricilla had to accompany us, and when we arrived in Paris, we were all taken by carriage to the George Cinq Hotel, which had just opened. We were escorted to our respective suites, each of which was equal in size to a large apartment, consisting of a bedroom with a four-poster bed, a dressing room, large bathroom, and a large drawing room with a study attached. The furnishings were exquisite and the general ambience one of complete luxury and elegance. I remembered that Tory and I stayed there in the 1990's as guests of The Chrysler motor cooperation and the suite we had then was similar, I could not discern any significant difference.

The next day we arrived in Luxembourg after three full days of travel from London. We caught the train from Paris to Metz early in the morning, and when we arrived at the station there, we found that Count Heidelberg had kindly sent down his chauffeur in a Mercedes 45hp 4-Seat Tourer, a vehicle that had a look of the Rolls Royce about it. The journey to his castle took less than two hours. Despite being in Luxembourg, the castle was very Germanic, situated on a hill with spires seeming to sprout from every corner of the

VIANDEN CASTLE

large building. It reminded me of the castle in The Sound of Music.

The car rumbled over the drawbridge into a perfectly delightful, cobbled courtyard decked with flowers. Much to our surprise, lined up in the courtyard, were all the house staff, all very smartly turned out, with Count Heidelberg and his wife Sophia and his now four young children standing in front. It was a huge honour, and I was extremely impressed, as was Victoria. Priscilla hung behind somewhat overawed by the welcome. I assumed that we had been seen approaching the castle from one of the upstairs rooms with views over the whole area.

Count Heidelberg was in the full military uniform of a colonel in the German army, and he moved forward clicking his heels and putting out his hand to shake mine. I proffered my hand, and he shook it with a firm handshake, you are most welcome Herr Alexander, he moved on to formally shake Victoria's hand and then Priscilla's. Victoria moved across to Count Heidelberg's wife, who came forward and hugged her, discounting formality and she did the same with Priscilla. She then introduced us to her children, Wilhelm, Adolph, Anja, and Angela. Angela was only three years old. We then had to be introduced to all the senior staff, and by the end of it all, I felt rather like a general inspecting the troops. After this, the butler took us through the Grand Hall to our allocated rooms inside the castle. The staircase was broad, but I counted over 400 steps until we reached the floor where we were to stay. We were told that our luggage would be delivered to our rooms within 5 minutes and that dinner would be served at 8 p.m. precisely, but that we would meet for an aperitif 30 minutes before in the Grand Hall.

I found that my room had two communicating doors, one on each side. Priscilla was on one side and Victoria on the other. I knew Victoria had dallied with the Count's wife, and I had seen Priscilla going into the last room, so I was confident that Victoria was in the next room to mine on the left. I tried the door, and it opened but only to another locked door. I knocked as quietly as I could, and it was opened. I steeled myself in case I had made a mistake, and it was Priscilla's room. However, I was correct in my assessment, and it was Victoria who opened the door. I immediately caught her around her slim waist and embraced and kissed her. She pulled away rather breathless, 'James, you beast, there'll be plenty of time for that, they'll come up with our luggage shortly, when they've brought it,

I will let you back in. By the way, Count Heidelberg's wife is called Sophia, and the Count is Helmut. We will be expected to use their given names. I don't know if you are aware of what Count means in terms of rank.'

I shook my head.

'A Count is like an Earl in Britain, and it is usually hereditary,' said Victoria.

Just then there was a knock at her door, and she pushed me back, closing the communicating door and locking it. I did the same on my side. I had just walked away from it when there was a sharp knock on my door. With the luggage came a maid who started to unpack and place my clothes in drawers and a cupboard. When she had finished, she curtsied and asked if there was anything else, I said there was not, so she left. I noticed that there were no locks on the doors into the passageway. I went back to the communicating door and opened it and found Victoria had already opened hers before me. This time she hugged me and kissed me. 'Let's explore,' she said, as she pushed past me and went to the large window facing the green fields beneath. I realised we were high because of the many stairs we had to climb to reach the rooms, but my bedroom view was stupendous showing the whole valley beneath us, and the hills in the far distance. I looked down from the window and felt an unpleasant feeling of vertigo as we were at least 300 feet from the ground. We both turned around and saw the bed was large and relatively high off the floor. 'Big enough for two, I think,' said Victoria, smiling. The bathroom was almost the full length of the room on the right-hand side and stopped at the heavy communicating door that would lead into Priscilla's room. 'Hmm, I suppose you could have two women if you so desired,' she said, frowning...

'One is quite enough for me,' I replied wrestling her to the bed where we fought playfully, with me eventually landing on the floor with a bump. Victoria got up, 'do you realise James, that this will be the first time we have slept together in a bed?' I nodded and savoured the idea as I hugged her again.

'Well duty first I guess, I'm just going back to my room to bathe, and then we can go down for drinks. I think they've gathered several local notables for us to meet, so it's going to be a busy night, one way or the other,' she said mischievously, ducking under my arm and fleeing through to her room. She came back and poked her head through the door, 'oh, I forgot to mention it, Helmut has said he'll be free tomorrow after 10.00 a.m. for any business we want to discuss.' She gave a quick wave and was gone.

I took a more detailed look at my room and noticed a large wardrobe with drawers where my clothes had been folded and hung. My shoes were on racks specially made for them. There was quite a large writing desk, a leather chair, and two Queen Anne armchairs near the window. The room was a bit warm as we were facing south, so I opened a window to let in some air, but it would only open by about four inches, not far enough for anyone to fall out. There was a tassel above the bed to call servants and surprisingly a telephone on the desk, but I was not sure whether it was an internal or external line. The carpet on the floor was thick Moroccan, and there were rugs spread about on it. I went into the bathroom and tested the taps, they worked, and I found the water was piping hot.

I was not particularly looking forward to the evening. The night with Victoria was different, and as I sank into the warm water in the bath, I began to think about how I would broach the subject I had come all this way to discuss on the morrow.

While I was dressing, I looked out of the window again down to the valley below. I suddenly saw a vision of thousands of soldiers running up the valley, machine-gun fire mowing them down. Then the reverse was the case as soldiers ran down the valley. This was to be the situation in only four years. *My God, I thought, what stupid people we are. My vision was prescient, as I had forgotten that the*

German army would be invading Luxembourg as well as Belgium.

When I made my way down to the reception held in our honour, I felt rather depressed, but I comforted myself, realising that I could not change history.

I cannot remember how many people we met that night, certainly over 100 including the Duke of Luxembourg. Helmut was an excellent host, and he apologised for initially meeting us in uniform, but he explained they had attended a special commemoration for the dead of the Franco Prussian war.

The dinner that night was a much more intimate affair, but it was still after midnight when we got to bed. I allowed a decent period for Victoria and Priscilla to retire, and then I went up the endless stairs to my room. I saw Victoria was in my bed, but fast asleep. After undressing, I climbed in beside her and snuggled up and she to me, but it was not quite the night of passion we had both planned.

The next morning, we arrived at breakfast at around 9 a.m. I remember I was first, and Victoria and Priscilla came down about 9.15 a.m. Sophia joined us shortly afterwards, and we talked for some time about politics and the state of Europe.

At 10 a.m. The butler took Victoria and me across a wide corridor to Helmut's study. We were shown to two armchairs placed in front of a small round table and sat down, and after the servant poured us some tea from a nearby dresser, he left the room.

Helmut said he hoped that we had enjoyed the evening and we assured him that we had and thanked him for his hospitality. He quickly turned the conversation to the business in hand. I had brought down a folder with me, and I picked it up from the small table where I had placed it.

'Lord Crowley has written to me regarding your position at Crowley's Bank, for which I congratulate you,' he looked at me and smiled. 'I understand that you are a trusted member of the Crowley family and that you and Lady

Crowley together have Lord Crowley's permission to act on his behalf. I am sorry that he is unwell, but hope he recovers soon. Lord Crowley mentioned that you James have been brought in to investigate certain suspected irregularities at the Bank and that you or your associates have come across an item that concerns our interests here. Lord Crowley said he did not wish to put anything about this in writing, and that you'd explain the position.'

I was surprised at his excellent English and remarked on it. He smiled; 'I suppose being married to an English woman may have something to do with it but thank you for the compliment.'

I drew a breath, 'the problem we have come across is two-fold. We have discovered that soon after the 2nd Lord Crowley died, an account was set up at your bank by a Mr. H. Truscott. The account has received £100 a month since then, so approximately 24 payments have been made. Now we can't find any authorisation for this payment, and there's no time limit for the payments to end, there's no investment made either to or through the bank in the name of Truscott. You'll appreciate, therefore that we were concerned with this matter, but it's linked to your bank in another way.'

Helmut was taking careful notes, and he raised his eyebrows.

'We have come across another account with our bank in the name of Herr Dieter Schneider ... '

I got no further... 'WHAT? Did you say Herr Dieter Schneider?' Suddenly Helmut was showing extreme concern.

'Yes, but we have no address and no other information for this man, other than the fact that there is £100 per month put into this account by your bank, and the balance is always drawn down every three months, and it has recently been emptied.'

Helmut sat back in his chair to assimilate the information I had given to him; I could see that it had taken him completely by surprise.

'Mien Gott this may be serious,' said Helmut quietly. He obviously recognised the account name, and he started to stand up, 'I'm familiar with this account, and it's clear to me that such an account,' he paused, 'should not have been opened with Crowley's Bank or indeed any other bank. I want to thank you for bringing this matter to my attention.'

I was about to ask him about the Truscott account when Helmut interrupted, 'forgive me, I need the rest of today to carry out my investigation, and be sure I will be thorough, I hope by this evening I will have some answers. If so, we can meet to discuss my findings. You will know that my bank carries many secret accounts, but in this case, to enable this matter to be dealt with, I will not hold anything back from you,' Helmut smiled grimly, 'now if you'll excuse me, I must go. I will, of course, also investigate the matter of the Truscott account at the same time. Please treat my castle as though it was your own home, there are many things to do and see here, and Sophia will be happy for your company,'

I interjected, 'just one more thing Helmut,' I took the photograph that I had taken from John Crowley's study. In the hotel room in Paris, I took the actual picture from its frame, so that it just looked like a bunch of well-dressed males with no caption to identify them. 'I would be most grateful if whoever you are talking to, you would ask them if they knew anyone in this photograph?'

Helmut took the picture and looked at it closely, he nodded and put it into a folder along with his notes and with that he ushered us out of the room with a smile and an Auf Wiedersehen, minutes later we saw him being driven off at speed in the Mercedes.

I must admit that I was puzzled, I expected a blank wall, as Helmut's bank had a similar policy to those in Switzerland, all of which guaranteed privacy to account holders. Quite obviously, the Schneider account was more important than we had realised.

The rest of the day was delightful, it was a little chilly, but we dressed up well, and Sophia took Victoria, me and Priscilla around their vast Estate, Sophia drove, which surprised me as I knew it was not normal for women to drive cars in 1910.

'The nearest village is Vianden, and the castle is locally known as Vianden Castle, it was built in the 14th century on an old Roman fortress. It is huge, and some is sadly in disrepair, so we only live-in part,' said Sophia. 'Helmut was left the property by his uncle and one day we hope to restore it. There's a nearby lake, Schenbielg Bieerboesch, which is a beautiful area; you can see it from your rooms. The surrounding land crosses into Germany as far as Roth an der Our and is about 10,000 hectares with many farms that we lease out.'

I was surprised that we crossed the border into Germany on our trip, and I thought that we would have had to produce identification, Sophia was obviously well known to the border guards on both sides. We were saluted through.

Although I had been to Luxembourg City in my former life, I had never been to the countryside, and I was enchanted with its beauty. 'Is Helmut from Luxembourg or is he German?' I asked. Sophia laughed, 'it depends on who he's talking to,' she said, 'he is legally both, but his family are very firmly German from Bavaria. Although he's in the German military, it's an honorary position, and anyway, Germany will never go to war, why should they, they have everything they need without belligerence.' I wondered why she referred to war; perhaps it was something she feared deep down in her consciousness.

I liked Sophia, she was down to earth, very accommodating and a superb host, but her view of Germany was like the British upper class, comfortable and complacent. *I wondered what would happen to her and their lands in only four years. Perhaps if I get back to my own time, I will research their history and write a book about them.*

Before lunch, Priscilla and Victoria had spent some time with the children, and I noted a look of sadness in Victoria's eyes when playing with them. She would have made an excellent mother I decided and wondered why life sometimes appeared to be so cruel.

We had a late lunch, which was more like a banquet, the amount of food and wine was far too much for me, and I went to my room soon afterwards. After I retired, Sophia took everyone else on a tour of the castle.

It was after 4 p.m. when a knock on the bedroom door awoke me. We had both locked our communicating doors so that the servants did not get the idea we were sleeping together. I climbed down from the bed and asked who was there. When I knew it was Victoria, I let her in, carefully hiding my naked body behind the door.

She came in and laughed, 'James, you really must learn to sleep in a nightshirt,' she said fondly kissing me fully on the lips. 'Helmut is back and appears to be quite excited with what he's learnt, so I've agreed that you and I will meet him in his study at 4.30 p.m., so you'd better get some clothes on before you come down,' she smiled.' I will see you down there,' she opened the door and was gone.

I reported to the study at exactly 4.30 and knocked on the door. I was bidden to enter and found Victoria already there. She had a glass of sherry in front of her. Helmut rose and shook my hand. I felt he was much friendlier than he had been up to now, and I detected an undercurrent of suppressed anticipation. He offered me a sherry, which I accepted, and when I sat down, he started with his story. 'You will be pleased to know that I have partly got to the bottom of the problem. The man I employ to handle major accounts is a Herr Adolph Schwienbeck, and I, with the director of the bank questioned him this morning, after some deliberation, he confessed to his crime. In return, we agreed that the bank would not report him to the authorities. It would not have been in the interests of my bank to do so anyway. The story goes back two years when he met Mr. H. Truscott at a Geneva bankers conference. They got on very well, and it appeared that Mr. Truscott was not happy with the change at the top of Crowley Bank, so this must have been when the second Lord Crowley died suddenly. Mr. Truscott told Schwienbeck that he had a perfect way of siphoning off funds from the bank that were unlikely to be detected. He suggested that he set up an account with the Banque Les Germain in his name, and he transferred £100 each month to that account. Truscott said it would be unlikely to be noticed but to cover up the hole, he asked Schwienbeck if he had any accounts, he handled that were not checked. Schwienbeck said that he did know of one, which only he dealt with. Truscott then suggested that Schwienbeck open an account with Crowley Bank in the name of that account and pay into it exactly £100 per month. Thus, the books in both banks would remain in balance.'

'If there was a single-entry financial system,' I said grimly.

'Ya, it's true that we also have not moved to a double-entry system,' answered Helmut.

'Do you know why your man, Schwienbeck would have agreed to such a dishonest suggestion?' I asked.

'Ya, that's a gut question,' I noticed Helmut interspersed German with English when he was concentrating. 'Schwienbeck was being blackmailed, he had an affair with a man during a previous conference, and someone found out about it. Somehow Truscott found out too and knew that Schwienbeck was desperate for money to pay off this man.'

'Okay,' I said, 'now we must find who Truscott is because we don't employ anyone with that name, but the man who oversees our financial department must be under suspicion because he's one of the people who is living above his means.' I was thinking of Smith.

'Ah, I may be able to help you there,' said Helmut, 'the photograph you gave me was shown to Schwienbeck, and he told us that Truscott was in that photo, and I, therefore, assume that this was a picture of your senior staff?' Helmut raised his eyebrows.

'Yes,' I concurred,' it was taken about three years ago before the second Lord Crowley died.

Helmut nodded, 'I thought it was an older picture, this is the man you call Truscott,' he handed over the photograph, with his forefinger covering the man's face. Victoria who had remained silent until now almost shouted 'My God. It's Anderson.'

It was indeed Anderson, the executive head of Crowley's Bank. Everything started to fit into place, his objection to a change in the accounts, his luxurious living, and his almost demonic control of the bank and its resources. I was nevertheless surprised, as this almost certainly meant that Smith was implicated too, as Anderson could not have organized this without Smith's knowledge. My mind was racing now, so Smith appeared to own more property than he could have afforded to buy from his salary. I doubted that it could be from the Truscott account so there must be some other source he was tapping into, as I was now sure that Smith would not have complied with Anderson without some form of reward.

Victoria had one more question. 'Obviously, the Schneider account was special. Otherwise, it would have been subject to checking,' she raised her eyebrows.

Helmut looked mildly uncomfortable; *he was uncertain as to whether he would divulge the name of the owner of the account. Then realising that James Alexander had done his bank a considerable favour, as if the account owner had noticed the matter, the repercussions for the Banque Les Germain would have been disastrous.* 'I must ask you never to disclose this to anyone else,' he said. Victoria and I agreed that it would be kept entirely confidential.

'The account is personal to Kaiser Wilhelm II, and the fact that he deals with us brings in a huge amount of business from the German establishment. He has never to my knowledge checked his account as he trusts the bank implicitly. Of course, the bank will have to repay the stolen funds and tell him what has happened, but it won't be general knowledge, you understand?'

'Of course, we do,' I said, and Victoria nodded in assent. 'Now we need to unravel the payments,' I said, 'I assume that the Truscott account is bare? '

'Ya, except for the last payment, which we have stopped, we pay the sum out in cash to a lady who is authorized to collect the funds. Her name is Frau Magda Schuman. I understand from Schwienbeck that she is Truscott's German mistress, although I am not sure how he knows.'

'Perhaps he made it his business to know, to have some sort of hold over Anderson,' said Victoria.

'Ya, that's possible as she lives just across the border in Germany, not far from here,' Helmut explained.

'That's fine,' I said, 'we will close the Schneider account, and you can cancel the Truscott account. We may be able to recover some of the stolen funds, having said that, there may be other matters we have to deal with because we don't yet know if Anderson and Smith have found other ways of siphoning funds from the bank.'

'Where did the money go from the Dieter Schneider account?' Victoria asked Helmut.

'Apparently to Schwienbeck, but we haven't yet found out how it was received or who drew the funds out from the Crowley Bank. I regret that our employee has been dipping into other funds too, so perhaps this was to be his pension, but that need not concern you, we now must find out just what else he has taken.'

'What will you do with him?' I asked.

Helmut smiled, 'once we have discovered the full

amount he has taken from the bank, he will retire early. Any other funds he has taken will be deducted from his pension. I suspect that he will not have an easy life as he will never be able to secure another job in banking. For our part, we will not report him to the authorities as it would then impact on the bank's reputation. When this matter has been completed, I am going to follow your advice and move the financial system on to a double-entry system, so that this cannot happen again.'

'I think that decision is wise Helmut, but I regret even with the best financial system in the world, we will always find dishonest people attracted to banking, it's something to always watch out for. It's called greed, and I suspect the more banks that become publicly owned, the more we will see greed.' I was thinking about the banking crashes in England, and I guessed there would be others in the future.

The next day Helmut loaned me a gun so that I could take part in a boar hunt that he had arranged for me. We eventually did find a boar, but I had the distinct feeling that the animal, imported into the closed part of the estate was especially for my benefit. Helmut shot the unfortunate beast after my shot missed. We had it for dinner roasted on a spit, and I had to admit it was delicious.

The following day we said our goodbyes and were driven by Helmut down to Metz, which was his way of saying thank you. Sophia accompanied us without the children. The three of us caught the train to Paris, where we stayed again at the George Cinq, and this time, I organized suites with intercommunicating doors without Priscilla's knowledge. Victoria and I spent some time talking about the bank, and as Priscilla had gone off with some American ladies to see Paris at night, we had our dinner brought up to my room where we celebrated with champagne. I told Victoria that *méthode champenoise* was possible because of an Englishman who had invented a bottle strong enough to enable the pressure of the gas to be contained in it. Hitherto the French had tried to reduce the bubbles to get rid of the gas content, considering it a fault of the wine.

Victoria laughed, 'James, your knowledge of things is impressive.' she kissed me as we toasted each other.

There was an exceptionally large bath in the bathroom, big enough for two. We made love in the warm soapy water, but the splashes we made in our exuberance somewhat dampened the walls and the floor. I am not sure, therefore that we would be welcome again. We eventually reached the bed exhausted and immediately fell asleep.

The next morning Priscilla told us that the American ladies she had met up with were on a tour of Europe and she had been scandalised at their views on sexuality and their general feeling of equality with men. We continued to be amused by her stories of the perceived low morals of the New World on our trip back to England.

I found Priscilla an interesting subject and quite sad in a way. She always kept well in the background, either through shyness or an inferiority complex, I was not sure which. She was undoubtedly a prude compared with women in 2010, but her upbringing was strictly Victorian, so perhaps that was not surprising. She read a lot and was quite interesting to talk to, but I always got the impression that she was sexually repressed. I suspect she did not have much love in her life from her parents and probably no experience at all with the opposite sex. Victoria told me that her education had been via a Catholic convent and that she had suffered abuse from the nuns. Unfortunately, she was not the type to break away or rebel, rather sinking into her thoughts and perceived injustices. I discussed this with Victoria, who was almost opposite, and she agreed. 'Perhaps, when we have a moment, we should try and hold a function and invite some serious young men for her to meet, as she would probably make a good solid wife for someone of the same demeanour.'

I decided to keep my eyes open for the right opportunity, as Priscilla was not unintelligent, and knew of the feelings between Victoria and me. I felt we owed it to her to try to help her find happiness if we could.

10 - THE BOARD MEETING

We arrived back at Crowley Hall eight days after we had left for the continent and I reflected that the trip had been quite exhausting, because of the length of travel time, particularly in open cars on dusty roads. The trees were starting to lose their leaves, but the autumn colours were stunning, and as we arrived back on a Friday, we decided to pay a last visit to our secret place until summer returned. We rode out at our usual time and spent happy hours just talking. But any idea of jumping in the river or any other regular practice was out of the question, as there was quite a cool breeze.

On Sunday, John looked entirely rested, and after breakfast, we sat in the drawing-room and told him the story of our visit. He was visibly moved by the fact that two of his senior employees had cheated the bank, obviously, taking advantage of his father's demise.

'How do you see us proceeding James?' he asked.

'Well, obviously Victoria and I discussed this in some detail on the way back from Europe. The first thing we should do is to announce an EGM formally.'

John raised his eyebrows, 'An EGM, you mean an extraordinary general meeting of the company'.

'Yes, and a board meeting to run concurrently. The EGM is necessary because you don't control the board, whereas between you and Victoria, you control the company and if you just had a board meeting you could be outvoted. Under the company's constitution, you've to give 15 days' notice of an EGM, so I suggest we do that first thing tomorrow. A board meeting has a similar notice of the time, so even if they get a whiff of what is going on, they could not hold a board meeting before the EGM. I'm hoping to receive a copy of Schwienbeck's written confession from Helmut, he is sending that by special messenger. We should receive that tomorrow, and once we obtain it, I suggest that we confront Anderson with the evidence. I expect him to try and wriggle out of the accusation, but Helmut is also going to send a letter from his bank stating that a certain lady, who we now understand is known to Anderson, has been collecting the funds from the Truscott account. He will have great difficulty in refuting the evidence. We need to find out what other matters he has been involved with including whatever deal he's done with Smith. If he's not cooperative, we should call in the authorities.'

'Is that wise John. Surely if this matter is made public, the bank will suffer?'

'Only in the short term, it is not quite the same as Helmut's bank, who have secret accounts with the German hierarchy. I believe we will be able to bring confidence back to Crowley's quite quickly by providing clients with first-class advice, and you can leave that to me to sort out. On the one hand, if he's cooperative, we can retire him and deduct what he has taken from his pension.'

John turned to Victoria, 'are you happy with what James is suggesting?' he asked.

Victoria realised that John had never considered her opinion even though she was the major shareholder, and she was pleased that he should have consulted her. 'Yes John, we have a nest of vipers in the bank, let us clean them out, and the quicker, the better,' she was quite surprised at her vehemence. 'One point though, it may be in our interest to transfer some shares to James so that he can officially be present at the shareholders meeting,'

'No need,' I said, 'you can simply invite me as Lord Crowley's executive officer, you've enough shares to outvote anyone else easily.'

John smiled. 'I've long felt uncomfortable working with these people, and I must thank both of you and particularly you James for the work you've put into sorting out the mess that I've allowed to continue.'

I could see tears in his eyes, and to move things on to a more comfortable area for him. I suggested we should break out a bottle of champagne. John brightened perceptively and called Porter to bring a vintage bottle from the cellar. When it came, I held my glass up, 'to the new prosperity of Crowley's Bank.' We clinked glasses and moved our conversation to the beautiful day outside, and the dropping of the autumn leaves.

The three of us set off first thing on Monday morning, arriving at the bank by 9.30 a.m. Victoria travelled on to Langham's, where she was to leave her luggage and return by 11.30 when we were to schedule a meeting with Anderson. Gerald was already in the office, and he told me that he had uncovered more revelations regarding Smiths circumstances. He had bought the Hyde Park properties with a bank loan but had paid not one penny to reduce it. The loan had been signed off by Anderson, with a moratorium of ten years. 'Well, that's a nice deal to have,' I said, 'as it means that no repayments are made on the properties either interest or capital for ten years.'

'It's even worse than that,' said Gerald, 'the loan is free of interest, and when repayments are due, he still has fifty years to pay!'

I nodded, I rather expected something like this, and I went on to explain to Gerald how we got on in Luxembourg.

'Good Lord,' he said, 'it's almost unbelievable and added to all the other matters we've found, these people have gone a long way to breaking the bank. I have got a full written report from the investigation team and one separately from me,' he handed me a thick document and one lesser one. 'What are we going to do?'

I told him that we had formally put out a notice

regarding the EGM, and that Lord Crowley, Lady Crowley and I would be seeing Anderson at 11.30, after that we would interview Smith. 'As you've put in such sterling work over the last few months Gerald, I would like you to be present at these meetings, you can take notes,' I added.

At 11.30 John, Victoria, Gerald, and I were sitting around the board table in John's office. When Anderson came into the room, he did not knock. He sat down, insolently at the head of the table, opposite John. He opened a folder. 'I've been told that you've evidence against me regarding the Truscott account,' he sneered. 'I've here a letter signed by Herbert Crowley that gave me permission to open such an account and to transfer £100 per month to it.' He threw the document on the table. John picked it up and read it, passing it to me when he had done so.

It was on the bank note paper and was addressed to Cecil Anderson.

To: Whom so ever it may Concern:

This letter confirms that Cecil Anderson has my permission to create an account with the Banque Les Germain in the name of H. Truscott and to allocate funds of £100 per month to this account in perpetuity. This is a payment of a favour done by Cecil Anderson to the writer.

Signed

Lord Herbert Crowley,

1st December 1907.

'If there's nothing further, I wish you good morning gentlemen.' Anderson went to get up. 'Not quite so fast Mr. Anderson,' I said. 'I would strongly recommend you sit down, as we have several matters to discuss.'

Anderson took his timepiece out of his waistcoat and sniffed. 'I'm a busy man, I have a bank to run, but I'm prepared to give you 10 minutes of my time.' He sat down and stared at me. 'We're not aware of the document you've produced,' I stated, 'it is not in any files we've seen, there are no minutes in any board meetings, and it's not declared at the end of year accounts. We will establish if the signature is valid in due course, but it doesn't have any validity in law because it hasn't been declared.' Anderson was about to speak, but I held my hand up. 'This matter won't take me ten minutes, and so until I've finished, I would appreciate the courtesy of your attention. if I don't have it, you will be suspended, and we will call in the authorities, not something we wish to do, but if you force our hand...'

'You wouldn't dare make these private matters public,' he said folding his hands.

'I must admit that to make public that the bank's chief executive has been carrying out illegal actions would have a deleterious effect on our status, but it would be short term, as we would immediately hand the contents of this file to the Times newspaper with a report of how we are now going to deal with the inherent problems that the bank has experienced due to extraordinary incompetent management.'

'Under the guidance of Lord Crowley,' Anderson shrugged.

I did not know who had tipped Anderson off of course, but I suspected strongly that the letter was a forgery, and by him producing it would throw us into a state of indecision. I did not know either what he knew of our meeting with Count Heidelberg. I was racking my brain when it clicked. I remembered Helmut saying that he had put a stop on the last payment to be collected by Anderson's mistress in Germany, and she would have gone to collect it, finding it stopped, she would have contacted him immediately by wire. It would not have been difficult for him to find out that we were in Luxembourg, all he would need to do was call Porter at Crowley Hall to ask for me, and Porter not knowing the reason for our trip would almost certainly have indicated where we had gone. With the investigation almost finished he would have known that he was on thin ice, although he would naturally try and sidestep the issues, blaming others as he was now clearly trying to do.

'I'm afraid the game is up Anderson, you see we've just received a letter from Count Heidelberg with a full confession from an employee called Schwienbeck, someone you know well I imagine.'

Anderson went white. His bluff had failed disastrously.

Victoria interrupted, 'as a precaution James. I've here a letter of credit from Credit Suisse in Switzerland for £10,000 that I will pledge to Crowley's Bank in the event of there being a run on the bank if this story gets out. I talked to John yesterday, and I understand that this amount would more than support the bank in the unlikely situation that Anderson has just threatened.' *I was aware that the sum equalled £3 million on a 2010 valuation*, 'and there's much more available if it's needed,' she affirmed. She waved the piece of paper before Anderson before handing it to John.

I saw Gerald was writing everything down, and he gasped at the amount of funding offered by Victoria.

I smiled at her, 'thank you Lady Crowley, but I would hang onto it for the moment, I don't believe that Anderson will be too interested in spreading the news, not by the time I've finished with him.

'Now Mr. Anderson, I need some answers:

'Why did Smith get an extraordinary loan to buy two houses in Hyde Park?

'How do you expect to pay the bank back for the funds paid to the Truscott account?

'Who received the funds from the Dieter Schneider account?

'Why were the gold and exchange rates manipulated to appear to be greater than the real value?

'Why was the bank building overvalued?

'There are various duplicitous accounts with Byron's bank, I want the details, please.

'Now, depending on your answers, we will consider what we do with you. There are two options; you'll be retired immediately and won't receive any pension until you've satisfied us with your answers. If you don't do so, we will call in the authorities, and we will sue for any monies owed, we know exactly where your properties are situated.

'The alternative is that you come clean and cooperate.'

John, who had not said a word, was upset and called Anderson a traitorous bastard. He got up from the table and went to the internal phone asking for security to come to his office.

While we waited for the man to appear, I turned to Gerald. 'Gerald, I want you to sit down with Anderson, and take a statement from him with answers to all the questions I've asked, indeed you may have some of your own, I don't want him to leave until you are satisfied that he's made a clean breast of all the skulduggery he's been up to.'

Gerald nodded. 'Don't worry James, I will not leave any stone unturned.'

I turned to John, 'John, would you write a letter to Anderson suspending him with immediate effect, pending the final decision at the board meeting and EGM.'

There was a knock on the door and John called 'Come,' the security man entered.

This time John gave the instructions. 'Geoffrey, this man,' he pointed to Anderson who was slumped in his chair all arrogance gone, 'will be leaving the building after Mr. Phipps has finished with him. You will go to his office now and remove any personal effects he has there, such as a hat and coat, family pictures and so on and then later you will escort him from the building. Please inform all the security staff that Anderson is not to be allowed into the bank under any circumstances in the future. Also, please ensure that he hands over all keys that he may hold, then telephone the locksmiths, to change the locks on all external doors and re-set all the vault combinations. They should be instructed to give me the new keys as well as the new combinations.'

Geoffrey, an ex-military man, saluted and left the room.

I made a sign to Victoria and John pointing to my

office; we all went in closing the side door.

'Well done, James,' said John, 'I must admit that I was thrown completely off course by that letter, as the signature looked to be true.' John held it in his hand.

'Is it your father's handwriting?' asked Victoria.

John grimaced, 'it's difficult to discern,' he answered, 'but I can't imagine him signing such a thing.'

'I suppose Anderson could have tricked your father into signing a blank piece of paper,' I said, 'but it doesn't matter, as with Schwienbeck's confession it wouldn't help him. However, I will ask Helmut if he can get something out of Magda, his mistress, as he will have a fair amount of power in that area. In the meantime, it might be a good idea to put it in the hands of an expert on signatures.

'Make sure you circulate the EGM and board meeting to be held in fifteen days. Probably be a good idea to get your secretary to give a copy to Anderson before he's let go, and make sure she gets a signature from him, he's still a director until we formally move him off the board,' I said.

John nodded, 'what about Smith?'

'I think we will leave him until tomorrow when we have the full report from Gerald.'

'Do you think that Gerald is the right man to tackle Anderson?' Answered John, 'he's young and inexperienced.'

I laughed. 'Gerald has done more work on this case than any of us, he's suffered all sorts of indignities from Anderson and Smith, when trying to elicit information from them, oh yes, I think he's exactly the right man.'

Victoria agreed. 'Well, after all that excitement, I would like to take you two for lunch at my hotel.'

'I for one will accept,' I said, 'because I've never eaten at the Langham's.'

The lunch was a great success, and I could see that John was greatly relieved to the extent that he drank rather too much, and I had to support him with the help of a man from the concierge into his cab at the end of the meal. I then had the horse-drawn carriage take him back to his club, and once I had taken him to his room, I walked back to the bank. Things are starting to shape up I thought, one more to go...

The next morning, I received Smith who resigned. He told me that he had been aware of Anderson's dishonesty, but Anderson showed him the letter that had allegedly been written by Herbert Crowley. Although he found it difficult to believe, he was not prepared to risk his position, particularly as Anderson had offered him a large sum of money to buy his Hyde Park properties. I told him that we would accept his resignation, but that the properties must be handed over to the bank as Anderson had acted illegally. Surprisingly, Smith did not argue, and he said he would get his lawyer to transfer the deeds. He also told me that the money from the Dieter Schneider account had been drawn down on a quarterly basis. We subsequently found it went to an account held by Anderson at Byron's Bank.

John had not turned up, and I went around to the club to ensure he was okay. He was but said he did not feel well enough to come into the bank for that day.

On returning to the bank, I had a call from Auchinleck, who then came up to see me with his resignation. He said that Byron's Bank had offered a position to him and Smith some time ago and as he was very friendly with Smith, he had now decided to accept. I realised that was why Smith was so quick to settle his affairs with Crowley's.

I scheduled a meeting with Gerald Phipps later in the morning, and I did some work on the various minutes to be presented to the board meeting in two weeks.

Gerald came in with a big smile on his face. 'Well, we are having a clear-out,' he said, 'I've just heard about Auchinleck.''

'Yes, that was a surprise,' I answered, 'but it does clear the deck of senior managers and makes it much easier to reorganize the bank into a more modern organisation.'

'Does it not complicate matters though, as Auchinleck has quite a following of investors, which could be quite a loss to Crowley's bank?' asked Gerald.

I shook my head, 'no, his advice was outdated, so we will be able to get back the business, the bigger problem is how we present this to the press, as they'll soon be on it.'

'Do you have any ideas?' Gerald asked.

I nodded, 'Journalist are lazy people, so I have always found it's best to write a better story than they can, adding a few confidential matters to add spice, and hope that they'll print what you've given them. It usually works,' I smiled, 'so as soon as we've dealt with the Anderson matter, we will work on a press bulletin, now tell me how you got on.'

Gerald sat down at the table and spread out his papers. 'I assume we can dispense with the loan to Smith.'

'Yes, he's handing the Hyde Park properties over to the bank,' I confirmed.

'Okay, regarding the Truscott account, I suggested that Anderson hand over the Belgravia house to the bank as part payment, but of course, this wouldn't cover the amount he has removed. He does have a reasonable pension, and we could have that transferred to the bank, but even then, there would be a shortfall of £550. Plus, the amount removed from the Schneider account that adds another £3,600 but of course that's owed to Helmut's Bank, so it's up to him how he deals with it.'

Hmm, that's still over one hundred and sixty thousand in 2010 money I thought to myself, 'what about his estate near Haywards Heath?' I asked.

'That appears to be worth about £833,' answered Gerald.

'And cash?'

'He swears he doesn't have more than £100 in various accounts.'

Okay, I will discuss this with Lord Crowley, and we will come to a decision, now what else?'

'The gold and US dollar holdings were inflated as you know to cover losses, and I've reckoned that we must recommend a write off about £1,000 and the building about the same. There is an account that has a deficit of £150 that is still outstanding by a Mr. Edward.'

'Have we chased it?' I asked.

'It's a bit difficult,' said Gerald, 'the man is dead.'

'Presumably, he had an estate that we could call on.'

'It's still a bit difficult,' repeated Gerald.

'Stop being obtuse, Gerald, what is the difficulty?'

'The name Edward is a cover for His Royal Highness, King Edward VII.'

'Ah, yes, I see what you mean, leave that one with me too.' I smiled at Gerald's obvious embarrassment, 'and finally the situation with Byron's and other banks?'

'It was mainly Byron's Bank where we accepted some quite large charges from them, amounting to £550. The largest amount was regarding Mr. Joseph Ward involving the Portuguese government for a deal that was done on behalf of him. Byron has acted as an intermediary.'

'Have we paid it?'

'No, I put a hold on it until I had discussed it with you.'

'Excellent, cancel it, Joseph Ward is no longer going ahead with the deal. Now, what I want you to do is add up what our true loss is, considering all matters and assuming we can claw back some from Anderson and Smith. Oh, and there is a £100 coming from Banque Les Germain as the last payment was stopped. When the total figure is available to us, we will see where we stand.' I stood up, 'thank you, Gerald, you've done an excellent job. When I've spoken to Lord Crowley, we will sort out our final figure, talk to the staff and then issue a press release. After that, we will make suggestions for where we go from here.'

Victoria had gone back to Crowley Hall, and I left the bank early. I checked that John was okay, and I had an early meal and turned in.

The next morning, I met John at breakfast, and we discussed current matters. He was apprehensive about Auchinleck leaving at the same time as the others, not because he particularly liked the man, but because of how it might look to outsiders. He also made the same point as Gerald, that he could damage the bank by taking clients away from it.

After breakfast, we walked to the bank and were surprised to see the press outside the door. When we saw them, we immediately backtracked and went in a rear entrance.

When we reached John's office, I walked over to the telephone and called in Gerald Phipps, and we all sat around the board table.

'First things first,' I said. 'yesterday I asked Gerald to see how much our suggested write off would be after claiming back certain funds, Gerald?'

Gerald produced a piece of paper with figures printed on it.

Suggested write off	£6,300
Return of funds from:	
Cancellation of Byron account	£ 550
The Banque les Germain (Truscott A/c)	£ 100
Value of Hyde Park houses (Smith)	£1,000
Value of Belgravia House (Anderson)	£ 750
Pension Funds (Anderson)	£1,000
Haywards Heath Estate (Mortgaged)	£ 300
Edward account (Write off)	£ 0
Anderson Mortgage – 5 years	£1,250
TOTAL NET	£1,350

Gerald tidied the papers in front of him. 'Right, the investigation suggested a deficit or hole of £6,300. Now assuming the following, we can recoup about thirty-nine percent as shown in my statement and perhaps more depending upon your final decisions.' He then laid a paper in front of John and me.

'Okay,' I said, 'that will leave a write-down of assets of around £3,150. including the over-valuation of the building, gold and dollar stocks, and a deficit of £250 on the Anderson account assuming we took his estate. The remaining debt is from bad loans, which we may or may not get back. What I suggest is as follows: We take all except the Haywards Heath estate. I assume that he earns something from that, and Anderson should commit to repaying the £250 over say five years. We'll take a mortgage on the estate to ensure he pays. It would mean that the amount can be put in as a bone fide loan and needn't be written off. The pension fund can be taken in full as can the Belgravia House.'

I turned to John Crowley, 'I recommend that the Edward account be cancelled as goodwill but let King George know that we have done so, as we may need a good friend in high places in the future. If we do that, that'll reduce our write off figure to £1,350, considerably less than first indicated and it may still be possible to recover some bad debt too. Let's not fool ourselves, this is still a lot of money to write off,' *£405,000 in 2010 I thought to myself,* 'but it represents only 6.85% of the net equity instead of the original 32% so that after the 46% capital we must hold, it leaves 47.15% to loan or invest. 'I reckon I can recover the 6.85% within 12 months,' I said confidently.

John looked much relieved, 'but what about Auchinleck?'

'I honestly do not think he was of much help to the bank, John, he gave bad advice to Joseph Ward, and his thinking was steeped in the last century. I didn't give him my list of suggested investments, so he will undoubtedly continue as before. We may well lose some clients, but I promise you, it'll be short term,' I smiled.

'What about the press...?' asked John.

'Right, give me fifteen minutes, and I will be back with a suggested statement.' With that, both Gerald and I left John's office to go into our own. While Gerald carried on with his work, I created a draft of the press release:

Crowley's Bank
City of London

Crowley's Bank announces that it has carried out a fundamental and far-reaching reorganisation of its business methods to bring it into the modern age. This is because three senior executives have left the bank, and further appointments will be announced shortly.

Crowley's will be concentrating on investment opportunities in this ever-changing world, and it's streamlined service will be of great benefit to its clients.

I felt that a short release would be enough to whet the press appetite and that we could release a series of articles on the bank in the future, thus keeping it very much in the public eye.

When I had finished, I took it through to John, who was on the telephone, so I left it on his desk.

Ten minutes later, he came into the office, handed a piece of paper to me, and left without comment.

I picked it up when I finished some figures I was working on and was startled at the changes made:

Crowley's Bank
City of London

Crowley's Bank announces that it has carried out a fundamental and far-reaching reorganisation of its business methods to bring it into the modern age. The result of this is that three senior executives have left the bank and Mr. James Alexander is to be appointed the chief executive officer at the next board meeting, in less than two weeks. Lord Crowley will continue as the chairman of the board. Gerald Phipps will be appointed as the chief financial officer with management status.

Crowley's will be concentrating on investment opportunities in this ever-changing world, and it's streamlined service will be of great benefit to its clients.

When I had finished reading it, I rushed into John's office. He was grinning like a Cheshire Cat. 'I know what you are going to say James, but the fact is I've already discussed this with Victoria on the telephone this morning, and she's agreed wholeheartedly.' He became serious. 'The bank is initially going to come under pressure because of these sweeping changes, and we feel that there is no one better than you to lead the bank. It is important it is seen that we have taken quick action to replace Anderson and Smith. As far as Auchinleck is concerned, I suspect you will want to deal with that yourself, with perhaps Gerald's help. I feel he has done such a good job for us that. despite his youth, he should be given a chance. You will notice that he has been promoted to a managerial position, not a director yet, but that does not prevent him from attending board meetings, of course, he would not have a vote.'

I sat down in the chair opposite John's desk, 'but what about you, John? What are you going to do?'

'Much the same as I did before, but I am going to spend much more time at my estate, perhaps coming in for one day a week just to be appraised of what is going on. Victoria is also going to be spending more time in London to assist you if indeed you need any assistance, which frankly I doubt.'

I drew a deep breath, *I had been involved with the bank for less than four months, and here I was leading it. I thought back to my financial position when I left 2010* and had to smile.

'Now, about salary,' John asked.

I held my hand up. 'The salary I have is more than enough thank you John, but what you can agree to is that I receive a percentage of every new deal that's done by the bank, this means that if no new deals are done, I remain with my basic salary. The figure I suggest is two per cent of the net profit of each deal, and this ensures that each deal must show a net surplus if I'm to receive my percentage.'

John smiled; 'well, the bank cannot lose on that basis. But if that does not work for you, I want you to come back to me and we can re-negotiate.'

'Agreed,' I stood up and shook John's hand. I was about to leave the office when John passed me a piece of paper. It was written on notepaper belonging to Byron's Bank. I read it carefully. It was addressed to Lord John Crowley of Crowley's Bank. "My son Jules and I will deem it a pleasure if you'd join us for luncheon at my Club on Thursday next as we have a serious proposition to put to you." It was signed your obedient servant etc. signed

Arthur Byron.

'What does this mean, John?'

'It means, the Wolves are out,' he laughed, 'I've no doubt that they are hoping to pick up the bank for as little as possible, but I intend to go, just to see what they've to say. The only condition is that you are invited too.'

'Should be fun,' I said smiling.

'Don't bank on it James, they are not gentlemen.'

'Neither am I...' I laughed as I left the office to give Gerald his news. He was delighted with the promotion and the new salary he was being offered. He told me that it would enable him to propose to the Lady Penelope, to whom he had been unofficially engaged for the last eighteen months. I told him I would expect to be invited to the wedding and he assured me that I would be. I detected tears in his eyes.

I gave him the press release asking him to pass it to the typing pool and circulate among the day's major press.

On Thursday we walked from the bank to the club where we were to have lunch. Arthur Byron had reluctantly agreed to me accompanying John, and he had given way when John had made it plain that he would not accept the invitation without his chief officer being present.

We were taken through to the luxurious lounge where the two Byron's were waiting for us. John introduced me to Arthur Byron first. While being very courteous, he shook my hand with a limp handshake. Arthur was a tall man with slicked-back grey hair and clean-shaven. He had a nose like an eagle's beak and piercing blue eyes that he used to try and intimidate one. I met his stare until he broke away. His dress was out of fashion for the present day and looked more like a Dickens character. His voice was slightly accented, and I guessed correctly that he originally came from the north of England. By his manner, I received the impression that this man was utterly ruthless. His son Jules was much more polished, presumably having had a very much better education than his father, his eyes were shifty, and he paid little attention to me, obviously considering my position of no account. His face was florid; I guessed his lifestyle was not healthy as he was undoubtedly overweight, and he smoked incessantly, which was extremely unpleasant. His almost black hair was combed carefully back and had no discernible grey showing which suggested that his hair was dyed as I put his age at around my own. He had a small moustache, which was neatly trimmed, and I assessed him as vain, without having the looks to be so. His dress was expensive, and he had a penchant for gold, as his watch-chain showed prominently across his waistcoat and his large studs were also gold as was his cigarette case. I took an instant dislike to Jules, but strangely I liked his father, though I was fully aware that he was not the sort of man that one would want to turn ones back on.

We had a drink in the lounge and then moved to the table set carefully in a corner to be private. We enjoyed the first-class lunch discussing the world at large when over coffee, Arthur came to the point of the meeting. 'We're aware of the problems you've had at your bank,' he said smoothly, 'and it is obvious to us that you are losing business and will not be able to meet your commitments if such a situation continues. We at Byron's are prepared to make you a generous offer for your interests.'

John Crowley asked why they should wish to buy the bank if they considered it was failing.

Jules chipped in, 'everything has a value,' he almost sneered, 'and we are interested because you still have some clients we would like to be involved with, although we will win them to our bank in time. This is your opportunity to get out while you can, and we can then merge the two operations, making Byron's the principle private bank in Britain.'

'And what are you offering?' I asked. The fact that I had entered the conversation appeared to surprise both men.

Jules looked at me as though I was not part of the conversation, and turned to John, his eyebrows raised as he blew smoke from his lighted cigarette in my direction.

John looked at me, 'perhaps you would answer Mr. Alexander's question?' he queried.

Arthur took over the conversation, 'we would buy you with an exchange of Byron shares at say 20 pence per share...'

I laughed aloud, 'your offer is, in my opinion derisory, it isn't one I could recommend to John and Victoria.'

Jules then showed his real character, 'then we will crush you like an insect.' He said, stubbing his cigarette out on his plate.

I smiled, 'I'm a Scorpio, so you should beware of my sting when you try to crush us, you'll not find us as easy a prey as you currently think my friend.'

John Crowley nodded, and turned to Arthur Byron, 'is this the way you intend to conduct your business?' he asked.

'Oh please, Jules got a bit carried away, but we do know that you'll not be able to continue for much longer so consider our offer, and we may be able to up the figure slightly, that's open to negotiation.' The older man was looking at me, and I knew that he'd initially underestimated my position and clout in the bank and was thinking how he could bring me round to support his bid.

'Perhaps Mr. Alexander would like to visit us at Byron's to see how we do things there? You would be very welcome, and I will arrange a date that is convenient to you,' he smiled, like a hungry alligator I thought. Jules was still seething but remained quiet.

Looking at John, I said we would be happy to look around his organization, and it was left at that. The lunch finished, we left the club, and as we did so, a photographer outside took our picture. Because we were moving the photograph would be blurred but enough to report that we had been to Arthur Byron's Club. 'They'll not give up that easily,' said John.

'Oh, I'm sure you are right,' I agreed, 'but we will beat them at their own game, you'll see, the old man is the one to defeat, Jules is an over-opinionated fool, dangerous, but a fool just the same.'

The board meeting was held as planned, and the various changes were passed as we had agreed. Afterwards, we talked to the management and assured them of the bank continuing and flourishing. I now had to put my money where my mouth was.

The press had printed a story about our visit to Arthur Byron's club, but other more important matters in Europe soon submerged the speculation of such a meeting.

11 – TEMPTATION

My intervention with Joseph Ward was starting to pay off, and the fact that Auchinleck had gone over to Byron's was beginning to help us re-establish ourselves. Joseph had recommended several clients, and I had used my list of countries and companies to good effect. The word was starting to spread. The cancelling of the Edward account had also brought an unexpected bonus. We were advised by the Kings Private Secretary that the King wished to maintain an account with Crowley's and would be interested in our advice on investments. This Monarch was quite different from his father, who had enjoyed spending money. George was far more interested in investing in the future. The primary advice I gave him was to pull out of his considerable interests in Germany, which he did much to my surprise. I think he was much more aware of the problems to come than were the politicians of the day.

My assignations with Victoria continued, and we had become almost like a married couple, although our time together was mainly at the weekends at Langham's hotel suite. Of course, we could not hide our love for each other completely, and I knew that rumour abounded in certain circles. Still, the bank's success overcame any damage from gossip, we were very circumspect, however, and did not flaunt our affair in society. Because I was now living in London and Victoria was travelling back to Crowley Hall during the week, it was no longer necessary for Priscilla to stay there, so we decided to organize a ball at Crowley Hall to ensure she was introduced into society. The primary purpose, of course, was to find her a loving husband, and to this end, Victoria made it known that Priscilla would receive a yearly income of £200 a year and would also be mentioned in her will. This ensured a considerable amount of interest and Priscilla suddenly found herself substantially more popular than she had been hitherto. Victoria had warned her that she must choose wisely as she would now receive much more attention from the male species that would not necessarily be connected to making Priscilla happy.

The ball's result was successful in this regard as she received several advances, but unfortunately, she did not choose well, and the resulting relationship was an unhappy one.

We received the promised invitation from Byron's Bank, but it came at a time when John Crowley wasn't at all well, as I'm sure Arthur Byron was aware, so I went on my own. I was reasonably impressed by the way they conducted their business, and the controls they had over their finances, although no better than ours, had been in place longer. As I expected, they made me a generous offer to join their bank, but I told them that I was not interested. Arthur said to me that I would regret my decision and left it at that.

Soon afterwards, I received an invitation to go to Paris with several other organisations to meet with French and other bankers, I found it to be more of a junket than a serious discussion on international banking, but I considered it worth going if only to contact important people over there. It was therefore surprising that Jules Byron approached me, he was standing in for his father, and he invited me to join a party for dinner that evening. I had nothing else to do, so I agreed, thinking it was perhaps a party of fellow bankers. When I arrived at his hotel, I was introduced to a quite lovely French woman who had obviously been picked to be my partner for the evening. Jules was accompanied by a young girl of around twenty years of age. I realised that this was the party, and no others were invited. I was immediately on my guard, but I found my partner for the evening a Madame Leclerc to be vivacious, witty, and excellent company and despite Jules, who appeared to be drinking heavily, I started to enjoy the evening. The champagne liberally served to our table was good, but I noticed Jules had his own bottle, served uncorked, which was not the custom. It was when Jules got up to go to the men's room that I supposedly in error picked up his glass and drank from it. He was not drinking champagne, but some fizzy concoction that was not alcoholic. When Jules returned, he had the appearance of being slightly tipsy, but I now knew this to be an act. So, what was he up to? *I ran certain situations through my mind. Was he trying to disgrace me by getting me to sleep with Madame Leclerc? I decided not, as such a matter would not be disgraceful. Did this woman have the same disease as the prostitute he had introduced to John Crowley all those years ago? She was certainly showing no signs of it, but I had read somewhere that a woman can contract syphilis and yet not suffer from it. I discarded that idea, however. I suddenly realised what Jules was planning. Firstly, he was to ply me with as much champagne as he could, and it would be Madame Leclerc's job to get me up to a bedroom in the hotel where she was staying and then when in an embarrassing position a man would burst into the room claiming he was her husband, who he may well be. A photographer would record the event, to provide evidence in a divorce situation citing me as a correspondent. The scandal would certainly damage my standing in the city, but worse would also damage my reputation with Victoria, who he must know was one of my major benefactors.*

I pretended to get rather drunk, and after a while excused myself to go to the men's room, but instead entered the hotel kitchens, much to their consternation, and found a back door, through which I exited. Although my hotel was some distance away, I decided to walk to clear my head. I arrived back at my hotel and using the notepaper provided, I scribbled a note dating it for the next day, packed my bags and hired a carriage to take me to the station where I caught a night train to Calais. The note for Jules Byron, which was to be delivered to him the next day apologised profusely for my disappearance but said I was taken ill suddenly and so as not to embarrass him, I returned to my hotel. I asked him to send my apologies to Madame Leclerc. I did not add that I was returning to England, but he would find that out soon enough. I reckoned he could not take offence at that, even if he did not have any devious plan in mind, and the worst he could think was that I could not hold my drink. I was sure, however, that I aborted his scheme, and it was an illustration to me as to how far he would go.

I returned to London the next day and telephoned Victoria telling her of what happened. 'Do be careful James,' she said, 'the more successful you are, the more desperate they'll become.'

12 - THE INVESTITURE

I received a note back from Jules some days later saying how sorry he was that I was not well and hoped that I was now better. He said that Madame Leclerc was most disappointed, and perhaps he would arrange another meeting in the future. *Over my dead body*, I thought,

Time went on, and autumn passed into winter and winter into spring. Now the bank was doing well and not a week went by without some investor or other asking for a meeting. I knew that we were hurting Byron's Bank and that fact made them more desperate to find out our investment strategy, the more they did so, the more mistakes they made until in 1911 they sacked Auchinleck, still they could not make headway against us.

It was with some surprise that John, Victoria, and I were summoned by the King to attend Cowes week on 21st July 1911. I was quite pleased with the invitation, as a keen sailor in my own time, sailing in the Caribbean, I also realised that I might meet people who could be important to the bank.

John was extremely pleased with the invitation, and although I felt he was holding something back, I happily went along as I had not had a break since the previous July in 1910.

I assumed that we would be staying at some hotel on the Isle of Wight, so I was surprised to find us heading out on a tender to the Kaiser's yacht Hohenzollern, moored just off Cowes. We were shown to our cabins, and I noticed that Victoria's cabin was separate from John's obviously at her insistence. We were due at a banquet that evening, and we went down for drinks beforehand. Winston Churchill, also a guest due to his recent appointment as First Lord of the Admiralty, made his way toward me. I tried to dodge meeting him, but it was apparent that he was intent on seeing me. I was with a group of people when Winston dragged me away into a corner of the huge cabin. He looked at me keenly, grinning, which I suppose was better than the last time we met. 'You will of course be aware that I have recently been appointed as the First Sea Lord?' he said.

I answered rather vaguely, 'I believe I read it somewhere, I must offer you my congratulations,' I smiled.

'Hmm, you'll have not forgotten that you forecast this over a year ago.' He growled, as only Churchill could.

I shrugged my shoulders, 'A lucky guess,' I answered.

Churchill shook his head, 'I don't believe in lucky guesses, there's more to you than meets the eye,' he was still staring at me as though trying to read my thoughts. 'Your startling success in the city is the talk of London, as you appear to be able to guess,' he laid emphasis on the word, 'which investment is going to go well, and which is not. To this end,' he said, 'I would be honoured for you to have lunch with me at the Admiralty, as there are many things, I would like to discuss with you.'

Of course, to have refused would not only have been churlish but bad-mannered too. I said I would be delighted to have lunch with the First Sea Lord, and the honour would be all mine, I said diplomatically, thinking that Churchill would probably forget the idea when he returned to London. The next statement surprised me. 'Next Wednesday at 12 then, I will inform the guard that you are to be brought directly to my office.' He smiled, grabbed my hand, shook it and was gone into the mass of people holding drinks.

I made my way to John and Victoria talking to some officials, I felt a little self-conscious as I hardly knew anyone, and I had a few looks from people present as though to say. Who are you?

John started to introduce me to various people who

suddenly took an extreme interest in who I was. I realised I was known by name far more than I thought, but of course few had met me. I found intense interest in my views for future investments, and I parried by saying that today was my day off, and I left my work behind. However, I received promises from various landed gentry that they would make appointments to come and see me.

I remember the banquet with a blur. Kaiser Wilhelm II gave a speech about close friendship with England, and George V responded in the same manner. Again, I found the food too much and too rich, and I was glad to reach my cabin after the meal. I was tempted to knock at Victoria's door but thought better of it.

The next morning after breakfast, when people were leaving the boat, John and Victoria held back, and I was somewhat surprised at this; shortly afterwards a very smart officer in the German Navy came and whispered in John's ear. 'Time to go, I think,' he said, 'just follow me.' I saw him walk towards one of the larger state cabins on the boat, he opened the door, and I was ushered in. I was amazed that several military men were present, and at the end of the room was the Kaiser with King George. A flunky then announced us, and I was asked to step forward to meet the Kaiser. He also stepped forward and suddenly produced a grand cross from a cushion held by an equerry and pinned it on my breast pocket. The Kaiser spoke. 'This is an honour I bestow upon you for a personal service to the crown of Germany and to me,' he said in excellent English. I suddenly saw Helmut in the background and realised what the honour was for.

I thanked the Kaiser and said I had no idea that this ceremony was to take place. He grinned, 'that was my idea,' he said. 'Thank you,' as he clicked his heels, I was then steered away by a British naval officer and presented to King George V. 'I also owe you a debt of gratitude,' he said,' this isn't the time or the place to show it, but I've not forgotten.' We talked for a few moments, and then I was led away back

163

to John and Victoria, I was handed a glass of champagne, and we all drank the health of the Kaiser and King George.

When I eventually got outside, I upbraided John and Victoria for not forewarning me, but they said they had been sworn to secrecy and congratulated me. I looked at the rather colourful cross pinned onto my coat and asked what it was. 'It's quite an honour, particularly for an Englishman, as it bestows on you a Baronetcy but because it's given for a personal favour to the Kaiser it ranks above other honours of the same rank,' said John.

THE KAISER WILHELM II

KAISER WILHELM II

We spent some days watching the racing, and we returned on the Monday 25th July, me to the bank, Victoria had decided to stay in London for the week and John went back to Crowley Hall as he appeared quite tired after all the proceedings.

I remembered that I was having lunch with Churchill

on 27th and I put it in my diary when I reached the office.

I travelled to the Admiralty by Hackney Carriage, and it took no longer than it would have done in 2010. *That's progress for you,* I thought.

I was met at the door by a commander in Navy uniform who had been instructed to show me around the Admiralty building, after that we went directly to Winston's office.

He greeted me affably enough and had a huge cigar sticking out of his mouth, which made me smile. He had arranged lunch at the House of Lords he said, and we walked the short distance over to the commons, crossing from the green carpet to the red.

We sat down and ordered. After the red wine came, Winston turned to me. 'Tell me, James, what sort of intelligence system do you have to enable you to forecast future events?' I was tempted to be flippant, but I thought better of it, as I felt he might take offence if I wetted my finger and held it up to the air.

'Well,' I started, 'I study history as you do and come to conclusions. I've no method, no secret organization, but you must know that I have an instinct if you like, and I can't say where that comes from.' I shrugged.

'So, what gives you the idea we will be at war with Germany in 1914?'

'The fact that Bismarck has created binding treaties that were right at the time for Germany, but he did that on the basis that he would be around to undo what he'd done if it became in Germany's interest to do so. As you know, Kaiser Wilhelm came on the scene and it's public knowledge that he's not the stable man his father was and by sacking Bismarck he's opened Germany up to extreme dangers.

'Let us just make some assumptions,' I continued. 'There are problems between Serbia, which is Slav and Austria Hungary, let's say that an important member of the house of Hanover travels to Sarajevo on an official visit. Let's say that someone shoots that personage visiting and he is killed by a Slav assassin, who would be blamed?'

Winston sucked on his cigar, 'Serbia?'

'Right,' I said, 'So Austria Hungary uses that as an excuse to move into Serbia... but Serbia have a treaty with Russia. Assume that Russia mobilises its forces, then what do Turkey and Germany do?'

'They support Austria Hungary.'

'Now, who does France have a treaty with?'

'Russia,' said Winston, suddenly starting to realise where this is going.

'Right, so we have Russia, Serbia, and France, possibly lining up against Italy, Turkey, Germany, and Austria Hungary. It may be that Italy would decide to change sides because their treaty gives them a let out, but that's not so important in this scenario.'

'Yes, but that supposition comes because of just one senior member of the House of Hanover being murdered by a Serb.'

'Or someone allied to the Serb cause such as a Bosnian,' I said.

'It's surely most unlikely that a country would go to war over one man, however senior,' said Winston.

'Yes, of course, you are right,' I replied, 'who kills who isn't important in the scale of things, the fact is that Austria is looking for an excuse to go into Serbia anyway, it's just a matter of time.'

'Hmm, well your logic is not altogether faulty, but I don't see where we come in?'

'What if Germany invades France?'

'We don't have a specific treaty with...'

'No First Sea Lord, we don't have a specific treaty with France, but what if Germany invades France through Belgium?'

'But why should Germany consider invading France through Belgium, instead of taking the shortest route through the east say, Alsace Lorraine?' Winston frowned.

'Put yourself in the shoes of a German General, where

would you create the most surprise if you were invading France?'

'Through Belgium a Neutral country of course,' Winston looked thoughtful, 'but why do you pick 1914?' he asked.

'Because if you are wise, you pick a time when you are strongest, to create a war, Austria Hungary won't be ready until 1914 either militarily or politically.'

'Your proposition has two weaknesses,' said Winston. One is that Austria Hungary would be mad enough to create a general war over Serbia, and Germany would be mad enough to invade a neutral country that had treaties with Great Britain.'

I grimaced, 'frankly even without Belgium, we could not allow France to fail on our doorstep; if we did, think about the situation where the Germans would have access to all the channel ports.'

'We have our navy, and you seem to have discounted that,' said Winston.

'Yes, we do, and it'll be able to defend Britain, but it isn't much good at fighting land armies.'

He was impressed and determined that he'd take up the point at the next military meeting. He did so, but he guessed correctly that he would be shouted down.

'So, do you have any thoughts for our future,' asked Winston as our food arrived. 'By the way, please call me Winston.'

'Thoughts for the future can be dangerous Winston, as if I told you certain things I believe will happen, even if I kept my criticism to mistakes you might make, it could change history, and may not be in the interests of our country. I will therefore make one more prediction for you, but don't press me any further. I believe there will come a time when a German corporal comes to be head of Germany, and he'll be extraordinarily evil. Watch out for him and never believe in his promises because they'll be false. Now let's move on to current affairs, shall we, how about the

Marlborough account?' I smiled.

We parted company as friends, Winston Churchill was no fool, and while part of him refused to accept what I had told him, there was a part him that accepted the possibility.

Just before parting, he told me that the Duke of Marlborough was having a shoot at Blenheim and if John and I would like to partake, he would see that we were invited. It would also be a way of being introduced to the duke, 'but I must warn you that both Arthur and Jules Byron have been invited too.'

I laughed, 'we don't object to competition, and therefore I'm sure we would both like to come if invited.'

Winston told me the shoot was the following weekend, and he would ensure we received an invitation.

Later in the week, John travelled up from Crowley Hall and came into my office telling me that he had received Churchill's invitation and he had agreed for both of us to go. He thought it would be easier for us to travel from London, so he was going to stay at his club until Friday when we could travel to Blenheim in the Rolls. The invitation included Victoria who would join the ladies, but they would not be shooting. 'I've taken the liberty of bringing both Purdie's up with me, I took the one I loaned you from the bedroom you used,' he said.

John also told me that he had arranged for the bank to lease me 1,000 acres of land near Crowley Hall, where he suggested I could build a house for myself. I started to think about the sort of house I would build and how much it would cost me.

He told me that there was already a house on the property, but I could pull it down or have it re furbished. I determined to go and look at it and see what would be involved.

13 - THE MURDER

We all met up at Langham's and Sydney arrived with the Rolls at around 2.30 p.m. on Friday. Sydney had packed our luggage, guns, and cartridges in the back of the car, and we set off towards Woodstock. It was a two-and-a-half-hour drive, and we arrived at the gates at 5 p.m. where livered attendants let us in. The Rolls swept up to the grand entrance to the building, with steps leading up between six columns. The baroque architecture is probably the finest of its kind in England and the gardens; designed by Capability Brown, were superb. We were greeted again by livered footmen, who escorted us to our three rooms in the East Wing. Beautifully furnished, the bedrooms were a delight as they had been recently modernised. When we had settled into our rooms, Victoria and I went for a walk in the gardens and enjoyed the well laid out paths. We started from the

Great Court entrance leaving the main lake to our left and headed for Vanbrugh's Grand Bridge, which we crossed, leaving the Queen Pool to our right. We passed the site of Woodstock Manor on the same side walking up to the column of Victory. From there we headed east around the main lake, crossing near the Grand Cascade and pump

house. We then continued via the Garden Lakeside, walking back around the east wing to the Great Court to see others arriving.

Going back to our respective rooms, we found the servants had unpacked our luggage for us, and hot water was already drawn in the baths. We were due down to dinner around 8 p.m., but Victoria and I went down earlier to look at some of the interiors, where everything was on a grand scale.

In the Grand Hall, there was a plan for the shoot. I noticed that John and I were being placed in a line about fifteen feet away from each other. My position was near the centre of our group, and I noticed that on my left was Arthur Byron and on my right John Crowley, Jules Byron was to the right of John.

The next morning the men assembled in the Grand Court area, and the open carriages were standing ready to take us to a farm nearby, to stand in front of a large area of woodland, from where the gamekeepers and the beaters would walk through to chase the pheasants out. As I passed the set-up board, something made me double-check to ensure I remembered my position correctly. When I looked,

170

I was surprised to see that Jules had been placed next to me on my right and John Crowley to his right. I wondered why a change had been made but assumed it was because he was left-handed and needed to be nearer the centre.

At 10 a.m., we were all in position, and at 10.15 a.m., the first pheasants started to appear, being immediately dispatched by the various people to my left. Gradually the number of pheasants increased until there were hundreds in the air at one time. I heard guns discharged all around me but something made me turn slightly to my right, at the same time I heard John shout 'JAMES,' because I half turned, I saw out of the corner of my eye that Jules' gun was pointing directly at me. I took a split second to react, and I did so by throwing myself backwards while allowing my knees to bend and felt the wind of the double bore shot as it whistled past the front of my head. I dropped my gun, and if Jules had reloaded, I doubt whether I could have responded. I heard a scream of pain from my left, and when I looked, Arthur Byron was down on all fours holding his head. He then slowly sank to the grass, dropping his gun as he did so.

John Crowley had run up to Jules and snatched his gun away from him. Jules realising where his shot had gone rushed over to his father and joined others who had dropped their guns to help the older man, who was laid on his back and his collar loosened, someone called for a stretcher and one of the shooters, a doctor, knelt by Arthur Byron's side. Then Arthur Byron opened his eyes and saw Jules. 'You bloody fool,' he said and slipped into unconsciousness. They were his last words.

Jules was beside himself, saying that it was a terrible accident. And the duke who was present said they would discuss the matter back at Blenheim.

The duke cancelled the shoot immediately, asking all those near Arthur Byron to meet in one of the dining rooms where he held a court of enquiry. The doctor and the chief gamekeeper were also present.

'Gentleman,' said the duke, 'I regret that we must

discuss this matter so soon after the terrible accident, but it's important to establish what everyone saw before memories start to fade. Mr Alexander, perhaps you would like to start?'

I told the story as I experienced it, including the warning from John, and said that I would have received the full blast from the shot if I hadn't fallen backwards.

'Are you saying that Jules Byron fired directly at you deliberately?' asked the duke.

'I can't say that' I replied, 'but his gun was certainly not pointing at the birds.'

The duke nodded and took evidence from the person on the other side of Arthur Byron. He only saw the man fall he said, but he heard the last words spoken, and it appeared that they were directed to Jules Byron.

The next man to give evidence was the doctor. He said that the wound was quite deep, surprising for a widespread shot at that range. He said that he believed Arthur Byron had died from shock rather than the wound, although he could have died from that before we got him to a hospital.

John Crowley was called next. John looked grim. 'There's no doubt in my mind what happened,' he said, 'I saw Jules Byron turn his gun directly at James Alexander and fire. Had I not issued a warning, and had not James acted immediately, we would be looking at his death and not that of Arthur Byron.'

Jules shouted 'it's a lie, I slipped, and the gun went off...'

The duke intervened, 'is that all John?'

'No, I've here some cartridges that Jules dropped, you'll see the size of the shot is large, used more for wild boar than for pheasants, he wasn't shooting pheasants he was out to kill James Alexander.'

'That's a grave accusation,' said the duke, 'may I look at the cartridges?'

John handed them over.

I then spoke out, 'there's one other thing I remember,

the set-up board was changed from early this morning to when we went out. On the first board, I had John on my right, but on the second board, Jules had replaced John.'

The duke turned to the gamekeeper, 'why was that done Gervis?'

'I can't say, sur, but Mr Alexander's right that was the original placing, someone must have moved it.'

At that moment Jules raced for the door and fled through it. By the time anyone could react, Jules was driving off in his father's Rolls.

The duke walked to the entrance, 'don't worry, he won't get far, I will inform the authorities accordingly, and they'll deal with the matter.' He turned to me 'I'm extremely sorry Mr Alexander, this has never happened before to us, and I hope to God it never happens again.'

At that moment Winston Churchill sidled up to me, 'didn't foresee that old man, did you?' he grinned.

I laughed, 'it just shows, nobody is infallible, besides, it wasn't in my history book.'

Victoria had been told of the accident and rushed outside to see me, 'Thank God you are safe,' she said.

'No, god had nothing to do with it, had it not been for John, I certainly wouldn't be here.' She turned to John, who was standing next to the duke. 'Thank you, John,' there were tears in her eyes. John nodded, 'you see, I'm still capable of looking after my assets,' we all laughed at that.

On Monday I was in my office at the bank when the Duke's secretary phoned me.

'I have been asked to inform you that the authorities went to the house of Mr Jules Byron this morning and he was found dead,'

'Dead,' I repeated, surprised at the news.

'Yes, the police found him hanging from his four-poster bed it appears to have been suicide.'

I thanked the secretary and put the phone down.

I felt strangely depressed that two lives had been lost due to pure greed. I felt no animosity towards Jules just sadness, particularly for his wife and six children. I suppose it was from that date I started to re-evaluate my life and what I was becoming.

1911 proved to be an excellent year for the bank and me personally. Byron's father and son deaths had created a vacuum in the banking system, and more and more of their clients were searching for a new investment banker, most came our way. By 1912 I had created a department of 30 people to enable us to handle the extra business.

I had placed the first stone on expanding the house on the leased land, and all the new area was at the rear and could not be seen from the front as that was covered in ivy. The whole of the interior was being ripped out and new floors put in. Electricity was one of the innovations, as was a pump for water. It wasn't to be a large mansion such as Crowley Hall. More a comfortable gentleman's residence with ten bedrooms, a study, drawing room, lounge, a sitting room that could double as a smoking room, a large dining room, kitchens, pleasant servant quarters behind the house and behind that the stables and outhouses. The building area in total was about 10,000 square feet, large but not huge. The house was to face south across the rolling countryside that I had had designed by the landscaper of the day. I used to travel over there once a week in my Rolls Royce 40-60 Tourer, the nearest I could buy that could in any way be called a sports car.

1913 brought more business and as often happened when everything goes well, the year sped by.

1914 saw Gerald, Penelope, and Priscilla Fortescue's marriages, hers to a poor but ambitious draper. He founded a large department store in York, but the marriage proved to be an unhappy one.

14-PETROGRAD

LORD STAMFORDHAM

During the week after the wedding, I received a call from the King's Private Secretary, Lord Stamfordham.

'Good morning, Alexander, I hope this call finds you well?'

'Yes, thank you, my Lord, what can I do for you?'

'Can you confirm you are on your own and no one can listen in to this conversation?'

'Yes, I'm in my own office now.'

I was puzzled at his questioning. *I remembered that he'd started his life as Arthur Bigge and had been ennobled in 1911 after being the private secretary to Queen Victoria, a post he took over from Sir Henry Ponsonby in 1895.* His northern voice brought me back to listen to what he was saying.

'The King has requested me to contact you regarding a personal matter, and asked if you could call on him at his residence at York Cottage at Sandringham House?'

I frowned, it was most unusual for the reigning monarch to invite someone to his home, and I wondered whether it was regarding the investments he'd made through the bank.

'Yes of course,' I answered, 'I assume it's something to do with his private investments.'

'No, Alexander, this is a matter of the utmost secrecy and sensitivity, and I would be obliged if you didn't tell anyone you are visiting the King.'

'I see, very well, when would his Majesty like me to call?'

'I've his diary in front of me, and he's at home tomorrow, but that may be too early for you, as I realise you are a busy man.'

'Sandringham is just north of Kings Lynn, and just short of the Wash?'

'Yes, but if you catch a train to Kings Lynn, the King's Chauffeur will meet you from the train rather than you having to drive up there. The King has suggested that you could stay the night; they've plenty of room.'

I'm sure he has was my thought. 'Very well, tomorrow it is, I will look up the train times and...'

'Oh, my dear fellow, no need to do that, I will organise everything for you here and we will deliver the tickets to the bank later this afternoon, and thank you, I know the King will be most grateful.'

The next morning, I walked up to Kings Cross and caught the train at 12.30. I bought a Times newspaper to read and noted the date. It was 12th of February 2014. It was extraordinary. Here we were speeding towards the bloodiest war in history, and the most interesting article in the paper was about laying the first stone for the Lincoln Memorial in the USA. There was also a piece about the threatened civil war in Ireland over home rule in Ulster. *Does nothing change, I wondered?*

I was thinking back to what else happened in the area the train was heading for, and I remembered reading an article in 2010 where the Kings Lynn line was the first to be successfully bombed by a German Zeppelin just after World War One was declared. Four people being killed. There was a large protest at the Germans bombing a civilian target. The Germans had retorted that the shore guns fired on their Zeppelin. Not surprising considering the Zeppelin was uninvited and carrying ordinance.

The train drew into the station, and as I had slept for the last hour, I looked at my timepiece. The journey only took two and a half hours despite stopping at various stations on the way up, probably not hugely different from the time taken in 2010 and arguably a lot more comfortable. I felt a little sleepy as I found the King's Chauffeur waiting for me on the platform. He immediately took the bag I had with me and appeared amazed that I had only brought one suitcase.

The drive in the Rolls Royce took only twenty minutes, and when we arrived, the butler met us at the main entrance of York Cottage.

It was not a cottage, the building from the front was equivalent to approximately six separate houses joined with a further six behind. Dwarfed by Sandringham house nearby, it was nevertheless large even by standards in 1914. As the butler bade me welcome another servant took my suitcase, I managed to see the part of the gardens with the lake in front of the house, and I could see why the King preferred to live there rather than his other palaces. It was a scene of complete serenity.

I was shown up to my room, and my suitcase was safely delivered soon afterwards. I had become used to the idea of someone unpacking and hanging my clothes, so I left them to it as the butler asked if I would like to join the King for tea in the study. I followed him down the sweeping staircase, and he led me to a large door in the middle of the house. He walked in, bowed, and announced, 'Mr James Alexander, sir.'

The King, who had been reading the Times, got up and smiled. He was wearing a beige smoking jacket that wouldn't have been out of place in 2010. He beckoned me to a large chair near a small table, and he sat opposite. 'It's good of you to give up your time, and I'm most grateful to you for coming up to see me so quickly.'

He offered me a cigarette, and I declined saying I didn't smoke.

The nonsensical tradition that you were not supposed to speak until spoken to was obviously a more modern rule. No doubt introduced by some senior highly paid Royal flunky, in a mistaken attempt to elevate their benefactor to a God-like figure. If it were in place in 1914, I wasn't aware of it, and wouldn't have followed it anyway.

I opened the conversation, 'I have to say that I can understand why you love this place, it's so relaxing, and the gardens I could see are magnificent.'

The King nodded, 'yes, we lived here when I was the Duke of York, you'll know of course that I wasn't brought up to be King. When my older brother died of pneumonia, I had no choice but to accept the reins of power, such as they are, so this place is my place of tranquillity,' he leant forward smiling, 'the place to which I can escape.'

Just then a maid brought in the tea along with home-made scones and fresh strawberry jam. 'I take it you drink tea, James, if I may be so bold as to call you by your first name.'

'Of course, your Majesty.'

Before leaving the servant poured the tea and offered me a scone, which I took, as I suddenly felt hungry.

'You are an interesting man, James, I am told you can foretell the future,' he looked at me quizzically in half amusement.

I smiled, 'people wonder how I'm able to predict certain things, but logic has a great deal to do with my predictions, plus of course keeping abreast of current world affairs.'

'Churchill tells me you've foreseen a great war on the horizon. Tell me, do you think Great Britain will be involved?'

'I'm afraid so, which is why I recommended to you that you shouldn't invest in Germany or Russia.'

'Yes, and I took your advice, I'm still not sure I was right to do so. I recognise there are problems between Austria and Serbia, but I can't see that being anything more than a minor political upset, the Austrians have a powerful army.'

'Well, sir, if I'm wrong, we will know by the first week of August of this year.'

'As soon as that?' He looked surprised.

'Yes, it'll be sudden I'm afraid, catching most of us and particularly the Cabinet off guard.'

'And you are saying that Germany will be implicated?'
'Yes.'

'I have to say that I've never been happy with Willie. He's a megalomaniac of the worst type. His understanding of the geopolitical situation is virtually zero, most of his advisers are military, so it's no surprise that he may well lead all of Europe into some form of conflict. Still, I can't see how that ties up with outright war, nor why Britain should be involved.'

I didn't answer.

The King continued, 'Nevertheless, this subject is interesting, because you are not the only one that sees into the future, and that leads me to why I've asked you to see me.'

'Oh.' I raised my eyebrows. I admit that what came next dumbfounded me.

'Have you heard of a man called Rasputin?'

'Grigori Yetimovich Rasputin the man who has some sort of hold over Princess Alix of Hesse Darmstadt,' I answered. 'He appears to be able to mitigate the alleged haemophilia suffered by her son Alexei Tsarevich. I understand it's because he can hypnotize the youngster, thus easing his condition.' *In 2010 I had read up on my Russian history when I had written a piece about it for a local newspaper that was producing an article about the Russian revolution. Recent medical investigations suggest he more probably suffered from aplastic anaemia, a severe condition caused by damage to the bone marrow but not necessarily inherited and more likely acquired due to hepatitis or other problems. I didn't mention this fact to the King because he would not have understood it anyway.*

Now it was the King who was surprised. 'you are exceptionally well-informed James; I thought his illness was supposed to be a secret.'

'Well, it's obvious what condition he has because his blood does not clot when he's cut or bruised. If it is haemophilia, it is usually handed down from the female line, and in fact, Queen Victoria was the carrier.'

'Good Lord, how do you know that?'

I shrugged, not wishing to pursue that side of the conversation, so I changed course.

'I know Rasputin isn't a particularly nice person and that the Russians are understandably concerned at the influence he has over their Royal family. He makes matters worse because of his questionable lifestyle. It's known that he drinks heavily, gambles and is known to frequent whores, not quite what one would expect of a monk.'

King George shook his head in disbelief and then smiled. 'Is there anything you don't know about, James?'

I did not mention that Rasputin was shot and killed by a British agent called Captain Oswald Rayner of the BMI a friend of Prince Felix Yusupov, accused of the act. The stories about him being difficult to kill were all made up.

I laughed, 'as I say I keep up to date on all current affairs, it's my job to do so to ensure I can advise my investors accordingly.'

The King exhaled the smoke he'd inhaled from the cigarette he had in his hand and leant forward. 'Well to the problem, the predicament is that Rasputin has frightened the Tsarina with talk of a future war that Russia will lose, and he's told her they will all be murdered. She's so affected by this story that the Tsar wrote to me to ask if they could send the Tsarevich and his elder sister Anastasia to England to be in our care until the situation is clearer. I have agreed, under certain conditions.

'As his first cousin, I have a responsibility and recognise that if things went terribly wrong for Russia over the next few years, then it may become politically difficult for us to get the Royal family out.

'I also have another reason for agreeing, and indeed this may be the real reason the Tsar has made this request; it will end the influence of this terrible man Rasputin, that's doing so much damage to the crown of Russia.

'Having said all that, I don't for a moment believe that Russia will fall or that there'll be a hugely damaging conflict, simply because it wouldn't be in the interests of any the countries involved.'

The King sat back in his chair, drawing on another cigarette he had just lighted, a sign of tension, I thought.

'You mention other conditions, what are they, sir?'

' In a situation where there's a collapse of Russia, the children would be brought up as any other English child, they wouldn't have a rank, and they would never be able to claim any privilege either from Russia or from England.'

'So, in that case, who would bring the children up?'

'Perhaps a member of the Ponsonby family, the mother was a Lady in Waiting to my grandmother. They're discreet and would educate the children from their home in France, but that's not fully decided yet.'

'So, they would lose all their titles and take on the name of the surrogate?'

'Yes, it is the only way we could arrange things. Otherwise, we would get heavily involved in Russian affairs, and that would not be in the interests of Great Britain.'

'I understand, sir, so what do you want of me, is it a question of money?'

'Good Lord no, James, I want you to fetch them from Petrograd. I trust you implicitly never to discuss this matter with anyone, and I feel the Tsarina would trust you with her children, as it will be a huge wrench for her. I would go myself if I could, but of course, that would be impossible, because of the current volatile political situation.'

I frowned, 'Of course, but why me, you must have many trusted people you could have called on?'

'I could not ask a Royal, I could not ask anyone from the military, I had to have someone both the Tsarina, and I trust, who better than the man with whom I place my money. Also, the one fly in the ointment, is Germany and to have someone who has a German Baronetcy given personally by the Kaiser must be helpful should you be stopped.'

Yes, I thought and someone expendable, but I answered, 'yes, I can't fault your logic, sir,' I smiled, 'I understand perfectly, and of course, I will do as you ask, but do you have a suggestion as to how I would get them out of Petrograd?'

'You could travel through France and Germany into Russia without any problem; indeed, the Kaiser thinks highly of you.'

I shook my head, 'it would be too public, and the Kaiser would wonder why I was going to Russia. It would also be impolite for me not to call on him should I go through Germany, and if I didn't, and he found out he'd feel slighted. If I was then to take the children back the same way, the Kaiser might find an excuse to hold them in

Germany.'

The King nodded, 'yes, you are right of course, the only other way is by sea.'

'I agree, but to start taking a Royal Navy ship through the Baltic at this time could create difficulties too.'

'Hmm, yes... I know, why not take my yacht?'

'You mean the Victoria and Albert, no sir that would also send the wrong message.'

'No, no, I was thinking of Britannia, I could lease it to you and make the public aware that I have done so. Thus, it would be up to you where you sailed it.'

'Isn't Britannia a racing yacht sir?'

'Yes, it is, but because of my official duties this year, I've just had it re-rigged as a cruiser, she's being put in the water in Cowes as we speak.'

I nodded; 'I seem to remember that Britannia is over 120 feet long so I would need a crew...'

'Absolutely, you could use my people, they're all Royal Navy of course, but I am sure we could persuade them to leave their uniforms in England. They would be discreet, although apart from the captain, they would not be aware of who your two young passengers would be.'

'That's fine sir, just one problem, how urgent is this matter?'

'It's not life-threatening, why do you ask?'

'Only that it's February now, the North Sea isn't particularly friendly at this time of year, and bearing in mind the frailty of one of the intended passengers, may I suggest we sail toward the end of May? In the meantime, I would like to meet the captain of the vessel to assess the crossings speed, and what we would need on board for such a trip.'

'The timing is eminently sensible, and I will let the Tsar know that you've kindly agreed to make the journey, I will ask the Captain of Britannia to contact you and arrange a visit.'

'Now that's settled, how about a stronger drink?' The King leaned across and pressed a bell near the fireplace.

I met the Queen at dinner that evening and was impressed not only by her intelligence but the evident love they had for each other. We discussed many things, and I found her very well informed and relatively modern in her thinking. The meal was tasty but quite ordinary fare. I think it was partridge shot on the estate. Afterwards, we had coffee in the drawing-room. I was surprised that the walls were covered in a light wallpaper quite different from the heavy drapes that typified Victoriana, the furniture was good quality, but not ostentatious. Family photographs adorned every surface, and there was a blazing fire that tended to have a soporific effect, on the King in particular. After about an hour he excused himself as he said he was tired after all the talking during the day, added no doubt to the several brandies he'd consumed.

The Queen, however, was wide awake. Once the King had left the room, she turned to me, 'Now Mr Alexander, what is all this nonsense I hear about you coming from the future?'

I laughed, 'I can't say that I've come from the future ma'am, only that I appear to remember being alive in 2010. Whether this is a fabrication of my mind, I've no idea, but certainly, things that happen in this time do appear to be coming true, I truly wish that this were not the case.'

She leaned forward, 'give me an instance of what is going to happen tomorrow.'

'I'm afraid it doesn't quite happen like that, think of a situation where you were thrown back into history by one hundred years, what would you remember?

'You would remember the big things that had happened to you in your old life, and you would remember the history you had been taught at school or you had picked up through reading. You wouldn't remember what your Queen did yesterday unless it created a huge story, and even then, you wouldn't remember it unless it influenced your life.'

'Yes, I see that,' she looked serious, no longer making fun of me, 'therefore do you know the next most important thing to happen that you do remember?'

I had drunk a few brandies, and I remembered the time I made a prediction when I met Churchill for the first time, so I was wary, and yet I had the feeling that whatever I told her would go no further.

'Yes, Archduke Franz Ferdinand and his wife will be murdered in Sarajevo on 28th June.'

Her face went white with shock, and she recoiled, perhaps thinking for a moment that it was something I had planned.

'Oh, how awful, was all she could say.'

'I'm afraid it is, as it'll start a huge war of European nations that'll cost millions of lives and bring down several monarchies, including Russian, German and Austrian.'

'So that dreadful man, Rasputin was correct?'

'Well, I'm not sure exactly what he said, but he certainly was right to warn the Tsarina.'

'You don't think he was from the future too?'

I laughed, 'I don't think so, although we do have a man called Putin who heads Russia, and he's reportedly not a very nice man either.'

'You are talking now as though you were back in, when it was, 2010?'

'Yes, I do slip up sometimes, because it's as real to me as is talking to you now.'

'What about the British monarchy...?'

I shook my head, 'it'll thrive, but in 2010 there's a Queen. She is head of state and will in a few years exceed the reign of Victoria.

'In 2010 the Empire will have gone. The cost to Britain for the war will be horrendous both financially and in the lives of our youth, everything will change but unfortunately, within thirty years from now another war, arguably caused by the one that's coming here soon, will decimate economies worldwide. Britain will lose its supremacy in the world to the

United States of America. But better that than to a dictatorship.'

'So, my poor husband will have a lot of problems to deal with in the future...'

'Yes, but I've already told you more than I should and...'

She held her hand up, 'you've been exceedingly kind, and I understand you must be tired, but one more thing and then I will let you get some rest. When will these horrendous affairs start?'

'Britain will declare war on Germany on 4th August this year.'

'Oh, my goodness, as soon as that, is there nothing we can do to stop these events happening?'

'Well, I suppose you can suggest to our security services the danger the Archduke and his wife face, but frankly, I don't think it'll change anything. He'll certainly go ahead with the visit, and even if he didn't the Austrian Empire are itching for a fight, they would find another excuse.'

The Queen nodded, 'I fear you are right, Mr Alexander, you must therefore try and save Alexei and Anastasia, but one thing puzzles me.'

I raised my eyebrows.

'If your mind is half in 2010, you must know from your history what happened to them.'

'I know what the history books say, but that doesn't necessarily mean that's what happened.'

She frowned; 'I don't understand.'

I took a deep breath; 'I will tell you what our history books say. That the Russian Royal family were captured and murdered by those who had taken over Russia, it was a people's revolt. However, when the graves were dug up in my time, they only found the bodies of the Tsar his wife and three of his daughters. There was then general consternation in Russia because if the heir to the throne was still alive or indeed, he had a family, under those circumstances, the Russian people may decide that they would prefer a monarchy based loosely on the United Kingdom. So, orders were given for the two children's bodies to be found, and hey presto they found them in another grave nearby. Russian scientists were brought in and confirmed that these bodies were, in fact, belonging to the two children, sine qua non. So, do we believe them?'

'You don't?' said the Queen hopefully.

'No, I don't, it seems odd that the Royal family were not all buried together, why would they have buried the two youngest children separately. It can't have been due to there being no room in the grave, so it tends to suggest that the children weren't there, but politically they had to be declared dead.'

'How horrific and yet you are right, which means that if you manage to save the children, they must never surface as members of the Russian Royal family.'

'Yes, that's correct, as the King has intimated, they would be brought up as English children and be sworn never to reveal their identity. The King realises the importance of that. Otherwise, it could create huge problems in the future.'

'You mentioned to my husband that the haemophilia that Alexei suffers from comes via Queen Victoria, but happily, our children appear to be safe.'

'Yes, haemophilia is a gene passed on via the female line, which is why Royals tend to suffer from the disease, it comes from intermarrying. The Jews were the first to discover this when they circumcised their male children to the extent that if the first two male children had died, they could forgo circumcision for any following children. In my day, there is a cure in the sense that haemophiliacs must take medication for the whole of their lives.'

The Queen rose to suggest the conversation was ended, she held her hand out, and I kissed it as was the protocol at the time.

'There's just one more question I would like you to answer, my husband... and my first son?'

187

I knew what she wanted to know, but I was firmly resolved not to tell her how long George would live.

'It would be unfair for me to go into detail, and I can never be sure that what happened in my time will necessarily happen in this time, but I would say this, Edward will only rule for a year but will never be crowned, it won't be illness or death that brings about his downfall. Your second son, the Duke of York will take over and rule successfully, and for the final question, your husband should give up smoking, goodnight, ma'am.'

She wanted to ask more but knew I would not give her what she wanted, so she gracefully thanked me as she left the room.

The next morning, I had an early breakfast on my own and left a note thanking the Royal couple for their hospitality. I wondered afterwards if I had said too much, but I believe that our conversation that night was never revealed even to the King. I received a note from the Queen after the murder of the Archduke and his wife in Sarajevo. It said:

Dear Alexander, I am forever in your debt for the information you gave me, it has prepared me for the worst that will enable me to support the King through what is going to be a challenging period.

Soon afterwards, I had a call from a Captain Smith-Jones of the Royal Navy. He referred to my conversation with the King and asked if he could see me. I agreed that we should meet the next day, but because of the subject, I felt it was better that we should meet in the privacy of my office rather than over lunch.

Captain Smith-Jones was a man of about forty, straight as a ramrod but with a pleasant sense of humour. He wasn't a tall man, I would say about five foot eight, but he was well dressed and sported a tan that he certainly hadn't picked up in Britain. He was one of those men that appeared to have no grey hair whatsoever and he'd a quiet way with him, precisely the sort of man you'd be able to rely on in a difficult situation.

As he'd travelled around the world, he had some good stories to tell, and he was interested in my travels to Africa, the West Indies, and the USA.

After we were served with coffee from the Bank's new canteen, he got down to the business he'd come to discuss.

'The King has explained what he wants, and you and I are to be the only ones to know the real identity of the children we are to pick up. I've hand-picked the crew of twelve men who will be sailing Britannia, I've also arranged for a distant relative of mine, who is a nurse, to accompany us. I feel that the young man may need medical attention on the trip. She will also have to be a party to the secret.'

'That's fine,' I said, 'did the King mention to you the approximate date when we should sail?'

'Yes, he said that you'd suggested the end of May, and I agree that we would have the best weather conditions in the North Sea, which can be brutal at times.'

I nodded, 'yes, the last thing we need is for the young man to be thrown around in rough weather.'

'Actually, that's an excellent point,' said Smith-Jones, 'I will organise some thick padding for his berth, so in case of a rough sea he can be strapped in.'

'How long do you think the trip will take?' I asked.

'Well, as you know the Britannia is a gaff-rigged sail ship originally designed specifically for racing, she's been re-rigged as a cruiser, which is safer for a long sea voyage. Nevertheless, she's still a fast vessel, and I hope to maintain around fourteen knots, that's sixteen miles an hour. We're looking at about 1,864 miles give or take, starting from Cowes, and assuming we can maintain say fourteen knots. It'll take us five days at best, probably six to seven days if we hit the wrong wind. Have you sailed before Mr Alexander?'

'Please call me James,' I said, 'yes, as a matter of fact, I've spent two years sailing the whole of the Caribbean, but that was in a Bermuda rigged vessel and about half the size of Britannia.'

'Ah it's good you are used to the sea, I will be extremely interested to hear more of your experience there, as I would very much like to do something similar when I retire. My first name is Evan by the way it comes from my Welsh heritage. It's the same as the Scottish Ian or English John.

'The Bermudan rig is faster to wind than a gaff-rigged boat, but on a long voyage, the latter would be faster due to the sail area. Of course, you need a larger crew to handle the sails, but twelve will be fine considering were going non-stop to Petrograd.'

'Do you see any problems on the way?'

Evan grimaced, 'I hear the Germans are very suspicious of private boats sailing in the Baltic and are illegally stopping and searching vessels despite the area being in international waters. The Foreign Office has complained about it, of course, but it doesn't appear to have made much difference.'

'Hmm, that may be a problem, there's little they can do to stop us going to Petrograd but returning with our young passengers it could be disastrous, particularly if we are stopped by the same German boat or ship.'

'I agree, but we could argue that they belong to the nurse and that we had picked them up from a holiday in Petrograd.'

'That's if we can carry this off without their spies in Petrograd learning of the abduction, I will give this some thought,' I said.

'There's another way,' said Evan, 'but it's top-secret so I would have to get permission to discuss it with you.'

'You mean by submarine?

Evan Smith-Jones was surprised at that revelation. 'How do you know that? Even the King hasn't been apprised of our submarines slipping into the Baltic.'

I laughed, 'I had no idea that our submarines were in

the Baltic, but, logically, they would be.'

It was a week later when I travelled down to Cowes to view the yacht. It had been cleaned and refurbished and was back in the water, as the King indicated. I was immediately taken with her, and just as I was studying the boat's lines, I felt a tap on my shoulder, it was Evan Smith-Jones. 'She's a beauty isn't she; would you like to go aboard?'

'I would indeed, is there a dinghy...?'

'Oh, my dear chap, we have a launch just over there,' he pointed at two sailors manning quite a large tender. We walked over, and Evan introduced me to the two men, both of whom were to help sail the yacht. I climbed in, and we were quickly transported to the vessel. As we approached, I imagined her in full sail, what a magnificent sight that would be. The steps up onto the deck were clearly made for older visitors, not at all like the boat steps I had been used to in the Caribbean that were simply metal attachments slung over the side.

I stood on the deck and inspected the beautiful, planked woodwork that ran the full length. I noticed that the mainmast was well forward, about two thirds from the aft of the vessel. The boom ran back to the stern, suggesting a large sail indeed although being gaff-rigged it wouldn't, of course, reach the top of the mainmast as a Bermuda rig would. Nevertheless, the sail would still be large. Evan led the way down to the cabins. The doors were polished mahogany, and the broad steps were located about thirty feet from aft. Once inside, Evan showed me the lady's cabin that we had just walked over. It took up the whole width of the interior aft. It had two double beds, one each side with a large sunken bath in the centre. I followed Evan and inspected the first cabin on the port side that again had a double berth with its own bathroom (called head in boat terms), I assumed correctly that it was the captain's cabin. There was a small cabin on the starboard side with a single berth and head and then the King's cabin that was about the same size as the ladies' cabin but with only one double berth, the head sporting a stand-alone bath. Coming out of there, one entered the salon, a large area with luxurious seats adjoining all sides. This was an area where people congregated after the sail and ate or where drinks were served. It included a small galley at the far end that incorporated a bar area. Going further forward there was another large cabin on the starboard side with a double berth and opposite, two smaller single cabins both with their own heads. Finally, in the forward part of the boat were five single berths. I assumed there were showers and heads, but I didn't see them. In this area were also replacement sails and there was a hatch above this area to enable the crew to get on deck without disturbing the other inhabitants aft.

It appeared that twelve people could live exceptionally comfortably on this yacht for a period. The interior was mahogany and all highly polished. It was a beautiful environment, and I fully understood why George loved the craft and the selfless way in which he'd loaned it to me to save at least the younger members of his family.

When we had finished the inspection, I turned to Evan and told him I would dearly love to buy such a boat.

Ah, I think you'll have the wait for the King to die, he will never part with her. *I happened to know he was right, upon his death in 1936, he left an instruction the yacht should be taken out to sea and sunk, and so it was.*

'Well, I'm certainly looking forward to sailing in her.'

'Me too, especially so soon after her refit, now let me buy you lunch at the clubhouse.'

Despite my experience sailing yachts in my previous existence, I had always wondered why one referred to the right and left of a boat or ship as starboard and port. I asked Evan if he knew the history behind the terms.

He smiled, 'Port and starboard are nautical terms for right and left, and they never change as they are unambiguous references that are intendant of a mariner's orientation. They use these nautical terms to avoid confusion. When looking forward, toward the ship's bow, port and starboard refer to the left and right sides, respectively.

'In the early days of the Vikings, before ships had rudders on their centre-lines, seagoing vessels were controlled using a steering oar. Most sailors were right-handed, so the steering oar was placed over or through the stern's right side. There may have been another reason for this, to prevent the rudder from being damaged when in its berth. So, they always manoeuvred the boat's left side against the quay. The Anglo-Saxon word for starboard was steorbord, which means the side on which a vessel is steered and bæcbord. This was referencing that on larger boats, the helmsman would often have to hold the steering oar with both hands, so his back would be to the ship's left side.

'After bæcbord came laddebord-laden meaning to load and board meaning ship's side, referencing the side of the ship where loading and unloading was done. This gave rise to larboard in the 16th century, rhyming with starboard, and again just meaning the side of the ship that usually faced the dock or shore. (Of course, most ships had central rudders by this time, so it was just a way of naming the side of the vessel from standing at the wheel.)

'Presumably, the fact that port and larboard first popped up around the 16th century is no coincidence. Once laddebord was slurred down to larboard, to rhyme with starboard, there was a problem with the words sounding so similar. There was now a good chance of people mishearing which direction was given, particularly in stormy settings or in a battle or the like. As such, around the early to mid-19th century, port popularly replaced larboard for this reason. At first many just made the switch on their own, but by 1844 the change from larboard to port was made official in the British navy and two years later in the U.S. Navy and has pretty much become ubiquitous since.'

I gave some thought to our forthcoming trip and decided that to ensure its success. I would need the King to produce some documents for us to carry with us. *Passports weren't yet available. It wasn't until November 1914 that the Nationality and Status Aliens Act 1914 produced a passport. It consisted of a single page, folded into eight and held together with a cardboard cover. It was valid for two years and included a photograph and signature, featuring a personal description, including details such as shape of face, complexion, and features. The entry on this last category might read something like: Forehead: broad. Nose: large. Eyes: small. Not surprisingly, some travellers found this dehumanising.* However, this wasn't available before World War 1, so I asked Evan to see my plan and together decide what sort of document we would need. My original suggestion was to produce one set indicating that I had permission to use the Britannia for my purposes. The second document would show my honour given by the Kaiser. The third suggests that Mr James and Mrs Alexander were travelling to Petrograd to collect their two children who have been on holiday with a distant relation. If stopped by a German naval ship, the German honours reference would undoubtedly carry some influence.

When he called at my office, he read my dissertation.

'I'm not sure about mentioning the German honour, as it wouldn't cut much ice with the Russians, in fact, quite the reverse.'

'Do you think we would be stopped by the Russians?'

'It's possible, they're as paranoid as the Germans. On the other hand, you will be the guests of the Romanovs so should be treated as such, but they may want to make sure that we're not a band of assassins. I agree that you set yourself up as a married man. The nurse relative I mentioned to you would almost certainly go along with that, as she's a little younger than you so it wouldn't look in any way odd, and she's certainly old enough have had two children because she does have two children,' he smiled.

'I think we should ask the King to contact the Romanovs to indicate that you'd be arriving by George Vs yacht for a private visit. This should ease the way for us to sail up the river Bolshaya Neva so we could tie up right in front of the Winter Palace. It'll be safer to get a tow before we get to the river in case the wind is in the wrong direction.'

'So, do we need two separate letters from the King?'

'No, what I suggest is that the King simply appoints you as his emissary and the document shouldn't mention your German honour, simply take that with you to produce if the Germans board us.'

I nodded, 'in that case, if we have the children on board, we would not be stopped by the Russian naval forces?'

'Correct, the problem would come if we were stopped

GREAT BRITAIN TO SAINT PETERSBURGH

by the Germans on the way back, particularly if it were the same German ship that stopped us going out.'

'I'm beginning to think that it would be preferable to arrange for us to meet a submarine once out of the Gulf of Finland, around say the uninhabited island of Gotska Sandon, just north of the island of Gotland. I realise there could be problems from depth charges...'

'From what?' Asked Evan.

'Depth charges, you know a specially designed bomb thrown over the side...'

Evan looked at me blankly and shook his head. 'There's been some talk about such things, and they may be in an experimental stage,' he said cautiously. 'I assure you nothing like that exists, apart from ramming or firing at a submarine when on the surface, we don't have an ordinance that can threaten a submarine once it is submerged. The biggest problem we would have is from mines, and in a restricted space such as the channel between Sweden and Denmark, mines are hazardous to a submerged craft.'

'Yes, I hadn't thought of that,' I said, 'and I suppose modern submarines can't stay submerged for too long either?'

'Correct,' answered Evan, 'it depends on the speed, but not more than a few hours, the area inside one is extremely cramped, not a good environment for a future King, or Tsar,' he corrected himself.

'Hmm, so the King's yacht would be the safest bet?'

'Yes, we will just have to bluff our way through.'

King George duly provided the documentation we requested, and his Equerry delivered them in person to my office. He told me that a personal letter was contained in the sealed envelope that I should read and destroy before taking the trip. I read it after the Equerry had gone and it merely explained that he'd been in touch with the Tsar and his naval forces had been instructed to look out for us during the first week in June, which meant the Russians would not board us.

During May 1914, I handed the reigns over to Gerald Phipps saying I was going on a continental trip to assess the channel's situation. The only person who knew the truth was Victoria. 'Oh, do be careful, James, that part of the world is dangerous.'

'Yes, my darling, I know the risks we're running, but we've assessed them very carefully, and with god's help we'll be back within two weeks safe and sound. I could not deny the King's request anyway, not that I would have wanted to.'

Victoria sighed, 'I know, I'm just afraid of losing you, oh, and the woman you are temporally married to I trust it will be a platonic affair.'

I laughed, 'that I can promise you. I will bring you back

a Russian present, perhaps a Russian doll.'

Victoria shrugged, 'actually I would prefer an egg.'

'Okay, I will see if I can find a chicken...'

'If it's a Faberge chicken,' she smiled, and I received a hug.

I reported to the yacht the next day, and Evan told me that they had readied the King's cabin for me. The Ladies cabin was given to Alice Waterford, the nurse who had agreed to sail with us. Alice was an attractive woman whose husband had been killed during the Boer War in 1901, leaving her with two young children. I soon found out that she and Evan were much closer than he had indicated, not that it mattered, if she could do the job. Alice was independently wealthy as were many that took up the nursing profession in those days. She was also highly educated, which made the sail much more interesting as she was well travelled, particularly in southern Africa so that we could swap stories.

One morning, I noticed her exiting from Evan's cabin looking embarrassed that I had seen her.

Evan told me that he'd decided to take only ten crewmen, all Royal Navy but without any sign of uniforms. Although we were travelling non-stop, which meant night sailing he thought it would be a little too crowded on the return trip. I insisted that I did my turn on the helm, usually a four-hour shift.

On Saturday we spent time purchasing stores for the trip and stowing them in various receptacles under seats and cupboards in the galley.

We set off at 08:00 hours on Sunday 31st May. The weather was fair with a south-westerly. We expected some rain, and although there was plenty of foul weather gear on board, the rain wasn't heavy enough to use it. We crept slowly out of the Solent before the full sails were hoisted. The yacht was like a racehorse, she took off, she was beautiful to handle, and one could feel the power as she almost glided through the water. I was at the helm when we hit the narrowest part of the channel, passing Dover to our port side. When I finished my shift, we were leaving the English Channel and heading for the North Sea.

The weather freshened, and the expert crew reduced the sail area, we stayed on a north-easterly tack for the next six hours, but then the wind changed to north-easterly. We spent an uncomfortable period sailing close to the wind until it changed again to a westerly, which brought torrential rain. By the late evening, it became apparent that we were approaching storm conditions, so we battened down anything that moved below. Alice was decidedly queasy, so she missed her dinner, returning to the Queens quarters. By 20.00 hours we were well into the North Sea and were struggling against gale-force winds that reduced our speed to around 10 knots, so much for the weather forecast, I thought. The next morning the wind had abated, and as we cleared the Netherlands, Evan changed course towards the south of Denmark but keeping well clear of the German coast. As we neared the Danish shore the wind changed again, now becoming north-easterly, but we were able to tack almost due north by this time, and with the protection of the lee of the Danish land mass our speed increased to

THE ROYAL YACHT BRITTANIA

over 17 knots. I had gone to my cabin at around midnight on Monday evening, having had little sleep the previous night and despite the still choppy seas, I slept soundly, not appearing until 08.00 on Tuesday 2ⁿᵈ June. We made excellent progress entering the Skagerrak, the sea between Demark and Norway, at around midday and turning sharply to starboard around Skagen Head at about 14.00. Our course was now south-east passing the Coast of Byrum Island to starboard, and then the smaller island Kattegat to port, heading south-east for the narrow channel between Copenhagen and Sweden at 18.00. Evan was pleased that we had cleared the narrow channel in daylight. However, because the shipping in the area was quite heavy, it took us three hours to pass the peninsula west of Trelleborg in Sweden. We were now entering the Baltic Sea, and we altered course. Unfortunately, the wind was directly from the east so we had to tack south-east which meant that it would take us nearer to the German coast than we had planned, so instead of sailing north of the island of Bornholm, which lies south of Sweden we were headed south leaving the island to port. This gave us a fair wind, but we were now about four miles from the north German shore, and before we entered the three-mile limit we changed course again to the north-east which would, with small adjustments and assuming the wind remained constant, get

us up to the Gulf of Finland, when we would again change

course almost due east for Petrograd

I knew that not all nations followed the three-mile law. The cannon shot law meant the boundary was the distance of the average cannon shot. It was not until 1989 that proper limits were agreed, but there were still a few disputes. Germany at that time ignored any convention but did appear to stay clear of Swedish waters.

When Evan woke me. 'we have problems,' he said, 'there's a German destroyer that's been following us since about 04.00, and now they've signalled for us to hove to, what do you advise?'

'We do what they ask,' I answered, 'there's no way we would outrun a destroyer, and we've nothing on board that could in any way be termed contraband.' I shrugged, 'we can, however protest, as we're arguably in international waters, not that it'll do us much good to do so.'

'Yes, I agree', answered Evan, 'but let's not give up quite so easily,' he grinned.

'He signalled back that the yacht was in international waters flying a British flag and should be allowed to proceed unhindered.'

The next minute a shell whizzed over the yacht landing some 50 metres in front of the bow.

'Not a bad shot,' Evan exclaimed, 'assuming it was sent as a warning.'

He ordered the sails to be dropped, and we could see several sailors climbing into a tender, which headed toward us. Britannia was now wallowing in a lumpy sea. Ten minutes later, they were alongside. They were all armed and looked extremely unfriendly. The boarding party consisted of ten sailors and one Lieutenant. Once they were on deck, the Lieutenant asked who the captain was, and Evan stepped forward. 'Your papers please,' he said in perfect English. I stepped in front of Evan. 'I'm in charge of this yacht Lieutenant, your boarding of the King's yacht is a gross insult to Great Britain, and your actions will be reported as soon as I return.' I put on a stern face glowering at the officer in front of me.

'I'm simply obeying orders...' *Some things in Germany haven't changed I thought.*

'Is that so,' I said, 'and are your orders to board a yacht belonging to his majesty the King of Great Britain and, I added, to insult the holder of the German Grand Cross invested in me by the Kaiser himself?' I presented him with the leather-covered box that contained the cross. 'My name is James Alexander look at the rear of the cross.' He did so, and went pale, as his men had already started to search the yacht. There was an extraordinary change in the man's demeanour; he stood to attention and saluted clicking his heels as he did so.

'My sincere apologies, Baron, we didn't realise that such an important personage was on board, I will let my Captain know immediately.' He curtly told the seamen to stop the search, and they all left the yacht in quick time.

I said to Evan afterwards, 'they were quite happy to search the King's yacht, but once they knew there was a German Baron who held the Grand Cross on board, they immediately gave up, how strange.' As I spoke, there was a signal from the Destroyer wishing us god's speed. It turned away, looking for easier prey. It had been an interesting experience and an insight into the German military mind at that stage of the early twentieth century.

Evan nodded, 'it's typical, the autocracy in Germany is paramount, and the fear of insulting someone who had received a high personal honour from the Kaiser would be considered an offence against the Kaiser himself, not something a military officer could countenance.'

The sails were hoisted, and the loss of time was only about two hours. On the current wind, Evan reckoned we would reach the Gulf of Finland at about 05.00 the next morning, 'which means, we should reach Petrograd by about 21.00,' he said, 'not bad for a sailing yacht.'

I agreed and wondered how long it would have taken a cruising yacht in 2010, about the same, I thought.

When we reached the mouth of the Gulf of Finland, we were met by a Russian destroyer which signalled to us that they were instructed to escort us to Petrograd. There was no question of anyone boarding us. We had to tack several times because of the changeable winds due to the landmass on either side, and we arrived there just after midnight, later than planned. As we reached the harbour area, we reduced sail just as a small launch came alongside and asked for our sails to be dropped as they would tow us to a berth opposite the Winter Palace. It was after 02:00 before we got any sleep that night, it felt strange sleeping without the steady rocking we had all got used to feeling.

The next morning, we rose about 06.00 and were surprised to see two guards outside on the land. At 09:30 a carriage, pulled by four horses arrived and what appeared to be the Tsar's Equerry, (*Konyushy in Russian, translated it means Master of the Horse*). I was invited to travel in the carriage and took Alice with me. The view of the Winter Palace was quite breath-taking, being set in white and green. The main building on its own was huge, certainly considerably more extensive than Buckingham Palace, but the two wings either side were almost as big again. The carriage drove through the centre gilded gate into the interior, where I learned the Tsar and his family had their

WINTER PALACE - SAINT PETERSBURGH

apartments. A senior officer of the guard met us, but

THE TSAR & TSARINA

who I'm sure checked us for any concealed weapons, not by searching but by scrutiny while remaining courteous and pleasant. At 11:00, we were granted an audience by the Tsar and the Tsarina, who looked extremely pensive. Alice was whisked away with her to meet the children.

The furnishings were extraordinarily luxurious, and everything appeared to be gilded, the walls, the furniture, which was certainly French, and carpets Persian. Around the walls were pictures of previous Tsars and Tsarinas and a massive picture of the Summer Palace. It was difficult to understand how they could live in such splendour when most of their countrymen found it hard to earn enough to eat.

The Tsar himself could have been taken as a twin brother of George V, but his eyes protruded, and I recognised this, as it was well known that both he and the Tsarina were avid takers of cocaine and a concoction of other drugs.

I commented on the similarity to his cousin.

'It's true,' he answered in perfect English, 'except that he's a little portlier than me,' he laughed.

I recognised the fact that George was of a heavier build, but the facial likeness was there.

After being presented to the Tsarina; Alix of Hesse as she was known before her marriage, she excused herself, as she wanted to spend time with Alice and the children.

The Tsar took me to a room that he used as an office, and we talked for several hours about the current situation in the world and many other things.

'You are very well-informed, James,' he called me by my first name; 'I've heard that you can see into the future?'

'Ah, that's not quite true,' I said, 'I appear to have the knack of being right about things that are about to happen, but of course like anyone else, I can't be sure.'

He nodded, 'the world situation is very grave, and I regret that war is getting closer. It's those damned Austrians and my cousin Willie who thinks he has the finest military in the world that is causing the upset to the geopolitical situation. Of course, the Russian Army is huge, and his little force will be crushed if he uses it against Russia.'

I stayed silent.

'Gregori Rasputin has frightened the Tsarina into believing our younger children aren't safe in the present situation, you know that my son, the heir to the throne has a health problem?'

'Yes, he is reputed to have haemophilia,' I answered, 'but that's not a fatal disease providing he's careful with his movements.'

'Hmm, difficult for a young boy, he's prevented from the normal thing's youngsters do, which makes the Tsarina unhappy for him.'

RASPUTIN

'Well, you'll know that Prince Leopold, Queen

Victoria's younger son has the same affliction, and he manages with it quite well.' *I didn't tell him that he died at the age of thirty due to falling on the stairs.*

'Do you think we're doing the right thing sending our younger children to England? I want a frank answer.'

I nodded, 'yes, sir, I do, they'll be safe there, whatever happens in Europe, and your son's condition will have the best doctors in the world, there's already some revolutionary medicine being tested in the USA, which may help.'

'Well, the decision is made; the Tsarina is reconciled to the fact, and I trust my cousin above all others to do the right thing. I'm grateful to you for making this dangerous journey, and I would like to give you something that indicates our gratitude for what you are doing for Russia.' He stood up and walked over to his desk and took a medal out of a blue box.

'It's the wish of the Tsarina and me to bestow on you the order of Vladimir, it's our highest order for a civilian.' He pinned it on my chest.

It came as a complete surprise; I admit I was deeply touched and thanked him for such generosity. We drank an excellent brandy to celebrate, and I was shortly escorted away by the Equerry to meet the Tsarina with the children. The Tsar had a prior meeting with his military chiefs. I felt she was a sad person and torn at the idea of letting her two young children be taken, but she was strong enough to go through with her original decision.

We dined at the Palace that night, and at just after 21:00 hours we were taken by the Equerry to a carriage with windows completely blacked out. I was in the carriage first, and Alice came in with the two completely unrecognisable children, they were dressed in large overcoats with hoods that helped cover their faces. Alice told me that the Tsarina was inconsolable at the loss of her children on the short drive to the yacht, but her belief that it would save their lives was firm.

The Equerry travelled with us. When we reached the yacht, he climbed out and dismissed the soldiers. When they had returned to the Palace, we could disembark and get the children out of the cold into the cabins. We decided that both should sleep in the second bed in the Ladies cabin with Alice so that she could keep an eye on them.

Evan had decided to sail immediately the children were on board and had agreed with a Russian Admiral that we would be escorted by a Russian warship as far as the island of Bornholm. A Russian navy launch again towed us, but this time through the north entrance via the River Malaya Neva past some huge fortifications at the entrance. Once in the Gulf, we were released and joined by the naval destroyer.

The sails were raised, and because of the wind, Evan told me we could take a more northerly course this time leaving the island of Bornholm on our port side, thus not sailing anywhere near the German coast. We made particularly good time as the wind continued blowing from the north-east, which allowed us to sail quite close to the Swedish coast. As we reached the north end of Bornholm, the Russian ship signalled that it was returning and wished us good luck for the return journey.

We allowed the children to come up on deck once the Russian ship had disappeared, but when we were approaching Copenhagen, we sent them below, but only for the period when we were passing the narrowest part of the channel. Anastasia told me neither of them had been to sea before, despite Alexei being brought up wearing a sailor's uniform. It was as if a new world was opening before them. I hadn't realised just what a restricted life they had lived in the cocoon-like environment within the royal palaces.

From there we made good time through the Skagerrak

and the North Sea that had calmed somewhat since our trip north several days before.

Two days later, we arrived just off the east coast of Great Britain at about 03:00 hours where we were met by a Royal navy launch that escorted us into the mouth of the River Great Ouse. We dropped sails just before leaving the Wash, and the navy launch towed us to a point about one and a half miles in towards Kings Lynn where there was a small jetty next to an isolated country road. It was there that Alice disembarked with the children. They climbed into a carriage that had been standing by for over twenty-four hours. I understand it transported them to York House on the Sandringham Estate.

Fortunately, the sea had been kind to us, so our concerns about Alexei being thrown about in rough weather never materialised. At 05.00 hours just before dawn, we were towed back to the Wash where we put up the sails and headed south for the Channel and Cowes where we arrived later that afternoon.

After thanking the crew and Evan in particular, I drove my car back to London, where I stayed the night at my club. The next morning, I met Victoria and was extremely glad to see her, promising to take her out for dinner that night to tell her the story of my adventure. I told her that I could not find a suitable egg for her but gave her the medal bestowed on me by the Tsar.

About two weeks later, the King's Equerry came to see me and give me a sealed letter. The Equerry was insistent that I should destroy it after reading it. I did so in front of him.

Dear Alexander,

Thank you for the journey you took on my behalf. We returned Alice to her home after she'd left the children with us. They are now safe with someone in whom we have absolute trust and who will bring them up as normal children. Of course, Anastasia at fourteen and Alexei eleven will have to learn that their background must be secret. Unless they eventually return to their family in Russia, they will be forever lost to their heritage. You will be interested to know that we have renamed them as Alexander and Anne; we thought you'd be pleased with Alexei's new name.

It was signed *George Rex.*

The Equerry told me that they had received reports from Germany that the Kaiser was advised of the King's yacht being sailed through the Baltic and he had ordered that we should be stopped and searched on our return. Whether this was due to information received from spies in Petrograd or simply that the Kaiser was suspicious of us being in the Baltic, I will never know. It was fortunate that the wind enabled us to steer clear of the German coast.

Discussing the situation with Victoria the evening after receiving the letter, I told her that although there were a few women who claimed to be Anastasia, none were accepted and all subsequently disproved due to DNA testing. *I've often wondered since, what became of the two young children, as their secret has never been revealed. I assumed that their education must have been by tutors, but that wasn't unusual for the time. In 2010 they would have been 101 and 98 respectively, so I suspect they took their secrets to the grave.*

I was also involved with another situation at the request of the King, but this time it didn't have a particularly happy ending. Prince Edward had an assignation with a beautiful French woman, which caused the Royals some embarrassment. I was asked to persuade the prince to return to England, and he did so with some reluctance. I always felt he'd have been far better with her than with his future wife, Mrs Simpson. After that, I got the impression that I wasn't one of his most favourite people.

The bank was approached at the end of 1914 by a

wealthy builder to develop a complex in south London. The scheme appeared to be a good one financially, but subsequently, I was horrified to learn that he'd bought the homes on the ground for a pittance and had ruthlessly evicted poor people from them, some families had lived in them for generations. I was appalled, but it was too late for the bank to pull out, so using my own money I bought a large piece of land nearby and created small modern houses that could be rented at affordable rents. I was an admirer of George Peabody, an American philanthropist now long dead, who did much the same thing in the middle of the nineteenth century. I ensured that all those displaced were offered a good home and instructed that any future developments consider the social aspect.

It was in June 1914 that I was summoned to the palace to receive a knighthood. The honour wasn't for my contribution to banking or my recommendation to cancel the Edward debt, but for my charitable works, which pleased me immensely. However, I realised that I was one of the few that had earned my knighthood, and I became critical of the extensive corruption in current society and the treatment of those not born to privilege.

My relationship with Victoria strengthened if anything. We rarely missed a weekend of being together, although we could never appear as a couple in public, which probably hurt her more than me. John had stopped coming to the bank altogether now, and in his way, he was happy on the estate, but although the symptoms of his illness slowed due to less stress, it was slowly but surely killing him. I was pleased, however, that he and Victoria had become firm friends.

My house was to be finished by the end of the year, and I was pleased with the progress but not realising the effect the forthcoming war would have on skilled labour.

The war started at the beginning of August, and there was what I would call war fever in Britain as almost all young men were desperate to show their wives and families that they were true patriots. The thought of the excitement and glory pulled thousands of young men into the slaughter.

When I reached my office one morning, I received a handwritten note from Winston Churchill with an Admiralty seal on the envelope. I opened it and read the contents.

Dear James,

Damn you for being right. If it is as bad as you forecast, and you have always been right up to now, I fear for the British Empire and those thousands of young men who will perish in the mud. If only I could have stopped it.
I am looking out for the corporal!
Yours
Winston

Gerald came into my office the same morning and said he was joining the colours. I immediately asked him to bring Penelope to the office before he made his final decision. He agreed to do so.

The next morning, I told them my whole story, I wasn't concerned whether they believed it or not, but I told them of the horrors of this war and the complete inadequacy and incompetence of the Generals to fight a war they didn't understand.

I showed them Winston's letter, which moved them both.

I turned to Gerald. 'You owe a commitment to your country, and you'll not dispose of that commitment by being killed in a muddy field in Flanders. The country will need men like you when the war is over, as there'll be precious little expertise left. You also owe a commitment to Penelope and your future children, and finally, you owe a commitment to the bank. We're going to have to work hard to supply Great Britain's needs, as this war will be costly not just in lives but in money. Now, go away and consider your position very carefully.'

I stood up, and Penelope came toward me in tears, 'thank you, James, oh thank you,' I told them both to go home, and that Gerald needn't return until they had the time to consider the future.

It was a very sober man who entered my office the next day. 'I've decided to stay,' said Gerald, 'I know people will say I'm a coward, but it would be easy for me join the colours and in a sense that would be cowardly.'

I nodded, 'you'll see that you've made the right decision, now I'm going to write to Winston and ask him to ensure that you are not called up because that's what will happen when they run out of bodies. I will tell him truthfully that the bank needs you to help ensure that the government has a ready supply of finance to win the war. He of all people will understand.'

When Gerald left my office, I felt that at least I had been able to change one life for the better.

By the end of 1914, the war was proving to be disastrous, and the alterations to my house were now moving at a snail's pace due to the lack of labour. My finances were increasing in leaps and bounds, war regrettably being very profitable for those with money and not involved in the fighting. I kept my money in cash in a personal account with a secret code, it was 23234-D, which was part of my old army number, and I put this in my safe along with my list of further investments I had worked on up to 1945.

I started to think more about my Tory and how she'd have been able to manage without me in the intervening years. Did she think I had abandoned her I wondered, would she have married again, all these thoughts kept running through my mind to the extent I became depressed. The war news continued to be bad, which didn't help.

The bank was now running well. I received enquiries from the new team at Byron's Bank asking if I would be interested in merging our interests.

I turned them down because I guessed that if I investigated their bank, I would find things that would destroy them.

From a strict business point of view, it would have been a good decision. But I wasn't interested in getting bigger, simply better, and more efficient.

The year, 1915 came, and I was concentrating on completing my house that promised to be ready for me to move to in early May. I bought furniture and the latest equipment, and some costly pictures including Monet's, Renoirs, one or two of Van Gogh including the Harvest at La Crau and The Peach Trees in Blossom I liked, and later I added Turners Venice. All were put in store to await my move.

15 - THE INTERLOCUTOR

I was sitting behind my desk dealing with some personnel problem that had come to my notice when the internal phone rang. 'Excuse me, sir, but I have had Mr Churchill on the line, he has asked that you call him at his house this evening,' she gave me his number. I assumed it was to invite me to one of his private dinners, for which he was famous. He used these to stay connected with what was going on outside politics. They were always attended by industrialists and senior people from all disciplines and walks of life and were always male. I looked at the date on my desk. It was Monday, January 11[th,] 1915, I frowned, something about the date stirred in my memory, but I could not remember what.

While I had come to like Winston, I was very much aware of his fierce ambition, and he could be quite boring as he was always keen to ensure that everyone concerned was made aware of his importance to the nation.

I decided that I did not wish to be subject to one of Winston's diatribes and resolved to excuse myself when I phoned, which I did later that evening.

I had stayed late in the office to phone him on a secure line and dialled the number. I was surprised that the phone at the other end was picked up immediately and even more surprised that it was Winston not one of his lackeys.

'Are you on your own?' he asked

'Good evening, Winston, yes, I'm phoning you from my office on a secure line, everyone apart from the security people have left. '

'Mm, good. I need to talk with you privately. It is a

matter of national importance.'

'Of course, Winston, would you like me to see you at the Admiralty?'

'Good god no, we must meet where we are not seen talking to each other.'

'Do you want to suggest ...'

Winston interrupted, 'I suggest you invite me to join you on the Royal Yacht at Cowes, you still have the use of it I assume?'

'Well yes, but I didn't realise you were a sailing man Winston.'

'I'm not, dammit, but it must appear that after a hectic week I am simply relaxing. The yacht will not move from its berth, and there should be no one else on board.'

'Not even someone to serve food and drinks?'

'No, I can pour my own. If you can organise some cold fare for dinner that will be fine. I will arrive at about 7 p.m. that's after dark, and you should advise the security that you are expecting a friend. I will be travelling under the name of Lord, he paused, yes Lord Newcastle.'

'I wasn't aware there was such a title,' I said.

'Oh yes, there was, it was held by a man called Thomas Pelham-Holles. He was a protégé of Walpole. He was depicted as the epitome of unredeemed mediocrity and a veritable buffoon in office. Clearly, Walpole wanted someone who would in no way be a threat to him. He died in 1768, and the title moved to Lord Lincoln.'

I smiled to myself; 'it sounds a little odd you should choose such a man to impersonate.'

'Not really, obviously I am his complete opposite, and the title is now unused, but is impressive enough for your security.'

I nodded, always impressed by his knowledge of history, 'Okay Winston, when do you suggest?'

'I would like to get there on Saturday 16th, and I will be leaving later the same evening, things are going to be very busy the following week as you will hear, and I need to be back at the Admiralty. By the way, I will be on my own.'

I realised that this was to be a unusual meeting as Winston was not bringing any advisers with him. There were rumours that he had disagreed strategy with Lord Fisher, the head of the Navy and that something big was about to happen that could end the war during 1916, I admit to being on tenterhooks for the remaining days of the week. Could it be, I wondered, that my current reality was different, and that history was about to change?

I contacted Captain Evan and asked him to sail the yacht to Portsmouth, where I would meet him for a bracing sail back to Cowes.

Leaving the Rolls in the naval shipyard, where I parked it in a secure area, I boarded the yacht at around midday on Saturday.

When we arrived at the berth in Cowes, Evan said he had a previous appointment, so could not join me for a drink and left the crew getting everything secured, I told them that they could have the weekend off, as I wanted some space to work on some private matters. The looks between the sailors gave me the impression that they assumed I was entertaining some lady or other.

The food was delivered later in the day, and I sat down in the cabin to read some reports I had brought down with me. When it began to get dark, I drew all the curtains before putting on the lights. It was just after seven that I heard heavy steps coming on to the yacht, and a profanity when the intruder tripped on some protrusion on deck. Seconds later, Winston's very red face appeared at the bottom of the galley steps.

'Bloody boats, I hate em.'

I found that rather amusing coming from the First Lord of the Admiralty, but I refrained from commenting.

He almost threw himself down on one of the comfortable chairs and looked around.

'Brandy?' I asked.

His eyes lit up, 'large if you please.'

I poured out a generous amount of a vintage Armagnac.

Winston gulped it down as though it was lemonade and held his empty glass out for more.

I apologised for not providing Cognac, a better-known Brandy in 2010.

Winston shook his head, 'my dear fellow, Armagnac was one of the first brandies produced in France, beginning in the 13th century. That's when medieval monasteries began promoting brandy as the miracle cure for everything from gout to senility. That's why I have neither,' he grinned.

He pulled himself up from his slouched position and leant forward. 'What I am about to tell you is a state secret, which you will hear about before the end of this month.'

I raised my eyebrows.

'I intend to cut this appalling war short by attacking the Turks at Gallipoli, take them out of the war and then attack the underbelly of Europe in a pincer movement landing in southern Russia to support a major Russian offensive from the south-east.'

Of course, I thought, I had forgotten about the Gallipoli invasion and realised that my previous thoughts had not realised that Gallipoli came so early in the war. I was amused at his comment about the underbelly of Europe, a term he used in WW2.

'Well, what do you think?'

I struggled with Winston's question, should I tell him that it would be a disaster both politically and militarily?

I decided to answer vaguely that if it were organised properly, it could be a wise move and certainly shorten the war. 'Even if it doesn't work as planned,' I said, 'it will still have the effect of bringing Turkey down as it will serve to weaken them thus making it easier for Allenby to defeat them from Egypt.' I was thinking of the story of Lawrence of Arabia who was under the command of Allenby.

Churchill frowned, 'Allenby, Allenby he repeated, he's

in France, not Egypt, and quite a junior General,' he added.

'There you are you see, I'm not infallible.' I smiled, *deciding not to tell him that it would be General Allenby who would eventually be appointed to the Middle East's command.*

Churchill frowned, but my answer had changed the direction of his thoughts.

I quickly intervened. 'But you didn't come all this way to tell me about your plans,' I cocked my head on to one side.

'Hmm,' I gathered Winston was somewhat disappointed with my response to his secret, but his voice dropped. 'The war is a disaster for us' he said. 'Even if we finish it by the end of this year, we and the dominions will have suffered huge casualties, estimated at more than half a million. Just think, it is our best men that are being destroyed, and if it goes on as you predicted, it will be almost a whole generation.'

'Exactly, Winston, and then what do you do when it's over, those families that have given up their sons and in some cases their daughters, will not be satisfied with the status quo. Society will change, and the old guard submerged.'

Winston nodded. 'It's this I have come to talk to you about. We were frankly not ready for a major land war. Our generals are still in the 1800s as far as tactics are concerned. We have foolishly given the French overall command, which means that politically they must ensure they do not give up land to the Germans. So, instead of retreating tactically to reform, and counter-attack, French soil is being held uselessly by our blood. Our infantrymen have the Lee Enfield rifle which can shoot 15 bullets a minute, the Germans the Mauser with only 5. But they have now developed the maxim machine gun that can fire over 600 bullets per minute, and their guns are water-cooled to prevent jamming. We started the war with only 1,350 machine guns, it was not considered cricket to use them, now Lloyd George is increasing supply one hundred-fold, but in the meantime, our soldiers are suffering impossible odds. This will be a war of attrition and technology, but we must increase the latter if we are to prevent massive casualties. Lloyd George wants to make mortars that would help redress the imbalance, but the war office has refused to fund their production. Kitchener thinks the tank is akin to a child's toy...' Churchill was understandably exasperated.

'But we still have the Navy...'

Winston grimaced, 'yes, it's the most powerful in the world by far, but we need to utilise all our forces to work together. Fisher, who as you know heads the Navy is way above the Generals in intelligence, but he is stuck with the idea of blockading the Germans and starving them. He feels that we should withdraw our troops and let the French deal with the Germans. The problem then would be giving up France, but as they are no match for the Germans alone, they could be overrun by them. The problem is that they refuse to give up French ground to buy time to retreat, re-arm and counter-attack properly.

I knew that Fisher's ideas conflicted with Churchill and that he was partly right, as almost a million Germans starved to death due to Fisher's blockade. There is little doubt that it was partly due to civilian unrest that brought down the Kaiser towards the end of the war. To combat this tactic, the Germans concentrated on the building of Unterseeboots. They came to be known in Britain as the U-Boat, which initially we had no defence against apart from mines. Paradoxically, it was one of these vessels that sank the Lusitania in the Irish Sea, which together with the publication of the Zimmerman telegram helped to bring the USA into the war, cementing a victory for the Allies.

I turned my attention back to the discussion. 'Well Winston, you didn't come down here just to tell me about the state of the war, so how can I help?'

Winston sat back, lighting a large cigar, which I found most unpleasant within the confines of the cabin. 'You have a huge following among those who have become rich through your advice, and you are well respected overseas within financial circles. We need money, James, so that Lloyd George can work his miracles without the pettiness of the establishment, later Great Britain will need huge sums to pay for war pensions, which will cost hundreds of millions at the end of the war and beyond.'

'Yes, I see that the one country that could give huge financial support is the USA, but Fisher's blockade is hurting a substantial number of businesses in the US who were trading with Germany.'

'What about the Swiss?'

'No, too close to Germany. I agree that you will need to borrow, and there are several ways of doing this. Lloyd George has already taken steps by leaving the Gold Standard and creating paper money not backed by Gold, but there is a limit as to how far you can go without creating hyperinflation. The war bonds invention was an excellent idea, as most patriotic subjects with money have bought into them. But I assess that you will only raise about 25% of the total cost by these innovative methods.'

Churchill looked surprised.

I continued, 'the US dollar is trading at about U$4.80 to the pound now, so that is where we must find the bulk of our money. It will further help if we buy military equipment from our cousins as soon as their neutrality act has been abandoned, as this will help their employment problem and soften the blow of those trading with Germany. It will mean me going to the USA to meet their principal bankers, but I will need to go with the British Government's backing.

'Having said that, it must be secret, I do not wish it to be known outside a few people what I have gone to the USA for. It would not do for the Germans to be aware of our need to raise funds to continue the war. Also, we must not forget that it was reported that the English language was adopted by only one vote in the United States against German as a language. It is untrue, and there was never such a vote. Nevertheless, there is a strong German lobby over there, and it would be important to keep my visit extremely low key.'

Churchill nodded, 'I agree absolutely, do you know the people you should meet over there?'

I smiled, 'there is only one worth speaking to, and that is Jacob Schiff of Kuhn, Loeb and Company.'

Churchill frowned, 'but surely the Rothschilds own that company, and their background is German.'

'So is our Royal family, but no one would suggest that is where their loyalties lie. There is something the Rothschilds want more than anything else that only the British can deliver, and that is Palestine.'

Winston looked shocked. 'Are you suggesting that we should give up Palestine to the Jews?'

'Why not, Winston, the area is currently under the control of the Ottoman Empire, it's worthless and assuming we push the Turks back to their original borders, having a Jewish state in the area would be a counter to future Ottoman ambitions.'

'Hmm, I would have to clear that with Asquith, and we could only make a secret undertaking at this stage.'

'Very well, you want the finance, these people can raise it, and they are also capable of making it much more difficult for the German alliance to continue to raise funds.'

'So, if Germany loses the war, it will be thanks to the Jews?'

I remained silent.

Winston looked at me, raising his eyebrows.

I nodded; 'it should also be remembered that any final armistice will depend much more on the terms of any settlement. If they are too harsh, then the German people may react in a way we could not at this stage, imagine.'

'Is that a warning?'

I smiled but didn't answer.

I continued, 'In the meantime Winston, I may be able to help obtain some free finance from a wealthy customer of ours, which will solve the mortar problem that Lloyd George has, and I will get back to you on this.'

Winston stubbed out his cigar. 'In that case, there is nothing else we can discuss now, why don't we eat that food you have had prepared, and then I will return to London.'

We talked about several matters, mainly politics, and he took his leave after cleaning his plate with a promise of contacting me during the following week. It rather amused me that he went back to the mainland by a fast navy tender, so much for a secret meeting, I thought.

I decided to stay on the boat overnight and left for London the next day to be ready to get to the bank on Monday morning.

I got to my office early, caught up on my mail and at 9.30 a.m. called the war office. A pleasant female voice answered.

'I am looking for Colonel the Maharaja Bhupinder Singh of Patiala,' I said.

'Ah, do you mean Sir Bhupinder Singh? I will see if he

IR BHUPINDER SINGH - MAHARAJA OF PATIAL

is available, may I say who is calling?'

'Of course, I'm sorry, it is James Alexander of the Crowley Bank.'

'Is that Sir James Alexander?'

'Yes, I replied.'

There was a short pause on the line.

'Jimmy how are you?' said a booming voice, 'it's nice to hear from you.'

He was the only person who called me Jimmy and my retort was, 'I am well thank you Bopa, I hear you are now a Colonel, are congratulations in order?'

He laughed, 'an Honorary Lieutenant Colonel, the military have not yet quite got used to a dark skin with pips.'

'Well, how would you like to become a dark skin with three pips and a crown?'

'Will that give me more money?'

I roared with laughter, 'Bopa was probably the wealthiest Maharaja in India. It was rumoured that when he travelled in India, he was supported by 20 Rolls Royce's in his cavalcade. He had been impeccably educated, and it showed when he spoke.'

'I was wondering if you were free for lunch at my Club Bopa, I have a small favour to ask you.'

'Just name it Jimmy, beautiful women, I have dozens, a large mansion in Patiala, or...'

'Stop Bopa, or you'll corrupt me, are you free?'

'Of course, I will meet you there at 13.00.'

I had met the Maharaja Bhupinder Singh some months before when he requested that we meet to discuss his setting up a bank in Patiala. I gave him some useful advice and offered to help him if he decided to go ahead. When he asked me how much he owed me, I waved my hand and told him there would be no fee. Since then, he had become a good customer and a great friend. He eventually opened his bank in 1917.

I made sure I arrived at the club before the time arranged, and precisely on time Bopa arrived resplendent in full military uniform but with a turban instead of an officer's hat. He was a delightful luncheon guest, and we talked of many things, including cricket which was his passion. Patiala was renowned for the highest cricket pitch in the world at 2,443 metres.

I told him of Lloyd George's problem, and Bopa immediately agreed to an open account so Lloyd George could draw as much as he needed. The only caveat being that our bank would control the account and give his financial people a quarterly report. It was an incredibly generous gesture.

BRITISH MORTAR

When I passed on the news to Churchill, he was delighted. I told him that I had promised Bopa three pips, and a crown (a Brigadier) and Churchill said they would do better than that. *He was as good as his word, as by the end of the war Sir Bhupinder Singh rose to a rank of Lieutenant General, the highest level for an Indian in the Army at that time.*

'That is great news James,' said Winston, 'I will pass that on to Lloyd George at the end of this phone call.

'On the other subject we discussed, I have received the authority to inform you that we would be prepared to offer the area we discussed under certain circumstances, assuming we capture it of course. Your point about it being a harbinger of peace in the Middle East is well taken, and I can confirm we would be able to make a public statement perhaps as early as 1917. I can, however, give you a draft of what that statement would look like.'

I frowned, 'I didn't say that it would be a harbinger of peace Winston, but it would certainly create a buffer state against Turkey and even the Arabs.'

'Yes, yes, I understand that, but we would still control it of course, and the Arabs are of no account, hardly any of them live there anyway.'

I did not answer.

After receiving the confidential draft from Churchill, the next day, I sent a telegram to New York asking for a meeting with one of the most important men in world finance at the time. I received a reply from Jacob Schiff, inviting me to stay at his mansion in Manhattan. In his return telegram, he wrote that he would be delighted to see me and would send his chauffeur to meet me off the ship when it arrived.

Within a week, I had handed over temporary control of the bank to Victoria and planned to sail in the Lusitania from Southampton to New York. I knew of course that this was the ship that would be torpedoed in the Irish Sea during May 1915, so I felt the crossing would be safe in January. I decided to be extravagant for a change and booked one of the premier suites of which there were two on the ship, called the Regal Suites, one on the port side which is the one I took and one on the starboard side.

The captain of the vessel graciously honoured me with a seat at his table during the voyage, which was most pleasant, although we hit some rough weather about 200 miles out of Liverpool, thankfully it only lasted for 24 hours. The ship, at least the part in which I was situated was ostentatiously luxurious.

On the second day, he proudly showed me around.

RMS LUSITANIA

The *Lusitania*'s first-class accommodation was in the centre section of the five uppermost decks, mostly concentrated between the first and fourth funnels. When fully booked, *Lusitania* could cater to 552 first-class passengers. In common with all significant liners of the period, *Lusitania*'s first-class interiors were decorated with a mélange of historical styles. The first-class dining saloon was the grandest of the ship's public rooms; arranged over two decks with an open circular well at its centre and crowned by an elaborate dome measuring 29 feet, decorated with frescos in the style of François Boucher. It was elegantly finished throughout in the neoclassical Louis XVI style.

CAPT. RAYNOR

The lower floor measuring 85 feet could seat 323, with a further 147 on the 65-foot upper floor. The walls were finished with white and gilt carved mahogany panels, with Corinthian decorated columns required to support the floor above. The one concession to seaborne life was that furniture was bolted to the floor, meaning passengers could not rearrange their seating for their convenience. All other first-class public rooms were situated on the boat deck and comprised a lounge, reading and writing room, smoking room and veranda café. The last was an innovation on a Cunard liner and, in warm weather, one side of the café could be opened to give the impression of sitting outdoors. This was a rarely used feature given the often-inclement weather of the North Atlantic.

The first-class lounge was decorated in Georgian style with inlaid mahogany panels surrounding a jade green carpet with a yellow floral pattern, measuring overall 68 feet. It had a barrel-vaulted skylight rising to 20 feet with stained glass windows each representing a month of the year. The lounge had a 14-foot-high green marble fireplace incorporating enamelled panels by Alexander Fisher. The design was linked overall with decorative plasterwork. The library walls were decorated with carved pilasters and mouldings, marking out grey and cream silk brocade panels. The carpet was rose, with Rose du Barry silk curtains and upholstery. The chairs and writing desks were mahogany, and the windows featured etched glass. The smoking room was Queen Anne style, with Italian walnut panelling and Italian red furnishings. The grand stairway linked all six decks of the passenger accommodation with wide hallways on each level and two lifts. First-class cabins ranged from one shared room through various en-suite arrangements in a choice of decorative styles culminating in the two regal suites which each had two bedrooms, dining room, parlour, and bathroom. The port suite decoration was modelled on the Petit Trianon.

I could not help but think about all the work and money that had gone into building this fine ship, only for it to be sunk by a German torpedo within the next 12 weeks or so.

We arrived in New York to a cloudy, freezing day, and as I disembarked, I noticed the outside temperature was at minus 15 degrees centigrade. I was glad to be met immediately after clearing immigration. The man waiting at the outside area was a smart gentleman in a dark grey uniform and a peaked cap. He recognised me straight away, and I was about to ask him how when he told me that he had been given a New York periodical, which told the story of Crowley's Banks huge success. It had a picture of me at the beginning of the article. I never did find out how they obtained my photograph, but as the text was generally supportive of the bank, I was quite pleased, particularly so bearing in mind my Quest.

ROLLS ROYCE BREWSTER

I learned his name was Robinson, strange I thought, as he was black and then I remembered from my visit to the Worthy Park plantation in Jamaica where I was shown a book with the names of all the slaves employed there in the early 1800s. Quite a number took the name of the plantation owner, and I guessed his ancestors were perhaps from the West Indies, which he later confirmed.

The car was close by, parked in a V.I.P. area, and I recognized it at once. It was a Brewster body built on a Rolls Royce chassis and engine. It was quite beautiful in that it was wholly enclosed, for which I was grateful. It was finished in dark blue with a cream interior. There was a glass divider between the front and back, and I noticed when I got in that there was a handle for the passenger to roll the centre window down. Robinson had taken my luggage and put it in the boot, what the Americans more appropriately call the trunk.

He seemed surprised, and he asked when the rest of my luggage would be brought off the ship. I had only one large case and a briefcase. I told him that when I was travelling on my own, without a wife or mistress, I always travelled light. He nodded sagely and grinned as he climbed into the driver's seat. The ship had berthed at Pier 54 in Lower Manhattan, and Jacob Schiff lived in mid-Manhattan. The drive took less than fifteen minutes, and as we turned into a gated driveway, I was utterly taken aback at the scene in front of me. We were stopped at the gate where there was an armed security detail and then waved through. The gardens on either side were quite beautifully manicured, much like one would expect with a Royal Palace in England. The mansion, however, was relatively new, finished in white. There were south, and north wings and the main entrance was in the centre building between the two wings. In many ways, it reminded me of Blenheim, but not nearly as large.

As Robinson drew up at the front entrance, a butler emerged with two young flunkies. As the luggage I had brought with me hardly required the helpers who had obviously expected a substantial number of cases and boxes, I smiled.

The butler welcomed me in an upper-class English accent, I learned later he had been born and brought up in Huddersfield, England, but there was no trace of a Yorkshire accent.

'Welcome to Greenway House,' he said smiling, 'er when is the rest of your luggage arriving, sir?'

'As I told Robinson, I am travelling light, because I am

booked to sail back to England in the Lusitania within the two days,' I answered.

'Oh, I see, sir, Mr Schiff will be disappointed, as he was hoping to show you, New York.' He steered me towards the entrance telling one of the young lads to put my luggage in the Royal Suite. 'Mr Schiff is in the drawing-room, sir, and I have instructions to take you there straight away unless of course, you wish to see your suite first.'

I told him that was unnecessary, but I noticed the young man struggling with the exceptionally large case I had brought with me eventually disappearing up the broad staircase in the centre of the house.

The butler, who told me his name was George; named after the King, he said with some pride, took me from the reception area to a room at the end. He opened the door, and I was ushered into a stunning drawing room, beautifully furnished with paintings on the walls that a museum would have given their eye teeth to get their hands on.

George announced me and asked if we would like tea, and I said I would. He then closed the door behind him, and Jacob Schiff, who had been on the telephone, walked around a sofa with his hand held out. 'Sir James, I am so pleased to meet you at last, did you have a good trip?'

I said I had, and we spent a few minutes chatting about mundane matters until the tea arrived along with delicious home-made cakes.

JACOB SCHIFF

When seated, he said he had hoped to meet me in Paris at the bankers meeting but was disappointed when he learned that I had returned to England due to being unwell. I smiled and told him my real reason for leaving. 'Unfortunately, the man concerned committed suicide after accidentally killing his father,' I said, 'by the way, please call me James.'

'And I am Jacob, but is good to

229

meet you, because I have heard so much about you and the huge turnaround of the Crowley Bank since you took over. I am told, however, that you were brought up in the United States.' He looked me quizzically.

'No, Lord Crowley invented my ancestry to give me some background, as you probably know. I turned up on his estate with a loss of memory, and because there is a physical likeness, he put it about that I was a long-lost cousin from the Crowley family who own estates in Virginia.'

'So, you have never been to the USA?'

'I have a memory of being here, but not in this time frame. I realise this is strange, but it is what it is,' I shrugged, hoping to move away from the subject.

Jacob nodded, 'Yes, I have heard about your loss of memory and the fact that you appear to be able to forecast future events with some accuracy. I must say, it is a beneficial attribute for a banker, I wish I had the same problem,' he laughed.

As he was talking, I studied him. He was good looking, certainly for a man of 68, which he was at that time, He sported a moustache not quite like Jimmy Edwards in his day, and a King George type beard, both completely white. He was almost bald at the front of his head, but had an abundance behind, cut but not too short. He wore a dark suit with a waistcoat and a dark red tie that matched the small rose in his buttonhole.

His eyes were brown and intelligent, one could imagine that he would quickly size up who he was talking to, and he looked at me with some interest.

'Tell me, James, why have you chosen me for your short visit, because the shipping line has indicated that you are returning on the same ship in two days?'

I nodded, 'you are certainly the most respected banker in the USA, and you are responsible for the Rothschild family interests over here. From my perspective, you are also a major contributor; using your wealth to help others and society generally. I admire that, and in my small way, I have tried to copy another American called Peabody, who was a major benefactor to the not so well off.'

'Yes, I'm aware of what you've done, which is admirable. You indicated in your telegram that you wanted to meet with me to discuss an extremely sensitive matter that I assume involves money?'

I nodded, 'yes.'

Jacob raised his eyebrows, 'for your bank. Surely not, as your balance sheet is strong.'

I was surprised at this comment, as I wondered how he had seen our balance sheet, and then I realised that we might have joint investors.

'No, it's for my country.'

'Ah, I see,' he said slowly, 'but why doesn't your bank...'

I shook my head, 'we already loan to the British government of course, but what I'm asking for is way beyond one bank, I'm effectively asking for a blank cheque.'

'Now you have the advantage on me, Great Britain is by far the richest country in the world, and it rules a third of it, surely the assets you hold are more than enough for your purposes?'

'Yes', I answered, 'you would think so, but the war is becoming hugely costly in terms of lives, munitions, and military materiel. It was thought that it would all be over within 12 months at the most, now we know that is not going to be the case. We have Russia, France, Italy, Japan and the Dominions against Germany, Austria Hungary, Turkey, and their dominions. It is effectively a world war that is already affecting world trade to a huge extent, and we are a trading nation.'

'Yes, I understand that, but you are blockading the German ports, which is causing a huge upset to US trade with Germany. so surely you will eventually starve the populations of both Germany and Austria Hungary as they are both effectively landlocked, except for the Baltic Sea of course.'

'The British navy is indeed by far the strongest in the world, but the innovation of the submarine is starting to some extent level the playing field as we do not yet have an effective method of dealing with this threat, only by laying mines, but in the deep sea, they are of limited value.' I leaned forward for emphasis.

'Do you indicate when it will be over?' Jacob asked.

'I do, yes, it will be toward the end of 1918, at least another three and half years. It is my view that Russia will collapse, Italy will be almost bankrupted, and the Allies and their dominions will suffer huge casualties, mainly because our generals are still not capable of realising that technology needs a different approach to battle.

'Not only will the military expenditure be huge, but the cost of paying out pensions to those in the fight will be astronomical and go on for years after we have won the war. The industry's disruption will be enormous as it will have to revert to a peacetime scenario, thus putting out of work most of the women now employed doing jobs that were originally done by men. Society will change, countries will change, and power blocks will be altered, Empires will fall. The world will change dramatically.'

'Hmm, interesting, you know of course that our Senate recently turned down the idea of having women vote in the USA?'

'Yes, women do not have the vote in Britain either, but that will change too.'

Jacob screwed his face up, 'change is rarely good for us bankers unless we can forecast it well in advance, which we can't of course. You mention that Empires will fall, are you referring to the British Empire, because as you know, many in the USA would like to see you beaten, and that is not only the German immigrants.'

'And no doubt the Irish.'

He nodded.

'Well Britain does have a lot to answer for, particularly as far as the Irish are concerned, but Britain will not be on the losing side in a sense that it will not lose the war, simply its financial ability to continue to control its interests.' I leant back in my chair.

Jacob pursed his lips; 'I understand that Churchill's idea to attack Turkey through the Dardanelles has been launched. It appears that this will be successful and take Turkey out of the war, allowing a pincer movement through the Black Sea to support Russia.'

'No, Jacob, it won't succeed, it's a brilliant plan, but our Army and navy coordination are not yet tested, and it will fail.'

'I see, so, to sum up, you are saying that Britain needs an amount of borrowing that it cannot yet substantiate, and you cannot even be sure that the Allies will win. That is not a particularly good prospect for me to put to my fellow banker colleagues.'

'I understand that the risk is there,' I said, 'but Germany and Austria Hungary will lose, as even though Germany has a better-trained army, they will lose in a war of attrition, which it is becoming. They will also start to sink your ships, bringing materiel to the Allies; it will not take long for the American public to turn against the Axis powers in such a situation.'

'Well, I must admit that as bankers, we agree with that assessment, as we have come to a similar conclusion, although we thought it would be over more quickly. You do know, however, that my background is German? Let me explain.'

'The sire of the family, Mayer Amschel Rothschild, established a small business as a coin dealer in Frankfurt in 1743. Although previously known as Bauer, he advertised his profession by putting up a sign depicting an eagle on a red shield, an adaptation of the City of Frankfort's coat of arms. He added five golden arrows extending from the talons, signifying his five sons. Because of this sign, he took the name Rothschild or Red Shield. When the Elector of Hesse earned a fortune by renting Hessian mercenaries to the British to put down the American colonies' rebellion, Rothschild was entrusted with this money to invest. He made an excellent profit both for himself and the Elector and attracted other accounts. In 1785 he moved to a larger house, 148 Judengasse, a five-story house known as The Green Shield which he shared with the Schiff family. That is our connection. My family moved to the United States, where we saw new possibilities after independence and were very much aware of the hardening of the populace in Germany against the Jewish community. I now look after the Rothschild interest over here.

'My view is that Bismarck, when Chancellor of Germany made alliances that made sense at the time, but when Wilhelm II sacked him, he was no longer in control. Had he been, he would have almost certainly not made the error of attacking France through Belgium, a neutral country, which brought Great Britain into the war.'

'I agree with your comments,' I said, 'nor would he have supported Austria Hungary attacking Serbia thus bringing Russia into the war. It indicates the problem of untrained and unelected Royals having too much power, although it may be that the Kaiser has allowed the German military to gain too much power and perhaps, he is now unable to control them. The Tsar in Russia, Emperor Franz Joseph, and Kaiser Wilhelm II will all disappear along with their ilk,' I said.

'Along with any chance of lasting peace in Europe I expect,' answered Jacob, 'how stupid we are to allow this to happen.'

I agreed.

'Well, I've listened to your proposal, but due to the conflicting interests of most of the bankers here, I am concerned that they may not relish the risk.'

'I have not finished my proposal,' I smiled, 'I have something to offer you that you and most of your colleagues may be interested in.'

Jacob looked surprised. 'Come with me,' he got up

from his chair and walked over to the French windows. 'What do you see?'

I looked out and saw the skyline of New York.

'You see all those large buildings?' he asked.

'Yes,' I wasn't sure what he was driving at, and I looked at him quizzically

'It is my banker colleagues and me that financed most of them. Do you see the beautiful gardens in front of you?'

I said I did.

'I have a beautiful house, I have castles, and houses and châteaux in Europe, and I have a beautiful wife and many children. I have everything I require to eat and more, now, what can you offer me that I do not have?'

I looked at him, 'Palestine,' I said.

He was genuinely shocked and stared at me for several seconds without replying. 'Palestine,' he repeated.

'Yes,' I said, 'A permanent homeland for the Jewish people.'

'But how can you give us Palestine, it's owned and occupied by the Turks, and you've already said that the military incursion in the Dardanelles will fail.'

'Yes, but we will take it from the south, from Egypt. The Ottoman Empire is finished, it will be beaten, and they will be driven back to the original Turkish borders, leaving the French and us with the Middle East.'

'How can you demonstrate this?'

'If you and your banker colleagues agree to my request, as soon as we take Palestine, and we will, a public declaration will be made by the British government, and I have here a copy.'

I pulled the document out from within my jacket and read the contents aloud.

MOST SECRET

His Majesty's government views with favour the establishment in Palestine of a national home for the Jewish people. It will use their best endeavours to facilitate the achievement of this object. It is clearly understood that

nothing shall be done which may prejudice the civil and religious rights of existing non-Jewish communities in Palestine, or the rights and political status enjoyed by Jews in any other country.

Signed: Winston Churchill.

'The document will be signed by the Foreign Minister of the day, and that may not be Churchill, but he has the full authority of the cabinet.'

I saw tears appear in Jacobs eyes, he could hardly believe it, and he had to go back to his chair and sit down, realising the enormity of what he was holding.

'How do I know this will be carried through?'

'I can guarantee it,' I said, 'but you should know this will be a declaration only. It will tie the British government to this policy until it is delivered.' *(I didn't mention that it would take a further 31 years to be accomplished)*

'But you are not a Jew, what does it mean to you?'

I sat down. 'My great grandfather was also called Beaur, he also lived in Germany and was attacked by the local community because he was successful. His house was trashed, his goods stolen, and he was murdered. An Englishman diplomat friend of his called John Alexander initially took pity on his wife and later fell in love with her, and he got her out of Germany into England, where they were married.'

Jacob thought for a moment, 'so your Great Grandfather was a Jew, but that doesn't make you a Jew.'

'No, of course not, but I did come from the female line; nevertheless, I am an Englishman, and my loyalty is to that country. I give you this offer from my country for your support to help us win this dreadful war, which is killing gentile and Jew alike, but it is also having a detrimental effect on the US economy. In my view, it is also essential to the US that democratic countries come out on top.

'I despise any type of racial discrimination, which is prevalent in the Axis countries and in lot of cases go as far as ethnic cleansing. It is for this reason that I understand

236

that you and others set up the Galveston Movement to help Jews who were being persecuted in Europe.'

Jacob grimaced, 'yes, but it was disbanded last year,' he shrugged, 'it appears that most are content where they are.'

I did not tell him of the holocaust to be carried out by the Germans in the Second World War, but said, 'my advice is to keep going, I am afraid that more, much more, is to come from the country of your ancestors, and none of it good.'

He looked at me with a penetrating gaze, 'is that a guess James or can you truly read the future?'

I laughed, 'I realise it is hard to comprehend, but I am simply reading from the past.'

Jacob looked puzzled. 'I thought you said that you had lost your memory, how then can you remember that your great grandmother was Jewish?'

'I didn't say I had lost my memory; it is others who have argued that I said I remembered my life in another time frame, and that is a fact, strange as it may seem.'

Jacob got up, 'James, whatever memories you have, the offer you have brought to me is astonishing, and I am now going to contact a few of my friends to see what we can put together. As you are leaving the day after tomorrow, time is not on our side.

'In the meantime, I will ask my wife and eldest son to show you the sights of New York tomorrow. I will meet you in the evening before dinner to discuss what I have. You are our guest for dinner tonight, and I have invited Woodrow Wilson and his wife, plus a few other notables. We will not discuss what you have just told me.

'I expect you could do with a rest after your journey, and we can meet for drinks in the room next to the banqueting hall, George will show you where to go. Please consider my house as you would your own, and you are free to wander either inside or in the garden, but perhaps it is a bit cool there now.'

George came into the room soon after Jacob pressed a button, and as I left, I noticed him picking up the telephone. George accompanied me to my room and asked me if I would like him to run a bath. I said, yes. The bedroom was just one of many rooms as it was a large suite. When he had left, I undressed and slid into the warm water and must have dozed off, because I noticed it getting dark outside the bathroom window. I quickly got out and dried myself. My clothes had been unpacked and placed in a large wardrobe. I noticed a note on the double bed, which indicated that there would be drinks in the drawing-room at 7.30 and the dress was a black-tie which was already laid out on an adjoining sofa.

The dinner was an amenable affair with just a few important guests, including the President and his wife. Wilson was particularly keen to get up to date information from me on the state of the war, and I told him my view. He would have received regular updates from his Ambassadors in Paris and London, so he was looking for confirmation more than anything else. He was particularly interested in the German U-boat development as US ships were already shipping Materiel and food to England.

'There is no doubt where the sympathy of my government is, and that is to the Democratic countries of Europe, particularly Great Britain. But there is a strong feeling in the United States that we should not be drawn into the war, but remain neutral to be able to intervene diplomatically when the time is right,' he said.

I nodded, 'yes, I understand your position, Mr President, but I'm afraid the time for armistice talks have gone, there is now too much at stake. The Axis powers are bent on securing the whole of Europe, and if they are successful, you would have a situation where three people would virtually dictate world policy. Should they win, they will not stop their plans of expansion, spreading discontent around the world.'

'And take over the assets of the British and French Dominions?'

I realised what he was getting at. 'Yes, but we are ruled by a Democratic process, and we have already given power away to Canada, Australia, and New Zealand, and more will follow as time goes by. There is a strong body of opinion in Great Britain that countries still controlled by us should become independent once they are capable of good government.'

'What about India?'

'Ah, as Mr Churchill said when asked that question by an American, he reportedly answered. "Are you talking about the Indians in India who are thriving under British rule, or the American Indians who are being corralled into reservations and their population being hugely depleted?"'

'As you know Mr Churchill is half American but has extreme views on the British Empire. He is a great friend of mine, but we disagree with his view of India and other British possessions. I believe he is wrong, and time will prove him so.'

PRESIDENT WILSON

We continued our discussion as we repaired to the smoking-room, without the ladies as was the custom at the time, and it was there that the President took me on one side and asked if I would do him a personal favour. I have a dear friend, a retired Democratic Senator who is travelling to England on the Lusitania tomorrow for a specialised medical procedure that is not

239

available here. The problem is that he is in a wheelchair and needs constant care from the nurses and his wife, who will travel with him. Unfortunately, the two suites capable of putting up his small medical team and his wife have been taken. I wonder if you would consider allowing him to take your suite and for you to move to a first-class cabin, which I understand is available. I have made enquiries, and I am assured that the shipping line will not charge you for the return journey if you agree to this.'

'Of course,' I agreed immediately.

'Thank you, I am most grateful to you,' said the President. 'In that case, would you be kind enough just to give me a brief note for the shipping line, and I will get my office to organise the changeover.' I went over to the desk in the room and wrote the note he required. Little was I to know that my generosity would save my life.

It was quite late before the President left, and he thanked me again, shaking my hand warmly.

The next day I was taken on a delightful tour of New York, and I made comparisons of the New York I knew in the 1990s when I was a regular visitor there.

We returned to the mansion at about 4-o-clock, and Jacob was already there. I got the feeling that he was quite excited by the news he had.

He steered me into the drawing-room on my own and took a bottle of champagne that had been left on ice, pouring me a glass, and ushering me to a seat. 'Well, James, I have some exceptionally good news. But let me start with the difficulty, which we have managed to overcome. Secretary of State Bryan was very much against anyone loaning funds to any of the warring nations as by doing so, the United States would no longer be able to claim it was neutral. However, your talk with the President has brought about a change of policy, it is not public and will not be made so until a situation presents itself. The upshot is that the financiers I have put together have a green light to offer a carte blanche amount to the British, which will carry a two per cent interest rate. I understand that this is rather higher than normal, but there is no designated repayment time.'

I nodded, 'I think that is an excellent deal Jacob, an amount of funding that is completely open without a repayment schedule is probably better than the British Government could have hoped for at this stage of the war. It will, in my opinion, eventually help to defeat the Axis powers.'

'Yes, but there is more,' said Jacob. 'The President has said that he will do his utmost to bring the United States into the war. He feels that it is his duty as a Democrat to be seen to support like-minded institutions. He cannot enact such a policy publicly. Still, he will ensure that American non-military goods continue to be sent to Great Britain and will authorise arms and ammunition to be carried by passenger liners like the Lusitania, to mask America in supporting the Allies.'

Of course, I knew that the Lusitania's sinking would start to change the American public view of the European war. However, it would be the Zimmerman telegram in January 1917 arguably decrypted by the British, that would cement it.

It was that and the threat in anticipation of Germany resuming unrestricted submarine warfare on any ships carrying goods to the allies that a decision was made. By April 1917 the United States declared war on Germany.

Jacob also told me that they expected the US treasury would eventually take over the loans when the USA declared war. His group had received assurance from the President that would be the case.

Before leaving, he handed me a letter signed by all the financial houses involved, stating the loans basis and terms. He also issued a warning, which I was to remember before the trip was over.

'Remember, James, this letter is highly confidential, if some unauthorised person got hold of it, it would be hugely damaging politically. Several people could benefit from its contents, and although we have created this deal in secret, we should expect that someone will add two and two together and wonder why you came all this way to see me. I will put out that the intention of your visit was for you to assess the financial market in the USA with the possibility of opening a branch here, believable, as your bank is so successful in Great Britain and the fact that you already have American clients. Finally. Be careful,' he looked at me seriously, 'you have already experienced what greed can do in your own country, and there are people here who are quite capable of murder to establish what they want.'

16-THE ASSASSIN

I said my goodbyes to the Schiff family and was driven back to the ship by Robinson to whom I gave a pound, forgetting just how much that was worth in 2010 money. He was delighted. On my person was a letter from Jacob and as I entered the ship from the gangplank, I saw the captain waiting for me at the top. He held out his hand, 'James, it's good to see you again, I just wanted you to know that you are on my table again, and we have some interesting and very wealthy people who you'll meet. I also have a request from the wife of Senator Tugwell, who you have given up your suite for, she would just like to thank you personally, and she will be at the table for the first night so she can meet you. After that, she will stay with her husband in the suite.'

That evening I had the pleasure of meeting Annabel Tugwell, who was at least 30 years younger than her husband, I understood he was 81. She was a bubbly individual and interesting to talk to as with her wealth, she had travelled to many obscure places in the world. I escorted her back to the suite and arranged to meet both her and her husband the next day.

I thought about the letter I had been given and took it out of my pocket to reread it. It was an historical document, though it would never be published. Was it to be so, it would ultimately compromise the neutrality of the United States and the political fall-out would be devastating? Arguably it still circumvented the current law of the United States. I thought that perhaps I should put it in a safe on-board ship, but I decided it would be safer on my person.

I was rudely woken in the early hours of the morning by the shrill ring of a telephone in my cabin. I looked at the clock after turning the light on above my bed. It was 2.30 a.m. I clutched for the phone and clumsily dropped it on the floor having to get out of bed to retrieve it. Picking it up, I heard the worried voice of Captain Daniel Dow.

'James, are you, all right?'

'A bit sleepy, but I'm now awake, why do you ask?'

'Something terrible has happened, I'm coming down to your cabin now, whatever you do, do not open your cabin door to anyone but me, it's a matter of life and death.'

I assured him I would not do so and thinking of the letter. I put it into a drawer and covered it with my socks.

There was a knock on the door, and I heard Daniel Dows gruff voice. I opened it carefully to ensure that there was no one else there and then opened it wide. He came in, and I closed the door after him.

He sat down heavily on a chair.

'I apologise for waking you, but you should know that Senator Tugwell and his wife have been murdered in their suite, your old suite,' he said for emphasis.

I frowned, 'but why, was it a robbery?'

'It appears not, as the room was thoroughly searched and there were at least two hundred pounds in cash and Mrs Tugwell's jewellery, but it was not touched. I have a Pinkerton man on board who has indicated that the murder was around 10.00 p.m. The Senator was still in his chair with his back to the door. He was shot in the back and fell forward on his face. This must have alerted Mrs Tugwell who was shot emerging from the bedroom, presumably alerted by the sound of shots. Both were shot twice in the head, and our Pinkerton man tells me that it is a classic assassin's method of dispatching people. His view is that the murderer did not expect to find more than one person in the suite, and Mrs Tugwell would have recognised the assassin, which is why she was killed.'

'But how did the assassin gain entry to the suite?' I asked.

Captain Dow nodded, 'I asked that question too, but apparently, because of the Senator's condition, they left their door unlocked to allow our staff to enter without disturbing him.'

I suddenly felt cold. 'do you think the murderer was after me, as after all, no one else knew that I had swapped cabins? Indeed, if such a person were watching me, he or she would have seen me walking back towards the suite when I escorted Mrs Tugwell last evening after dinner.'

Daniel Dow nodded. 'The man from Pinkertons thinks that is a strong possibility, but do you have any reason to believe someone would want to murder you?'

I had to be careful, as there was no way I could divulge that I had an explosive document, if I did, the captain would reasonably ask for it to be placed in his safe. I could not take that chance. Then it dawned on me that I did not have to reveal the detail.

'I certainly have knowledge that is important to the ongoing war situation that will be useful to our government, but it is not something I can put to paper.'

'Umm, well our assassin obviously thinks that you have a document that is important, and whether you have or not, it appears he may be prepared to kill you to prevent such knowledge reaching your government.

'I have here a Webley .455 pistol, it is common for us to be issued with side-arms, and I would like you to hang on to it until you disembark. In the meantime, with your permission, I would like to call security and ask the Pinkerton man to come down to meet you to see if there is any way we can catch this man before he does any more damage.'

I agreed.

Captain Dow strode across the room and picked up the telephone. 'First Officer,'

'Yes sir,'

'Please ask the Pinkerton man to come to Cabin four on the upper deck, and when he knocks, he should issue the number 463, so we can be sure he is who he says he is.'

Five minutes later, there was a knock on the door and the correct code given. Captain Dow stopped me from opening it, and he did so himself, locking it once the Pinkerton man was inside.

'Mr Andrew, this is Sir James Alexander, and from what I've heard, I believe Sir James was the intended victim, so what suggestions do you have?'

Andrew looked at me carefully noticing that I did not show any form of concern. After Captain Dow told him of our conversation, he said, 'your life is in danger. We have two options: you stay in your cabin for the rest of the trip, and we suggest you have been killed. The second option is to try and find the perpetrator, and that will carry some risk on your behalf.'

'Very well,' I said, 'logically we should consider option two for the simple reason that our assassin may have already realised that he has made a mistake and be on the lookout to find my cabin. I realise that Tugwell fell forward on his face as Captain Dow told me, but even then, it would have been obvious that it was not me even viewed from behind, but it is highly likely that the murderer turned the dead Tugwell over as he searched him, so what is your plan, Mr Andrew?'

'Your logic is correct; we should assume that he knows he shot the wrong person and so he will be desperate to find you. This assassin is a hired professional, so I have already telegrammed New York with brief descriptions including passport numbers of everyone on board. But unless we are lucky, it is doubtful that they will recognise likely suspects before we dock in England.

'My plan is as follows: My assistant Charles Frobisher, who was born in England incidentally, his parents immigrated to the USA when he was a boy, will stay with you in this cabin. He will be armed. Neither of you will leave the cabin for any reason whatsoever, even if we find this person, we cannot be sure there is only one.

'Then we will ensure that our bar and restaurant staff are made aware that you are unwell and confined to your cabin. It would not be difficult for someone to find out exactly which cabin you are in.

'I would expect that he would attempt to gain entry by indicating he is from the cabin service with food. So, we will ensure that only English-speaking waiters are sent, so if you hear an American accent, you can be sure that the person is unauthorised.

'In the meantime, the rest of the Pinkerton security staff will unobtrusively keep an eye on the corridor and the remaining passengers.'

I nodded, 'of course, the perpetrator could be a member of staff as no doubt you take on new people at each port.'

'Yes, good point, which is something we will consider'.

'Will you announce what has happened to the Tugwell's?' I asked.

Captain Dow pursed his lips, 'No I think that would send the wrong message, in any case, we have closed off the area and will hand that over to the police when we arrive in England.'

'Very well, there is one thing I would like you to do for me, and that is to send a telegram to Jacob Schiff,' I handed over a scribbled note:

An attempt made on my life, but assailant killed the wrong person STOP we are investigating at this end and would be grateful if you could do the same among your colleagues. STOP. James.

'I will have that sent straight away,' said Captain Dow, 'I will also arrange for a single bed to be brought in here for Mr Frobisher, and I will simply announce during dinner tonight that you are indisposed and have taken to your bed.'

It was on day four that it happened. I received a telegram from Jacob Schiff saying that his colleagues were above suspicion. Still, his security had caught a young woman assistant in the New York office going through the files. There was no copy of the letter of course, but there were minutes of the meeting I had with the other financiers. She was able to use the telephone before being caught. She has now confessed who she passed the information to, and the new department of the Bureau of Investigation is following that up. Jacob.

At 1.30 p.m. there was a knock on our door, and an English voice called out room service. Frobisher got up, pistol in hand and opened the door. What happened next was a blur, the waiter was thrown forward by someone behind him, which sent the tray and the waiter crashing to the floor. Frobisher was slightly behind the door as he opened it with his left hand, and therefore, his gun in his right hand was between the door and the assailant. I was walking across the floor holding the Webley as I had got used to, but I had forgotten to take the safety catch off the pistol. I saw the man move his gun toward where I was standing, and I went to fire, but nothing happened. I realised that I was about to be shot, so I dived to the floor, and at the same time Frobisher fired his gun through the door, but the bullet deflected, and the assassin moved his pistol round to deal with Frobisher, at that moment the waiter who had brought the food, bravely threw a glass that hit the killer. This deflected the shot at Frobisher, so he was only wounded in the arm which threw him backwards, his second shot going into the carpet. By this time, I had removed the safety catch and fired towards the assassin, which in turn threw him back against the door which had swung shut due to Frobisher's first shot. Despite a bloody stain appearing on the assassin's shirt, I saw he was recovering and his gun steadying to fire at me again. Although quite gravely wounded on the floor, Frobisher fired two shots as I fired again this time the three bullets hit the man squarely, and he fell to the floor dead.

I rushed over to the body, took the gun from the

assassin's hand, and threw it across the room. The waiter got up and said that there was a man in the corridor who was severely hurt. I picked up the phone and asked for emergency medical services, and within two minutes, the cabin was full of medics and Pinkerton's men. It transpired that Frobisher had been hit in the shoulder, which had broken his collar bone and so he was in considerable pain, the Pinkerton man in the corridor was dead, he had had his throat cut.

Talking about it afterwards to Mr Andrew and Captain Dow, I told them the action could not have taken much more than five seconds from the entry to the last shot being fired. What the assassin had not contemplated was that he had three men to deal with, two of them armed, and the waiter certainly saved the life of one of us, and I suggested he should be rewarded with a commendation.

On leaving the ship, I was escorted by a special naval military guard sent by Winston, and before I left, I thanked Captain Dow and Mr Andrew of Pinkerton's for their help.

I told both that they should not be on the ship after April of 1915. When asked why, I simply said that with the resumption of German U-boats in the Irish Sea, the dangers would increase ten-fold. I am not sure whether Andrews took my advice, but Captain Dow certainly did, as he took sick leave and handed the ship over to Captain William Thomas Turner who was one of the 761 survivors out of a total complement of 1198 when the ship was torpedoed in May of the same year.

On my return to the bank, I heard from Jacob Schiff that an arrest had been made of a senior man who worked within the office of one of the financial institutions and evidence was found that he had connections with both the German Embassy and the Mafia.

I had had a close shave, and when I met Winston the next day, I told him the story.

He looked at me strangely. I had the feeling that he wished he could have been there with me as I'm sure he would have enjoyed the trip, particularly the subsequent action on the ship.

'You realise, James, that you have achieved something that no one else could have done. It would have been impossible for our diplomatic staff or any of our politicians. This paper, he waved it in air, will secure the winning of the war. I am going to recommend you for a seat in the House of Lords, there is no single person more entitled than you, dear friend, and I am honoured to be your colleague.'

I saw tears forming in Winston's eyes, and I shook my head. 'It is not necessary, Winston, thank you all the same, but it was simply my duty to help my country, god knows the sort of privations thousands of our men and women endure who lay down their lives for our Democracy.'

'Yes, it's true, but without people like you and me, their lives would be wasted. You will accept a Seat in the House of Lords; we need people like you.'

He took the paper I had given him; he shook my hand warmly and was gone. It was the last time I saw him.

THE LUSITANIA IS SUNK;
1,000 PROBABLY ARE LOST

17 – KITCHENER

I did, however, hear from him again. I remember the date well, as I had just had the confirmation of the sinking of the Lusitania and the substantial loss of life connected to it, which made me feel depressed because I could not prevent the disaster.

I was aware of some changes in the high command of land forces. Field Marshall Herbert Kitchener had been moved sideways, due to criticism of his ability to ensure the delivery of enough rifles and shells, both items of which the army was growing short. As a result, he lost control of both munitions and strategy. There were criticisms that he found it difficult to delegate, and it was clear to some that he was becoming overtired. I did wonder whether the sinking of the Lusitania was partly responsible for the loss of arms, as it was rumoured that the ship had a substantial supply on board.

I received a note from Winston during the second week of May 2015. In it, he told me that he had suggested to Kitchener that he should call me for a meeting. A new coalition government had been formed under Prime Minister Asquith's watch because of criticism of the war and shortages of armaments. Winston indicated that while some of Kitchener's responsibilities had gone to Lloyd George, he still had a following from the public. So, it was deemed that the sacking of the Field Marshall, could create a general loss of morale.

I confess that I was not sure what Churchill expected me to say to Kitchener, but I indicated I would be happy to meet him should he call.

Within two days, I was told by my secretary, that a Captain Roberts had telephoned and requested that I report to the War Office at 10.00 hours the next morning for a meeting with the Field Marshall. I was irritated at the summons, but after careful thought, I decided to go, after all, Kitchener was still an influential figure, and he still had significant military responsibilities.

It was a lovely day, so I decided to walk to the War Office, which threw the guard at the entrance. He asked me who I was and what I wanted. I told him that I had come to see the Field Marshall and that an appointment had been made. He told me to wait and pointed to a chair in an anti-room. I went and sat down and reached for a copy of the Times that was on a table nearby.

Some fifteen minutes later, another man appeared in uniform with three pips, and I assumed this was the man who had made the original call. He spoke with an affected accent, which suggested he was highly educated, and his manner gave the view that he felt somewhat superior.

'Excuse me sir, but you did not confirm that you would be attending the meeting with the Field Marshall.'

'I did not, because it appeared the Field Marshall had already given the instruction that I should appear, however, if he is too busy, I will return to my office.' I got up and prepared to go.

'The Field Marshall is a busy man, but...'

I lost my cool. 'Well, young man, he may well be, but he is obviously not well served by arrogant young officers like yourself, now, either he is free, or he is not, I too am a busy man trying to ensure this appalling war has enough money to purchase the arms that are necessary to win it.' I turned to go.

'Er, the Field Marshall has instructed me that he will see you now, sir.'

'Fine, perhaps you would lead me to his office without any further delay,' I snapped.

The young officer now rather red-faced, turned and led the way up two staircases, and knocked at a large double door at the end of a corridor on the second floor.

Come,' came a voice from inside.

As I walked in behind the Captain, I saw the Field Marshall in full uniform behind a large desk. He didn't get up or offer his hand in greeting. The captain closed the door as he went out.

'You are Alexander, I presume?'

I was still standing in front of his desk. 'Yes, General, my name is James Alexander, and you asked to see me, well I'm here. What is it you require of me?'

He seemed a little shocked at my attitude. I assumed he was used to toadies cringing in fear by being in the same room as the great man.

'Please sit,' he waved his hand to a chair in front of his desk. 'I understand from Churchill, that you've recently returned from America.'

'Yes.'

He frowned, 'there is some rumour about what you might have achieved over there, would you like to elucidate?'

'No,' I saw him narrow his eyes, obviously not used to being refused. 'The matter is classified,' I said, 'and you will have to ask Mr Churchill for any details. I am not empowered to discuss secret government information, even with someone as senior as yourself. Now, is there anything else?'

He gave a watery smile, 'it appears we have got off on the wrong foot, Mr Alexander?'

'I confess to you that I despise rudeness, particularly when there is no reason for it, I decided to comply with your rather abrupt request to see you, and I expect some respect, even from a Field Marshall. We are both on the same side, and both interested in winning this war.' I said, smiling.

'All right, Alexander, I was asked by Churchill to see you, because you appear to have the knack of seeing into the future. Quite ridiculous of course, but I understand you and your financial institution have been helpful to the war effort, and I would be interested in your view from now on. I assume you have not served in any military organisation.'

'Not that you would be aware of, sir, but the world of finance is intertwined with war and its repercussions. As a result, it is important that we view what is going on currently, but even more important what sort of situation we will be faced with when we have won.'

'Oh, do you think we will win? That's comforting.'

'Yes, we will win militarily, but it will break up the Empire, so in that sense, we will lose financially and politically.'

'That's rather a sweeping statement to make.'

'Is it? You were one of the few people that made the prophecy that the war would not be a short one. You are right, and French are wrong for thinking it will be over before the end of 1916.'

'What gives you that view?'

'Two things. The Axis powers have been planning for war over the last four years, and they are well trained, well-armed, and believe that they should be the rulers of Europe. Germany is by far the strongest and the most belligerent. Their weapons are better. They have a substantial number of mortars, (I made that point because of the War Office refused to finance them.) ideal for trench warfare, heavy artillery, a great machine gun and their trenches are designed for an extended stay, as against ours which are too shallow and filled with mud. Hence the low morale of our troops.

'The second thing is that we have made a huge error in giving control of our armies to the French. They cannot afford politically, to give up one inch of French soil to the Germans. So, instead of being able to retreat tactically, reform and counter-attack, we stand and are killed in our thousands, all because the French do not want to give up their land.'

I could see that Kitchener, agreed without stating the fact. 'That may be, and I did my best to alter their opinion, but was overruled by Joffre, and subsequently by our politicians.'

'I understand you did not complain too much, because you thought there was a good chance of you being given overall command, but frankly, that would not have worked with the French breathing down your neck.'

He scowled but didn't reply.

'One more thing,' I said. ' Wars in the future will be won by technology; those with better weapons and tactics will win because most cannot afford an extended conflict. Germany, while being strong militarily, has major weaknesses. Their geographical position makes it vulnerable, surrounded by enemies, both on land and on the sea. Russia should be a key to defeating them, creating a front behind their lines, but in the end, despite our control of the sea, it will be the Americans that will supply the necessary human resources. But by then, Lord Fisher's strategy of starving the German civilian population will have started to bite.'

Kitchener raised his eyebrows at this and thanked me for my views. I had no idea whether he took in what I had said, but I believe he really couldn't win. He was already tainted by the concentration camps he created during the Boer war. His lack of understanding of the supply chain for armaments and new technologies, coupled with faulty tactics, would be the death of his career. However, he did take my advice regarding Russia, and I understood that he planned to sail there from the Orkneys during the following month. Unfortunately, this was a part of history I had not studied in my other life, and my advice may have been different had I done so.

18 - THE REQUEST

I told Victoria what had happened on my way back from America, and she was angry that I had taken such a risk. 'In future when you travel, I will go with you,' she said, and it was left at that.

We got back into our routine, and I was told confidentially that I would receive a peerage at the next investiture at the beginning of 1916. Victoria persuaded me to accept it as she argued that it would add to the bank's reputation. I had however, already decided to defer the honour until 1918 when I would feel more comfortable in receiving it.

The summer was full of bad news, and the number of stories of death on the front kept hitting the headlines. The incompetent generals on both sides would not have lasted more than a few months in the second world war. The problem as I saw it was the intransigence of the French, who were surprisingly given command of all the armies involved in the struggle. Even in the battles of the First World war there was some sense in armies retreating and counter attacking, but the French were steadfast in not giving an inch of French territory thus multiplying the casualties more than necessary.

The autumn arrived with little change. Churchill's idea of taking on Turkey had been a dismal failure, more due the incompetent generals and admirals than to the plan. The eventual demise of the Turks was more due to General Allenby moving up from Egypt, but that was to come later. Admiral Fisher's plan to embargo Germany with a blockade was starting to hurt but it was not until after the battle of Jutland in May of 1916 that British ships completely controlled the North Sea.

Following my return from America I began to feel guilty. I had to admit to myself that everything concerning my financial affairs was working so well that a touch of boredom started to creep in. My affair with Victoria had blossomed, the bank was hugely profitable, and now because of the war we were now making millions on a regular basis.

It is strange I thought, here I was, a hugely successful man with a happy relationship, the world at my feet, and yet there was an emptiness, a lack of purpose. By the end of October, I was moving into a state of depression, and it was in that state of mind when I was sitting in my office feeling sorry for myself that there was a shrill from the internal telephone on my desk. I picked up the receiver, 'yes?'

'It's Donald from the front desk, sir.' A picture of Donald entered my mind, an ex-sergeant-major now retired and in charge of the large reception area behind the entrance to our building. It was unusual for Donald to call my office directly and I found myself slightly irritated. 'Yes sergeant-major?' my irritation was noticed as he apologised for calling my office without first going through my secretary. 'I have a lady and a gentleman here who are insisting on seeing you. sir, and that no one else in the building should be contacted including your secretary. I asked if they had an appointment, but they said no.' Donald lowered his voice. 'I have sat them down in the reception room. The lady is heavily veiled, and the gentleman is unquestionably a senior officer, a type I recognised from my military experience. But the lady is obviously the senior of the two, which is puzzling, I'm sure you agree sir?'

I immediately thought about my recent experience on the Lusitania. 'Are they American?' I asked.

'No, sir, the gentleman is English, and the lady has a very slight foreign accent. But neither will give their name, the gentlemen said it was a matter of state security.'

I made up my mind, 'very well sergeant major, I assume you have one of your colleagues who can look after the entrance.'

'Yes, sir.'

'Accompany them to my office but make an assessment that they are not carrying any weapons as they alight the stairway.'

A few minutes went by and there was a knock on the office door. I opened it and was immediately caught by the vision of the dress the lady was wearing, it was obviously

coutured by a top designer. I sat them down on the sofa and took an armchair opposite. I was about to speak when the lady took off her veils.

I gasped; it was the Queen.

KING GEORGE V AND QUEEN MARY

She laughed at the expression of surprise on my face. 'I am sorry to surprise you like this,' she said, 'but after you kindly dealt with the other matter,' she was referring to my bringing the tsarevich and his young sister to the UK.

'The king needs your help once again, and again absolute secrecy is paramount.' She turned to her companion; 'I would like to introduce you to Captain Godfrey-Faussett who is Equerry to my husband.' I leaned forward and shook his hand. It was a firm grip. 'You may have heard that my husband recently had a fall from his horse, he was thrown while reviewing troops in France. The accident occurred while he was visiting President Poincare, and he was badly injured, otherwise he would be here himself. This is a matter that cannot be discussed or even come to the notice of the government.' She continued. 'The king has been deeply depressed at the rate of casualties in France, and his reason for going there was to discuss matters with the President. After the accident, Captain Godfrey-Faussett was asked to immediately return with a letter for my eyes only, but Godfrey-Faussett will explain.'

I nodded, 'how is the King, Ma'am?'

I noticed her eyes glisten with a sign of tears, but she immediately recovered herself. 'He has damaged his leg severely, and may not walk again, but he is in the best of hands medically speaking, and we are hoping he will return well before Christmas.'

'Please convey my best wishes to his majesty and I wish him a speedy recovery.'

'Thank you, Mr. Alexander, I will ensure he receives your kind message.'

'With your permission, Ma'am,' Godfrey-Faussett intervened, 'I will explain exactly what the King desires and how I am to be involved.' He looked at me. 'If you agree to this venture, I will be spending quite a lot of time in your company, therefore, against the general social preference of our time, I would like you to call me by my first name which is Bryan.'

I nodded.

'Now, sir, as the Queen has already said, the King is extremely concerned at the number of casualties Great Britain is suffering at this time and thus there is one consideration upon which he wishes to be informed. It is for us to meet with General John French who is the current commander of the BEF (British Expeditionary Force) and his number two, Sir William Robertson, the latter who the King believes should be brought back to be appointed Chief of Staff in London.'

I frowned, 'that would make him senior to French.' I raised my eyes.

'Yes, it would, but Robertson would almost certainly sack French and replace him with Douglas Haig who the King feels would be better equipped to deal with the French.

'I will introduce you over there as one of the principal funders for the war. However, this will serve as a cover for the real purpose of our trip which would be for me, in the first instance to drop you off at the Swiss border opposite Geneva where you will be met by Helmut Heidelberg, someone you have already met I believe?'

CAPTAIN BRYAN GODFREY-FAWCETT
EQUERRY TO KING GEORGE V

'Yes, I have, and consider him a gentleman of the highest repute. He is not only an honorary Colonel in the German Army, but he manages the Kaiser's private funds.'

'You are quite right, but he is now a General by the way, and he is concerned that the Kaiser is being sidelined by his military who now only give him the briefest of notice. You will not be surprised to know that the King has many relatives in Germany, and he has kept in touch with those sympathetic to Great Britain but not necessarily the French. Our understanding is that Helmut has some documents created by the German foreign office that would be of interest to us. He is travelling on behalf of a very senior person, but the trip may be dangerous as if a certain section of the German army has any suspicions, and get wind of your presence, they would be delighted to use their well-known persuasive methods for you to visit the fatherland.'

'I see, I gather from your explanation that it is not known who may show an interest in our proposed meeting, apart from Helmut?'

'There are names I could expose to you, but it is better that you have no knowledge of them at this stage, I am sure you understand.' Bryan smiled; 'however, this is not the place to discuss either the details or the timing of the suggested operation. I will call you in seven days, and if you are agreeable in principle, we should meet again, and I will discuss with you a plan which has been put forward for action.'

The Queen stood up, smiled, and held her hand out to receive the cursory kiss. 'We are already most indebted to you and what you have achieved for us and the country. You can trust Captain Faussett absolutely and if you decide to take on this mission, the King will be hugely grateful.' After pulling her veils across her face she glided through the door opened by the captain who held his hand out before leaving the office. The sergeant-major, who had remained in the corridor took them down to the entrance where a carriage awaited.

I met Victoria that evening and discussed the meeting with her. She insisted that should I decide to go, she would accompany me. I shook my head, 'no Victoria, this really is man's business, if there is a problem, I need to be able to extricate myself without being responsible for you or indeed anyone else.'

Victoria pursed her lips, 'very well then, I will stay in Paris and if you do not return within a set time, I will raise the alarm.' Her countenance implied there was no argument, so I left it at that.

The next week went quickly and true to his word Bryan telephoned me. I told him that I was agreeable on the basis that I had full details of the plan and what it could achieve. It was arranged to meet at my office on the following Monday and I told my secretary to leave the day completely free.

Bryan arrived on time, as any good military man should and after coffee, he pulled his briefcase onto his knee and extracted a file marked TOP SECRET. 'Anything that does not suit you in this plan can be changed.' He looked up at me for a reaction. I just nodded. He started reading.

'We will leave on February 24th, 1916,' he smiled. 'We will sail on HMS Westminster at 07.00 hours from London Docks and arrive in Le Havre later in the day. From there two embassy cars will pick us up and take us to Paris where we will spend the night at the British Embassy. The next morning, we will have a meeting with the British Ambassador, and we will tell him that you have arrived in France early to allow a Lady Ponsonby, who will accompany Lady Crowley to do some shopping, my wife will also accompany her.' He obviously knew of my liaison with Victoria. It rather surprised me, because such matters were not normally accepted in society, on the other hand even George V had been known to have mistresses from time to time.

'The next day, you will then move from the Embassy to the George Cinq hotel which I know you are familiar with. There are four suites booked there for the period. One for yourself, one for Lady Crowley, one for Lady Ponsonby and one for me and my wife. The following day the ladies will be accompanied on their shopping trip by Lady Ponsonby who will be their guide. The same morning early, you and I will be driven to the Swiss border, just south of Geneva. You will cross over by foot and be picked up on the other side by Helmut who will drive you to the Fairmont Le Montreux Palace on the shore of Lake Geneva. Next morning both of you will meet one other person who will be known as ''K.'' K is a close relative of the King. He is a highly placed and a well-connected German.'

I raised my eyebrows, 'so you will not be joining us in Switzerland.'

'Regrettably no, I am forbidden to travel to a foreign country outside Britain and France. I am in possession of too much military information, in fact all the information that the King holds. That means if I were captured all military plans would have to be scrapped, which would not make us popular with the French nor Parliament.'

So once again I am disposable, was my thought but I didn't say anything.

Bryan continued, 'the person you will meet in Switzerland you may recognise, but you should never use his name and you should expect the duplicitous Swiss to have some system of listening to your conversation, so you should only discuss matters of importance in the gardens attached to the hotel. Of course, it is probable that Helmut will have arranged for your meeting to take place somewhere else, but I am not privy to arrangements once you are over there.'

'Do we know what this gentleman is offering?'

Bryan shook his head. 'No but he is loyal to the Kaiser and to the future of Germany, which means he is not happy with the current management of the war, but he is not able to stop it. Apparently, he has some information that he believes will ensure Germany will lose the war within the next two years and as such it will create a situation where Germany will have some negotiating power in trying to force an armistice. He wants to ensure that Germany is not occupied by foreign forces. Having said that, he wants something in return.'

'What?'

'We don't know, but we assume it is something in the power of King George V to grant. He is paranoid that such negotiations do not reach the ears of the French, which is why he does not trust the British government who would be duty bound to pass any secret negotiation over to them.'

'If a treaty is to be signed, governments must be involved,' I said, frowning.

'No, once you have been told the details of what is on offer, you will impart that to me on your return. The king will then consider what they want and whether he is able to gift it. Should he decide to do so, the reply we receive from them will not refer to your visit but come as a secret letter of confirmation and will include incontrovertible evidence by way of original documents which will be sealed and handed to the British Ambassador in Berne, Switzerland, and brought to the foreign Secretary in Britain via a diplomatic bag. It will be addressed to the King for his eyes only.

'Now, when in Switzerland, should you be apprehended, the story will be that you have been asked to meet Helmut to discuss part of Vianden Castle being turned into a hotel after the war, this to be financed partly by Helmut and the Kaiser, your bank picking up the difference. It is not unusual for banks to do deals to be implemented after a conflict. It will be a genuine proposal from Helmut which you can bring back with you and if opened at customs, it will verify your visit.

'If the King agrees to the proposal sent by ''K'' then you will be asked to certify the Hotel agreement which will be taken as approval of the secret deal.

'Of course, all this will be based on trust, but as only royalty on both sides is involved, there should be no slip up.'

I smiled, 'it seems you have thought this out very carefully, but what happens if (a) I cannot agree to the hotel deal and (b) I am apprehended?'

'The King will guarantee the bank should you need to be covered; however, the contract will be worded in such a way that will give you a get out clause. You may be searched, but not apprehended, because you will be travelling under diplomatic immunity, and you will be contacted by our ambassador at the hotel during the following day, he will arrange to meet you there when you are free. He has meetings in Geneva which he will discuss with you, but he will not be party to the agreement with Helmut nor the secret meeting.

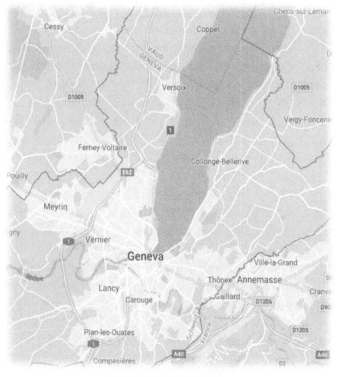

FERNEY-VOLTAIRE

'We know the Germans do not consider diplomatic immunity, and if they suspect a plot, you will certainly be watched but remember you are not, so far as I am aware visiting the German speaking area. Geneva is on the French side of the lake and is close to the French / Swiss border, Helmut is a General in the Wehrmacht, so it is unlikely to go wrong unless Helmut is not loyal. The British Ambassador will be armed, and he will be accompanied by a senior British officer, who will also be armed.

'I have arranged with our military based in Ferney-Voltaire, a French town which straddles the border to be on alert. It would be easy to cut across the access road north of Geneva if there is any funny business. I have told them that our ambassador will be having a secret meeting with certain individuals in the company of the King's representative. This brings me to the second reason for your visit.'

I must have looked surprised, 'oh,' was all I could say.

'It seemed to us that our Ambassador should take the opportunity to meet with two highly placed individuals to establish their plans regarding Russia, as it could have a major effect on the war, Our Ambassador 'Sir Evelyn Mountstuart Grant Duff KCMG who is normally at the Embassy in Berne, will brief you. You in Geneva provides him with an excellent excuse to be there at that time. His family has close connections with the crown however and he can be trusted. He will not be aware of the true purpose of your visit, only that you are meeting Helmut to discuss a deal regarding property and hopefully eliciting information out of him regarding the morale of the German population.'

'So, the Ambassador will not be present at my meeting with Helmut?'

'No, that will be private and if the Ambassador asks you should tell him that your visit is purely regarding the hotel scheme.'

I laughed, knowing that history handed down through the years, was not always quite true to what really happened.

It is often created by the person who wrote it and sometimes twisted it to suit a purpose.

'Of course, your meeting with the Ambassador will simply be as an observer and Helmut will not be aware of such a meeting.'

'Who will we be meeting?'

'I am not sure at this stage, but I am advised that it will be two important people who could influence the war.'

'So, I will be there for two days?'

'Yes, no longer as the word will get out and then it could be harder to extricate you if there is a problem.'

'Why are we are not moving until February?' I asked.

'Oh, that is easy to answer, we must make very careful plans, as what we are doing could shorten the war, and almost any plan that could do that is worth an extra effort.'

And so it was, we had a series of meetings during the interregnum but amazingly we boarded the HMS Westminster on 24th February 1916 as planned, recognising that the Battle of Verdun had started only three days earlier, which I knew was to be the longest and bloodiest battle of the war.

The trip in HMS Westminster was not a comfortable one. The sea in the channel was very rough and

HMS Westminster during the First World War

we were pleased to disembark. We were met by two Rolls Royce's supplied with army drivers that took us to Paris and as planned we stayed the first night in the British Embassy. On the way down to Paris I was struck by the amount of army vehicles on the road travelling both ways. Some carrying fresh troops and supplies towards Paris and others carrying wounded troops back towards Le Havre. The sight of the wounded could not have increased the morale of those heading towards the battle. It struck me that someone should have organised the use of two different roads, one going east and the other west. I am proud to say that I was able to change this when I met with General Robertson.

We enjoyed a dinner that evening at the hotel, and we all turned in early as both Bryan and I had to set off early the next day.

We reached the Swiss border in good time as the roads south of Paris were reasonably clear of military traffic. On the way there Bryan told me of a new situation that I might face once in Geneva.

'I have heard from Evelyn Grant Duff that the Germans have opened a consulate in Geneva, probably because they realise that it is an excellent place for foreign diplomats to cross the border from France to meet with what they consider are dissidents, people against the war. This means that they will have used their presence to infiltrate the border guards and will almost certainly know of your forthcoming visit. I mention this as you should take care.' It was good advice as I was to find out.

I got out of the car and walked to no man's land and into a small building straddling the road. There was a counter with two uniformed men who appeared rather disinterested in their new arrival. I was asked for my identity papers which were briefly checked and returned. I was asked what my business was and how long I would be staying in Switzerland. I told them I was meeting a businessman and would not be in their country for more than three days. The final question was where I was staying and when I told them, they appeared impressed and told me that the hotel carriage was outside, presumably awaiting my arrival.

I did not show them my embassy papers, as they didn't request them, and I felt the less divulged the better. As I walked through the building, I saw Helmut coming toward me. He grabbed me in a bear hug which was rather a surprise, 'it is really gut to see you again, James,' slipping into bastardising the English language. 'And me you,' I answered, 'how are Sophia and the children?' I enquired. 'Gut, gut, Sophia sends her love, but come, the carriage will take us to the hotel and after you have had time to freshen up as the Americans say, we can talk. This appalling war has ruined everything.' A lackey had picked up my bags and placed them in the carriage, and we climbed in. It was rather a grand affair drawn by four horses and despite the metal ringed wheels was quite comfortable. We talked about my time with him at the Vianden Castle and he asked after Victoria, that nice lady that accompanied you, was how he described her. I congratulated him on his promotion to General. He waved his hand, 'it carries no responsibility, it is just an honorary title.'

'But you must be responsible for something?' I said. He laughed, 'it is a title to encourage me to ensure my bank supports the financing of the massacre that is going on in Northern France, but confidentially I have to tell you that the vast amount of the bank's funds have been transferred to Switzerland, that way I can control the profligate spending of the military.'

I nodded, 'I wish that Great Britain had been able to keep out of it,' I said, 'but Germany invading Belgium left our politicians no choice.'

Helmut grimaced, 'Ya, the German generals were overconfident and thought that the British would find an excuse to opt out of the treaty, but I did warn them that they had misunderstood the honour of the English,' he sighed. 'Germany has the best trained army in the world and is better equipped than all its adversaries. It's air combat facility under Baron von Richthofen is also the best in the world. But Germany is a land state and surrounded by its enemies. If the generals had been able to take over France as they did during the Franco Prussian war, we would have made short work of it. The difference is that in the Franco Prussian war it was masterminded by a clever politician.'

'Otto Von Bismarck,' I said,

'Ya, and he was careful to ensure the English were kept out of it. Unfortunately, the treaties that he fashioned should have been adjusted according to circumstances, but the young Kaiser was pushed by the military to sack Bismarck, and he had no one to take his place. Politicians work by devious ways. Military men think only of force. They ignore the public, they ignore where the funding is to be found, and they ignore the strength of their allies. At the start, they will always carry out spectacular victories but unless they can completely subjugate their enemies quickly, they will always lose. Napoleon was a good example of this.'

'You are quite right Helmut, Britain is essentially a country of defense, which is why it has concentrated on its Navy, the largest and arguably best in the world. War to us is an anathema as it interferes with trade. Now our future is in the hands of the military as is yours. It will end badly for both sides and there will be no winners in this current conflict.'

'Ya, but there is something else the British excel at which our military did not consider.'

I frowned, 'something else.'

'Ya, you have the best intelligence operation, it is a silent weapon, but quite devastating.'

'Umm, I hadn't thought of that, but I suppose there are a lot of Brit's throughout the world. But wherever they are situated they remain firmly British.'

Helmut did not elucidate. 'Today we are travelling to the hotel where we will dine this evening. Tomorrow we will ride in a military vehicle to Chillon.'

I raised my eyebrows, 'Chillon?'

'Ya, it is in the German speaking part of Switzerland and just the other side of the lake, there we will meet "K" and discuss an offer that he will make. We will lunch there and return to the hotel in the evening where we will hopefully agree on the proposal, I have for your bank regarding Vianden Castle in Luxembourg. You will remember that there is a large section of it that requires a considerable upgrading and that is the area in question, but I will give you full plans of how we should proceed. The documents I will give you will be genuine and if you should be stopped you can produce them for the reason you are in Switzerland.'

'Am I likely to be stopped?' I asked.

Helmut sighed, 'it is a possibility, they know we are meeting, and there are German spies everywhere. They would not dare to interfere whilst you are with me, but they will be curious why you are staying an extra day to meet with your ambassador.'

'To be honest with you, I have no idea why the Ambassador wishes to meet with me, but I plan to leave Switzerland as soon as possible after my meeting with him.'

Helmut nodded, 'I think I have an idea, but it won't work.' He looked at me with a smile.

I decided not to take the conversation further in case it led me into something I did not wish to discuss. Helmut changed the subject. 'The castle of Chillon is built on the island of Chillon, an oval limestone rock near Geneva between Montreux and Villeneuve, with a

CHILLON CASTLE

steep drop on one side and on the other side the lake and it's steep bottom. The placement of the castle is strategic: it closes the passage between the Vaud Riviera (access to the north towards Germany and France) and the Rhone valley which allows quick access to Italy. Moreover, the place offers an excellent view of the Savoyard coast. A garrison could thus control (both militarily and commercially) access to the road to Italy and apply a toll. According to the Swiss ethnologist Albert Samuel Gatschet, the name *Chillon* comes from the Waldensian dialect and would mean "flat stone, slab, platform "castle built on a chillon" on a rock platform.

'The first construction dates to around the 10th century, although it is likely that it was already privileged. *Castrum Quilonis* (1195) would therefore mean military site before that date. Objects dating back to Roman times were discovered during excavations in the 19th century, as well as remains from the Bronze Age. From a double wooden palisade, the Romans would have fortified the site before a square dungeon was added in the 10th century. Sources from the 13th century link the possession of the Chillon site to the Bishop of Sion.

'A charter of 1150, where Count Humbert III grants the Cistercians of Hautcrêt free passage to Chillon, attests to the domination of the House of Savoy on Chillon. The owner of the castle is mentioned as Gaucher de Blonay, a vassal of the Count of Savoy. At the time it was a seigniorial domination of Savoy within the framework of a feudal society and not an administrative domination.'

'How interesting,' I said, with conviction, 'and why is the gentleman we are meeting residing there rather than travelling to Geneva?'

Helmut smiled and looked at his watch, 'you will see in precisely 10 minutes time, there are currently too many Germans in Geneva, and it would not be safe for him to be seen there.' It took that time to reach the gates of the castle and as we approached them some unseen hand opened the large double doors and we drove into the courtyard.

As we alighted from the car, 'I noticed what appeared to be an old man walking towards us, I noticed his left arm was tucked into his jacket. Because of his shabby clothes I assumed he was a gardener from the estate. As the man approached, I saw Helmut snap to attention and salute. I looked around to see who he was saluting, but there was only the old man who had stopped in front of us. I peered more carefully at the person and gasped, it was Kaiser Wilhelm II.

'I think we have met before,' the man said, in clipped English. 'You must forgive me, but I am here in disguise because of the delicate matter I wish to discuss with you. Only General Heidelberg knows who I am.'

Over lunch I was amazed at the revelations that were imparted. He revealed that he was a virtual prisoner in his palace and that the military had effectively cut him out of the command structure. 'Of course, I managed through my trusted doctor to get admitted to hospital with a made-up illness and from there I was able to sneak out in disguise in these old clothes, and I have arranged for my chauffeur to pick me up from here and I will appear back in the hospital gardens in uniform, so no one will be any wiser. It would have been difficult for me to get away from the palace without being noticed and certainly impossible to get back in.

'You may be surprised that I have called for you to meet me as the war appears to be in our favour, but I know that Germany cannot win the war nor will the French allow any sort of negotiation, so the killing of our young men, the flower of our future will continue on all sides. You will know that we are attacking Verdun at this moment, but in my view the French can never afford to give up that fortress. The stupidity of our military going through Belgium and thus virtually dragging England into the war was a mistake. The British army is no match for ours, but their sea power is huge and is already interfering with our supplies. The only way we could have won was a swift strike into France and they could not have survived with the Austrian Empire supporting us against Italy.'

'It is probably true,' I said, 'but are you not forgetting Russia?'

The Kaiser grimaced, 'Russia is dead, it is close to revolution, their army, although large, is badly formed, their equipment is old, their command is hopeless, the military will take Russia out of the war with ease.'

'In that case, Austria Hungary will benefit as without Russian support, they will have a free ride against Serbia despite Turkey supporting them from the south.' I said.

'Ya, it is true, but there is Italy on their flank and the British attacking from Egypt. It is a war of attrition and the longer it goes on, the weaker Germany will be, and I will be blamed for it. While Bismarck's planned allegiances will be ignored.'

'Let us say that you are right, and Germany will lose. Why did you want to meet me?'

The Kaiser looked across at Helmut. 'Because our generals have conceived a plot to ensure America will not enter the war, it will only be used when it dawns on them that all is lost.'

I looked surprised.

'They are planning to send a telegram to Mexico and Japan to inveigle them to join the war. An offer of military and funding support will be offered to both countries, in the case of Mexico, they would be encouraged to capture the states of Texas and Arizona, areas which America took from Mexico and with Japan, they would have a free reign in China. The military believe that such a telegram would almost certainly prevent America joining the war against Germany.'

I frowned, 'but only if it did not became known by the United States,' I said.

Helmut interjected, 'that's where you come in, you need to persuade the government to pass on the information to the Americans.'

I frowned again, 'but surely that would be against the interests of Germany, I don't understand.' I was thinking of some dastardly trick to draw me in to helping the Germans and the more I thought about it, the more puzzled I became. Here in front of me was the head of Germany who arguably started the whole thing off, now bringing about its demise.

Helmut saw that I was struggling with the enormity of what I had just heard.

'It depends whether you are thinking of Germany and the German people or the military who have now taken command of the war,' said Helmut. 'Let me explain.' We were sitting around a huge table and had just had our soup served. When the person who had brought it had left the room, there was a brief interlude, when we finished our soup, Helmut sat back in his chair and took a deep breath. 'The German military promised that this war would be over in weeks and the Kaiser was promised that would be the case. Remember the Franco Prussian war was over in 7 months. The German military assumed that England would keep out of it. After all, the heads of State were cousins and both states are Protestant, the French Catholic. Why would Britain get involved? The military mind did not consider that by over-running Belgium the British would act with a military force, they thought reasonably, that the British would react by intervening in the diplomatic area. They did not assume that the British would put their military under French command either.

'Germany had become a military state with little attention to politics, so there was no one of any note that had the political experience to see where the military action would take them. There was no one who foresaw how the war would be paid for and in the end, it is all about money and supply.

'When war broke out, the Allied powers possessed greater overall demographic, industrial, and military resources than the Central Powers and enjoyed easier access to the oceans for trade with neutral countries, particularly with the United States. The British Navy had 532 warships including 65 submarines, Germany had 264 warships including 28 submarines. Although the German ships were technologically better, the other naval vessels in the Central powers were inconsequential. So, the lack of supply from overseas has to some extent been dealt with by innovation, but as more and more men have been drawn into the military, our manufacturing industry has suffered, and we now lack skilled and trained men to run our factories.

'The Schlieffen Plan was drawn up mainly for attack and defence. Knowing the mindset of the French, it was realised that once French territory had been taken, they would move heaven and earth to dislodge the invader. Thus, our trench system, communications and weapons were designed to take out those attacking. Therefore, our machine guns, mortars and artillery are vastly superior.

'No one realised that the enemy would throw the cream of their armies into such an unequal battle. The German military had not considered the cost of such a long-drawn-out war. At the end of this year, 1916, we will have used up 70 percent of our gold reserves, which means even now we are printing currency that is not supported by value. We are also supporting the Hapsburg Empire and the Turks. Inflation is already growing and there will come a time when it becomes difficult to feed our people, particularly if the embargo by the British Navy continues.'

The door to the room opened but the waiters were waived away by the Kaiser.

'Even with a fleet technically superior to the British and French navies, we do not have sufficient submarines to make a difference. I fear that the generals who know nothing about sea power will make the mistake of throwing their ships into battle against the most powerful navy in the world. We cannot possibly win such an unequal contest.' *I remembered from my history that the battle of Jutland was only two months away, but of course I said nothing, only nodded in agreement.*

The Kaiser continued, 'as we grow weaker, you will grow stronger. I would imagine that Britain will bring to bear more of the assets from the empire, particularly in the south against the Turks and take a more aggressive stance in France by getting rid of General French who appears to be incapable of dealing with his namesake to the detriment of the British army.

'Our civilian population is already fragmenting; we are a relatively new state and like America we have attracted many immigrants who do not necessarily share the views of our military. For instance, we have a large Jewish population, and it is suspected that after war was declared and war bonds were offered by the state, the Jewish population sent their money overseas, mainly to the USA, thus causing a rift that could disable our country in the future.'

I nodded, now understanding why the Kaiser wanted the war to end. If the Americans came into the war, they would be a foil against the French and would be much more likely to be against occupation of a beaten country. It was also a fact that the USA had a very large German population that were loyal to their homeland.

'There is one other factor that has come to my attention from our spies in Germany.' Smiled Helmut.

'Oh, what is that?' I asked.

'The USA industrial might is already helping Britain to finance the war, something I believe you were part of.'

I ignored confirming the point he had made. 'So, as I understand it, you will give me evidence that Germany will indicate to both Mexico and Japan that they will be supported financially and diplomatically by Germany to attack USA interests, in the case of Mexico to attack the states of Texas and Arizona and in the case of Japan, to attack American interests in Japan and China, is that correct?'

'Ya,' answered the Kaiser.

'But from what you have already told me you could not afford to fund such an operation?'

'We couldn't,' answered Helmut, 'but the military have no conception of the financial situation and no conception of the industrial power of the USA. Their prime objective is to stop the USA becoming involved in the European war, which arguably may dissuade America from becoming involved if their border and other interests were threatened. They are assuming America would deploy their forces to prevent that happening, but that is a huge underestimation of American power. It may delay their reaction to the European war, but in that case, there would be civil war within Germany. Such a situation would put France into a situation where they could occupy Germany and an armistice would be denied to us.'

'Okay,' I said, 'let us assume that the British can somehow convince the USA that they have managed to obtain this information, it does not follow that they will believe it. They may well think that it is a ruse by Britain to involve the Americans into the war.'

The Kaiser looked at Helmut. 'Ya, we have thought of that possibility,' answered Helmut. 'The German foreign Minister is called Arthur Zimmerman; he plans to send a telegram to the Mexican and Japanese Foreign offices in January 1917. We would expect the British to pretend that they have intercepted that message and announce it to the world. Arthur Zimmerman will then confirm publicly that he has sent it. You see Arthur is a patriot and a royalist and is disgusted at what the military are doing. Here is a copy of what the telegram will say:'

"We intend to begin on the first of February unrestricted submarine warfare. We shall endeavour despite this to keep the United States of America neutral. In the event of this failing, we make Mexico a proposal or alliance on the following basis: make war together, make peace together, generous financial support and an understanding on our part that Mexico is to reconquer the lost territory in Texas, New Mexico, and Arizona. The settlement in detail is left to you. You will inform the President of the above most secretly as soon as the outbreak of war with the United States of America is certain and add the suggestion that he should, on his own initiative, invite Japan to immediate adherence and at the same time mediate between Japan and ourselves. Please call the President's attention to the fact that the ruthless employment of our submarines now offers the prospect of compelling England in a few months to make peace." Signed, ZIMMERMANN."

I read it through twice and raised my eyebrows. 'You will appreciate that it is unheard of for a secret document to be confirmed, what excuse will Zimmerman give for doing so?'

The Kaiser answered. 'He will say, when defending his action that it was a logical precaution in the event of the American entry into the war.'

I would have been much more suspicious if I were unaware of the Zimmerman Telegram and the furore it caused. Obviously if Britain had made such an announcement and it was not confirmed, the action would not necessarily have been helpful, indeed it could have had the reverse affect.

'Very well sir, I will memorise this message, and take this back to the King, and report my meeting with you. Now my understanding is that providing the King agrees to hand this on to our government you would require something in return.'

'Ya, I want to receive from the King a solemn promise that in the event of Germany losing the war, myself and my family will not suffer any prosecution nor disgrace and be allowed to live in my mansion which I intend to buy in the Netherlands.

'You will simply send an affirmation of the separate commercial deal you have discussed with Helmut. That will be taken by me that the King has agreed. As soon as that is received, and the telegram sent, I will reply with a secret sealed letter through the British Embassy in Berne addressed to King George V for his eyes only.

'King George will presumably give the telegram to your secret service with instructions that they should declare it publicly. When that happens Zimmerman will indicate that it was sent by him.'

I could hardly believe my ears, but of course I was aware of the Zimmerman telegram and how it brought America into the war, but not quite as quickly as the Kaiser hoped.

I do remember however that King George V did insist that the Kaiser was allowed to move to the Netherlands after the war and despite many calls for him to be tried and shot, particularly from the French, the King stood his ground. What I did not know was that it was due to me that this arrangement was carried through.

'Well, sir, I will carry out your instructions to the letter.' I confirmed, ' I hope to god it works and many lives can be saved.' It struck me afterwards that by me doing so, may have saved my father's life, as he was due to return to duty after being wounded on the Somme. I felt very strange at this thought as if he had been killed, then I would not have been born.

'Gut, gut, now call in the servants and let us finish our lunch.'

On the drive back, Helmut explained that the Kaiser had taken a very difficult decision. While it may appear that he was looking after his own interests, the opposite was the case.

'He has been advised by me and others that it is highly unlikely that Germany will come out well in this war. Armies move slowly and we are not yet in a position where speed is our friend. Perhaps things will change in the future. If Germany had waited for another two years things may have been very different. He knows that his action may well cause difficulties for Germany, but by bringing the war to an end he believes he will save thousands of lives and importantly ensure that Germany is not occupied by foreign troops. There is already some disquiet within the population, and as the lack of food and increasing food prices take hold, it will become a fight on two fronts, the enemy, and the people.'

Helmut dropped me off at the hotel in Geneva and wished me god speed. He ensured I had the documents pertaining to the loans available for his hotel and he left me with a warning. 'My gut friend, I know you are spending another day here, but I have been informed that the military know you are here, and you may find that they will try to prevent your return, so it would be good if you stayed close to your Ambassador. I realise that you have diplomatic immunity, but you are not accredited and thus you could be in danger. I happen to know that there is a military mission in the area that are involved in a meeting later this week.' We shook hands and he drove off. I never saw him again and learned later that he was killed in a civilian riot in 1918 just days before the armistice.

I went to my room in the hotel and found a message from the British Ambassador that he was arriving that evening and suggested we meet for dinner.

While Helmut was talking at Chillon, I had pencilled in the details of the Zimmerman Telegram, as I knew I could not remember it without doing so. When I had finished, I realised if I was stopped, it could easily be found on my person, so I spent some time concocting a letter to Tory. It took me almost 2 hours to encrypt all the items within the letter enclosing all the individual words to remind me of the text.

I was quite pleased when I had finished as the text could only be interpreted by someone who knew the contents of the Zimmerman telegram and even then, it is unlikely that a connection could be made.

I then burnt the notes I had made and put them in the wash basin in my room and turned on the tap.

I met Sir Evelyn Mountstuart Grant Duff KCMG that evening and regretfully we did not hit it off. I think he was peeved that I was on his patch, but he did not know why. He clearly did not believe that I had come over to discuss the financing of the Vianden Castle and was constantly trying to find out what the deal was. Eventually I showed him the document signed by Helmut, but that didn't satisfy him.

At our meeting I called him by his first name, I should have known better, but there were some things that I still clung to from 2010.

He looked down his nose at me. 'People normally call me, sir,' he said haughtily.

'I too am used to being called, sir,' I said, 'but usually by those who I employ. However, if you prefer that we address each other as, sir.'

I don't remember him calling me anything after that, so I stuck with Evelyn.

During dinner he told me that he was on a special secret visit to Geneva, and although he had been instructed to include me in any meetings he might have, he made it plain that I should simply act as an observer and not to enter any conversation. The resultant discussion over dinner was uneventful.

The next morning, I met Evelyn at a small conference room booked within the hotel and it was shortly filled by another four people. Two of them were translators but I immediately recognised the names of the other two. It appeared the senior one was called Vladimir Ilyich Ulyanov, better known as Vladimir Lenin and the other Lev Bronstein born to a Jewish-Ukrainian family, better known as Leon Trotsky. We listened to a tirade of the unfairness of the countries governed by the upper classes and who kept the downtrodden peasants in their place, with no chance of a proper education and advancement.

LENIN   **TROTSKY**

I listened carefully and could agree with everything that was said. That this man was to be responsible for many thousands of deaths was an eye opener as he proved to be no better than the people he was criticising.

Trotsky was rather less of an intellectual than Lenin, I knew he became the leader of the army in the oncoming civil war. He fell out with Stalin and was assassinated in Mexico under his orders.

I was not sure what Evelyn thought he would gain by meeting these two, as they gave nothing away. I learned later that they really came to Geneva to talk with the Germans who were very keen to meet them. Subsequently they were transported by a secret train through Germany to Saint Petersburg where they managed to create the revolution and eventually take over the state and pull the army out of the war.

I did not fancy having lunch with Evelyn, so I telephoned Bryan and asked him to meet me at the customs area telling him the time I hoped to pass through into France. I persuaded the hotel to find me a driver and car and the man drove me to the border. As I alighted from the car, I had just received my luggage when I was approached by two men in similar suits, a large car with driver was standing by. They told me that they were customs officials, but I suspected that they were not as their accent was German.

'Herr Alexander?'

'Yes,' I answered. I noticed Bryan in the French part of the building some 200 yards away from where I stood. He looked concerned.

I turned to the two men. One of them flashed a card in front of me, but too quickly for me to read what was on it. 'Herr Alexander, you are under arrest for border irregularities, and you are to come with us.' The one not speaking turned to open the car door.

I smiled, 'yes of course,' I said I picked up the larger piece of luggage and moved toward him and literally pushed the case into his arms. He reacted by trying to catch it but became unbalanced and stepped back hitting the man who had just opened the car door. I threw the other smaller piece of luggage at the car and ran. I assumed that they had guns, but I guessed it would take them a few seconds to get their balance and draw their weapons, in which case they would be firing at the Swiss border guards, who, alerted by Bryan were rushing toward me. Bryan told me afterwards that the two men grabbed my luggage and bundled it into the car, did a swift U turn and drove away at speed. The only thing I had was the document signed by Helmut and the letter I had compiled for Tory which I had put into my inside pocket in case I needed to show the former at customs.

I was passed through at lightning speed and was soon sitting in the car next to Bryan who was rather out of breath.

'Well done, James, that could have been tricky. I noticed that the two were standing by their car on the roadside, so I alerted the Swiss Guards, which is why they were so fast in moving towards you.'

'Thank you for that, I noticed that there were a lot of Germans in the hotel last night, most were certainly military in suits.'

'How could you tell?'

I laughed. 'By the accentuated way they walked, almost as though they were on the parade ground. I also noticed a couple standing to attention when speaking to what was obviously a senior officer. I have the feeling that they were there to meet Lenin and Trotsky but let me fill you in on what happened on my trip.'

To say Bryan was surprised at me meeting the Kaiser was an understatement, he was as shocked as I had been and even more so when I told him of what I had been told.

We reached Paris in the early afternoon, and I learned of the successful shopping trip from the ladies. In fact, so successful was it that they needed a van to accompany them when they returned to England.

Later that evening we met the ambassador who told us that the meetings with General French had been arranged for the next day as well as separate meetings with General William Robertson and General Haig. Although I am told there were grumbles from General French, because the meeting was requested by the Kings equerry, he could hardly refuse.

The next morning the ladies were tired from their previous day's exertions, so they decided to stay in the hotel.

The embassy driver came for us at 10.00 hours and drove us to the British Embassy where we were taken up to meet the Ambassador Viscount Bertie of Thame. He had been the ambassador to France since 1905, so he was well acquainted with the French. We were greeted cordially and offered a drink which we both declined but Bertie took a large scotch just the same. He reminded me of Father Christmas with his white whiskers and portly build. He asked us if we spoke French, he turned to Bryan. 'My apologies, sir, of course I know you do,' He looked at me, 'I'm afraid not,' I said.

'In that case we will stick to English,' he answered.

He pointed to two comfortable chairs in his office, and we sat down, Bertie smiled, 'well I understand you want to discuss the situation with the generals. I am of course extremely sorry regarding the Kings accident with a horse, damned silly to give him one that was frisky if you ask me. But that's the French for you. Wouldn't be surprised if it were on purpose.' He lowered his voice, 'you see they know the King doesn't rate General French, but they like him because he does as he's told, don't you know. Good chap, but not up to the job. He's a gambler, but I expect you know that.' he looked at Bryan.

Bryan nodded.

The Viscount Bertie of Thame
GCB GCMG GCVO PC

Lord Bertie of Thame 1915

'If it hadn't been for Haig, he would have been declared bankrupt. It just is not on, that the commanding general had to be saved by a more junior member of his staff.'

He sniffed and looked at his timepiece, 'should be here shortly.' As he finished talking, the internal telephone on his desk rang. He answered it, 'ah yes, bring him up,' he turned to us, 'it's

French. I will leave him alone with you if you don't mind, I have got other things to do.'

I took an instant dislike to General French, not something I normally do. Despite Bryan representing the King, he treated him with some disdain, and it quickly became clear that he thought the meeting a waste of time, his time. He then dropped a bombshell. 'I am afraid that neither Robertson nor Haig will be available. The French are fighting for their lives at Verdun and need support from us on their flank, the generals are therefore fully engaged.' He sat down on one of the comfortable chairs and lit a cigarette the smoke from which was unpleasant. I learned afterwards that they were Russian. He looked at his time piece impatiently, 'so gentlemen, what can I do for you?'

I thought Bryan was extremely courteous in the circumstances as he did not show any form of annoyance. 'You will be aware that King George has been injured...'

'He fell off his horse, I believe.' interrupted French, raising his eyebrows. 'I am sorry gentlemen, but the King visiting the troops on the front line would have been a morale booster, visiting the President did not help at all.' He tapped cigarette ash on the plush carpet.

'I would have thought that the King would have had to contact the head of state before going to meet the soldiers,' I said, 'to do otherwise could have been taken as an insult.'

He looked at me for the first time, I read on his fac a disdain for someone who was a civilian.

'And you, sir, have you ever been in the military?'

I was caught, I couldn't say I had, when I had served for three years, so I answered that although I had not, I had studied military history, which was true. He looked faintly interested.

'Oh, what period?'

I smiled, 'Waterloo, the Crimean war, the Boer war, the American war of independence, Khartoum.' I could see that he was going to ask me questions and so I added the 'Naval battles of Copenhagen, the Battle of the Nile,

Trafalgar, the Russian naval battle in the China Sea...' I was about to add the Battle of Jutland, but realised it had not yet been fought, so I stopped.

Once I moved to sea battles he lost interest, which was perhaps fortunate.

He then launched into a brief assessment of the allied plan which was to support the line in Picardy while the French army was bogged down in Verdun. It seemed to us that he was content to allow the French to take the brunt of the war while at the same time obtaining the credit for any victories. The British were under strict orders from the French not to give up any French territory irrespective of the position, which was not necessarily the best plan for us, as it restricted our movement and created heavier casualties.

Bryan interjected. 'Mr. Alexander is helping to provide funds for the war effort, without him and others like him, you would not be able to continue, particularly so as our army appears to lose almost more weapons than we can supply. Anyway General, I was asked by the King to meet with both General Robertson and General Haig, so if they cannot come here, which is understandable in the circumstances, I must go to them.'

French raised his eyebrows. 'Impossible, it is too dangerous, our line is fluid, and the German artillery is accurate, and there are the German flying machines that fly behind our lines to strafe the vehicles supplying our troops. No sir, I could not allow it.'

Bryan pulled a document out of the brief case he had with him. 'You do not understand General, this document is one signed by King George V, and it is an order that I should be given all assistance to meet with your good self and with the two aforementioned generals, and I am going to carry out that order, irrespective of the danger.' He handed the document to French.

General French frowned. 'In that case, sir, I will have a document typed up for you to sign. It will allow you as a civilian to go through various military check points and I will advise General Robertson that you will be heading to see him. This document will also absolve me of any responsibility for your safety.' He got up and left the room.

While he was gone, I turned to Bryan. 'I have the feeling that we are not going to get much out of General French, what do you think?'

Bryan smiled, 'I agree, I think he knows that the King is unhappy, Lloyd George called all the Generals butchers, but he was really aiming at French, so he is aware of the political feeling at home and will probably sidestep any questions we put to him, Robertson is really the man we need to talk to.'

We waited about fifteen minutes and whilst waiting we scanned a map of northern France which was shown predominately on the wall of the office. There were some markings on it which showed the front line which in some places was quite near to the road we would have to take to reach the BEF Headquarters at Montreuil-sur-mer.

'It seems to me that if we are to embark on this journey, then the ladies cannot accompany us,' I said.

Bryan nodded, 'of course you are right, we will arrange for them to return on HMS Westminster that is awaiting us at Le Havre.'

I smiled, 'let us hope the weather is better on their return,' I said, remembering the trip to France.

'Yes, but we can go via Calais, probably we will be able to catch a hospital ship, which will be much quicker,' said Bryan.

'I trust we will be passengers not incumbents,' I laughed, 'don't forget that Calais is not far from the front line.'

'In that case, perhaps we should not tell the ladies?' said Bryan.

General French returned with two documents for us to sign, which we did, he kept one. He indicated the best route to take out of Paris but warned us that the nearer we got to Montreuil-sur-Mer, the busier the roads would be.

We returned to the hotel and explained to Victoria and Bryan's wife what our plan was, and Victoria immediately became alarmed. I told her that we would be quite safe as the Military headquarters were quite deliberately located in a safe area, but the trip we were to take would not be suitable for them. After some fierce argument they both appeared to be mollified and so it was settled.

Bryan and I set off at first light in another army car, but we noticed that the driver was heavily armed, and he was accompanied by a captain of the Scots Guards who was also armed.

It took several hours to reach the BEF headquarters, not only because of the seemingly endless convoys taking troops and ammunition to the front, but the constant roadblocks manned by the military police. When we arrived at Montreuil-sur-Mer we were directed straight to the fine building that was originally the town hall.

Montreuil-sur-Mer is a small French town. The only maps in the book—and the only ones needed—locate the town in far western France, about 80 miles from the Atlantic coast. A peaceful place, it was chosen as the **BEF HQ** partially because it is not near anything, giving it a constructive isolation from the world.

General Robertson met us at the entrance and shook hands warmly. 'I must apologise, I am afraid Haig will not be able to make it, he is embroiled with a problem further north. He led us into a large, covered area which I assumed had been a council chamber. Once seated and drinks served Robertson gave a thorough briefing of the up-to-date situation. He did not assume that we were incapable of understanding the military aspect and answered all our questions firmly and concisely.

He did not criticise French, but it became clear in the conversation that he felt that the British were too soft with the French generals and that as the British negotiating power was substantial, our interests should be more powerfully argued. We discussed options for the next two hours and by the time we left headquarters it had become obvious that it was Robertson and Haig that were running the whole military operation leaving French to play politics in Paris and not always on the side of his own country.

It was early afternoon by the time we moved off towards Calais, with the same car and driver as before. We took the main road almost directly north and again met a huge amount of military traffic. We had just managed to get in front of a large military ambulance when I was aware of machine gun fire. Both Bryan and I were slouched in the back seat and had been asleep. The trip had been very tiring, and we had eaten only sandwiches prepared for us by the hotel in Paris. It was thus a shock as bullets whistled around us and I saw the driver slump over the steering wheel. We were not going fast, so we were not in danger except for bumping into a large lorry in front of us. For a split second I thought that we had been ambushed by the German army but then I heard a roar as an aircraft cast its shadow as it passed overhead. The glass at the back of our car had been shattered and the ambulance that we had recently overtaken was stationary and in flames. I was furious that an enemy aircraft should have fired at a vehicle obviously carrying wounded personnel and I swiftly opened the rear door and looked up. I reached into the car and leaned over the driver who was obviously dead and noticed the Captain in the other front seat had been hit by a ricochet, so I grabbed the rifle by his side and once in my hands I balanced it on the roof of the car, winding the web strap around my arm to steady the gun and aimed it at the plane that had just done a sharp turn behind us ready to carry out another strafing attack.

I waited as long as I dare and then fired five shots in quick succession. The plane red in colour, suddenly jerked upwards, and the right wing dropped. It hit the ground some two fields away where it burst into flames.

A soldier from behind ran up to me and said breathlessly that I had just shot down Baron von Richthofen. He pointed breathlessly to the burning wreck. 'You see it is red, only the Baron flies such a plane.'

I was dazed, as my adrenalin boost subsided, and I just felt overcome with tiredness. The captain had a nasty wound in his right arm, so both Bryan and I helped him into another ambulance that had available room further down the line.

BARON VON RICHTHOFEN

I took over the driving and we reached Calais just in

time to board a hospital ship, but we were nearly turned away by an officious Major who oversaw boarding.

As we went up the gangplank, he shouted at us. 'Hey, you two, where the bloody hell do you think you are going? You don't look wounded to me.'

Bryan was not in uniform, so it appeared to the major that two civilians were hitching a free ride. Fortunately, Bryan still had the Kings document with him, so the major very quickly climbed down and apologised. He was rather concerned that he had sworn at the equerry to the King, but we told him that he was quite correct to shout at us, but perhaps in future he would modify his language.

We had a speedy trip back to England and I was rather dreading that the story of me shooting down Baron von Richthofen might have superseded me, but there were others shooting at the plane at the same time. It certainly looked like his aircraft, and I suspect that it was his plane, but I knew from history that he was apparently killed by an infantryman near the end of the war in 1918. There is just a slight suspicion that the Germans may have concealed his death in 1916 as his demise would have had a huge demoralising effect on German troops.

Field Marshal **Sir William Robert Robertson, 1st Baronet**, GCB, GCMG, GCVO, DSO (29 January 1860 – 12 February 1933) was a British Army officer who served as Chief of the Imperial General Staff (CIGS) – the professional head of the British Army – from 1916 to 1918 during the First World War. As CIGS he was committed to a Western Front strategy focusing on Germany and was against what he saw as peripheral operations on other fronts. While CIGS, Robertson had increasingly poor relations with David Lloyd George, Secretary of State for War and then Prime Minister, and threatened resignation at Lloyd Georges attempt to subordinate the British forces to the French Commander-in-Chief, Robert Neville. In 1917 Robertson supported the continuation of the Third Battle of Ypres, at odds with Lloyd George's view that Britain's war effort

ought to be focused on the other theatres until the arrival of sufficient US troops on the Western Front.[2]

Robertson is the only soldier in the history of the

British Army to have risen from an enlisted rank to its
highest rank of field marshal.

GENERAL HAIG – GENERAL FRENCH

ZIMMERMAN

19 THE NEW HOUSE

When I arrived at the office, I had two messages waiting for me, one was from Scotland Yard, a Chief inspector Healey and the other from the King's Private Secretary, Lord Stamfordham. I rang Lord Stamfordham, but he was overseas at the time, so I called Inspector Healey, who asked if he could come and see me urgently. I made an appointment for the next day and then updated myself with what had been going on at the bank while I was absent.

The next day, Inspector Healey arrived on time and appeared somewhat mysterious. Seated in my office he leaned across my desk and spoke in hushed tones. He told me that he was head of the foreign section and they had been informed of a person who had entered Britain from the United States. Unfortunately, by the time the information on this man had been received, he had disappeared. Healey told me that he was a known assassin and my name had been mentioned by the FBI. I was quite surprised as I didn't know that the FBI had been formed but learned later that it was created during 1908. The message was that this man had come to the UK because of a connection with some dealing I had in the USA. I knew immediately what he was referring to but did not wish to impart that information to Inspector Healey.

''It has come to my notice, that you are soon to move into your new house in Buckinghamshire,' he said, 'I think you would be wise to employ some security as soon as possible, in the meantime I will have the site checked over to ensure everything is okay and have someone to keep an eye on the place until you move in. I would recommend you consider buying some guard dogs as well.' I thanked the Inspector for his advice and promised I would investigate it. The next telephone call came from Bryan and took the previous meeting with Healey out of my head. Bryan told me that the King had decided to ennoble me with the Order of the Garter, the oldest honour of Chivalry given by the King personally. Bryan said he was to call me to Buckingham

Palace for the investiture on June 8th.

In early May, I moved into my new house, and although all the equipment and furniture were in place, time was too short to have my valuable pictures delivered and hung before the planned housewarming party.

RE **FURBISHED IVY BANK HOUSE AND GARDENS**

I decided to invite just a few close friends, as the war news was getting worse all the time and I considered it would be inappropriate to be seen spending a lot of money on a party during such difficult times for the country.

Afterwards, I walked around my house that I had put so much effort into refurbishing and purchasing the contents and realised that all I had achieved was an empty vessel. Beautiful, yes, comfortable, yes, luxurious, quite definitely, but it was empty of life.

I felt an overwhelming sadness for my previous life and again felt a huge responsibility for my Tory that I had left behind in 2010. She came constantly into my mind and the thought became overwhelming.

It was the night of 7th June when it happened, I had gone to bed early, and I awoke suddenly to a pungent smell of smoke. I was wide-awake now, and I jumped out of bed, hastily putting on a shirt, pair of trousers and shoes and rushed to the bedroom door. As I touched the brass doorknob, I let out a yell. It was unbearably hot. I realised that if I opened the door, I might have been enveloped in flames. The smoke was coming under the door, so I got a towel from the bathroom, put it under the tap to wet it and lay it along the bottom of the door. I then went and opened the window. The drop to the garden was about twenty feet, but I saw that I had left the blind out that protected the study underneath my bedroom, from the glare of the sun. If I jumped, it should break my fall, but whether it would hold me, I could not be sure. I could hear the fire now roaring within the house. I had no choice, and I had to jump.

The awning gave way under my weight, but it broke my fall, and I ended up in a flower bed, just missing a stone patio that had been designed for sitting out on sunny days.

As I picked myself up and stood well back from the flames, I realised there was absolutely nothing I could do to save the building. I don't know how long I stood there but was conscious of a car coming up my long drive. I turned and saw Victoria running towards me, she threw her arms out, 'Oh, my god, thank goodness you are safe,' she was crying. John Crowley and Sidney were close behind, 'Are you all right, James?' We heard an explosion and then saw the flames, so we came straight over. I hadn't heard an explosion but realised that was what had woken me. We all stood there as the house walls started collapsing. John wisely counselled us to go back to Crowley Hall. I was shaken when I arrived, and John got me a large brandy that I swallowed in a couple of gulps. He then said that they had prepared my old bedroom and that I should go straight there, we could sort matters out in the morning. Before leaving the room, I turned to Victoria and pressed two items into her hand. *When I had gone, she looked at what I had given her. The German Cross and the St Georges Cross were the honours I had received from both monarchs and the only items I had saved from the fire. She of course still had the Russian medal.*

I awoke with a start. For a moment, I didn't know quite where I was, except that my surroundings were vaguely familiar. I forced my mind to concentrate, and then I remembered. Yesterday had been a disastrous day for me. My new house with everything I had worked for, furniture, clothes, pristine Rolls Royce, and my beautiful Persian carpets, all disappeared swallowed up in a huge conflagration. Of course, I was still very wealthy, but three years of my life had been spent in the design and rebuilding of Alexander Hall, and its destruction in just twelve hours had left me somehow empty and bereft.

ROLLS ROYCE 40/60

That John and Victoria Crowley had immediately driven over to console me and had insisted I stay with them at Crowley Hall was kind, and here I was, in the same bedroom that I slept in when I first arrived six years ago.

John knew of my love for his wife and her love for me, although he didn't know we were lovers as far as I knew. Nevertheless, I felt that it must have hurt him deeply, yet he encouraged our friendship. I supposed as some sort of compensation to Victoria for the terrible hurt she'd received when he told her the truth of his scandalous liaison all those years ago. I was pleased that all traces of bitterness had left Victoria now, and she treated John more as a favourite brother. It had been impossible in the society in which we lived to divorce, and in any case, Victoria wouldn't have considered it, she knew her husband didn't have long to live.

We still managed to meet at least once a week. Both Victoria and I agreed long ago that we didn't want to make our liaisons too frequent as such meetings would have become too obvious and therefore public knowledge. It wasn't a perfect arrangement, but we both knew we would be together before too long, and we had decided we could not build our future on the unhappiness of John's misfortune.

I switched on the light and looked at my gold timepiece, it was 3.15 in the morning. A chink of light was appearing through the windows that heralded the first signs of dawn. I turned the light out again, and my mind slipped forward to the Tory I had known in 2010. How I loved her, and what she must have thought of me when I didn't return that day, six years ago. A silent tear trickled down my cheek as I thought of her having to struggle with the company's winding up and the bank. I thought of the irony of the situation. Here I was with the equivalent of millions of pounds to spare, but 100 years behind when it was needed.

My mind was in turmoil, and I knew I could not get back to sleep, so I got up. I felt that I needed to go for a walk, but then I realised that I only had my trousers and a shirt, the clothes I was wearing yesterday. I lay back on the bed again. Suddenly a thought came to me. I got off the bed, and went into the dressing room, opening a draw where I had left my tracksuit and tennis shoes some six years ago. They were still there, folded neatly as I left them, the shoes lying on top as though time hadn't moved for them. I hurriedly put the tracksuit on, and then the socks and shoes. I knew no one would be around at this time of the morning, and I didn't care anyway. I had to walk. I had to think. I was just going out of the bedroom door, when I noticed something gleaming on the floor by my bed, I went over and picked it up. I remembered that I had put it in the pocket of my tracksuit for safekeeping, and I realised that it must have fallen out as I was putting the tracksuit on. It was the gold chain and filigree locket that Victoria had insisted I keep after we had first made love in that wooded area by the river on a lovely summer day. It seemed like a lifetime ago. I snapped open the catch that was hidden on the underside, and it gave way showing a tiny painting of Victoria Crowley. I shut it and thrust it into my pocket. It made me feel more complete in a strange sort of way.

I had reached the hall when I heard a whisper from behind.

'James...'

I turned; it was John Crowley.

I understood that he'd not been well the night before, and had turned in early, having broken his sleep to come to the fire. But this morning he looked in good spirits. That's how the illness affected him, down one minute and up the next.

I could see him looking at my attire. 'I've nothing else I'm afraid, and you'll remember that I took all your clothes that fitted me some years ago.'

John laughed. 'I remember,' then he asked me where I was going, and I told him.

'Fancy a ride instead old boy?' I didn't, I would have rather walked on my own, but I felt it would have been churlish of me to say so.

I noticed he had his riding gear on.

'Why not,' I said, 'shall we saddle up?' We went out to the stables at the back of the house and lifted the heavy saddles into place.

I still rode Bright Star from time to time, and she was there waiting for me, her nostrils twitching nervously.

Soon we were galloping down the drive, the sun was

rising quickly from the east, and the sky's colours were a deep red. The saying red sky at night, shepherds delight, red sky in the morning, shepherds warning crossed my mind and gave me a trace of unease, but it was clear and fresh, and it was good to be alive. I turned Bright Star off to the left, cutting up near the old farmhouse, and then down towards the canal's tow-path. I don't know to this day why I chose that route, which I had not covered since the second day of my arrival, but I did. I slowed Bright Star down to a trot and then a walk. John Crowley caught up with me and rode alongside.

'I've something to tell you, James,' he looked across at me, and there were tears in his eyes. He didn't allow me to answer. 'I've enlisted in the Kings Own; I will be joining the British Expeditionary Force in France next Friday.' I looked at him, shocked. 'But you've no need to...'

'I know, I know,' he said quietly, 'but we both know I'm dying, and I want to die in a way that brings honour to our family, not from some wretched disease which... which I contracted from a prostitute. But you know about that, don't you?' I could not lie to him. I just nodded sadly. I knew he'd no intention of returning from France. We rode on in silence for a while, and then John turned to me again.

'There's one thing you must do for me...'

'Name it, and it's yours,' I said. ' You must look after Victoria for me, will you promise me? I know that you two have been lovers since shortly after you arrived.' He saw my startled look. 'No, don't worry, James, I was comforted that she obtained some happiness, but I've never been sure whether you would marry her after I've gone, you see I love her deeply.' His eyes were now so full of tears; they ran down his face and into his beard. But he was quite unashamed of them.

I pulled in the rein on Bright Star as she unaccountably showed signs of nervousness. 'I know you love her, just as I know the reason for you not being able to show your love in the physical sense.' I looked at him, wondering if I would have had the compassionate capacity that he showed in the same circumstances. 'I promise that when you've gone, I will look after her to the end of my days, assuming she will have me of course,' I smiled.

John relaxed and wiped his hand across his face. 'Thank you, thank you,' his voice broke as he kicked his mount sharply with his heels, and she surged ahead. I was surprised, and did the same seconds later, urging Bright Star into a gallop. Suddenly John Crowley seemed to be caught up in the morning mist, I was worried that he might do something foolish, so I urged Bright Star on faster. I was aware that she was nervous, not wanting to enter the mist that was now all around me.

Bright Star stopped very suddenly and being caught unaware I felt myself being thrown over her head, I tried to save myself as I fell, then I knew no more.

20 - THE RETURN

I was aware of something wet on my face. I painfully lifted my head. There was a Golden Retriever licking my face. I heard heavy boots running in my direction, and a rough arm pulling at mine.

'Are you all right old chap?' I sat up and blinked in the weak sunlight. In front of me was an elderly couple, the man was helping me up, and the woman who had now reached me was looking at my face anxiously.

'Oh, I'm so sorry, I think our dog may have tripped you up, we saw you fall, and... Here's, my handkerchief, it's clean,' she assured me, 'I think you've cut your lip in the fall.' I took the handkerchief gratefully and wiped the blood away from my mouth and offered it back to her.

'No, no, please keep it,' I stuffed it into my pocket. I must have looked a bit dazed because I was still trying to get my bearings. I saw the little bridge over the canal, and I was vaguely aware of traffic noise. 'Oh, my god, I'm back,' I whispered to myself, 'I'm back.'

'Are you sure you are all right, my dear?' the woman said. I looked at her. 'What day is it?' I asked. The woman looked at me, curiously.

'Why it's Tuesday,'

'Tuesday what?' I asked. 'Tuesday 8th June of course,'

'What year is it?' I asked desperately.

'The year,' The woman now looked thoroughly concerned.

'Yes, the year,' I insisted, 'what year is it?'

There was silence. 'It's 2010.'

I let out a sigh.

The whole thing had been a dream, some sort of weird dream. I noticed the man and woman had been talking. The woman turned to me, 'we are going to take you back to your home, our car is just in the car park over there,' she pointed.

I shook my head, 'It's quite all right, I've my car...'

She didn't let me finish. 'No love, you can't drive in your present condition, and we wouldn't let you, would we Freddie?' She turned to her male companion, who I assumed was her husband. He shook his head, vehemently.

I knew it was no good arguing, so I allowed them to steer me to a small Renault parked next to my BMW. The woman got into the back after the dog, and I climbed into the passenger seat. I put my head between my hands I could feel a migraine coming on. My eyes began to blur. It was something I was used to, but I knew the quicker I got home, the better. I had found in the past that if took an aspirin or two before the pain came, then the chances were the migraine discomfort would dissipate.

'Where do you live love?' the woman said quietly.

I told her. I was aware of her husband starting the car, reversing, and then going forward. I felt rather than saw us go over the little bridge, and then turn left on the main road. Within five minutes, I was being walked through the garden to my house. The woman rang the doorbell, while the man held my right arm by way of support.

Tory came to the door. She took one look at me and let out a stifled cry.

'What on earth...?'

The woman explained that I had fallen badly near the bridge. 'I don't know whether he tripped over our dog,' she pointed to the Golden Retriever in the back of their car, 'or whether he just passed out love, but he doesn't look too good to me...'

Tory got us all inside and sat me down on the couch. She brought me the aspirins I asked for, and a warm wet towel with which she wiped my face.

Man and wife were anxious to go, so Tory thanked them, and showed them out. They offered to bring our car back, but Tory said not to worry, she'd fetch it later.

When they had gone, she came back to sit beside me, she looked worried.

'What happened?' she whispered.

I found I was crying, uncontrollably. Tory put her arm around me and squeezed. 'What is it?' I took a breath and shook my head. 'I don't know, I could not sleep, so I went for our normal walk, and I had almost completed it when I became dizzy. I have had the most incredible experience... I can't explain it, not yet anyway,' Tory gently wiped my face again with the warm cloth.

I looked at her. 'Oh, I do love you,' the tears started to come again. Now she was crying, and we sobbed in each other's arms.

I lifted my head. 'I'm so sorry about the last few months, truly sorry. I was so afraid of failing for the second time in my life that I lashed out at those people who were closest to me. I must have been unbearable to live with,' I sniffed. 'I've decided to tell the bank that I'm closing the business, it'll mean giving up ten years of hard work and our house... but... nothing is as important to me as my life with you, and whatever our difficulties, well survive.'

'Of course, we will, besides,' she said looking at me and gently stroking my face, 'no material gain is worth wrecking our love for each other, life is far too short for that. But what made you change your mind?' She knew only the day before that I was determined to fight on at all costs.

I smiled, 'during my walk, I completed six years of thinking...' I didn't explain further.

'Well for my part I'm pleased,' said Tory, 'I know how difficult that decision was to make.'

'It'll be tough,' I warned.

'We were without money once before, and we were happy,' she smiled, 'the business isn't worth us ruining our health or marriage for. Now,' she became practical again. 'Take off your tracksuit, it's muddy, and I will put it in the wash.' I did as I was told, first taking off my shoes, and then the two track suit pieces. Tory felt something in my tracksuit pocket. It was the handkerchief, then she looked at me oddly, as her hand came out with a filigree gold chain with a gold locket attached to it.' I was rooted to the spot; my eyes riveted on the locket.

'There's a catch behind it,' I said almost mechanically.

Tory found it, and it snapped open. She looked at the miniature picture and then back to me. 'James, it's... it's beautiful, and the picture of me, how did you...? And how much did it cost you? It's solid gold.' she didn't know whether to be pleased or annoyed.

'It's for your... our twenty-fifth wedding anniversary,' I stuttered, 'and I promise you, it didn't cost me a penny, not one penny. It was given to me.'

'Given to you, this? It's an antique, and the picture is exquisite, even though I look a little sad,' she frowned.

My mind was racing as I put on the bathrobe Tory had given me. She came towards me with the chain in her hand, kissed me, then turned and asked me to put it around her neck. I did so and watched as she went to the mirror and looked at her reflection and then me through the mirror and smiled. I could see tears welling up in her eyes again, as she turned away, but they were happy tears.

My mind was still disturbed as I climbed the stairs to reach the bathroom, and it was while I was having my shower that a thought hit me. Had I bought the locket? I could not remember doing so, but the incredible thing was it fitted into my dream. The locket was certainly real I told myself crossly, I couldn't have been back in time. In any case, the proof was conclusive whatever my brain said to me about spending six years in a period near the beginning of the last century. I had been unconscious for less than a minute. I remembered seeing the Golden Retriever and the elderly couple just before I lost consciousness. But the dream or vision I had was very real too. I thought back as I allowed the water to cascade over my face and body. I could remember everything that happened very precisely, Tory Crowley and John Crowley, Crowley Hall and the bank, everything, just as though it had happened.

I dried myself and went to sit on my bed. The puzzle, I told myself, is the chain and locket, I tried to think back as to where I obtained it, but my dream came back to me each time. And the picture, it was painted, it was not a photograph. I sat up with a start. I remembered it showed the head of a young woman wearing a high-necked blouse. I knew Tory Alexander didn't have such a garment. Had I fulfilled my original promise to Victoria Crowley, was my Tory the same?

I realised that if my dream had been real, then I was worth millions as I remembered putting amounts of money into a bank account, there were at least five hundred thousand pounds there in 1915. My god, I thought, what would it be worth today?

The thought countered the initial euphoria, I knew of no Crowley Bank. There must have been hundreds of bank mergers in the last 100 years, and I wondered if there ever was such a bank as Crowley's. If so, had it been taken over at some stage, but if it had been in 1915 why had I not put my money into Credit Suisse or Lloyds even, a bank that I knew would survive the period. Then I realised why I could not have done so. Had I drawn my own money out of the bank I was running, it could have caused a panic if others had heard about what I was doing. I remembered, though, that in my dream, I did allow for the fact that I might get back to 2010. The instructions I gave were very clear. Anyone presenting to the bank the number 23234-D would automatically have ownership of the money. The code was easy for me to remember, as it was part of my old army number. But in my dream just in case, I left a copy of the number in my secret book that I kept in my safe at the office, the safe I shared with John Crowley. This was the book in which I kept notes of future events, recommendations to clients and deals.

I remembered that book. I would while away my leisure hours trying to remember events from the future that would affect commerce or the money markets in or after 1910. I wrote everything down I thought of right up to 1945.

Now I was thinking ahead again, the first thing I had to do was see if I could trace the history of a Crowley's Bank. Where better to start, I thought, than my bankers, Barons Bank of Lombard Street.

I felt cautiously elated. I finished my shower, and dressed in a white shirt, with a military tie, and dark blue suit with stripes. I put on my regular polished shoes and went down to breakfast. I decided not to tell Tory of the possibility of a bank account yet. The logical side of me still insisted that the whole thing had been a dream, and yet I knew the experience had been so stunningly real. Whatever the case, I could hardly lose anything by making a phone call.

MY VICTORIA

When I appeared downstairs, she noticed the

difference in my mood, and she looked at me quizzically. 'You're looking better, almost chipper,' she smiled. It was nice to see her smile.

I ate a hearty breakfast and then realised that I didn't have my car key. I asked Tory if it had been in my pocket before putting the tracksuit in the wash, but she confirmed it wasn't there. I must have dropped it in the fall, I said, but suddenly remembered that I had given the key to John Crowley and that further confirmed what I had experienced was no dream. Borrowing Tory's key, I walked back to the park, collected the BMW, and drove it back to the house.

I had a downstairs room in the house that I used as an office, and after I returned from the park, I went in and closed the door. My first call was to Debbie, to say I wouldn't be in the office today. She told me that she'd had a call from the bank. They had threatened to dishonour some cheques I issued. I had done so on the understanding from a large conglomerate client that they would pay me without fail by yesterday. The client hadn't done so. I told her that I would work on the problem and get back to her. The next person I called was my account manager at the bank. I got his assistant Mr Cardrew who told me Mr Jones, was too busy to speak to me. He confirmed that if I didn't have £5,000 in my account by 11-o-clock that morning, they would dishonour my cheques. I told him that I had been promised £13,000 from a client and I asked if he'd carry me for a few more days to enable me to get the money in. He said no, he was under instructions from the manager to dishonour them if the cash wasn't there on time. I told him the bank would have to do so, as I could see no way of finding the funds in such a short period.

I was beginning to prefer my dream life in 1915.

I just stopped Cardrew from hanging up the phone.

'There's one question I would like to ask you?' I added.

'Oh?'

'Have you ever heard of a Crowley Bank?' I expected

him to say no immediately, but his answer surprised me.

'Yes, of course, haven't you read our latest balance sheet and accounts?' I felt a thrill of excitement shoot through me. 'I regret that I haven't,' I admitted.

'Well, all our clients were sent a copy,' he said huffily, 'and the history of the bank is in there. It's put in every year, but if you can't find it, let me know, and I will send you another copy,' he said.

'I'm sorry, I don't follow, what has Barons to do with Crowley's?' I asked.

'Barons was founded on an amalgamation of two Victorian institutions, Crowley's and Byron's, read it and you'll see,' he said. I thanked him and rang off. I knew that I received something from them about a month ago, and I had brought it home to read. Not having had the time, I did not look at it.

'Now where did I put it...?' I murmured to myself as I opened my filing cabinet. I eventually found it misfiled amongst bills to pay. I unconsciously filed everything there I thought because that was where most of my mail went anyway.

I got it out, and turned the pages, stopping at the back. It didn't tell me much more than Cardrew had told me. There were two pages of relatively small print, headed

HISTORY OF THE BANK

Barons Bank was founded in 1919 with the amalgamation of the hugely successful Crowley's Bank and Byron's Bank. Crowley's Bank merged with Byron's Bank in 1917, but they traded as separate institutions although Crowley's were the controlling company. The Chairman was Lord John Crowley until he died in late 1917; Gerald Phipps controlled the main board until Lord Porter took over in 1918.

It then went on to a more recent history, which left me with a feeling of considerable unease. Who the devil was

Lord Porter, I certainly knew no Lord Porter on the board in 1915?

So, I thought, there was a Crowley's Bank, and I certainly did not know such a name before my dream. I decided that matters were looking up in my life, and I was quite excited when I rang the bank again and asked for Mr Jones's assistant. This time, he wasn't available either, which was probably due to my low standing, so I was transferred to his assistant, Miss Fellows. 'Miss Fellows,' I said, after giving my name, 'I want to give you a number that I've been given, and which should unlock a substantial account in my name, it goes back quite a long way, in fact to Crowley's Bank in 1915.'

Miss Fellows listened intently.

'The number is 23234-D, would you see if you can trace it and get back to me?'

Miss Fellows said that it would take some days to research so far back but promised she'd hand on the inquiry to investments. I could hardly contain myself now, and I began considering a few what ifs. I worked out what five hundred thousand pounds would be worth at say a net 4% per annum interest over the whole period. It came to the staggering sum of around or more than 1.5 billion pounds.

I wished I had not calculated the sum, as it made me completely incapable of doing anything else but thinking of how I could spend some of it. My mind was still very much in the clouds when I received a call from the bank at three forty-five the same afternoon. It was from a Mr Erdington, Director of Investments.

'Mr Alexander?

'Yes,'

He coughed. 'A Miss Fellows asked me to investigate your request, and because the amount was originally a very large one, we didn't take too long to trace the account in the Crowley archives. I must tell you that the account was closed in 1920, and the money was transferred to the account of the then owner of the bank, a certain Charles Porter...,'

'Charles Porter, the butler...' My 1.5 billion pounds evaporated in a flash, and my heart seemed to sink to my boots. I felt rather like the lottery winner who has given someone the money to buy his ticket and found out after drawing the winning number that the ticket wasn't purchased.

'I beg your pardon'.

'I'm sorry,' I said, 'but I happen to know that Charles Porter was the butler to Lord Crowley. I can't imagine how he got access to that account, or indeed how he came to own the bank in the first place.'

'Hmm, well I wouldn't know either, but perhaps the letters in the deed box will tell you something.'

'Letters?' My heart pounded.

'Yes, it's a most interesting deed box; it was left with two letters addressed to a Mr James Alexander, your namesake. Was he any relation to you by the way?' He didn't wait for me to answer. 'I understand that he was the true founder of the wealth and influence that our bank still holds today, I suppose there's some irony there for you Mr Alexander.' Obviously, Mr Erdington knew of my precarious financial situation.

'Anyway, it seems to me that as you've quoted the correct number of the account, I think the bank can reasonably hand over the letters to you.'

After my hopes of being an instant millionaire had been dashed, I was mildly excited again. I knew now that it had been no dream, incredibly I had been back to the first decade of the last century, I wasn't mad. But who were the letters from I wondered, and what did they contain? I had to know and knew I would never get any sleep if I didn't immediately fetch them.

'About what time do you leave the office, Mr Erdington?' I asked.

'Er... tonight, about 6 to 6.30 but I will happily wait for you if you are going to be late.' I looked at my watch; it was nearly 4 p.m. I just had time to catch the London train from the central Milton Keynes railway station and get to the bank before six. I told him I was on my way.

'Ring the external doorbell when you arrive dear boy, and I will tell the security guard to expect you,' Erdington put the phone down.

I arrived at the bank door at five minutes to six, and by the time the hour was striking, I was sitting in a plush board room awaiting Erdington's appearance.

A tall man entered; he had a pleasant face with a distinguished air. He wore a dark blue Saville Row suit with a red silk tie. There was a red rose in his buttonhole. I saw he was carrying a large deed box and a thin book rested on top of it.

He introduced himself and sat down opposite me, as he did so, he pushed over the deed box. There was no key, and I asked him for it.

'I'm afraid the key has long been lost if ever there was one,' I looked at him in amazement.

'Well, how on earth do you know there are two letters inside?' I asked. Erdington smiled and reached across the table where we sat. He turned over the box, and on the back was a piece of paper along the bottom, well and truly glued on with some small, neat writing. I recognised it at once as John Crowley's.

For Mr James Alexander's attention, please hold for 100 years from this date, 25th October 1917. This box contains two letters that should not be opened until Mr James Alexander comes to collect them. The key owned by Mr Alexander can only open this box. In the event of Mr Alexander not having the key on his person, the box can still be handed over to him on the presentation of the unique code and proper identification. He will remember the code.

The code starts at 23***-D

Signed and sealed by Lord John Crowley, 25h October 1916.

'You do have identification I assume Mr Alexander?' I

handed over my driving licence. He looked at it for a few seconds and called in someone to take a photocopy, he returned my licence back and presented me with a form to sign. 'And the missing code figures?' I answered that the whole code was 23234-D.

The formalities dealt with, I looked at the keyhole on the deed box, but it was an extraordinary lock, not at all like the ones I had come across in 1915. I shook my head. 'Beats me I'm afraid.' Erdington smiled, 'well it shouldn't be too difficult to get a locksmith to open it for you, but be careful it's very heavy, I think it must be cast iron.' He moved to get up, and as we both walked towards the door, he stopped. 'Oh, just one other thing, I found this book in our archives,' he handed me a small grey covered book, and I turned it over to look at the front of it. There was an unmistakable drawing of Crowley Hall on the front. It was titled The Crowley's of Buckinghamshire. I looked inside at the first page. it said. This is the tragic story of the Crowley's of Buckinghamshire written by Lady Crowley's cousin Priscilla Fortescue. It's a story of scandal and intrigue. The first print was dated 1934.

I looked up at Erdington. 'Thank you, I'm sure I will find this most interesting, and I will let you have it back when I've finished with it.'

Erdington shook his head. 'Keep it, dear boy, it's of no interest to the bank or me. I understand it caused a bit of a stir when it was first published though, one of the first Kiss and Tell books to be written,' he smiled.

In the taxi travelling back to Euston railway station, I scrutinized the box. It was very well made, I would have said almost certainly hand-crafted, quite unlike the tinny petty cash type boxes you can buy in office supply centres today. It was very heavy as Erdington had indicated, surprisingly so. I took it in both hands and shook it, half expecting to hear a heavy gold bar moving from side to side. I fantasised what if it was full of gold or valuables. I shook it hard. Nothing, there was no sound. I decided it wouldn't be easy to open, the division between the top and the bottom was almost invisible, and it had been painted with black paint since it was closed, which further disguised where the top and bottom met. The box itself, while square in overall shape was rounded at the corners and the edges, I could see where the metal had been beaten into shape; it was simple yet beautiful. John Crowley's crest was embedded into the top centre of the box, which was the only way I knew which was the top and which the bottom. I wondered why the box had been painted, and of what metal it was made. It was heavy enough to be cast iron. Just before the taxi turned right into the station, I examined the lock again. I was puzzled; it wasn't like any lock I had ever seen on any deed box, even the modern ones. The aperture was flat, and as I peered at it, holding the box out in front of me, I could see the top half of the flat piece thickened in the middle and then thinned out on the bottom, like two Ls stuck together, one the right way up, one upside down.

I had no more time to ponder the problem as the taxi had arrived at Euston station. I quickly paid the driver and walked to the large electronic board to see when the next train was due to leave. I noticed I was just in time to catch the seven-ten that was a fast train getting into Milton Keynes just before 8 p.m.

When I reached the train, I was pleased to see the coach I selected was not crowded, and I easily managed to find a section on my own. It was a single-seat with a table; the other single-seat facing me was empty. I put the box on the table and looked at it. The key aperture is flat; I kept telling myself, why should I have had the key? I sighed exasperated. The train had started to move out of the station, and I noticed an attendant at the top end of the coach with a drinks trolley. I wondered whether I should get a sandwich and then decided against it. I had left the car at the station, and it would only take me ten minutes from there to reach my home. I could ring Tory from the station when I arrived, and she'd have supper ready when I... I frowned, the car at the station, why was it that I felt the car was significant? To get me home, of course, came back my answer. No, a voice inside me said it's more than that. It was as the attendant drew level that I let out a whoop, much to his surprise.

21 - THE LETTERS

I had the key. I fished in my pocket and withdrew the BMW car key, I put it in the box, and it opened instantly. I sat staring at the open lid as my thoughts drifted back. I gave John Crowley my car key during the first few days of my visit to Crowley Hall, and he probably guessed that I had a duplicate somewhere, so he had the box specially made with a lock that could only open with my key.

I looked inside, it was lined with unpolished wood, there were two envelopes at the bottom and nothing else in the box. I took out the first envelope, but it was still easily readable. The writing was unmistakably that of John Crowley, and his seal was on the back, embedded in bright red sealing wax. The second letter was in neat small handwriting, and my mind went back to the note on the tray that second day at Crowley Hall. There was a Crowley seal on the back of that also. I put both the letters on the table; face up in front of the box. I felt tears well up into my eyes. A lump appeared from nowhere in my throat. I can't explain the emotions running through my mind at that moment, but part of me didn't want to open those letters.

Was I afraid of what I might find contained in them? I gritted my teeth and took John Crowley's envelope, and gently tore the flap open trying to preserve as much of the seal as I could. There were six pages of writing, and I started to read, elated with the contents. The crest was printed in the centre top of the first page, and then:

Crowley Hall

Buckinghamshire

25th October 1916

Dear James,

I feel most strange writing to you, not knowing whether I am writing to the ether or whether in the event of you living in 2010, you will come across the box and the message inside. I did not believe your story first, but your predictions of future events were too uncanny to be just coincidence. I finally realised the truth when you disappeared on that beautiful morning in June 1916. Do you remember? I had just told you I was joining the colours, and as I was becoming emotional, I spurred my horse on in front. I seemed to lose my way for about ten seconds in the ground mist we ran into, and when I didn't hear you following, I stopped and turned around. There was no mist, only Bright Star standing there quite motionless, trembling from head to foot. I trotted my horse back to her, but she wouldn't move and seemed rooted to the spot. I dismounted and searched the area, but there was nowhere you could have gone, and I knew then that we had lost you.

Tory was distraught when I first told her of your disappearance, but over the months, she came to understand the reason for your visit to us, as have I. The authorities were less understanding, and I had a challenging time explaining your disappearance. I thank god that you and Tory were discreet; otherwise, they would have had a perfect motive to pin your disappearance on me. Eventually, we put around that having brought the bank to profit you decided to return to America.

I knew then that I could no longer join the Army, and

I declined my commission when it came through. Last month I completed a deal with Byron's Bank merging Crowley's with theirs. Thanks to you we were able to come out very much the senior partner. Young Gerald Phipps now heads the organization, and although I am the Chairman, I take very little interest and rarely go to London nowadays. I realise you may be sorry to hear this, after all your hard work, as I know you were against a merger, but you made me realise that one should do what one is good at in life and what one enjoys. Go with the current, you once said, not force yourself to work against it. I could not have considered going back to running the bank, especially as it is now a much larger organization.

I was brought up to accept responsibility for others and conform to what society demanded of me. My frustration with being trapped in that box made me look elsewhere for my escape, with disastrous results. I hated the bank and everything it stood for. I hated the competitiveness, the dishonesty, the deceit but above all, the humbug. I would have loved to just work on my estate, as a farmer, and nothing more. I probably would have been happy for a while, but the family responsibilities would have weighed heavily on my heart whatever I had decided, and perhaps because of that, I could not have experienced happiness for too long. Was it my fate to be where I was at that time and to do what I did?

I now truly believe that my inner cry of anguish called myself from the future. I would look at you at times, and there stood the man I wanted to be, the man I strived to be. Since you left, I realise that to be myself, I must stop striving to be what I am not and consider my responsibility to myself rather than to others. By doing that, I have come to a greater understanding of me and how I fit into life's scheme. I believe the people around me have benefited from my new-found freedom.

Tory and I are close once again. Your loss drew us together as never before. Of course, our relationship's physical side has gone forever, but you brought us back to just being before there was nothing but bitterness.

The box I entrusted this letter to was made by an excellent craftsman with in-depth knowledge of how to fashion metal. The box I was given in the form of the human body was also fashioned superbly. I could not find the key, so I battered it to force it open with the equivalent of a large hammer. I irreparably damaged the outside of the box to the extent that the message inside was also damaged. I still could not find the key, so I cried out for a skilled locksmith.

You were my locksmith.

You held the key.

You showed Tory what love was again, and by doing so, she realised as I did that bitterness simply serves to burn the message. You relieved me of the responsibilities that I never wanted and gave me time to think about what I was and where I was going.

I had decided to give up all my responsibilities to myself and others by being killed in France. My compatriots would have said I was brave. I may even have won a medal. But I know that I would have been taking the coward's way out. My responsibility to myself would have been compromised.

You also came with a key that had been fashioned in the future, it made your existence here successful in the financial sense, but you were not truly happy. I hope, for my sake, that you find that true happiness that is so elusive to all but a few.

My illness is steadily worsening, and there are days at a time when I have no recollection of my movements. I seem to move between reality and other places, some wondrous, some extraordinary, some dismal. Some days I find they all merge into one, making my concentration on a human plane impossible. The doctors say I am going insane. I laugh at that, as I see so much insanity in our world, I am not sure they are qualified to judge.

I am feeling tired now, so I must leave. Remember

what you always told me. Follow your instinct, never use force against yourself or others, and be responsible for yourself first.

Yours

John

P.S. We removed your private safe to Crowley House for safekeeping, and the box is in the safe along with your notes.

I found I was crying. I was embarrassed as the man from the other side of the coach had noticed. I suppressed my emotions and dried my tears with my sleeve. I suppose he thought I had been reading a Dear John letter. The thought then crossed my mind. What did it matter what he thought; It's what I think that matters just as John Crowley had indicated in his letter, how stupid we were to conform to what others expect in us.

We were nearing Milton Keynes Station, and so I decided to leave Victoria's letter unopened until I got home. I was deep in thought as I got off the train and drove to Hammond Farm. If I provided the key for John Crowley, and if as he indicated I had been John Crowley, what had I learned? I thought about my own life. Abused as a child at numerous boarding schools I was packed off to, bullied by my peers at school, I developed a defensive mechanism to fight those people who threatened me effectively. My schoolteachers, my parents, my fellow students, and the world in general. I craved for love and acceptance. I found the love that I sought, but approval from my fellow man was harder to obtain. I decided that society accepted those who were successful, particularly those with money. I set my course, ignoring all other instincts.

I used tactics that had been used against me. I bullied, lied when it suited me, and dispensed with those who had helped me when they could no longer be of help, and I became rich. I think it was my conscience that caught up with me, rather like a fast speed boat that stops suddenly in the water. I cut the engine because I could see that I was heading for the rocks in human terms. The water engulfed me and threw me on the rocks anyway. All that I had built disappeared in a flash, just like the fire at Alexander Hall. Most of the friends I made crept away in case failure could somehow be transferred to them, and those that wanted me to know I was still in their thoughts, I was embarrassed to stay connected with.

I started again, determined that I would win this time, but my heart wasn't the same ruthless machine it had once been, and I started to question myself and my motives. Once I did that, I saw I was doing the wrong thing, but I convinced myself that it was what I had to do. I think it was fear that I would be less of a person that led me to make money, to ensure I wasn't financially dependent on others, to become independent to become admired. During all this time, my Tory had persevered through the difficult times, and she became the only person I could honestly take out my frustration on. The bond was inevitably breaking down when I had gone for that fateful walk.

I drove the car into my drive. So deep in thought that I had forgotten to telephone Tory, and I realised there would be no dinner ready. She came to the door when she heard me and kissed me full on the lips. I held her tight with the door still open. She laughed at me, and ever practical broke away and closed it. This time she didn't mind when I suggested we had dinner out, and after she had changed into a long dress, she wore the locket I had given her earlier in the day. We drove to a small Italian restaurant we had frequented in the past, in a little village called Aspley Guise.

The restaurant was quiet that night, and although Tory asked me about my visit to the bank, I was evasive, and she didn't press me. We spoke openly about the business and our future, about our children and now grandchildren and ourselves. She detected a change in me as I did. I wasn't just showing confidence to the outside world. I felt more confident in myself. The future wasn't important any-more, the evening with Tory was the most important thing to me, and we started to talk about life and what it meant to both of us. We didn't plan anything, we just let our thoughts drift into the open, as though we weren't really part of the world we were sitting in, but two people in love watching the earth roll by underneath us.

I wondered if one had other lives, whether the same mistakes were made time and time again, like some sort of merry-go-round that you could not release yourself from until you corrected the reason for those mistakes. I had a kind of visual apparition of one spinning off into space, and returning like Halley's Comet, always returning, always taking the same route, and entirely predictable. My thoughts turned to Churchill and his early warnings about Hitler, was that due to me telling him to look out for a German corporal? We shall never know, but he of all people must have realised that my sudden disappearance in 1916 was extraordinary. Did he believe that I was from 2010?

The next morning, I went into the office early to be there when Debbie arrived.

I decided to tell her about my decision to close my business, so I was surprised when she confronted me first.

She told me that she'd been looking for a job for some time and had now found one; she wanted to leave at the weekend. I thought afterwards of how worried I had been about her and of the excellent pay off I had decided to give out of my meagre reserves. I had acted in what I considered was a responsible way but she'd no qualms about putting herself first and effectively leaving me in the lurch. I realised afterwards that she was right, and I was wrong, why should she stay on in a precarious job that had no future. She acted in her interest, and it was my perception of what she should have done that coloured my thinking.

At the end of the month the bank took over our house and the assets we had worked so hard to build up over the last ten years, and we moved into a small, rented cottage near Oxford. For the first time in my life, I drew unemployment pay, something I could never have done previously, my pride being too strong to admit that I was unemployed and dependent on others, just the same as thousands of my fellow men.

We had been in our little cottage for just over a week, and I was conscious that Victoria Crowley's letter still sat in my desk drawer unopened.

Tory and I had just walked back from the village store, our car had to be sold after we moved, and I was sitting in the tiny room I had converted into a study. The sunlight was filtering through the trees outside, and I could hear Tory making some coffee, the clink of cups being a familiar sound.

I opened the drawer and took out the envelope. I used a paper-knife to slit open the top of the envelope to preserve the seal intact. As I opened it, I could have sworn that I could smell her perfume; it took me a second to realise that my Tory was standing over me, handing me the coffee cup. She kissed the back of my neck and left for the kitchen.

Crowley Hall

Buckinghamshire

25th October 1916

My Darling James,

How I do miss you. When John returned on that fateful day in June, I thought my life had come to an end. At first, I allowed myself to suspect the rumours that John had somehow got rid of you through jealousy. It was a hugely challenging time for him, but he had changed, and I started to see the man I once loved come to life again. His love for you and what you achieved for him was obvious, and I realised he could not have done you harm. This was further demonstrated when I took Bright Star out for a ride one morning, and I visited Hammond Farm, the farm building that you told me was your home. Bright Star reached the spot where John told me you disappeared, and she just refused to go further. I had to take almost a mile detour to reach the area where we used to meet. I often go there now, and I always think of you and wonder if you are thinking of me.

I know we will meet again, somewhere, sometime, and it's that thought that makes my life meaningful. John is extremely ill, although he does not seem to realise it. He must be watched constantly, as he's likely to think he is a bird and can fly from the top windows...

We laugh about it when he's himself. Strangely our love for each other has grown far and beyond what we had before, and I think John is truly happy with his life. It's difficult for me, not that I am complaining, but I know his time is limited, even now his periods of conscious reality are few and far between, and thus we live for the moment, not thinking of the future. Indeed, I shut out any thought of living without either of you, as the pain is too much to bear. What a lucky woman I am, to have had the love of two men, or have I only had the love of one? Were you, as John suggests, one and the same? I wonder if you know the answer to that question, whether all that marvellous technology in 2010 will give you an explanation?

Think of me, darling.

Yours always,

Victoria.

22 - THE SURPRISE

I had put off reading Victoria's letter because I was afraid of what it might do to me. I was relieved that I now felt free of the past. It was as though a weight had been lifted from my shoulders.

I opened the drawer, put Victoria's letter back in the box it came in and pulled out the little grey book Erdington had given me. It wasn't a very large book, as books go, but it gave all the essential details of Crowley's back to John Crowley's grandfather. I skipped that part and found the section that most interested me.

The Crowley's
By Priscilla Fortescue

I was invited to stay at Crowley Hall for the summer of 1910 when I first met James Alexander. The first thing I noticed about him was his family likeness to John Crowley, but he struck me as more intelligent, and he appeared to have inner confidence with him that I and others found a little frightening. People would listen to him in awe because he was so often right in predicting events.

I learned very quickly that my cousin hadn't invited me because of her love for my company, but because I provided a convenient chaperone for her passionate affair with James Alexander, later to be Sir James Alexander. I believe that Lord Crowley knew about and even encouraged the affair, but it was to be much later that I learned of the dreadful disease that finally killed him in 1917.

I've always believed that Alexander was the

illegitimate son of the second Lord Crowley, and therefore the two of them were close, but I never did manage to find out where his mother lived or who she was. Alexander seemed to have all the skills necessary to run the Crowley Bank, and there's no doubt that its success was due to his efforts, as it was losing favour in the city before he became involved. He found some dishonesty within the bank that involved the Banque Les Germain in Luxembourg, known as the Kaiser's bank. I suspect the problem involved the Kaiser because he honoured him when he visited Cowes in 1911. James Alexander was subsequently knighted by King George V for his services to charity. There was a rumour that on the day that Alexander disappeared he was due to be ennobled by King George V, but there was no statement from the palace regarding this or of Alexander's disappearance.

Alexander's involvement gave Lord Crowley more freedom, and he became a more contented man than I had known previously.

It's difficult to say if Lord Crowley was jealous of his younger illegitimate brother, if he was, he didn't show it. But had an affair between James Alexander and Victoria been known at the time of James Alexander's disappearance, I think events might have taken a different course. We subsequently understood that Alexander had returned to America, once the bank had recovered and that may well be the case as I'm sure the fire of his newly built house in Buckinghamshire must have deeply saddened him.

Although he probably never knew the fire's cause, it was later confirmed that it was due to a bomb placed near the back door. The security services brought in to investigate indicated that it had an American connection, but no reason was given as to why that should be so.

Lord Crowley applied for a commission to join the army on the outbreak of war, but when it came through, he refused it. Some said he was a coward, but it soon became apparent that he was very ill with the advanced stages of syphilis. Victoria Crowley devoted herself to nursing him, and she would not let anyone else near.

There were stories that he could become quite violent, and at one time he chased a member of staff through the house with an unsheathed knife. In 1917, Lord Crowley fell from an upstairs room, and he was killed instantly. Some say he threw himself off the balcony outside the glass windows, from the bedroom Alexander stayed in while he was there. Some say he was trying to fly to prove his new-found freedom. But no one will know the whole truth.

Despite the difficulties Lord Crowley created for Victoria Crowley, she seemed genuinely bereft by his death, and the last time I saw her was in the summer of 1917, at John Crowley's funeral. Soon after that, she became a virtual recluse, not accepting or even answering society invitations, and in the winter of that year, she took one of her horses, Bright Star out for a ride. The horse threw her near a place called Hammond Farm just by a small bridge that spanned the Grand Union Canal.

Victoria was paralysed but lived on for over a year being cared for by Lord Crowley's butler, Charles Porter.

When she died, it was said that James Alexander's honours in the form of medals given to him by the Kaiser, King George and the Tsar of Russia were clutched in her hand. I never found out why the Tsar should have given James Alexander a medal, it remains a mystery to this day. In return for Porter's devotion, she left him most of her estate and all her possessions, including some secret papers that James Alexander had left in his safe. Porter became wealthy from Victoria's inheritance, but shortly afterwards, he inexplicably came into a further fortune; some say it was secret money belonging to Alexander. Whatever the case he used his considerable wealth to buy a baronetcy and of course he already had control of Crowley's Bank. The irony of the situation didn't escape some when it was realised that Lord Porter as he now was, owned all the assets of the Crowley Empire and Byron's Bank. The irony comes when it's remembered that Porter's father was turned out of his farm by Lord Crowley's father and died in a debtor's prison as a result.

Lord Porter changed the new consortium name to Barons Bank in 1922, to celebrate his peerage. He prospered for some years, as he seemed to have inherited some of Alexander's skills. He too had the uncanny knack of forecasting events, and the bank grew under his stewardship. He never married, and in 1932 he was walking down Fleet Street and went to cross the road. He was hit by a tram and died within hours.

There was an editor's postscript on the 1947 reprint, which was the copy I was holding.

Crowley Hall remained empty for a time and was sold to the Potterton family by Lord Porter in 1924. It retained its original glory for a time but became run down after Sir Henry Potterton died in 1938. The War Office took it over during World War II and turned it into apartments for staff at the nearby Bletchley Park. The flats were pulled down in 1945 and replaced by a block of modern apartments.

I realised the only person who could have had access to the safe was Charles Porter when he was left Crowley Hall after Victoria's death, that's how he accessed my account and my notes. He presumably took the view that the box was of no value.

I put the book down.

There was even a further irony in the story, as it was now apparent that it was Porter's legacy that had just ruined me, how twisted can a story become I mused.

That wasn't quite the end of the tale. I had always wanted to write but had suppressed the urge because I felt I had to pursue other interests, like making money.

Now I decided I would become a writer. In true fashion, I determined that by writing an espionage thriller, I could make the most money, so I authored a book about the kidnapping of the prime minister of the day. When I finished it, I found it stilted, so I did a re write, and although

I nearly got a publisher to accept the story, but I was never quite happy with it. The next book I wrote was a true story about a part of my life. I forced the plot to be funny, and thus the writing became anecdotal, but it didn't have broad appeal. It was only when I remembered my own advice that I really started to become successful. I would think up my stories as I took my early morning walk and come back to my word processor and write them down as I imagined them. It was completely natural, nothing was forced, and I didn't care whether they were published or not. I had stopped writing books that I thought others might like. I wrote down the stories I liked. Suddenly others liked what I wrote too, my books sold by the thousands, films were made, and I became prosperous again. Subsequently, the early books were rewritten until I was happy with them. The millions I have made from writing allowed me to give funds to worthy charities. I now love what I do as there is no stress attached to the result. I know that happiness may be an illusion but take it while you have it. This time, I am my own locksmith. This time I found the key myself, and I wondered how many lifetimes it had taken me to learn what I had always preached to others: go with the current.

All this came from just an early morning walk.

Since my experience, I have often wondered if our current life is just a small passage in time within our real existence. Perhaps death is only a return to reality, and we choose to move our consciousness to other short-term realities to add to our total understanding of what is...

23 POSTSCRIPT

There's a final irony to this story. I kept the deed box in my desk drawer, with the original letters inside. I had long ago told Tory of my experience, of course, and we had come to accept that something very strange had happened to both of us. We now live in a larger house, not pretentious, but big enough to have our children and grandchildren to stay from time to time. We had been having a picnic on the lawn just near my study; the French windows, which led into it, were open. As sometimes happens with small children, little Antony had decided it would be more fun to investigate the inside of my desk, and he came out with the deed box. He was only five, and he staggered under the weight. As he reached the paved path just outside the doors, he could no longer bear the burden, and the box crashed to the ground. I rushed to pick it up, and as I turned it over, I noticed that some of the black paint had been removed. You may have guessed. It was made of solid gold. I subsequently had it assayed and found it worth more than two hundred and eighty thousand pounds. I felt a little stupid for not thinking about it earlier, but it never occurred to me. I sometimes wonder if my life would have taken a different turn if I had found out the box's value when I first received it. I would have probably used it to save the business and soldiered on with what I was doing. Of course, the box's true value wasn't its gold content, and I'm glad now that I didn't know.

Had I done so; you would not have read this story.

I still have it, it's still painted black, and it will remain that way until the end of my days.

Oh, yes, and I moved my bank account to another bank...

THOUGHTS

Since my experience I have given much thought to what happened to me, and it has led me to search for answers. The result is that between my writing I have been studying Quantum Mechanics and Entanglement. This section of physics is relatively new, but there are matters that we now know. The world and everything in it are composed of waves of energy. To all appearances, we, and everything else appear solid but it is not so. It appears that our brains, the energy that drives us, are creating a picture that is not there. We are all living in a dream world. Some scientists are now prophesying that everything we experience is not new, it may have been before, thus life is like a film simply being re wound. The universe is not there as we see it and yet it may be replicated to infinity. We humans may also be replicated but are only concious of being one. Time is an illusion just as everything else appears to be. Some scientists are coming around to the strange idea that the world is flat energy, did our ancestors know something we do not? Is it therefore possible that our conciousness can move between different realities, just as I did? But when you dream you cannot bring parts of your physical items back with you, or can you? As all material is a matter of the mind, in theory anything is possible. So, what is death? A move from one dream to another, or to reality?

James Alexander

HISTORY CONNECTED WITH THIS STORY

After my return, I came to understand that the Central Powers lost despite their superior tactics, weaponry, and technology. We caught up and the tank was a major factor (thanks to the British navy under Churchill who took on the creation and testing of it). The main fact was that Germany was not capable of surviving a war of attrition and did not have a powerful enough navy to ensure their supply routes were kept open. The length of the war also meant that they did not have the financial clout necessary.

The Zimmerman Telegram, the secret diplomatic communication issued from the German Foreign Office in January 1917 proposing a military alliance, between Germany and Mexico almost certainly shortened the war, but it may not have had that effect it had, if Zimmerman had not admitted that he had sent it.

The British intelligence claimed that they had decoded it thus greatly enhancing their deductive powers. Of course, I knew the true story.

The revelation of the contents enraged Americans, especially after German Foreign Secretary Arthur Zimmerman publicly admitted on March 3 that the telegram was genuine, which helped generate support for the United States declaration of war on Germany in April. The decryption was described as the most significant intelligence triumph for Britain during World War I. One of the earliest occasions on which a piece of signal intelligence influenced world events.

Despite the overwhelming call for the Kaiser to be tried and hanged, George V kept his word, and the Kaiser was allowed to live in peace with his family in the

Netherlands until the beginning of the second world war. He died in 1940. His plan worked; thousands of lives on both sides were saved, Germany was not occupied, which was his greatest fear but unfortunately the French insisted on huge reparations which was to be the reason for the second world war. Arguably it was the French that sowed the seeds possibly not realising the global monetary supply could not stand the financial drain. It was therefore France that was to suffer more than most in World War 2.

I was not to know it at the time, but Field Marshall Herbert Kitchener was killed shortly after I met him, in June 1915.

I referred to Kitchener as General when speaking to him, but he was a Field, Marshal. **Horatio Herbert Kitchener, 1st Earl Kitchener**, KG, KP, GCB, OM, GCSI, GCMG, GCIE, PC. Born 24 June 1850 and was killed on 5 June 1916. He was a senior British Army officer and colonial administrator. He won notoriety for his Imperial campaigns, especially his scorched earth policy against the Boers and his establishment of concentration camps during the Second Boer War, and later played a central role in the early part of the First World War.

Kitchener was credited in 1898 with winning the Battle of Omdurman and securing control of the Sudan for which he was made Baron Kitchener of Khartoum. As Chief of Staff (1900–1902) in the Second Boer War, he played a crucial role in Lord Roberts conquest of the Boer Republics, then succeeded Roberts as commander-in-chief. By that time, Boer forces had taken to guerrilla fighting, and British forces imprisoned Boer civilians in concentration camps. His term as Commander-in-Chief (1902–09) of the Army in India saw him quarrel with another eminent proconsul, the Viceroy Lord Curzon, who eventually resigned. Kitchener then returned to Egypt as British Agent and Consul-General (*de facto* administrator).

In 1914, at the start of the First World War, Kitchener

became Secretary of State for War, a cabinet minister. One of the few to foresee a long war, lasting for at least three years, and with authority to act effectively on that perception, he organised the largest volunteer army that Britain had seen, and oversaw a significant expansion of materiel production to fight on the Western Front. Despite having warned of the difficulty of provisioning for a long war. He was blamed for the shortage of shells in the spring of 1915. It was one of the events leading to the formation of a coalition government. And that stripped him of his control over munitions and strategy. Perhaps he was expecting a large shipment that was in the Lusitania when it sank?

On 5 June 1916, Kitchener was making his way to Russia on HMS *Hampshire* to attend negotiations with Tsar Nicholas II when the ship struck a German mine 1.5 miles (2.4 km) west of the Orkneys, Scotland, and sank. Kitchener was among 737 who died.

Deploying the BEF

At the War Council (5 August) Kitchener and Lieutenant-General Sir Douglas Haig argued that the BEF should be deployed at Amiens, where it could deliver a vigorous counter-attack once the German advance route was known. Kitchener argued that the deployment of the BEF in Belgium would result in having to retreat and abandon much of its supplies almost immediately. As the Belgian Army would be unable to hold its ground against the Germans; Kitchener was proved right but given the belief in fortresses typical at the time, it is not surprising that the War Council disagreed with him.

Kitchener, believing Britain should husband her resources for a long war, decided at Cabinet (6 August) that the initial BEF would consist of only four infantry divisions (and one cavalry), not the 5 or 6 promised. His decision to hold back two of the six divisions of the BEF, was based on exaggerated concerns about the German invasion of Britain. He arguably saved the BEF from disaster as Sir John French

338

(on the advice of Wilson who was much influenced by the French), might have been tempted to advance further into the teeth of the advancing German forces, had his force been more potent.

Kitchener's wish to concentrate further back at Amiens may also have been influenced by a mostly accurate map of German dispositions published by Repington in *The Times* on the morning of 12 August. Kitchener had a three-hour meeting (12 August) with Sir John French, Murray, Wilson and the French liaison officer Victor Huguet, before being overruled by the Prime Minister, who eventually agreed that the BEF should assemble at Maubeuge.

Sir John French's orders from Kitchener were to cooperate with the French but not take orders from them. Given that the tiny BEF (about 100,000 men, half of them serving regulars and half reservists) was Britain's only field army. Lord Kitchener also instructed French to avoid excessive losses and exposure to "forward movements where large numbers of French troops are not engaged" until Kitchener himself had had a chance to discuss the matter with the Cabinet.

Meeting with Sir John French

The BEF commander, Sir John French, concerned at heavy British losses at the Battle of Le Cateau, was considering withdrawing his forces from the Allied line. By 31 August French Commander-in-chief Joffre, President Poincaré (relayed via Bertie, the British Ambassador) and Kitchener sent him messages urging him not to do so. Kitchener, authorised by a midnight meeting of whichever Cabinet Ministers could be found, left for France for a meeting with Sir John on 1 September.

Together with Viviani (French Prime Minister) and Millerand (now French War Minister), they met. Huguet recorded that Kitchener was "calm, balanced, reflective" whilst Sir John was "sour, impetuous, with congested face, sullen and ill-tempered". On Bertie's advice, Kitchener dropped his intention of inspecting the BEF. French and Kitchener moved to a separate room, and no independent account of the meeting exists. After the meeting, Kitchener telegraphed the Cabinet that the BEF would remain in the line, although taking care not to be outflanked, and told French to consider this "an instruction". French had a friendly exchange of letters with Joffre.

French had been furious that Kitchener had arrived wearing his field marshal's uniform. This was how Kitchener usually dressed at the time (Hankey thought Kitchener's uniform disrespectful, but it had probably not occurred to him to change). Still, French felt that Kitchener implied that he was his military superior and not merely a cabinet member. By the end of the year, French thought that Kitchener had "gone mad" and his hostility had become common knowledge at GHQ and GQG.

1915

In January 1915, Field Marshal Sir John French, the British Expeditionary Force commander, with the concurrence of other senior commanders (e.g., General Sir Douglas Haig), wanted the New Armies incorporated into existing divisions as battalions rather than sent out as entire divisions. French felt (wrongly) that the war would be over by the summer before the New Army divisions were deployed, as Germany had recently redeployed some divisions to the east and took the step of appealing to the Prime Minister, Asquith, over Kitchener's head, but Asquith refused to overrule Kitchener. This further damaged relations between French and Kitchener, who had travelled to France in September 1914 during the First Battle of the Marne to order French to resume his place in the Allied line.

Kitchener warned French in January 1915 that the Western Front was a siege line that could not be breached, in the context of Cabinet discussions about amphibious landings on the Baltic or North Sea Coast, or against Turkey. To find a way to relieve pressure on the Western front, Lord

Kitchener proposed an invasion of Alexandretta with Australian and New Zealand Army Corps (ANZAC), New Army, and Indian troops. Alexandretta was an area with a large Christian population and was the strategic centre of the Ottoman Empire's railway network — it's capture would have cut the empire in two. Yet he was instead eventually persuaded to support Winston Churchill's disastrous Gallipoli Campaign in 1915–1916. (Churchill's responsibility for this campaigns failure is debated; for more information see David Fromkins *A Peace to End All Peace*.) That failure combined with the Shell Crisis of 1915 – amidst press publicity engineered by Sir John French – dealt Kitchener's political reputation a heavy blow. Kitchener was popular with the public, so Asquith retained him in office in the new coalition government. Still, responsibility for munitions was moved to a new ministry headed by David Lloyd George. He was a sceptic about the tank, which is why it was developed under Churchill's Admiralty's auspices.

With the Russians being pushed back from Poland, Kitchener thought the transfer of German troops west and Britain's possible invasion increasingly likely and told the War Council (14 May) that he was not willing to send the New Armies overseas. He wired French (16 May 1915) that he would send no more reinforcements to France until he was clear the German line could be broken but sent two divisions at the end of May to please Joffre, not because he thought a breakthrough possible. He had wanted to conserve his New Armies to strike a knock-out blow in 1916–17, but by the summer of 1915 realised that high casualties and a major commitment to France were inescapable. "Unfortunately, we have to make war as we must, and not as we should like" as he told the Dardanelles Committee on 20 August 1915.

At an Anglo-French conference at Calais (6 July) Joffre and Kitchener, who was opposed to "too vigorous" offensives, reached a compromise on "local offensives on a vigorous scale", and Kitchener agreed to deploy New Army divisions to France. An inter-Allied conference at Chantilly (7 July, including Russian, Belgian, Serb, and Italian delegates) agreed on coordinated offensives. however, Kitchener now came to support the upcoming Loos Offensive. He travelled to France for talks with Joffre and Millerand (16 August). The French leaders believed Russia might sue for peace (Warsaw had fallen on 4 August). Kitchener (19 August) ordered the Loos Offensive to proceed, despite the attack being on the ground not favoured by French or Haig (then commanding First Army). The Official History later admitted that Kitchener hoped to be appointed Supreme Allied Commander. Liddell Hart speculated that this was why he allowed himself to be persuaded by Joffre. New Army divisions first saw action at Loos in September 1915.

REDUCTION IN POWERS

Kitchener continued to lose favour with politicians and professional soldiers. He found it "repugnant and unnatural to have to discuss military secrets with a large number of gentlemen with whom he was but barely acquainted". Esher complained that he would either lapse into "obstinacy and silence" or else mull aloud over various difficulties. Milner told Gwynne (18 August 1915) that he thought Kitchener, a "slippery fish". By autumn 1915, with Asquith's Coalition close to breaking up over conscription, he was blamed for his opposition to that measure. (Which would eventually be introduced for single men in January 1916). And for the excessive influence which civilians like Churchill and Haldane had come to exert over strategy, allowing *ad hoc* campaigns to develop in Sinai, Mesopotamia, and Salonika. Generals such as Sir William Robertson were critical of Kitchener's failure to ask the General Staff. (Whose chief James Wolfe-Murray was intimidated by Kitchener) to study the feasibility of any of these campaigns.

Kitchener advised the Dardanelles Committee (21

October) that Baghdad be seized for the sake of prestige then abandoned as logistically untenable. His advice was no longer accepted without question, but the British forces were eventually besieged and captured at Kut.

Archibald Murray (Chief of the Imperial General Staff) later recorded that Kitchener was "quite unfit for the position of secretary of state" and "impossible", claiming that he never assembled the Army Council as a body, but instead gave them orders separately, and was usually exhausted by Friday. Kitchener was also keen to break up Territorial unit's whenever possible whilst ensuring that "No "K" Division left the country incomplete". Murray wrote that "He seldom told the absolute the truth and the whole truth" and claimed that it was not until he left on a tour of inspection of Gallipoli and the Near East that Murray was able to inform the Cabinet that volunteering had fallen far below the level needed to maintain a BEF of 70 divisions, requiring the introduction of conscription. The Cabinet insisted on proper General Staff papers being presented in Kitchener's absence.

Asquith, who told Robertson that Kitchener was "an impossible colleague" and "his veracity left much to be desired", hoped that he could be persuaded to remain in the region as Commander-in-Chief and acted in charge of the War Office, but Kitchener took his seals of office with him so he could not be sacked in his absence. Douglas Haig – at that time involved in intrigues to have Robertson appointed Chief of the Imperial General Staff – recommended that Kitchener be appointed Viceroy of India ("where trouble was brewing") but not to the Middle East, where his strong personality would have led to that sideshow receiving too much attention and resources. Kitchener visited Rome and Athens, but Murray warned that he would likely demand the diversion of British troops to fight the Turks in the Sinai.

Kitchener and Asquith were agreed that Robertson should become CIGS, but Robertson refused to do this if

Kitchener "continued to be his own CIGS", although given Kitchener's great prestige he did not want him to resign; he wanted the Secretary of State to be side-lined to an advisory role like the Prussian War Minister. Asquith asked them to negotiate an agreement, which they did over the exchange of several draft documents at the Hotel de Crillon in Paris. Kitchener agreed that Robertson alone should present strategic advice to the Cabinet, with Kitchener responsible for recruiting and supplying the Army, although he refused to agree that military orders should go out over Robertson's signature alone – it was agreed that the Secretary of State should continue to sign orders jointly with the CIGS. The agreement was formalised in a Royal Order in Council in January 1916. Robertson was suspicious of efforts in the Balkans and Near East and was instead committed to major British offensives against Germany on the Western Front — the first of these was to be the Somme in 1916.

1916

Early in 1916 Kitchener visited Douglas Haig, newly appointed Commander-in-Chief of the BEF in France. Kitchener had been a key figure in the removal of Haig's predecessor Sir John French, with whom he had a poor relationship. Haig differed with Kitchener over the importance of Mediterranean efforts and wanted to see a strong General Staff in London, but nonetheless valued Kitchener as a military voice against civilians' folly such as Churchill, however, he thought Kitchener "pinched, tired, and much aged", and thought it sad that his mind was "losing its comprehension" as the time for a decisive victory on the Western Front (as Haig and Robertson saw it) approached. Kitchener was doubtful of Haig's plan to win a decisive victory in 1916, and would have preferred smaller and purely attrition attacks, but sided with Robertson in telling the Cabinet that the planned Anglo-French Offensive on the Somme should go ahead.

Kitchener was under pressure from French Prime

Minister Aristide Briand (29 March 1916) for the British to attack the Western Front to help relieve the stress of the German attack at Verdun. The French refused to bring troops home from Salonika, which Kitchener thought a play for the increase of French power in the Mediterranean.

On 2 June 1916, Lord Kitchener personally answered questions asked by politicians about his running of the war effort; at the start of hostilities Kitchener had ordered two million rifles from various US arms manufacturers. Only 480 of these rifles had arrived in the UK by 4 June 1916. The numbers of shells supplied were no less paltry. Kitchener explained the efforts he had made to secure alternative supplies. He received a resounding vote of thanks from the 200 Members of Parliament who had arrived to question him, both for his candour and for his efforts to keep the troops armed; Sir Ivor Herbert, who, a week before, had introduced the failed vote of censure in the House of Commons against Kitchener's running of the War Department, personally seconded the motion.

In addition to his military work, Lord Kitchener contributed to efforts on the home front. The knitted sock patterns of the day used a seam up the toe that could rub uncomfortably against the toes. Kitchener encouraged British and American women to knit for the war effort and contributed a sock pattern featuring a new technique for a seamless join of the toe, still known as the Kitchener stitch.

RUSSIAN MISSION

During his other political and military concerns, Kitchener devoted personal attention to the Eastern Front's deteriorating situation. This included the provision of extensive stocks of war materiel for the Russian armies, which had been under increasing pressure since mid-1915 In May 1916 the Chancellor of the Exchequer Reginald Mckenna suggested that Kitchener head a special and confidential mission to Russia to discuss munition shortages, military strategy and financial difficulties with the Imperial Russian Government and the *Stavka* (military high command), which was now under the personal command of Tsar Nicholas II. Both Kitchener and the Russians were in favour of face-to-face talks and a formal invitation from the Tsar was received on 14 May. Kitchener with a party of officials, military aides and personal servants left London by train for Scotland on the evening of 4 June.

Death

Lord Kitchener sailed from Scrabster to Scapa Flow on 5 June 1916 aboard HMS *Oak* before transferring to the armoured cruiser HMS *Hampshire* for his diplomatic mission to Russia. At the last minute, Admiral Sir John Jellicoe changed the *Hampshire's* route based on a misreading of the weather forecast and ignoring (or not being aware of) recent German intelligence and sightings U-boat activity in the vicinity of the amended route. Shortly before 19:30 hours the same day, steaming for the Russian port of Arkhangelsk during a Force 9 gale, *Hampshire* struck a mine laid by the newly launched German U-boat *U-75* (commanded by Curt Beitzen) and sank west of the Orkney Islands. Recent research has set the death toll of those aboard *Hampshire* at 737. Only twelve survived. Amongst the dead were all ten members of his entourage. Kitchener was seen standing on the quarterdeck during the approximately twenty minutes that it took the ship to sink. His body was never recovered.

The news of Kitchener's death was received with shock all over the British Empire. A man in Yorkshire committed suicide at the word; a sergeant on the Western Front was heard to exclaim "Now we've lost the war. Now we've lost the war"; and a nurse wrote home to her family that she knew Britain would win as long as Kitchener lived, and now that he was gone: "How awful it is – a far worse blow than many German victories. So long as he was with us, we knew even if things were gloomy that his guiding hand was at the helm."

General Douglas Haig commanding the British Armies on the Western Front remarked on first receiving the news of Kitchener's death via a German radio signal intercepted by the British Army, "How shall we get on without him." King George V wrote in his diary: It is indeed a heavy blow to me and a great loss to the nation and the allies. He ordered army officers to wear black armbands for a week.

C. P. Scott, the editor of *The Manchester Guardian*, is said to have remarked that "as for the old man, he could not have done better than to have gone down, as he was a great impediment lately."

Conspiracy theories

Kitchener's great fame, the suddenness of his death, and it's apparently convenient timing for several parties gave almost immediate rise to a few conspiracy theories about his death. One was posited by Lord Alfred Douglas (of Oscar Wilde fame), positing a connection between Kitchener's death, the recent naval Battle of Jutland, Winston Churchill, and a Jewish conspiracy. Churchill successfully sued Douglas in what proved to be the last successful case of criminal libel in British legal history, and the latter spent six months in prison. Another claimed that the *Hampshire* did not strike a mine at all but was sunk by explosives secreted in the vessel by Irish Republicans.

In 1926, a hoaxer named Frank Power claimed in the *Sunday Referee* newspaper that a Norwegian fisherman had found Kitchener's body. Power brought a coffin back from Norway and prepared it for burial in St Pauls Cathedral. At this point, however, the authorities intervened, and the coffin was opened in the presence of police and a distinguished pathologist. The box was found to contain only tar for weight. There was widespread public outrage at Power, but he was never prosecuted.

FBI file photo of Duquesne

General Erich Ludendorff, General quartiermeister and joint head (with von Hindenburg) of Germany's war effort stated in the 1920s that Russian communists working against the Tsar had betrayed the plan to visit the Russians to the German command. His account was that Kitchener was "killed because of his ability" as he feared he would help the tsarist Russian Army recover.

Frederick Joubert Duquesne, a Boer soldier and spy, claimed that he had assassinated Kitchener after an earlier attempt to kill him in Cape Town failed. He was arrested and court-martialed in Cape Town and sent to the penal colony of Bermuda, but managed to escape to the U.S. MI5 confirmed that Duquesne was "a German intelligence officer ... involved in a series of acts of sabotage against British shipping in South American waters during the First World war"; he was wanted for: "murder on the high seas, the sinking and burning of British ships, the burning of military stores, warehouses, coaling stations, conspiracy, and the falsification of Admiralty documents."

Duquesne's story was that he returned to Europe, posed as the Russian Duke Boris Zakrevsky in 1916, and joined Kitchener in Scotland. While on board HMS *Hampshire* with Kitchener, Duquesne signalled a German submarine that then sank the cruiser, and was rescued by the submarine, later being awarded the Iron Cross for his efforts. Duquesne was later apprehended and tried by the authorities in the U.S. for insurance fraud but managed to escape again.

In the Second World War, he ran a German spy ring in the United States until the FBI caught him in what became the biggest round-up of spies in U.S. history: the *Duquesne Spy Ring*. Coincidentally, Kitchener's brother was to die in office in Bermuda in 1912, and his nephew,

Major H.H. *Hap* Kitchener, who had married a Bermudian, purchased (with a legacy left to him by his uncle) Hinson's Island, part of a former Prisoner of War camp from which Duquesne had escaped, after the First World War as the location of his home and business.

Nothing I read later, changed my opinion of Kitchener, a soldier who lived and fought the old way but was incapable of assessing and using new technology. His biggest problem being the difficulty in dealing with his political masters. It should be a lesson for us.

There is a sequel to the above story in that the family of Duquesne were taken to one of the British Concentration camps in South Africa, where they died of disease and starvation. The soldier who created the camps was Kitchener. It is not impossible that Dusquesne planned his revenge which was consummated in the North Sea with the death of the man responsible thus killing two birds with one stone.

THE LUSITANIA
There is a theory regarding the sinking of the Lusitania. The questions asked were. Why did the ship slow down, to make an easier target for German submarines? Why did it sail close to the Southern Irish coast just off Kinsale, the port that had the most modern RNLI boats, so that many lives could be saved? Was it because the British government required the ship to be sunk to turn the opinion of the United States in favour of the western powers? History will no doubt give us the truth in time.

WHAT IS TIME?

According to certain theories in physics, the time is not real and is nothing but a product of our consciousness. Let's explore these theories and the concept of the illusion of time.

Time is still regarded as a reality, and the statistical interpretation of causality principle within the framework of the Heisenberg's uncertainty principle is still respected. However, recent discoveries at the quantum level are now directing us to the idea of the illusion of time and the conclusion that **time may not exist** and that it exists only with regards to an arbitrary reference point. In order to make it simple, let us **have** a comparison between space and time coordinate.

It is a fact that the notion of left, and right is a relative concept that depends on the location of the observer; so, the concept of right and left cannot be an absolute property for defining the location of objects.

Left and right are relative and not absolute since they may be in the reverse order for another observer looking at the same set of objects. Generalizing the same concept to the time coordinate as the 4th dimension will lead us to the result that the past and the future may indeed be reversed for another observer at a different reference point. This simple comparison can be best described in a picture that is named *block universe*, which is presented overleaf.

This is the view of the universe by an observer outside of space and time looking from a vantage point at our universe. In this picture past and future are not absolute; rather, they depend on the reference point of the observer. In this theory, the concept of past and future for time are as relative as the concept of right and left for location.

Einstein's Block Universe

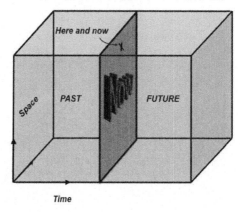

In the 1970s, the famous US physicist John Archibald Wheeler along with the physicist Bryce Dewitt, working on the unification of quantum mechanics and Einstein's theory of gravitation, developed an equation in which time as a separate concept had no role.

The theory was a big step towards the elimination of time from the description of the universe. This concept, although seemed weird and led to many controversial debates among physicists, was later developed to its extreme limit by the physicist Julian Barbour. According to him, the time is not real and what we regard as the time is no more than changes that lead to the illusion of time.

This notion of time is in total contradiction with the Newtonian concept of time as a linear and homogeneous passage of a river and that of Einstein as the 4th dimension. According to Barbour, what our mind records are moments that he calls "Now's" and what we perceive as the passage of time is just our move through a succession of "now's".

I show the incredible loss on land by 2050
Because of the rise of oceans.

Printed in Great Britain
by Amazon